THE CHOSEN CHRONICLES

CHOSEN A PATH

K.A. PARKINSON

Cover and title design by Deborah Bradseth
ISBN 978-1-942298-44-1

www.snowypeaksmedia.com

Books in The Chosen Chronicles

Author's Note

Welcome to the world of the Hidden, a place that shows in a very real way the constant struggle between good and evil, or in Hidden terms, the Light and the Dark. The appendix at the end of the book contains detailed descriptions of Hidden world terms and titles, as well as character and creature information, and a basic Hidden language dictionary.

I hope you enjoy being a part of Tolen and Macy's adventure!

○○○

Arwah…Animashta…Leenwa…Télora…
Lóklana…Kunamin…Honitahai…Dicernan…
Dembashi…To'Conchla Mindra…Degani…Ladonradi…
Darkness veils the Sight,
Those with Power lose their Might.
Shields to heal left to die,
Unending Night; a fallen Sky.
A failed Trust; Balance broken,
A Single hope; a simple Token.
But lo, Eight remain,
United under a Banner of pain.
One shall lead with Might and Shield.
With the breath of Radia, so nature will yield.
Water, animal, earth, light, unseen, fire, wind and Sight,
The Chosen will save this world from endless Night.
The Ninth shall lead them with Light's Aid beside,
To death or victory within the coming Tide.

—*The Prophecy, as revealed by Eamun Woodlore*

THE KEEPER

THE MOMENT OF his death drew near.

He could hear it in the echo of paws thundering toward him across the forest floor, and in the shrieks of the demon Raksasha carried on the winds of the Shadow storm.

Eamun Woodlore, Watcher and Keeper of the Last Shard, did not have long.

He dropped from his vantage point in the trees and glanced up at the darkening sky as tears splashed onto his cheeks.

There would be no stars this night.

He crushed the herbs between his palms, blew them into the wind, and closed his eyes to Watch them trickle into every footprint he had left behind. With his eyes closed, the nightmare became too real. The echo of terrified screams filled his ears and his eyes snapped open. He could not save them, but at least his son Sashan had escaped.

He pushed his feet forward, his own sobs mingling with the howl of the wind.

He paused beside a towering pine. His fingers trembled as he tugged the blood-red shard from its cradle within the scepter. It glowed red-gold in the dim light. He knelt at the base of the tree. Tears dripped off the end of his nose as he dug his hands into the cold earth, deeper and deeper. With a silent plea, he gently dropped the shard beneath a thick root, placed his hand on the rough bark, and whispered so that only the tree could hear. He pulled his hand away and a gleaming, golden symbol burned brightly in the wood and then disappeared.

With a surge of fierce relief, Eamun pushed the dirt back into the hole and waved his hand over the mound of earth. Thick grass sprouted around the tree until the ground surrounding it appeared undisturbed. He sprinkled another handful of herbs through the grass. His waist-length gray hair whipped around him as he paused to listen.

The shrieks of the Raksasha and the howls of the DéHool wolves were too close. He couldn't lead them here.

He waved his hands behind him as he ran back, careful to match each step. The grasses stood upright as he passed, hiding his footprints.

The howling grew louder and he felt an unnatural cold layering the air around him.

The Shadow Wraiths were almost upon him.

He emerged from the thicket to see the first line of DéHool. Their red eyes flashed to the trees behind him.

He clenched his teeth and dropped to his knees in front of them.

The wolves howled in victory and flung themselves on him.

Eamun threw his arms up toward the sky. *"Radi! Y'na hi y'takra!"* A burst of white-hot light engulfed him, and then all was silent.

The fire burned out as quickly as it started. The black, skeletal Raksasha uncovered their yellow eyes. The second pack of wolves rushed forward, but where Eamun had been, nothing remained but a dozen dead DéHool and a pile of ash.

A long, mournful cry echoed through the sky as the clouds released their rain and washed away the grisly scene. A silver great horned owl circled low over the destruction before spreading its vast wings and soaring through a hole in the clouds.

ooo

"Eamun is dead."

Forrest Bastian looked up at Zarin, leader of the Guardians—those charged with watching over the affairs of earth—as he scanned the scroll in his hands, his wings dragging on the ground behind him as he paced past the group of Guardians.

"I am sorry, Bastian. Word has just reached the citadel. His village was attacked." Zarin sighed and sat down. "Our Sight over the village has dimmed, but as far as we can tell, there were no survivors."

Bastian tugged on his long, white ponytail, his sapphire eyes bright with worry. "Do we know who is responsible?"

"The owl did not see him there, but Daemon's symbol was burned into the heads of the bodies of the slaughtered villagers."

Pain lashed through Bastian's chest. The Demon Master, back in the earth realm. Eamun Woodlore was Hidden-kind—like Bastian, like all the Guardians, and most who dwelled here in the Light Realm—a race of beings who exist outside the knowledge of humans and are behind all the worlds myths and legends. He was a gifted follower of Light and goodness, the speaker of the Prophecy of the Ninth, and Keeper of the immensely powerful Last Shard. "Eamun's whereabouts within the earth realm have remained a secret from the Dark for centuries. How did Daemon find him?"

Zarin shook his head. "We do not know."

"The Last Shard?"

"No sign." Zarin rubbed a hand over his eyes. "I am certain we would know by now if the Dark had it. The owl tells us Eamun sacrificed himself before the DéHool could take him."

Bastian stood and began to pace.

"We just sent word to the closest Hidden village off the island." Zarin's voice held the strain of leadership. "We have asked them to send spies to gather more information so we can plan how to proceed."

"If the Last Shard is still on that island, we need to go there, now." Bastian stopped mid-stride and turned to face them. "We must find it first."

"Sit down, friend." Zarin waved his hand toward Bastian's chair and waited for him to sit before he continued. "You know it isn't that simple for the Guardians to venture into the earth realm. Especially now as the Dark's power there increases daily. We will see what we can learn. We will trust in the two-fold protection over the Last Shard. A Seeker and Keeper. If the power works as it should, only the Seeker can find it."

Bastian's eyes narrowed. "You speak of the growth of darkness. Ancient power has been fading all over the planet. What if the protection guarding the Last Shard also fails? With the Keeper dead, the Dark will only have access to a fraction of its strength yes, but yet still too much power in their hands."

Zarin placed the scroll on the table in front of him, his face strained, his eyes weary. "This news has hastened our need for the Ninth Chosen. The fate of both Hidden and human kind is at stake. It is time to talk to the children."

Flashes of the future cut across Bastian's Second Sight and he raised both palms up. "I will speak with them…alone and separately."

Zarin's eyebrow rose.

Bastian kept his hands up but ducked his head as his eyes continued to shift for several minutes, shoving the truth of what was to come into his mind. As the Watcher for both Tolen and Macy, he had the ability to see small pieces of their future. A gift that aided him in the task of teaching them the ways of Hidden kind, training them in their gifts, and helping them understand the missions the Light asked of them. In his mortal life he had acted as a mentor and loved them like a father.

Not quite six weeks had passed since Bastian and his sixteen-year-old ward Macy had found Tolen Parks, a skinny, clueless seventeen-year-old boy, and told him that his true race was Hidden-kind, not human as he'd believed. They also began his training as a member of the Chosen, a group of children gifted with a single power from the Light and tasked with protecting the oblivious human race from the monsters of the Dark. But an unforeseen attack had forced Bastian to sacrifice himself to save Tolen. It had then fallen to Macy to guard the child of prophecy. Something that enraged her until their relationship took an unexpected and somewhat dangerous shift. Macy and Tolen had fallen in love.

Less than a month had passed since Tolen had discovered his destiny as the Ninth Chosen—wielder of all the Light's gifts and the prophesied final hope for all life on earth. Just days ago, Tolen and Macy had ended up here, in the Citadel of Light, understandably shaken after a terrifying, yet successful trip to the Shadow Prison to save Tolen's parents. They were pleased to find upon their arrival that Bastian had joined the Guardians at the end of his mortal life—that he had been and still would be watching over them from a distance.

Distant guidance, but not physical protection. A fact that increased his concern as he watched glimpses of their entwined futures flash by.

He must speak to Tolen first. Since Tolen also had the gift of Second Sight, the ability to see the future for those he was meant to protect, he must understand what he had been seeing in his dreams and accept the truth. As the Ninth, his ability to Watch for Macy will be much clearer, his feelings for her deepening the connection.

Macy…A burning, tearing sensation blossomed in his chest. How could he send her out there to face the uncertain, dangerous future alone? His life ending, ripped and slashed away by the DéHool's monstrous claws, had felt soft as feathers compared to this.

When the vision finally ended, Bastian raised his head and met Zarin's worried expression. "As their Watcher you *must* trust me," he said, his voice bleak, broken. "This is about more than just the Last Shard. The Dark is after the Relics."

A collective gasp passed through the group. "The Relics were hidden by a power even greater than what we wield. There is no way the Dark can find them," Zarin whispered.

"Just as there was no way for the Dark to find Eamun? The Light's power in the earth realm is fading. We are running out of time."

The leader of the Guardians took a deep breath, and for several uncomfortable seconds stared into Bastian's eyes while the tension in the room layered thick and heavy as mud.

Finally, with a slow sigh, Zarin nodded once. "Very well."

July 6

1 Poisonous Truth

Macy tucked a stubborn strand of her thick, blonde hair behind her ear, her emerald eyes glancing at the clock in the hall. 7:15 AM. Everyday for the week they'd spent in the Citadel of Light, Tolen had come to her room at 6:45 so they could have breakfast together before training. Now with just four days until Tolen turned eighteen and completed Transcendence—the moment when his gifts would reach the height of their strength—the Dominant trainers were working him extra hard. It was no wonder he had slept through his alarm. She'd decided to pick up their breakfast and bring it back to his room rather than wake him up to eat together down in the cafeteria.

In three days they would leave the Light Realm and head for the Zenith, the stronghold within the earth realm where Tolen would complete his training and his Transcendence—something she both looked forward to and worried about. The Zenith was supposed to be strong enough to shield him from being discovered by the Dark, but so far they'd underestimated Tolen at every turn. He was so powerful already that the Spheres here, who had the ability to shield people and places from detection of the Dark, struggled to hide him. If they were struggling, how could anyone possibly hide him once he transcended?

The closer she got to Tolen's room, the more her Radia shard, the source of her gifts, zinged with familiar energy.

She clutched the handle of the bag holding their pastries and milk tighter in her fist and picked up her pace. She turned the corner to see Bastian standing in one of the many tall windows lining the hallway.

"Bastian!" He stepped down and she threw her arms around his waist. His heavy wings twitched beneath her hands.

Her Watcher put his huge hand on her hair. "Hello, *LaUnahi,* my little bird." His voice sounded strained, sad.

She looked up into his face and her stomach turned at the agony she saw there. "What's happened? Tolen—?" she dropped her hold on his waist and took a step toward Tolen's room, but Bastian grabbed her arm.

"Wait, Macy. I need to speak with you. Now. It cannot wait."

Heart pounding she followed Bastian into one of the many private thinking rooms in the hall. Her hands shook and the bag of pastries rustled. Bastian gently took it from her, sat it on a small table, and guided her to one of the two cream-colored overstuffed chairs.

"What's wrong?" The Kuna—her gift of fire—heated her chest and tingled in her palms.

Bastian knelt at her feet and took her hands in his. The tingle slowed, but her heart raced from the look in his eyes. "Macy, how are you handling the weight of my shard?"

Her eyebrow rose. She'd been wearing his shard since his "death." She'd tried to give it back when they'd arrived and learned he was now a Guardian, but Bastian told her it was hers now. "Its power seems to be growing, but it's not that noticeable. Jonas told me it will get harder to manage once I am back in the human dimension, that the Light's power here helps to control it."

"He is correct." Bastian squeezed his eyes shut. "I must ask you to do something. It will be something extraordinarily difficult, almost impossible, but I know you are capable. Will you do it?" He opened his eyes but didn't go on.

"What is it that you want me to do?"

"I need you to trust me."

"Bastian, you know I trust you." The heat increased in her palms. Soon it would become an unbearable burn and have to be released.

"This is different, Macy."

Macy swallowed loudly. "You're starting to freak me out." She twisted her hands out of his and clenched them in her lap.

Bastian gripped her hands again. "I need you to trust that I will only ask something of you that I know in my heart you can do, but it will be incredibly dangerous and difficult."

"Well, that'll be a change." She tried to smirk. As a member of the Chosen, she was responsible for protecting ignorant mankind from the monsters of the dark, something that made every day dangerous and difficult.

He didn't crack a smile. "You and Tolen must leave the citadel today. But you cannot go with him to the Zenith."

"What?" Macy jumped out of her seat. "You're joking, right?" Anger boiled up inside her and a thin trickle of smoke curled from her palms. She shoved her hands into her pockets and took three deep breaths.

"Macy, you promised." He stood up and reached his hand toward her but she ignored it.

"Bastian! Why?"

"The Light has a vital mission for you and Tolen must complete his training. As the Ninth he will need the protection of the Zenith as he transcends. He cannot go with you and you cannot wait for him." He gently put a hand over her lips before she could argue. "*LaUnahi*, I am still your Watcher. Please trust me." His voice trembled and Macy's stomach twisted.

"W-what is the mission?"

"The future is too hazy for me to know the exact details. But I have seen that leaving today is best. Safest for both of you. You must hurry. Trust the Light to guide you. Focus on my shard. It will watch over you when Tolen and I cannot. It will link you to him even more strongly than your own."

She barely heard his last words. Her lungs were burning, her heart slamming against her ribs. It felt like someone was holding her to the ground and stepping on her chest. "But…the prophecy…I'm Light's Aid, and Tolen's trigger for his gifts. He needs me."

Bastian sighed. "And you need him." His eyes shifted black to blue swiftly, searching the future.

Her heart sank. "But it doesn't change anything, right?"

He barely shook his head. "Jonas wishes to speak with you before you leave, but it must be very brief. You need to be ready to go within the hour. I've had some food delivered to your room. Eat. You'll need your strength." He wrapped his arms around her in a final hug. "Goodbye my little bird." He touched her cheek, spun on his heel and left.

○○○

Time ceased to exist as Tolen lay on the floor beside the open balcony doors. He didn't remember how he ended up on the floor. It could have been hours or minutes ago that Bastian had left to speak with Macy, to deliver the blow to her as well.

Macy was like a daughter to Bastian. He'd been extremely upset when he flew off Tolen's balcony. Would it be up to Tolen to break the terrible news of their necessary separation? He needed to get up, but he couldn't move. His concrete body had become part of the floor, the thick carpet like razors against his cheek. Nothing, not even the warmth of the Citadel of Light, could ease the pain of this moment.

Soft blue light emanated from the Radia Shard he wore around his neck and he felt his gifts stir within him. Other Chosen received their gifts from their shard, but as the Ninth Chosen his gifts were born with him and right now they too were reacting to his pain. Kuna, one of his strongest gifts and the one most affected by emotion, heated his chest and flooded his palms. He must contain it, but as his thoughts continued, the heat intensified. His shard pulsed, echoing his agony as his mind raced through the events of the past few weeks.

When he first met Macy he didn't like her very much, but it didn't take long to fall for her once he got to know the real her. The time spent in Jonas's training camp had brought them together in more ways than one. While there he'd learned he was the Ninth Chosen, a child of prophecy meant to lead the Chosen in a Final Battle against the Dark, a prophecy in which Macy would play a vital role. Then one week ago she had helped him infiltrate the Shadow Realm, the Dark dimension where demons and evil thrive, and rescue his parents from the horrors of the Shadow Prison. They'd stormed through a literal hell on earth, fought against Daemon the Demon Master—a creature more terrible than any of Tolen's worst nightmares, scores of Dark servants, and survived. He'd believed the prophecy determined they would remain together as they moved forward into the future, but it had been a dream, a fantasy, as unattainable as grasping smoke.

Bastian's brief visit had begun as a conversation about how well Tolen was doing in his training with the Dominants then morphed into a poisonous snake of torturous truth that had wrapped itself around his heart, squeezing and sucking the life from him.

Macy must take a different path, and no matter how much Tolen wanted to, he couldn't follow and protect her against the evil that would be shadowing her every move. For days he'd pushed away the images of Macy he'd been dreaming about, refusing to acknowledge them for what they were—actual glimpses into her future. But Bastian had confirmed Tolen's nightmares. Being both Tolen and Macy's Watcher he'd also seen it.

As soon as Bastian left, the vision Tolen had been fighting against forced itself upon him.

His hands trembled where they sat curled into fists beside his head as the worst of the images returned.

Daemon was back in the earthly realm, trying to find a way to free Darsapean—leader of the Dark and the single most evil creature to ever walk the earth—from Misery, the prison kept by the Guardians. Bile rose in Tolen's throat. He swallowed hard and squeezed his eyes shut as the rest of the vision cut again through his thoughts. The slaughtered village, the sense of urgency on the side of the Dark.

A knock sounded at his door and he forced his body off the floor, but it wasn't Macy waiting for him on the other side. It was Keytleen—his emissary to the Guardians.

"Your parents wish to speak with you before you leave." She offered him a sympathetic smile before motioning for him to follow.

He glanced over his shoulder as he left the room to see Bastian leading Macy the other direction into a thinking room.

The relief at not being the one to have to tell her was fleeting. Tolen knew what he had to do, but he was afraid it would kill him to do it. Heat waves rolled off his hands. Whether because of the power she held over Tolen—the Ninth Chosen—or something more sinister, one thing was for certain.

Daemon was hunting Macy.

2 FINAL ADVICE

"Hello, McLacy." Jonas's quiet, gravelly voice came from the chair facing the window.

Macy took a deep breath and tried to force a smile. "Hey, Jonas."

Warm sunlight poured in through his open window. A soft breeze played in the curtains, coaxing in the sweet smells of the honeysuckle vine that grew up the side of his hospital wing, but it didn't slow the Kuna that was becoming too hot in her palms. Going to see Jonas first was only stalling the inevitable goodbye to Tolen, but she couldn't help hoping the ancient man would have answers, a concrete reason to do what duty expected and ignore her heart.

He waited for her to sit before he started to speak. "I am sorry for your pain."

Growing up Chosen, she'd learned many missions didn't make sense. You had to accept that those in charge of such things knew what they were doing. But never had she felt so much dread going into an unknown before. She'd feared when she first started having feelings for Tolen that their Chosen duties would pull them in separate directions, and that fear had come forward to slap her in the face. But she could not regret falling for him, no matter what lay ahead. She shrugged, but a pulsing ache shot through her heart. "It's part of the job, right?"

Jonas slowly shook his head. "The worst part."

Macy shrugged again, bit her trembling lip, and looked out the window. "Bastian said you wanted to talk to me, but apparently I'm supposed to be in a hurry?"

"You have heard of the growth of evil in the human realm in the short time you have been here, yes?"

Macy swallowed and nodded. "Yeah."

"Human news can tell only a fraction of what is happening." Jonas took a slow measured breath. "They do not understand the real cause behind fathers turning on their children, children turning against their parents, brother against brother. They do not understand that at the very root of terrorist attacks, political wars, and unexplained natural disasters lies the Dark in all its horror."

Macy could feel his creepy cobwebbed eyes on her face as he continued. "As humans slowly become desensitized to the violence around them, they become easier targets for the Dark and its ability to make them rationalize fighting violence and hatred with more violence and hatred. Once men fought with honor and treated their enemies fairly. Now, those who claim to fight for the good of man find themselves treating their enemies with the same kind of inhumanity they were supposedly fighting against.

"In the final battles that are to come, I fear it will not be the Dark that destroys the human race. The humans will *become* darkness and destroy themselves."

Goosebumps rose on Macy's arms. "Are you talking about the *Darkened*?"

The power emanating from him had her turning to meet his gaze, and no matter how uncomfortable his strange eyes made her feel, she couldn't look away. "Yes, the Darkened, those humans who have chosen to side with evil, the demons of the blackest nightmares. Their numbers are swiftly increasing. You must be careful." His voice rose a fraction and her palms tingled. "The role of the Chosen has shifted. You are no longer just protectors for the unsuspecting human race. You are its *only* chance for redemption."

Bastian's shard warmed where it rested against her throat, confirming the gravity of his words. The Kuna was becoming unbearable.

"You are going on a mission of faith. Faith is an acceptance of things unseen but that are real and true. It is courage to take each step as it is revealed to you, even if it means taking a step into the dark unknown. The Light trusts you, you must trust Them." He placed a gnarled hand over hers. "*Liosladon*, McLacy."

"Goodbye Jonas." She squeezed his fingers before she hurried out the door. She ran to the nearest open window and shoved her palms toward the open air. Fire burst from her hands as the heat left her chest, scaring a flock of birds out of the nearest tree and eliciting a frightened shout from the Honitahai gardener below. She yanked her arms back inside before he could see who was responsible. If she'd thought Jonas was going to help, she'd been sadly mistaken. If anything, he'd scared her even more.

The Chosen were mankind's only chance for redemption? How much more concrete of a reason to do your duty can you get than that?

ooo

Tolen's feet dragged as he walked behind Keytleen. Whatever his parents had to say would be brief, the people at the Zenith were preparing for his arrival, waiting to train him and help him fulfill his duty as the Ninth.

Keytleen paused just outside his father's healing room, motioned for him to enter, and then walked away.

Tolen's eyes were drawn to where his mother sat in her wheelchair beside his father's bed. Her once-vibrant red hair was streaked with silver and hung limply over her shoulders. Her face was fuller and healthier than when they'd left Green River, Utah a little more than a month ago, but she'd aged significantly since then. She was healthy, but unhappy. The wrinkles forming around her eyes and mouth gave her a harshness that intensified when she frowned at Tolen's disheveled appearance. He ran a shaky hand through his hair trying to smooth out the tangles, but he knew he couldn't hide the evidence of his pain.

His father's eyes widened with obvious concern. His silver-brown hair was thicker, shinier, and brushed into a smooth ponytail on his neck—much different from the thin, shaggy mess it had been when they'd first arrived here. His soft brown eyes held the sparkle Areen's had lost. His skin was still a little waxy and pale, but pink color had begun to rise in his cheeks, and a healthy diet was helping him to look less and less like a starved corpse. With time, he *would* heal. The strong Protector of legend still existed inside the ailing body. He'd survived months of torture. He was not a quitter. Tolen wondered if this was as true for his mother.

"Where's Macy?" Daedal asked.

The mention of her name brought snippets of Macy's current thoughts into Tolen's mind. "She's meeting with Jonas." His voice trembled and his father grasped his hand.

"I'm sorry son. I know you wanted her to go with you to the Zenith."

"It is what it is." He whispered, not meeting his father's eyes. "How's recovery going?"

Daedal seemed to sense his son's need to change the subject and glanced at his wife.

"Slow." His mother brushed at the blanket over her legs. "I wish we could go outside the citadel, but with the Dark growing, Daemon's power over me seems to be strengthening. I have to stay where the Sphere's power is strongest." Areen bit her lip and looked away.

Tolen squeezed her hand and glanced at his father. "How about you?"

Daedal's mouth twitched. He did that sometimes when the effort to speak was too difficult. Tolen let go of his hand, placed his fingers on his father's cheek and whispered, "*Lon'adras.*"

Daedal took a deep breath and a tiny smile touched his lips. What had been so difficult to do, trying to speak, would not cause him pain now. The little burst of healing wouldn't last—the Tormentors had done their job well. His father's physical body could heal in time, but the wounds inflicted on his life force, his mind and spirit, may never fully heal.

"Thank you, son." He patted Tolen's hand and pulled in a slow breath. "Every day is easier than the last, even though I am still too weak to leave this room. I have a long road before my body heals fully, but every time I see your face I feel better." Daedal sighed. "But we didn't ask you to come Tolen, to talk about our health. We know you will be leaving today," Daedal paused and his mother squeezed her eyes shut. "And we wanted more than just a chance to say goodbye. There are things we promised to tell you. Things we feel you need to know before you begin your journey. I'm sorry I have not been strong enough to discuss it before now and I'm not sure how long I will be able to speak, but your mother has promised to finish if I lose consciousness again. No more secrets."

Tolen's fingers twitched.

Daedal cleared his throat and shifted his position on the bed. He lifted a shaky finger. "Will you get that paper on the table?"

Tolen leaned over to the bedside table and picked up a faded piece of parchment. "This?" It was written in the Hidden tongue, with a variety of symbols and hieroglyphs.

Daedal nodded and motioned for Tolen to read it.

His eyes flew across the page and a strange feeling filled his chest. "This is an explanation of the Hidden Hierarchy, The Order of the Nine Realms."

Daedal sighed and closed his eyes. "Do you understand?"

"Not completely." Tolen shook his head.

"With time, you will." Daedal nodded sadly. "The Order of the Nine Realms is the system of harmony that allocates the highest followers of Light. It is how we govern our very lives. It is our direction, our faith, our divine purpose. To be in the Order is of highest honor and purpose. To dishonor the Order is worse than death." He put his hand over the parchment. "Keep it."

Tolen folded the paper and put it in his back pocket.

"I fell in love with your mother long before either of us worked at the citadel." His father continued. Tolen glanced at his mother, but her eyes were on her hands clasped together in her lap. "I was twenty-six in Hidden years; 178 human years, when I first saw her. She was the most beautiful woman I'd ever seen. I had but my final test and initiation left to become a full Protector. I'd come back to my village after nearly eight Hidden years of training to visit my mother and my younger brother, Daemon." Daedal squeezed his eyes shut and ran a trembling hand through his hair—a trait Tolen had inherited—took a ragged breath and licked his dry lips before continuing.

"My father was killed when I was fifteen and Daemon nine. After my transcendence at eighteen earth years, I accepted a call to join the Protectors, my mother was left to raise Daemon alone." Tolen's eyebrow lifted and his father clarified. "Once you have been chosen to train with the Protectors you leave everything else behind, including family. It is a sacrifice not to be taken lightly, but also a great honor. My mother was very proud to have her son in such a noble calling.

"Love for your mother came swiftly for me, but it wasn't until the first blood bath marking the beginning of the Radia Revolution that she agreed to marry me. We did not know if either of us would survive the escalating war. We wanted to be together for what was left of our lives. When the revolution ended nearly 100 years later, we had both survived, yet also lost so much. We decided to leave our stations and try to have a life together free of fighting and pain. It was a vain wish and one made without deep thought."

He looked back at Tolen, his voice quavered and dropped to a whisper. "I was a Protector, your mother a Sentinel Sphere. We were in the Order, part of the Second Realm, and we dishonored them." A tear slid down his cheek. "I am a disgrace. I had a duty, a responsibility, to you, to your mother, to the entire race of beings who dwell on this Earth and I failed. Our actions, keeping you from your destiny, hiding the truth from you…My selfishness nearly cost me not only my own life and that of my precious family, but had you never discovered who you are, could have led to the downfall of the Light in this world." His voice caught and Tolen put his hand over his father's heart.

"Your heart was in the right place, Dad. You only wanted what was best for me."

Daedal's breathing slowed, but his eyes still shone with unshed tears. He gripped Tolen's hand. "I know it isn't easy, son, but don't make the same mistakes we did. There's always purpose in the Light's expectations, even if we can't see it right away. There is a reason for everything."

Daedal's regret felt like a knife in Tolen's own heart and right now he couldn't take it. He could see why his parents had defied the Light and followed their own desires. But there was no denying the results of their choice had brought them to their current state and left their son unprepared to fight the Dark forces intent on killing him.

It was a warning.

Tolen had a duty to the Light, just as his father had, and he was afraid Tolen would follow his own desires instead.

What scared him most was the realization that his father's fears were legitimate. He felt as if there were two sides to himself, one that desired to be with Macy above all else, and the other that knew the importance of his mission as the Ninth *and* Macy as Light's Aid.

Daedal started to cough again and Tolen held onto his shoulder until he was finished. Areen watched with pain in her expression.

"Are you okay?" Tolen squeezed his father's shoulder.

Daedal dipped his chin but his eyelids fluttered and his breathing turned shallow.

Tolen leaned over the bed and touched his father's forehead. "He's exhausted." He looked at his mother. "Was there more?"

She met his gaze with moist eyes. "He wanted me to tell you about Daemon."

3 THE BRAND

"DID YOU LOVE him?" Tolen asked. "Daemon?"

"Yes." Areen's voice cracked and her cheeks reddened. Tolen sucked in a deep breath, and pushed back against the heat in his palms, holding it in.

"I was easily distracted and Daemon was exciting. My parents were very old fashioned. I liked trying different things with my gifts. I liked walking around the village and sensing the people around me, their character, and their strengths and weaknesses. I liked finding those in need of healing and helping them."

"That doesn't sound so bad," he whispered.

His mother's eyes hardened. "I wasn't doing it to genuinely help. I wanted their praise. Their notice. I wanted the glory. I reveled in my gifts. I believed they made me special, better—"

"You agreed with the Hidden who were against the humans." The disgust was there in his tone even though he tried to hide it. The effort to hold back the Kuna, to focus, was bringing forward the frustration he'd dealt with his entire life from her secrets. For so long he'd wanted to know everything, but never had he imagined her secrets would lessen his opinion of her. He thought he'd forgiven her for her deception—hiding him from his destiny and the truth behind his birth—but the resentment was still there. He hadn't dealt with it, he'd buried it, and now he could feel it pushing its way out, tainting the gentle image he'd always had of her.

She looked up and met his gaze. "I did. You have to understand Tolen, it was a very different time. The Dark was growing. Humans seemed to fall under its power easier than Hidden kind. Daedal didn't tell you how his father was killed. He was murdered by a band of Darkened humans when they attacked their peaceful village of Nature Speakers. Nearly everyone in the village was killed, ruthlessly, mercilessly—"

"But they were gifted. How could humans defeat them?"

His mother sighed. "Most humans can hide their darkness, Tolen, unlike the Hidden whose features change to show their choice, which makes humans all the more dangerous. But there are some humans who have turned so evil, who have wholeheartedly given themselves over to the Dark, that they too change, but it is subtle unless you know what to look for—a deadness in the eyes, an indescribable smell, a tremor in the Balance that sickens. Their powers are a combination of darkness and human skill. Deception, selfishness, greed, times a thousand. Shadows of their true selves they move like wraiths, no longer human. They are the Darkened. Demons in the truest sense of the word."

Tolen shivered.

"Hidden fight with honor. These creatures did not. With Dark on their side, half the village was silently slaughtered before the fighters even knew what was happening. Your grandfather made Daedal take his mother and younger brother and escape." She covered her mouth with her hand and turned her gaze out the window, lost in memory. "Until I met your father I was wholeheartedly involved with Daemon and his twisted dreams of Hidden domination. I believed every word he said about the need for the destruction of the human race. Part of me knew he was wrong. Part of me knew that the thirst for revenge was making him become the very thing he'd pledged to fight against."

She looked at Daedal and ran her fingers along his cheek. The harshness left her face and some of the heat left Tolen's chest. She held years of guilt and sorrow on her shoulders. It didn't excuse her actions, and he was still angry with her, furious even, but a tiny seed of sympathy began fighting for a place as she continued.

"Eventually, I realized what Daemon really was even before he turned into the monster he is now, and I began training to work at the citadel. A selfless career under the watchful care of the Guardians seemed to be the best option for me. Your father visited me as often as he could. I thought for a long time he still hoped I'd be able to change Daemon. It wasn't until he first asked for permission to kiss me that I realized his feelings." Her sallow cheeks glowed pink and love flowed from her eyes as she looked at her husband. "I couldn't believe someone like him could even be interested in someone as lost as I was. I ignored his advances for some time; I knew I didn't deserve him, but I couldn't help falling in love with him." Her voice caught and she touched her husband's hand. "We continued in our duties plotting and planning how to fight Darsapean. I gave them all the information I could on Daemon. We were able to stop Darsapean."

She was silent for a long time and Tolen mulled over what she'd said and not said. "What did Daemon mean when he said he found us when I was little?"

It wasn't fun to remember the reason for this question that had surfaced in the dark horrors of the Shadow Prison. Macy unable to move, his parents trapped, Daemon stalking toward them—yellow eyes filled with hate, black fangs bared, horns glistening in the pale blue light—filling Tolen's head with tales of his parents and terrifying oaths.

Areen wrapped her fingers around Daedal's limp hand. "When you were about a year old we were discovered by a Kludde—a soul tracker. I had been ill, a strange illness I couldn't overcome, and it weakened me enough that our tremors affected the Balance. I'd seen the crows, but I thought I was shielding us enough to keep us from discovery. I was wrong. A Doogar friend named Ishta, came to help take care of me. She'd been gone for an hour when Daemon's demon appeared in our home and trapped us. It opened a link to the Shadow Realm. Daemon threatened to kill you if I didn't go back to him. The demon forced my hand through the link, and Daemon sealed the promise." She absently rubbed a small mark on her left wrist.

"What's that?" Tolen turned her wrist to see it better. "I've never seen it before."

Areen tugged her hand free and folded her arms. "A brand. Daemon's claim over me. It faded after awhile, but my time in the Shadow Realm brought it back. It's proof of his power over me." Her breathing increased and she glanced again out the window.

The symbol—a solid black eye within a circlet of black leaves—the same symbol had been etched on Daemon's sword as Tolen fought him in the Shadow Realm. His stomach turned.

"Ishta and her brothers returned just in time. They killed the demon and took us underground. They welcomed me into their home in the Binithan until I was well. I contacted them again in Green River when I was no longer strong enough to shield you."

"And they sent Dane and Hank up to help." His heart clenched at the memory of his deceased best friend. A boy he'd believed to be exceptionally short, but who was actually a real live dwarf, like in story books, or as Dane had corrected Tolen, *I'm a Doogar, not a dwarf.* Without Dane, Tolen knew he would never have found any joy in that place.

She nodded.

"The promise to Daemon. Is there no way to break it?" Tolen's fingers trembled.

Areen shook her head. "No. At least no one here knows how." She looked up at him and tears trailed down her cheeks. "It's no less than I deserve, Tolen. I have made so many mistakes. I let fear rule my heart. I have always known what I should do, but never had the courage to do it. I don't want to let you go. I don't want you to face this destiny. But I guess it's a fitting punishment for what I've done."

Tolen swallowed back his feelings of betrayal, stood up, and wrapped his arms around his mother. "Dad will heal and I'll be okay." His next words were for both of them. "We just have to have faith."

4 SEPARATION

MACY TOOK HER time walking back to Tolen's room, her stomach in knots. She passed the giant windows without noticing the view, she passed other visitors and residents without noticing their faces. She knew how the Light worked. She would not be forced to go on this mission. It had to be her choice. But she also knew that her refusal could have dire consequences—Jonas's warning was proof. In all her years as a Chosen this was the only time she could remember actually not wanting to go on a mission.

Tolen's door was wide open by the time she returned. She knew before she even popped her head in that he wasn't there.

Her shoulders drooped. They wouldn't make him leave without letting them say goodbye, would they?

She turned back to her room, stepped through the doorway, and noticed a notecard standing on the table next to a plate of food and the bag of pastries she'd left in the thinking room. She rushed over and snatched up the card. It was from Bastian.

LaUnahi,

I already packed your bag. Do not leave your room and speak to no one. An escort will take you to the gate to the human realm in less than an hour. I shall not see you again before you go, but know I am always with you.

Trust the Light, trust your instincts, and you will know where to go.

I love you, my little bird,

Bastian

Her bag sat open on the chair, she could just see her MP3 inside sitting on top of a large bag of purple suckers. Under the card were four familiar objects. Bastian's battered compass, a Movan-made flash drive, and another Movan device the size of her palm that looked familiar, but she couldn't remember how to work. Movan could manipulate bioelectricity and were the geniuses behind all the world's technology, which meant the device could do any number of things. She'd worry about it later. There was also a set of keys she recognized as those he used to unlock the various storage sheds Bastian rented all over the country. Her eyes burned as she put the compass in a pocket of her cargo pants. The keys, drive, and device she tossed in the bag, zipping it shut. This was by far the hardest thing he'd ever asked of her. And that included how hard it was for her to try to befriend Tolen back when she thought he was the end of her world.

Tolen, the true *beginning* of her world. How could she leave him? Especially without saying goodbye?

Tears pricked her eyes and she pressed the note to her chest. Smoke started to rise from the edges of the paper.

"You don't really want to burn that, do you?"

"Tolen!" Macy dropped the note and spun around.

He was perched on the windowsill, a branch from a nearby tree curling back into its natural form behind him.

He jumped inside, dropped his pack to the floor, and she flung herself into his arms.

"Hey Mace." His voice was just as heavy and sad as Bastian's.

Standing on her toes, and keeping her arms around his neck, she pulled back to see his eyes. His blue Watcher's eye dilated and contracted so fast it made her dizzy. She tried to focus on his brown eye, but what was he *seeing* with his Second Sight? Or worse, what had he already seen? She opened her mouth to ask, but he was kissing her before she could get the words out.

She could feel fear, desperation, need in this kiss. He pressed his hands to her back and lifted her off her feet. Her heart raced with fear. The Kuna within her began to react to what she could feel coming from Tolen's life force. Pain, terror, heartbreak, betrayal and sorrow so deep it reminded her of the moment she'd sat holding Bastian's lifeless body in her arms.

She held in the heat as he ended the kiss and tucked her head beneath his chin. He stroked her hair and she clung tightly to him. Scared as she was, she couldn't deny the peace she felt when he held her this way. Love. Jun'tar—Dominant of the Kunamin—would say love was the only real power in this world.

Tolen cupped her face in his hands. "We don't have much time. Are you packed?"

She nodded. "Bastian took care of it. He said I was to wait for someone to take me to the gateway."

"I'm going to take you. My guards will be here any minute to guide us. Bastian feels that the fewer who know about our separation," his voice broke, "the better." He pulled her back under his chin and she pressed her cheek against his chest, listening to the fast beat of his heart.

"Tolen, it's okay." She swallowed. "I'm used to this sort of thing." He cocked his head to the side and she amended. "Well, I'm used to being sent on dangerous missions we don't always get explanations for, but this will be the first one I've ever attempted on my own."

"You saved me on your own." Tolen ran his finger down her cheek.

She looked up and met his eyes. "We saved each other." His eyes hardened and she knew she'd just made things worse. "Just a sec. I was saving this for your birthday, but," she pulled away and grabbed the small box she'd been keeping in her bedside table.

"Happy *early* birthday."

His fingers trembled as he pulled the thin blue ribbon off the box. Inside was a watch specially made for him by the Movan who lived and worked here in the Light Realm, silver with a deep-blue face.

He stroked the glass but didn't speak.

"It's Movan-made, so it has no batteries. It'll never stop working. It's waterproof, shatterproof, and glows when you tap the button on the side. They said it did a whole bunch of other technical stuff, but I didn't understand what they were talking about. I knew you were smart enough to figure it out. It's got an inscription on the back…" She trailed off and bit her fingernail.

Tolen gently took the watch out of the box and turned it over.

O'winishnee —Macy

"It means—"

"*I love you beyond time.*" Tolen rubbed his thumb across the inscription. "It's Hidden language."

"Bastian told me it's something they used to say forever ago in Promise ceremonies. I guess it's a little corny." She could feel her face turning red.

A tear rolled down Tolen's cheek. He dropped the box and wrapped his arms around her. "It's beautiful. Thank you, Macy."

She let him hold her, their tears silent yet steady, for a full minute before she pulled back and touched his chin until he met her eyes. This was part of the Hidden world, the Chosen path, whether they liked it or not. It hurt to say her thoughts aloud, but as the words left her mouth, she couldn't deny the truth of them. "Tolen, being Chosen isn't easy, but the world needs us. Jonas said we will be the only chance for the human race—at least I think that's what he was saying—and I trust him. I trust Bastian, I trust the Light, and I trust *you* completely. You'll train and become even stronger than you already are—which is really cool. I'll succeed in my mission, and we *will* meet again soon."

If this was to be a mission of faith, then this was her first prayer: that they *would* be together again. The Balance and the Light would not have brought Tolen and her together just to rip them apart before they really wreaked some havoc on the Dark's plans.

"Time to wreak some havoc." Tolen smiled as he spoke her thought aloud but the smile didn't touch his red-rimmed eyes. "I love you."

"I love *you.*" When their lips met and the fire started in her veins, she felt a shift take place somewhere in her body—a connection being solidified. Something had been molded into her heart. Tolen had become part of her as much as every other organ in her body, and she knew as long as they were separated, her heart would ache and bleed for the return of the whole.

ooo

Tolen wished he could extend this moment into a thousand moments, but he heard footsteps outside the room and broke the kiss. He gathered both their packs, tugged them over his shoulders, and waited for Macy to strap on her knife and belt loaded with her herb pouches. When she finished he grabbed her hand and led the way out of the room to where two huge guards stalked toward them.

The seven-foot tall Radia Warriors he'd met back in Jonas's camp had radiated power, but there was a kindness in their eyes that made you feel safe and comforted—once you got over the strange leather clothing, woven breastplates shining with glowing beads, and menacing weapons clasped in their huge fists. He even considered Incrah, leader of that Radia Warrior band, to be his friend.

These guards looked far more intimidating than friendly. They stood just as tall as Incrah, but were fiercer in both appearance and demeanor. Shiny armor gleamed over their chests. Heavy metal plates carved with strange runes were laced tightly over their arms and thighs, their bronze helmets tucked beneath their muscled arms—the thickness of their biceps equaling at least both of Tolen's thighs. Harsh lines carved deep paths in their brooding foreheads and around their unsmiling mouths. White scars marked their hands and thick fingers, and streaks of silver hair whispered at their temples. But it was the knowledge and experience in their dark eyes, the hardness centuries of battle had forged into their depths, that told him these were not men he would likely be making friends with.

The taller of the two, with thick, wavy red hair, held out his arm. Tolen held out his own arm and they grasped each other around the bicep and shook in the traditional Hidden greeting. He had a solid no-nonsense air. "I'm Brax." He pointed to his fair-haired companion. "This is Reed." The blond shook Tolen's arm with an iron grip and a look that said he wasn't thrilled to be where he was.

They greeted Macy as well, glanced at the knife she had strapped to her thigh, and nodded in approval.

Reed took a long silver sword with a golden hilt, sheathed in woven gray material from Brax. He motioned for Tolen to turn around and strapped the sword to Tolen's pack. The two turned on their heels and walked away, obviously expecting Macy and Tolen to follow.

The trip through the Forest of Grace didn't take long enough. Tolen wished in some ways he was alone with Macy so they could talk, but what more could be said that wouldn't add to their pain?

Ten minutes later the guards led them to a thick copse of trees where two men with silver hair, dressed in creamy white robes, stood waiting.

They motioned for Macy to join them, but Tolen followed clutching her hand. The men waved their hands in the air and a golden sphere appeared, widening until they could see a different, darker forest through the gateway. Tolen tugged her pack over her shoulders, pressed his forehead to hers and whispered, "I asked Bastian if he knew where your link would open, but he said not even the gatekeepers would know, only the Light. I can see that you need to head northeast, but that's all." He touched the shards by her throat, kissed her lightly on the lips, and held her hand as she passed through the link. "Stay safe."

"You too." She whispered.

He drew his hand back and the link slowly closed.

ooo

Macy knew that the last look on Tolen's face, fear mixed with pain, would haunt her in the days to come.

She felt her shard and Bastian's connecting her to Tolen, but the tug from her heart was stronger. She put her hand over the shards willing them and her heart to be calm. If she was going to put one foot in front of the other and focus on where she was supposed to go, she needed her head straight, a feat that would be virtually impossible if she couldn't stop thinking about him.

She took a deep breath, hoisted her pack higher on her shoulder, turned away from the Light Realm, and headed northeast—into the darkness of the unknown, focused on a light she could not see.

5 A Message From the Light

Tolen's hands blurred as his gifts began reacting to his pain. "I need a minute," he said without turning, his pack and the sword slipped off his shoulders and fell to the ground.

"We don't have a minute." One of the guards shuffled behind him.

"Give me a minute!" Tolen's body blurred out of sight and grasping onto the gift of the Dicernan, the unseen, he rushed from the spot, fighting to hold his other gifts inside.

He made it just beyond the guards before he let go of his hold on the Dicernan, reappeared, and collapsed in a small clearing. The trees around him swayed their branches, mimicking his pain with a horrible dance of their own. Wind rushed through the grass, stirring up a cloud of choking dust, and the once still and peaceful forest filled with the black cloud of Tolen's despair. Even the animals ran off, unable to bear his pain.

He pressed his hands to the earth and the ground rumbled beneath his palms, shifting and cracking as a scream built in his chest. The power growing inside him he'd been trying so hard to control let loose as the plea escaped his throat. "WHY?"

Instantly the rumbling stopped, the trees ceased their dance, and the dust settled. Tolen fell to his back as an unknown power overcame him.

"Destiny is not singular." The voice was loud, familiar and unfamiliar, echoing with the deep timbre of many male voices speaking at once. It moved through him until it touched his very soul.

The voice of Light itself.

Tolen shielded his eyes from the increasing brightness of the sky.

"You are in pain."

His heart felt like it was going to shatter. He had never truly understood the truth behind the analogy of a broken heart.

"Have peace, Tolen Daedal Téloran."

The pain in Tolen's chest *moved,* as if he were temporarily separated from it, but he couldn't stop the tears. It felt horribly selfish to ask, but the question couldn't be silenced. "What if I lose her?"

A soft sigh seemed to carry on the wind. "Macy was Chosen for a reason, Tolen. Do you accept this?"

Tolen swallowed. "I'm trying. I just—I don't understand why her mission couldn't wait until I could go with her, to help protect her from the evil I've seen in my visions."

"Sacrifices are often required that outweigh even the love between individuals."

Tolen squinted into the light. "But my parents had me even though Bastian said their forbidden union should have rendered them unable to procreate. That must mean, it has to mean, that sometimes love *should* outweigh duty."

"There is much you do not understand Tolen. The birth of the Ninth Chosen was necessary to the survival of the Light in this world. And it was not an accident that you were selected to fulfill this role. Love did not overrule duty in your parent's case. The Light selected them to be your parents and had they obeyed the rules of the Hidden, time would have allowed their union. Your birth would have been celebrated, hailed, and you would have been taught our ways. Their deception caused deep ripples in the watery paths of future. Only time will tell just how far the effects will reach. Already you question the Light and our intentions."

"I thought love was the epitome of Light. If that's true, how can loving someone be wrong?"

"Love is never *wrong,* Tolen. But as Bastian tried to teach you, timing is everything. Even love has to be shown and *lived* in the correct way and time. The needs of the many and the needs of the few must be weighed."

Tolen's fears began to take the shape of puzzle pieces in his mind, twisting and turning this way and that, seeking to make sense of the Light's words.

Bastian taught him that every infinitesimal decision affected the future. Tolen's parents had kept Bastian from finding him, which shifted the future and Tolen wasn't the confident warrior he would have been. Instead, he was an insecure teenager raised in the human world. Had he been confident and self-assured he had no idea if he would have ever been humble enough to look past Macy's outward faults to see the beauty in her heart. He'd fallen for her before they'd recognized the depth of their individual and joint purposes. This *early* fall into love had put a "ripple" in their future that would make following the path to their destiny all the harder.

He pushed his weary body until he was sitting cross-legged on the ground. His arms shook, and he felt extremely weak, as if the Light were pulling strength from him—or just from his gifts, preventing them from going haywire because of his tangled emotions. "So my needs—Macy's needs—are not as important as the needs of the entire world?"

"The many and the few encompass far more than that. Life, truth, future, past, present, death, pain, illness, sorrow. All things are interconnected as a circle with no beginning and no end. The needs of the many and the few change constantly. Although love will always be a compass to what should matter most to you in this life, you must learn to look past your own needs and desires in order to make your decisions based on the needs of the moment to achieve the necessary outcome. This is the duty of the Ninth."

His eyes burned as the light faded. The sounds of the forest met his ears, and the feeling of being cut in half returned—the half that was Ninth Chosen cut away from the boy who was in love with Macy—separating the person he was meant to be from the person he wanted to be, a dividing crack in his heart.

He stood up, his legs still trembling, dusted his hands on his pants, and trudged back to his guards.

6 BLOOD AND FIRE

WHEN TOLEN RETURED to the gatekeepers Bastian was standing beside the guards holding Tolen's discarded pack. He walked forward and put his hand on Tolen's shoulder. "This mission is not easy for either of us. I am afraid there is much we will not understand until it is over."

Tolen nodded once as Bastian helped him tug the pack and sword back over his shoulders.

"But—"

He looked up to see a tiny glimmer of hope flash in Bastian's eyes.

"—you must always do what you feel is best. Tolen, you *are* the Ninth Chosen. You have been selected to watch for Macy even more so than I have. You will best see what the next movements should be."

Bastian glanced at the guards and lowered his voice. "Do you remember what I told you of fate and destiny when you were in the Binithan?"

Tolen nodded slowly. "You said that choice plays a role in everything. That fate and destiny are not the same thing. That some things have been set in motion that can't be stopped, but my choices affect the final outcome of my life." He couldn't stop it—hope started to blossom in his chest, a slight smile wanted to lift his cheek. "We can't interfere with the destiny of others, but our choices can affect their circumstances."

Bastian tilted his head. He still didn't smile but his eyes twinkled. "Listen to the Light, Tolen. Follow the guidance of your shard. Train hard. You will be guided when the time is right for you to affect the circumstances of others." He nodded toward the white-haired men waiting to open the gate. "*Liosladon.*"

"Bye Bastian." He shoved his hands into his pockets, and turned to face the gatekeepers as they opened a new portal into a forest far different from the one Macy had entered.

Tolen ducked his head and followed the guards without a glance back.

He turned his thoughts to the kindness he felt from the wildlife that followed his steps. Their thoughts were hopeful and encouraging. It helped him place his feet one after another. He sped up slightly when he heard an impatient sigh from Reed. They must have hated what they saw as a babysitting mission. If Tolen had been trained from birth, as was the original plan, he would already be out there fighting, instead of being hidden and coddled. They didn't care it wasn't his fault. They didn't care that his mother hid him from his destiny, that he hadn't known his heritage until the truth showed up on his doorstep in the form of the Watcher Bastian and his ward, Macy.

Thinking about Macy was too painful. He straightened his shoulders and determined he wouldn't be a burden. He would make the trip to the Zenith as easy on his guards as possible.

Brax and Reed put on their helmets as they passed from the Light Realm into the human world. As the gate closed behind them, Tolen's body reactively tensed. The amount of evil in the human dimension had grown far more than he could have imagined it would in their short time in the Light Realm. The heaviness of the Dark pressed on his life force, alerting his senses and awakening his gifts. He pulled back on the warmth rising in his palms, maintaining focus, he would not react on feelings only. "Where are we?"

"Montana." Reed whispered. "Somewhere in the middle of Glacier National Park." The guards had been walking tall and confident in the Light Realm but now slowed their steps. Their eyes darted back and forth as they made their way deeper into the new forest with taller trees and deeper shadows. The sun's light, barely visible through the thick canopy of leaves, cast an eerie green glow over their lined faces. His guards unsheathed their long swords from behind their backs and motioned Tolen to do the same.

A weird sound met his ears, like the cry of a jay, but twisted, raspy. He shivered and the guards glanced up.

"Impossible." Reed twisted around, looking into the trees.

"They were ready for us." Brax looked back at Tolen.

An explosion of evil materialized, pressing in from all sides. "How?" Tolen spun around. "I'm shielding! I didn't draw them here!"

Brax didn't have a chance to answer. A black arrow slammed through his helmet into the back of his head and he collapsed.

Tolen stared at the lifeless body, unable to move.

"Get behind me!" Reed shouted.

It felt like Tolen was stuck in a nightmare where everything moved in slow motion. He shifted his body until he and Reed were back to back. They began circling, looking all around. Another arrow zinged by their heads; Reed raised his shield and a third bounced off the metal.

Tolen called to the wind and the trees and a fierce gale whipped through the forest. The trees burst to life, swatting and crushing, but he couldn't see what was attacking them.

A frightened bear came running toward them. Tolen tried to call to it, but as soon as it reached them it blurred out of focus and then it was a man, horribly grotesque and covered in shaggy fur, larger than a grizzly on its hind legs. Before any of this could fully register, the creature leaped onto Reed and sank its teeth into his neck.

Tolen twisted to the side, running his sword between the creature's ribs. It lifted its hairy head, screeched, and took off back into the trees with Tolen's blade stuck in its side. Reed seemed to fall in slow motion, his eyes meeting Tolen's once before the life left them and he fell to the ground.

Tolen watched in horror as animals of every shape and size appeared out of the shelter of the trees and surrounded him, their bodies blurring and shifting into hundreds of hairy man-creatures. Some held crudely hewn bows or axes, others simply stood there with saliva dripping from their pointed teeth, their soulless eyes filled with inhuman savagery.

Tolen stood weaponless in a pool of blood and stared into the hideous faces of his assassins.

7 FRIEND OR FOE

THE FOREST FELL dead silent as the hairy creatures circling Tolen paused. A horrible smell, like sweat and death saturated the air, gagging him. He watched those holding the bows, waiting for the arrows to fly. He could pick up one of the guard's swords, but one sword against this army would never succeed. Instead he concentrated on the weapons he held within his life force and focused on trees surrounding the battlefield, wanting to time the attack just right. He felt for the calming ability of the Dicernan—the Unseen. It was time to become one with his surroundings and disappear, but calling it into being was entirely different and far more difficult than when his gifts thought for themselves and exploded out of him. He tried to focus on what Vindi—master of the Dicernan—taught him.

Lose the fear of the situation and focus on the tremors of the life forces around you—move with *them. You are no longer apart from them—you are* part *of them.*

Tolen closed his eyes. *Now!*

The trees wrapped their branches around every creature they could reach. Tolen heard the loud crunch and snap of their bones at the same moment he felt the Balance settle around him, and he became one with his surroundings. He opened his eyes and all was chaos. The grotesque creatures ran blindly deeper into the forest as the trees ripped at their bodies. Tolen stayed still and silent, his back pressed against the bark of the nearest tree, until the air went quiet and every remaining dark creature lay dead among the dried leaves of the forest floor. He listened for the minds of innocent animals and made sure any fleeing creature was a good distance away before he broke focus.

Tolen let go of his hold on the Balance and bent over gasping with his hands on his knees. Using the gift of the Dicernan was one of the most difficult gifts, but it'd been a lot easier in the Light Realm.

He looked down, feeling their presence before he saw the claws of the Night Demons coming for the bodies strewn all over the ground. A quick silent request and two trees swept their branches down and gently lifted Brax and Reed's bodies out of reach. With a wave of Tolen's hand the wind gathered up the broken bodies of the Dark creatures and lowered them into a pile.

"*Mi'no ha!*" Tolen twisted his fingers and aimed the fireball at the pile. He opened his hands, pushing the heat from his palms into the heart of the pile. The fire burned hotter, hotter, the light increasing from red-orange to bright white, and the pile exploded into a shower of choking ash and dust.

Before the first Demon fully broke free of the ground, Tolen whispered the words that made the spot beneath Brax and Reed's trees into sacred burial ground. The Night Demon's screeching echoed from the dirt as they were forced away from the feast of death.

Tolen whispered a plea to the Earth. Slowly, a hole large enough to hold the bodies of the guards opened and the trees tenderly laid them inside. The ground rolled over them as Tolen spoke the words of the burial chant with his eyes closed tight. He did not shed a tear for the men who had died for him despite the burning behind his lids—he knew they would not like it. They died doing their duty, something no fighter for Light would begrudge.

He opened his eyes to see a sprinkling of bright purple and yellow wildflowers, and blades of tall field grass sprouting over the grave, hiding the gruesome truth of the battle, and creating a beautiful resting place.

Tremors rocked through Tolen's body as he fought against the horror of his situation. Barely an hour had passed from when he'd said goodbye to his parents, to Macy, to Bastian. He had no idea how to get to the Zenith on his own, and based on the fact that the Dark had been waiting for him, how could he guarantee they didn't know where he was headed and be waiting for him there as well?

He glanced down at the watch Macy had given him to see a strange rune glowing bright blue across the face. It looked like a black crescent moon eclipsing a sun. It flashed brightly once and disappeared. It was 1:43 pm, but the shadowy forest looked closer to sunset. He needed a safe place to come up with a new plan.

He'd accidentally opened a portal to the Citadel once. Jonas said that as the Ninth he could bend certain laws if the need arose. Well he definitely had a need, but the old man hadn't told him *how* he'd bent the laws or how to do it again.

He closed his eyes and concentrated on the good life forces that could help him find shelter. After minutes that felt like hours, as exposed as he was, the image of a small crevice in a rocky hillside about a half mile north cut across his vision, and he pushed his legs forward, hoping beyond hope it would really be safe for the night. Not only did he need to think, he needed to regenerate. His body felt weak and shaky. He had a sneaking feeling not even the Guardians could see just how powerful the darkness in this realm had become. This single battle shouldn't have drained him this much, not now that he knew how to control his gifts better. Despite the weakness he felt, he pushed the Kuna to his palms, the tingle reassuring as he moved forward, one measured step at a time.

ooo

The sounds of the surrounding forest disappeared. "Tolen!" Macy's scream came out more like a sob. She heard nothing but the pounding of her blood. Bastian's shard sent another painful jolt through her body. *Tolen is in danger!* it seemed to be screaming.

Her arms and legs shook violently—the panic and fear overwhelming her physical body. Her eyes blurred out of focus. Black spots danced across her vision. Her breath whooshed loud and fast from her lungs. Her stomach rolled and saliva flooded her mouth. She was either going to puke or pass out.

LaUnahi! Her Watcher's voice cut through the terror.

Bastian!

Sit down!

Her body instinctively followed the command, knowing her Watcher's voice, trusting he was there to take care of her, as he had always done.

Slow your breathing.

But Tolen! Her breathing continued toward hyperventilation.

Macy! He is safe! Breathe!

Her lungs reacted to the word "safe" and her breathing slowed marginally, at least her head stopped spinning. Bastian continued to speak, his voice filling her body with calm. If Bastian said Tolen was safe, then she trusted him. Bastian did not lie.

Your body reacted to the forceful emotions of my shard. You need to search past the emotion. The shard can tell you what you need to know if you stay focused. Focus!

Macy concentrated on the sound of Bastian's voice to help center her thoughts. The shard was pulsing gentle bursts of relief, but the relief paled in comparison to the forcefulness of the terror before. This must mean that Tolen was still in danger, but he was safe for now. She was no Watcher, the shard could send her emotions related to Tolen's circumstances but it couldn't show her what had happened.

"Bastian, what happened?"

But Bastian was gone.

Macy wrapped her arms around her knees, and concentrated on slowing her breathing. She closed her eyes and turned her attention to her own shard, trying to block out the strength of Bastian's. The connection to Tolen from her shard was as strong as ever. The ache in her heart throbbed. She shifted her focus to the Watcher's shard and concentrated on reining it in, calming it.

She could see now the reason Bastian was always so overbearing, so protective. The shard demanded it. A Watcher's shard was the greater half of their ward's. And Tolen and Macy's shards were each once part of Bastian's shard—the father shard. A very overprotective father.

Macy shook her head.

The drain of the Watcher's shard was incredible. If she didn't figure out how to search past the emotions, as Bastian had said, she'd never survive carrying his shard. She closed her eyes once more and concentrated on separating the emotions of the two shards—Watcher and ward. Hers would keep her aware of Tolen's life force. It would give her the comfort of his light, it would keep her aware of the Dark, her gifts at the ready. She would try to block out the stronger emotions of Bastian's shard, despite Bastian's advice, unless her shard didn't give her enough of a feel on Tolen and she had no choice but to focus on it. The overwhelmed, scared part of her wished she could simply take off Bastian's shard and put it in her bag, but the wiser, braver part of herself knew that was a very stupid idea.

She rolled onto her back and stared into the darkening umbrella of leaves above her. There was burial ground nearby, an ancient spot—she could feel it. She'd camp there for the night. She didn't have the strength to continue any further today. She pulled out Bastian's compass to make sure she hadn't strayed too far off course.

She was still heading northeast. If she were to venture a guess based on the climate and plant-life, she'd say she was somewhere in the eastern United States. She put the compass back in her pocket and pulled the Movan gadget out of her pack. The shiny silver device fit comfortably in the palm of her hand. She tapped the tiny screen, but it stayed blank. There were no buttons to try. Maybe if she could figure out how to turn the stupid thing on she'd remember exactly what it was.

She sighed and tucked the device back in her bag. *This is going to be a long trip. Take care of yourself Tolen.*

○○○

Macy's voice echoed softly in Tolen's mind. She wanted him to be safe. He concentrated momentarily on her thoughts. It was harder to hear her, whether it was the distance, his weakened life force, or the fact that the Earth realm was filled with so much more darkness, he did not know. But he'd have to think about it later. Right now he needed to figure out who was following him.

He had felt the presence just after leaving the grave of the guards. It did not feel sinister, yet he couldn't even be sure of that, because no matter how hard he tried he couldn't get a read on the thoughts of whatever was following him. He couldn't even tell if it was animal, human, or Hidden-kind, but he had no doubt someone, or something, was tailing him. He knew where his pursuer was, as the trees kept him informed of movements, yet they, too, could only sense a presence. He wished Ardia was with him—being a tree spirit her instincts would have been helpful and comforting—but after sacrificing much of her power to protect Bastian's body from the Dark she could no longer survive in the earthly realm and so would finish out her life-term in the Light Realm.

He leaned over and concentrated once again on becoming unseen. He was weak and tired and knew he couldn't keep it up for long, but maybe his follower would slip up as he tried to find him.

He didn't have to wait long. A tall man with a long, silver ponytail trailing down his back appeared from behind a thick tree trunk. He held a sword in his hand and a bow hung across his back. Long, pointed ears peeked from beneath his silver hair, and when he turned slightly, Tolen could see a white, puckered scar that split the right side of his face from temple to chin.

Tolen's breath caught. It was Quasar, Nova's guardian. They'd only met briefly in Jonas's camp, but the elf's disfigured face was impossible to forget. The memory of Nova's treachery that nearly resulted in Tolen's death and had caused her own, came back with bold clarity. Was the elf here to avenge her?

Tolen called to the tree beside the elf. Before Quasar was aware of what was happening, the tree wrapped him tightly in its branches. His sword fell to the leaves below with a *thud*.

"Come to kill me, Quasar?" Tolen released his hold on the Balance and stepped to where Quasar could see him from his leafy prison.

Quasar's violet eyes met Tolen's.

"*Iy'hika.*" Tolen spoke, meeting the elf's gaze. He reached for his thoughts.

Nothing.

Quasar smirked.

Tolen concentrated harder.

Nothing.

Quasar's smirk grew more pronounced.

Tolen's patience waned. The branches of the tree tightened and he heard Quasar gasp.

"All right. I shall let you in for but a moment so you may see my intent is good, but then my thoughts shall be my own once again. Fair enough?"

Tolen nodded once. "*Iy'hika!*"

The floodgates opened. In just a few seconds Tolen seemed to see Quasar's entire life. He saw the battle Nova had told him about between the Lafar and the Daklafar—Light elves and Dark elves. He saw thousands of dead or dying elves lying on a huge battlefield under a sky the same strange tint as that of the Shadow Realm, while Daemon stood over them triumphant. He saw scores of the Lafar led away to the Shadow Prison.

He saw two dazzling elves passing a beautiful baby girl with a shock of raven hair to Quasar's expectant wife, Nebula, while Quasar, a ghastly bloody wound on his face, held tightly to the hand of a small boy with the same dark hair as the baby. Nova and Bolide?

He saw and felt the love and concern Quasar and Nebula felt for these two children. He witnessed the pain of betrayal Quasar felt when he learned of Nova's treachery. He saw the farewell between him, his wife, and the grieving Bolide, as he set forth to right the wrong done by Nova and become Tolen's unseen protector. Tolen saw him running into the throng of man-creatures after the guards were gone, killing and injuring dozens as he headed toward Tolen. He saw the elf weep over the grave of Brax and Reed before he stood up and began to pursue Tolen once again, this time with the intent to let Tolen know that he was following.

He'd allowed himself to be caught.

The images stopped and instantly a wall was back in place protecting Quasar's mind. If Tolen hadn't been looking right at him he would have thought the man had somehow escaped and disappeared.

Though it was hard to doubt the man's clear thoughts, Tolen was still leery to fully trust. "How can you do that? Block me out?"

"Let me down and I will tell you."

The tree slowly lowered Quasar to the ground, but its branches still hovered nearby.

"Okay, talk."

Quasar's jaw clenched. "Under cover. We must get somewhere safe before nightfall. Then I will answer your questions."

8 INSTINCT

Tolen watched with his arms folded and his fingers twitching as the elf busily sprinkled herbs around their makeshift shelter—a small shelf of rock turned lean-to. From the outside, it looked like nothing more than a natural pile of leaves and sticks. Tolen told Quasar about the small cave the trees had shown him, even though it was likely not big enough for two, but the elf wanted to get even further away from the scene of the battle, just in case the Dark sent reinforcements. He pushed them into the thickest part of the forest—dropping herbs in their path to mask their scent and hide their footprints—until he proclaimed that he'd found a spot good enough to hide for the night.

All this effort should have helped calm Tolen's mistrust. But it didn't. In Jonas's camp, Tolen had gone against everyone's warning that the elves couldn't be trusted. He had ignored Macy and Incrah and befriended Nova, believing that any creature of Light could be good. But Nova had tried to turn him over to Daemon to save her parents. The possibility that Quasar was in league with the Dark, just as Nova had been, and was attempting to lead Tolen into some sort of trap would be stupid to ignore, no matter what the elf had shown him with his thoughts.

While Quasar worked, Tolen connected with the trees and wildlife nearby, asking them if the area had seen any Dark movements recently. They assured him there had been no evil through their part of the wood for many years, but he still asked them to inform him of any suspicious behavior. The desire for information battled with the worry he might not have the strength to fight Quasar if the answers to the questions floating around in his head proved deadly.

A sparkle on his arm caught his eye and he glanced down. The watch seemed to be pulling in the tiny beams of remaining light passing through the trees. The reflection that should be across the top of the glass instead was underneath, twisting and refracting into the many symbols and numbers that circled the face.

He tapped the strange watch and sighed. Thinking of Macy right now was dangerous. He had to focus. The screen suddenly glowed blue again showing the same eclipsed sun, only this time he could swear the black crescent had become larger, covering more of the sun symbol. Before he could wonder at its meaning, the symbol disappeared and Quasar motioned for him to enter the shelter.

Focusing on keeping his gifts as ready as his exhaustion would allow, he crawled inside and watched as Quasar pulled a door loosely woven with leaves and twigs across the entrance, plunging the shelter into near total darkness.

Tolen whispered, "*To' inreedo.*" His eyesight enhanced and Quasar's form took shape in the gloom.

"That won't be necessary," Quasar whispered back, and the tiny shelter filled with warm light. Quasar seemed to be holding a tiny flame in his hands. He gently placed it on the ground between them, and Tolen noticed it wasn't fire at all, but a palm-sized stone that emitted soft, orange light.

Tolen released his enhanced sight and the light dimmed marginally. "What is that?"

"A Fire Stone."

"I have one of those, but it's never done that."

"Have you ever asked it to?"

"No."

"You will never know what anything is capable of if you don't ask and believe that you will receive."

Tolen sensed Quasar was talking about more than just the stone, but he didn't care enough to ask.

Quasar pulled food from his pack and placed it on the ground in front of them. "Please eat."

Tolen picked up a lump of meat cake and twisted it in his hands. "I thought you were going to tell me how you blocked your mind."

"I will. I was simply being courteous. I know you must be hungry."

Tolen didn't respond.

Quasar cleared his throat and wiped his hands on a handkerchief from his pocket. "Our time in Jonas's camp taught you little about me—except that trust of one of my kind led to treachery and tragedy. You do not trust me and I will not ask you to. Trust is not something my race is granted easily."

Tolen raised his hand. "Look, I know Nova wasn't a bad person. I do. But I also know that people do desperate things for love. The fact that you can hide your thoughts from me says you could also have a way of hiding your real intentions as well. How can I know you aren't seeking vengeance for my part in Nova's death?"

"If I wanted vengeance, I would have left you to be discovered by the Dark or killed you myself."

The glow from the stone made Quasar's scar appear deeper, more grisly.

Tolen felt his temper rising. "Then how did you know where to find me? Jonas's camp is hundreds of miles away. Are you in contact with him?"

Quasar shook his head. "No. I am not."

"Then someone else at the citadel?"

Quasar shook his head again.

"Then how?" Heat trickled into Tolen's palms but he held the Kuna at bay.

The elf took a bite of meat cake and chewed slowly, increasing Tolen's frustration. "I am not in league with the Dark. I serve only the Light. I am going to do what is necessary. I am here to help you." His tone said he meant it, but didn't necessarily like it.

"That's not an answer."

"It will suffice." Quasar took another bite and a trickle of smoke rose from Tolen's palms. "I know where the Guardians were sending you."

The smoke increased. "Where?"

"To the Zenith."

The smell of cloves and earth filled the tiny space. Soon the heat would have to be released. "You shouldn't know that."

"I'm not the only one who knows."

"What do you mean?"

"Someone betrayed you. Someone told the Dark where you would come into the earth realm and that same someone most likely told them where you are going."

The heat in Tolen's palms became nearly unbearable.

"You have already accepted this conclusion. I can see it in your eyes. There is a leak within the citadel."

Only a handful of people knew of the plan. The Guardians, Keytleen, Tolen's parents, Macy. The Kuna fought for release and he closed his eyes trying to pull it back in. A fireball in this tiny space would kill them both. But the fears raging though his thoughts of a mole in the citadel were awakening all his gifts—self-preservation warring with exhaustion.

The ground rumbled beneath their feet, wind howled outside, and smoke once again curled from Tolen's palms. He fought for control, but his thoughts couldn't be silenced. The image of Daemon moving through the earth realm flashed across Tolen's vision and his control slipped. Vines ripped free of the ground and wrapped around Quasar, his gifts seeking the only recognized threat within reach. Seconds later the elf was on his side with vines tightening around his windpipe.

Tolen fought against the power surging from his body, but instinct had taken control of his gifts. His worst nightmare was coming true, his gifts were acting of their own accord to protect him. No matter what he said or did they wouldn't be stopped. His breath came in pants. Fear clutched his insides as Quasar's face turned blue.

Ding! Ding! Ding!

Bright white light shot from his watch, blasting him in the face and his control returned. "*Inasi!* Stop! Stop!" He screamed. Slowly, too slowly, the vines slithered loose from Quasar's throat and wound back into the earth, but Quasar didn't stir.

Tolen fell to the elf's side and started shaking him. "Quasar? Quasar!"

Quasar's body spasmed. He drew in a deep, grating breath and then fell into a hacking cough.

Tolen backed away, his whole body trembling. "I'm sorry, I'm so sorry. I lost—"

Quasar held up his hand and shook his head once.

"You need to leave. Now." Tolen looked down at his hands, hands that almost belonged to a murderer.

"Leave you to what?" Quasar coughed again. "Be captured by the Dark? Killed? You cannot stop me. I will follow you without your knowledge if I must."

"Why? I nearly killed you!"

"Because I believe the prophecy, *Conchla Mindra*—Ninth Chosen, and I am going to make sure you fulfill it!" The elf's violet eyes glowed with barely contained fury but also showed he meant what he said.

Giving the elf full trust would be foolish, but Tolen knew he couldn't rely solely on his precarious knowledge of the Dark and the Hidden world with only the direction of his sporadic and confusing visions to guide him. He looked at the red welts on Quasar's neck. "If I decide to let you come with me, I can't guarantee your safety. I'm…dangerous."

"I'm willing to risk it."

A long look passed between them and something clicked into place in Tolen's befuddled and exhausted brain. Quasar didn't believe Tolen was strong enough to succeed, but he did believe the prophecy of the Ninth Chosen. He cared for his people. He knew that if the Light said the world needed the Ninth, then he would do all he could to protect Tolen, even if it meant risking his life to be in the presence of a kid who couldn't control his gifts.

The desperation of his current situation had Tolen weighing all the angles. The Guardians had wanted him to get to the Zenith. He needed a safe place to train and transcend. But now his guards were dead and he had no idea how to find the Zenith. Whether he wanted to admit it or not, he needed help.

9 OF STARS AND ELVES

A HEADACHE STARTED ABOVE Tolen's right eye and he rubbed his thumb against it. "Fine. You can come."

Quasar started tracing in the dirt, possibly allowing Tolen a moment to think. "Protecting the mind is only achieved through extensive training and is incredibly difficult to master." His tone was light, conversational—an obvious attempt to soften the tense atmosphere by returning to Tolen's original question.

Tolen followed the elf's lead, stifling his guilt, turning his focus, shifting into a role. The exhaustion had returned in force and he slumped against the dirt wall, resting the back of his head against the cool surface. "Why would anyone be trained to block their Watcher?" he asked with his eyes closed.

"Not all *Dembashi*—Watchers—are on the side of Light, Tolen."

Tolen opened his eyes and noticed Quasar watching him. "But then only the person who the Watcher is responsible for, their Chosen ward, would be at risk, right?"

"Not only Watchers can sense thoughts, or the future for that matter."

"So you're trained to block more than just Watchers?"

"It's more complicated than that. The training is to achieve the ability to protect one's mind from intrusion from *any* unseen or unwelcome force. With time the individual can recognize when someone, or something, from outside is trying to get in and they put up a wall, for lack of a better word. After a while, it becomes second nature. I never enter an unknown situation without guarding my mind. It's instinctive."

Tolen's head reeled. Would the Hidden world ever stop throwing surprises at him? A sick thought entered his mind.

"Shadows—?"

Quasar's eyebrows rose.

"Shadow Wraiths can sense thoughts, can't they? That's why they can magnify Fear—the Dark's ultimate weapon. That's how they increase your greatest horrors and drown you in your own pain. They intensify the painful thoughts until you are driven mad. Tormenters—they can too, can't they?"

The elf gave a solemn nod. "Yes. That is why the Dark so highly values the Wraiths and those ghastly Tormentors. The horrors they discover in the minds of their prey can be passed along to their leaders, and then the Dark knows exactly what to use against them. Our fears are our deepest enemies. They betray us. If you do not overcome them, or learn to protect your fears from the Dark, they become your downfall."

Tolen felt the elf's last sentence was directed specifically at him and his hands went cold. The Dark knew his fear. When the Shadows held him prisoner they sensed his love for Macy and his parents. They passed that on to Daemon and Darsapean. His parents were safe under the protection of the Guardians, but Macy was out there alone, with Daemon hunting her. His fingers twitched and he clenched them into fists. "Can I learn to protect my mind?"

Quasar's eyes held a look of resignation. "The Dark already has a weapon to use against you. I can see you know this. But with time, yes, you can learn. It is a matter of concentration and focus. The more you learn to recognize the vibrations within your own mind, the more easily you will be able to sense when another's vibrations are trying to intrude."

Tolen dropped his head in his hands. Anger at his mother pushed at him, if only she'd been straight with him from the beginning. Explained this world to him. He squeezed his eyes shut once before looking up. He couldn't afford to dwell in the past. He could only move forward and focus on the future, although a different future than the one he had imagined two hours ago. But if anything happened to Macy because of him…

He shifted his thoughts from the pain, fearing the return of his anger. "How did you know where to find me?"

"I've staked out the permanent gateways to the citadel ever since word came that they hid you there. I knew you were too powerful to stay for long, and that they would move you someplace to protect you as you train and transcend. It stands to reason that such a place would be the Zenith, as it is the most powerful stronghold in the earth realm. I was right. I saw your guards come through the gate two days ago and heard them discussing their mission. I hid further on the path and waited, planning to follow."

"Wait. If you knew we were coming out there, why didn't you warn us about the ambush?"

Quasar sat back and put his hands on his knees. "I'm sure the way my kind is treated did not escape you at Jonas's camp. I am the last person they would have trusted. They would have tried to kill me as soon as they saw me, without pausing to question me. They would have believed that I set the ambush there to stop them."

Tolen didn't comment because he knew that is exactly what he would have thought. In fact it *was* what he'd thought.

"Despite what you may think, I did try to help, but I was too far away. Not since the creation of Misery have creatures of darkness been able to come out in daylight, and only the Kezgani have the ability to hide their evil from affecting the Balance. I didn't have any idea that they'd been released. I staked out the area for days and only came across a few of the usual Dark creatures, but no more than expected. The ambush took me by surprise as much as it did all of you. I was fighting my way back from the rear of the army, but I did not reach you in time." There was regret and shame in his words.

"Kezgani? Those bear things? But—how can they come out in daylight?"

"The Kezgani were once Animashta, but when they turned to the Dark their animal side took over. These shape-shifters can come out in day as their animal selves, but they do not live long once they shift to their twisted, half-human forms. Their numbers suggest that they assumed they would have an easy target, and would not have to stay in their half-human form for long."

Tolen let out a slow breath. "And I thought the Shadow Wraiths were bad."

"*Mindra*—Chosen one, you have no idea. Should Misery fall, the creatures released would quell your darkest nightmares."

Tolen shivered. Macy had said something similar when they'd first met. It was hard to imagine facing evil greater than that of the Shadows,

DéHool, or Raksasha. He shook his head. "I can't go to the Zenith." Tolen leaned forward. "If the Dark has somehow found out where it is, they will come after me there."

"After today's attack, I am afraid that by the time you reached it, the Zenith would no longer exist."

Tolen clenched his teeth. "What about all those people?" The bit of meat-cake he had eaten turned in his stomach. "We have to warn them somehow." He wouldn't leave them unaware. Great warriors or not, right now they assumed their borders were secret.

Quasar sighed. "Try to connect with the minds of the animals near us. They should be able to recognize the Kezgani as not truly their own. Send a message through those with thoughts you can trust. If you can locate an owl, that would be best, as they will know where to find the Zenith and they travel quickly."

Tolen swallowed. The Kezgani scared him more than he wanted to admit. At least everything else that attacked him he'd known was coming. He closed his eyes and felt for the animal minds around them. Most of the voices in his head were soft, subdued, almost frightened. They recognized the Kezgani and their evil. Tolen stayed away from the thoughts that were curious about the Kezgani.

It took him a few minutes, and the effort was more taxing than he felt it should be, but then he found an owl. It was in the process of hunting, but seemed to sense Tolen's intrusion and landed on the branch of a nearby tree. The owl's mind was the clearest of any animal mind Tolen had ever entered. As clear as a human's.

He focused on keeping his tone soft and gentle as he sent his request into the creature's mind.

One soft word echoed back in Tolen's mind: *Yatha.* Yes. The owl knew where the Zenith was and he would take the message to them. Tolen's words came out in a rush. "I found an owl. He's passing word to the Zenith now." Tolen could still hear the owl's voice as he gathered others to his cause and they set off in the night. "He's getting other owls to help him."

The relief in Quasar's eyes matched Tolen's feelings. "Well done. They will pass the message through the night, owl to owl. Word will reach the Zenith by dawn tomorrow." He lifted the Fire Stone to his mouth, whispered something, and the stone's light dimmed to a gentle glow. "Rest now, Tolen. Tomorrow we can answer more questions and come up with new ones."

Tolen's body responded to Quasar's words, and after a simple plea to the trees to watch over them for the night, he found himself curling up on his side watching the strange flicker of the Fire Stone as his eyes drooped shut.

JULY 7

THREE DAYS UNTIL TRANSCENDENCE

10 HIDDEN PAST

MACY TWISTED ONTO her side. Bastian had taught her that one of the safest places to sleep was burial ground. She felt the soothing comfort of the ancestors, but she couldn't help but miss the cozy bed, warm food, and indoor plumbing she'd enjoyed in the Light Realm. She wrinkled her nose. It'd probably ruined her forever.

The morning sun had yet to peek over the mountains and she guessed it probably wouldn't be up for another hour, making it unsafe to start moving.

The bigger question: *Where* the crap was she supposed to end up? Northeast wasn't exactly a lot to go on.

Her thoughts instantly shifted to Tolen. Was he safe? She absently rubbed the shards at her throat and shivered.

Focus on the task. Bastian's voice was a whisper.

She took a deep breath and sat up. Breakfast, and seeing what sort of things Bastian had packed for her, might be a good distraction. Maybe she'd get lucky and he'd given her a hint of what her next move was supposed to be. Going on faith was fine, but going on blind faith? Frustrating.

She dug out some jerky and an apple and began to nibble as she rummaged through the bag. Buried beneath her clothes was the familiar cracked leather envelope she knew contained various fake ID's, passports, fake birth certificate, and stack of money. But the stiff rectangle attached to the back of the envelope with a paper clip was not familiar. She lifted it from the pack. The unfamiliar envelope was rumpled, and the ink faded. The approaching dawn wasn't enough light to read by so she whispered the words to enhance her sight. Her fingers trembled when she finally made out the lettering on the front.

"For Macy."

It was not written in Bastian's hand.

Her heart bumped against her ribs as she turned it over. The seal had already been broken. Bastian had already opened it. She ignored the pangs of betrayal she felt. She slid several sheets of faded paper out of the envelope and opened them. The creases were worn almost completely through in places—obviously opened and closed many times.

October 23, 2000

My dearest McLacy,

So much I must tell you and yet I wish I did not have to. But if you are reading this then I am likely no longer with you. A father should always be there to protect his child. I am so very sorry—

Macy's eyes filled with tears. The letter was from her father. He had written it on her third birthday, exactly three years before his death. How long had Bastian had this? How did he get it? The questions swirled in her head as she caressed the page longingly once before reading on, scrubbing away the tears with her fists.

I would not have considered writing this if it weren't for a recent experience that leads me to believe I may not always be there to protect you, and therefore must do all I can to warn you. I can only hope and pray this is not the case, that you will never have to read this and can enjoy a normal human life.

Your mother does not wish me to do this. She wants me to leave the past in the past. Sometimes I wonder if she believes the truth of my history despite the evidences around us. I have kept no secrets from her, and I wonder if this was a wise decision. Time can only tell.

Before I begin, Macy, you must know I love you dearly, with all my heart and soul. My life was not complete until the day I first held you in my arms. From that day forward, I vowed to keep you safe from a world not everyone can see.

Knowledge can be a burden, but it can also be a protection, and as I can't be there to protect you now, I want you to know what you must in order to protect yourself. I can't explain it all in one letter so I am going to try to write a brief history for you explaining in more detail. I pray to have enough time to give you what you may need. So much of the future is veiled. The information will be hidden in a special place that you must find. You will know where to look if you remember what I have taught you.

As you read, please trust me. The world is not what you've been raised to believe.

Be safe. I love you and will always be a part of you.

Happy birthday, sweetheart.

Your loving father,

Max

Macy quickly sifted through the small stack and noticed charts and diagrams describing various Dark creatures and historical facts about the Hidden. He knew so much. How? She reached the final page. It was new, held the seal of the citadel, and was written in familiar hand.

LaUnahi,

As you read this, you will likely be very angry with me. I will not ask for your forgiveness at this time. I do not know why I felt compelled to go back to your home and search through the wreckage while you lay sleeping in a hotel. When I found this letter among the ashes I still did not understand completely. I did not feel the time was right to share it with you then. I followed my heart and that is all I can offer you. There are things you will likely glean from your father's notes that trouble me deeply. Over the years, I have sought answers to the many questions your father poses, especially about the Fallen, but I have come to no satisfactory conclusions. I was taught when I was young about the Fall of the Watchers, those who took their shards and their gifts to the side of the Dark, but I never wanted to believe them. I wanted to assume it was a tale to frighten and keep the young in line. I have counseled with the Guardians, but although the stories are a part of our history, we cannot connect to any Watchers who are not on the side of Light to prove otherwise.

Macy, if it is true, your task will be even more dangerous. My shard is connected to all Watchers, and all Watchers' shards are connected to the Chosen. If the Fallen do exist, they may try to use my shard to tempt you, as it is no longer in my possession to tame.

Maybe my reasons for not telling you are purely selfish. I have always wanted nothing more than your trust. I suppose I could not bear to find any truth to his words and possibly lose your trust.

I do not know exactly why the time to share this with you is now. I once again followed the pull of my heart.

Do what you will with the information you find here. Whether or not it will help you on your quest I do not know, but, LaUnahi, I beg you, stay true to your heart. If there be truth to your father's discoveries, do not let it sour your opinion of the Light. There are frailties in Hidden kind and men, even in those entrusted to lead, but there is no frailty in the Light. Please, please remember this.

I love you, my little bird, with every fiber of my existence.
Bastian

Macy flipped back through her father's notes until she found the one entitled *The Fall of the Watchers*.

Macy skimmed the page, her heart hammering. He said the Fallen were the inventors of Fear, using their vast knowledge of the human and Hidden psyches to create the perfect weapon. They worked with the Shadows—those creatures that had taken her parents from her—training them, honing them, controlling them. The words blurred on the page as the sharp point of betrayal cut into her heart, not from this new knowledge of the Fallen—it was scary yes—but from the fact that the one person she'd trusted and loved like a father had lied to her. Well maybe not *lied*. But keeping Max's letter from her, the only piece of her father she had left in the world, just to protect himself, felt almost worse than an outright lie.

Her hands shook so violently the papers fell out of her grasp and fluttered to the ground. The smell of eucalyptus and roses floated around her head, and the tips of her fingers glowed orange. Unable to stop the heat she aimed her fingers at the sky and the Kuna released from her hands. The burst of fire cast an orange glow into the leaves above and turned the thick branches into ghastly shadows. The image made her shiver and she dropped her still-smoking hands to her lap.

She closed her eyes and tried to rein in her anger. Bastian's shard pulsed against her throat and she could feel its emotion—it was *afraid* of her.

Bastian, how could you keep this from me?

I am so sorry, LaUnahi. I was a selfish old man. The whisper was full of chagrin, and Macy's anger evaporated to be replaced by something much worse.

Jun'tar told her love was more powerful than anger and he was right. She loved Bastian. With all her heart. But it was Jonas's words about how love was the only emotion that could cause two equally powerful, yet opposite emotions—incredible joy and crippling pain—that rang through her head. It hurt terribly that Bastian would keep this from her. She wasn't angry anymore. Instead she felt sick, disappointed, and afraid. Afraid that no matter what she discovered about her family's past, or the Hidden hierarchy—even if Bastian ended up being right to keep it from her—she might never be able to fully forgive him for it.

She took a deep breath, reined in the hurt, and turned her focus.

The fear slowly left Bastian's shard, but she could feel its caution. The constant flux of emotions could cause the shard to lose its allegiance to her, but she couldn't completely ignore the ache, it was part of her now, like an ugly crack in an otherwise flawless work of art.

But, if the Fallen really existed, it was probably better to keep the shard from connecting fully to her heart and mind.

She picked the papers up and began to shuffle them back together with trembling, although no longer smoking, fingers. As she tried to straighten them into a pile she noticed numbers penciled lightly in each corner. Instead of shuffling them together she laid them out on the ground and looked for chronology.

The letters from Bastian and her father had no numbers so she folded them together and put them back in the envelope. The numbers on the diagrams and charts were written in pencil that had faded, but after carefully going through the pages several times she realized several must be missing. Had Bastian kept them from her? She forced away the hurt, refusing to add more pain over something she didn't know for sure.

The sun crested the mountains and bathed the back of her head in its warmth. Something tugged at her memory and she pulled the ring of keys from her pocket. A quick sift and she found only one with a name engraved in the metal.

Whisper.

Breakfast and rummaging through the bag had given her what she wanted.

She knew *exactly* where she needed to go.

11 THE WARNING

DEMBASHI…Dembashi…

Tolen opened his eyes to tiny shafts of pale light streaming through the leafy door. He blinked several times and looked around the shelter. Quasar was kneeling with his back toward Tolen. Packing? Tolen sat up and looked at his watch. Just past five a.m. He was shocked he'd actually been able to sleep. After everything that had happened yesterday, he thought his rest would be riddled with nightmares, but for the first time in a long time he'd slept dream free.

"I've decided on a path for us to take." Quasar spoke without turning around. "I'll have you ask the trees and animals you trust if it is a safe enough route."

Tolen fumbled for his pack. "Where are we going?"

Quasar twisted around, holding a hand-drawn map and unfolded it in front of Tolen. The paper appeared to be a type of animal skin, mottled with brown stains and wrinkled with age. The faded writing was a language he'd never seen before, made up mostly of strange runes and dashes. The elf traced his finger along a winding black line. "Show them this."

"I have no idea what that map shows."

"They will know."

"Okay, so tell *me*. Where are we trying to end up?"

"There are several colonies of Hidden in the north. I have trusted contacts within them who may decide to help us. You need a safe place to transcend and the Dark knows you must issue the Call in order to bring the Chosen together for battle. They will hunt the Chosen ones as they will be hunting you. The strength of the united Chosen is not something they want to face. They'll see you all dead if they can."

Tolen looked up. "Bastian said the Dark doesn't want to kill me. They want to turn me."

Quasar sighed. "After the way you decimated their army of Kezgani, I think their plans will have changed. You have become too much of a danger to them. They will do all in their power to stop you. You will need an army to protect your mission if you hope to have any chance of success."

"We're gathering an army?" Tolen paused in the middle of loading his bag.

"Yes."

It made scary sense. Tolen took a deep breath. Staying calm was going to be a minute-to-minute challenge. He closed his eyes and focused on the gentle life forces of the trees. He envisioned the map and slowly they began to show him the path he and Quasar would take. For the most part it seemed unknown to the Dark.

"It looks clear for now."

Quasar nodded. "I'm going to look around and take down the shelter. Come outside as soon as you've finished packing."

Tolen nodded, waiting for Quasar to step out before whispering, "*Iy'hika* Zenith." He didn't know any individuals at the Zenith, but his Second Sight seemed to know what to look for. It was hazy, but he was able to skim through various thoughts. All hurriedly prepared for the Dark. Word seemed to have just reached them. The size of the encampment made Jonas's band seem small. The idea that the Dark had enough forces ready to destroy such a stronghold filled him with foreboding.

He didn't stay in the chaotic, anxious thoughts of the residents, instead he took comfort from the fact that they had at least listened to the warning. He pulled his thoughts back, wishing he could do more.

"*Pench Ni'yālo,*" Tolen whispered and fell forward onto his hands and knees, panting.

"The growing Dark is making it harder to project your gifts and shield them at the same time," Quasar said through the open doorway. "At the first colony you will have the protection of a Sphere again. It will help."

Tolen ignored his embarrassment as Quasar handed him some dried meat and a canteen. "But, it will only get worse once you turn eighteen. No Sphere—"

"I know, I know. No Sphere will be strong enough to shield me." Tolen popped the meat into his mouth, downed most of the canteen, and mumbled. "Everyone keeps saying things like that. I'm really not looking forward to my birthday."

"Don't worry. The Dark doesn't want you to turn eighteen, either."

"That makes me feel so much better." Tolen followed Quasar out and copied his movements as he methodically dismantled the shelter piece by piece until the space looked undisturbed. "I was supposed to train at the Zenith. What am I going to do now?" He wasn't really asking the elf. Seeing the one place everyone seemed to think was infallible about to be attacked made the task ahead—saving the world—seem even more impossible.

Quasar pointed to a narrow deer path between the trees, barely visible in the early morning light, and motioned Tolen to follow. "You do not need to train, Tolen. You need to learn."

Tolen fell into step behind the elf and combed his fingers through his tangled hair. "Sounds like the same thing to me."

"Training is preparation. Learning is absorbing the skills, talents, and truths that you already possess. You do not have time to prepare. The time for action is already upon you. You must take those blessings of the Light that have been a part of you since your creation and absorb them into your whole self. You must allow your gifts to be *who* you are; set aside the human world you cling to, and embrace your true birthright. You must *become* the Ninth."

Tolen followed quietly behind Quasar, unwilling to respond to the elf's words. He wasn't sure what he meant by *become* the Ninth, and didn't want to ask. Not yet anyway. The elf and his riddles were almost more annoying than Bastian when he'd refused to tell Tolen the truth of his destiny. He felt no darkness from Quasar, but he didn't feel a lot of light either. Somehow the elf was blocking more than just his thoughts and it made him leery. He focused on the life forces around them. He could sense the Dark everywhere. Not directly on their path, but surrounding them, subtle in some places, more deep and vibrant in others. The trees would keep Tolen on the path they were supposed to follow. He could leave the strange elf and allow the trees to show him the way to the colonies.

But would an army follow him without Quasar to talk them into it? Or would bringing a Lafar elf into their community hurt his chances of gaining their favor? Would they believe in the prophecy, like the elf, but not in Tolen? And how much danger would he be bringing to their doorsteps untrained and unprepared?

Only the uncertainty of his future was certain.

He felt the pull upon his life force of the millions of lives he was responsible for, even though they might not know they relied on him to save their way of life. He could feel the pull of Macy. It was all taking its toll on his mind and body.

"What are you thinking about?" Quasar paused beside a leaning pine tree and looked back at Tolen, his expression frustrated.

"Does it matter?"

"Yes," Quasar said seriously. "You must control your thoughts, your emotions. *Focus!*"

Tolen raised his eyebrows. "Excuse me?"

Fire flashed in the elf's eyes. "You are causing a block in the flow between the Balance and your life force. It makes you weak. You are selfish, and until you learn to get a handle on yourself and stop thinking only of your own pain you will not succeed!"

Heat rushed to Tolen's palms. He took several deep breaths to stop the Kuna from reacting. "You have no idea what I'm thinking about or who I am." He growled through his teeth. "I grew up in the human world wanting nothing more than to be just like the kids I went to school with every day, but I don't cling to that fantasy anymore. I didn't ask for this destiny. I'm not ready for it. I could royally screw things up. But I am going to give it my best. I don't want the Dark to win. I will follow the Light." A small burst of heat released from his palm and he clenched his fist. "I'm leaving, now. You don't know me or trust me and I don't trust you. We can't do this together. What if—?"

"What?" Quasar's violet eyes blazed. "Say it!"

"What if next time I actually kill you?!"

Quasar sighed and ran a hand over his chin. The fire in his eyes dimmed.

Tolen shook his head and turned to leave. He would become Unseen and let the trees guide him. He'd take his chances with the colonies. Whether by his own hands or because of the darkness that sought him out, he wouldn't be responsible for the elf's death.

"Wait." Quasar's calm tone caused Tolen to pause mid-step and glance back over his shoulder. "Do you really believe you didn't ask for this destiny?"

"What?"

Quasar stepped closer until their faces were just inches apart. "Tell me, *Conchla Mindra*—Ninth Chosen—I must know." The fire was back in the elf's eyes, but it wasn't anger this time. It was desperation. Hope burning.

Tolen swallowed, the pain in the elf's eyes grounding him. "I'm not sure what you mean."

"Imagine for a moment that you are standing atop a great building and below you a fierce battle rages." The elf's voice came out hard, frustrated. "People are dying, men, women, and children. Do you think for one second that you would turn your back on them? Do you think you would not wish to join the battle and offer everything you can?" His jaw clenched. "You knew. You chose your destiny. You were not a coward."

"But I am a coward now? Is that what you're saying?" Tolen's voice rose and the heat fought for release.

Something silver flashed across the elf's violet irises so quickly Tolen almost didn't believe he'd really seen anything—almost. "I hope you are not *Mindra,* I hope not."

Tolen's palms were scalding now, nearly unbearable, but he held it in, refusing to let his gifts take control again. "I am not a coward and I'm not selfish." He squeezed his hands into fists, still holding Quasar's gaze. "I braved the Shadow Realm to free my father. I'm sacrificing *everything* for this destiny." His arms shook by his sides, but he kept his fists clenched, holding the heat inside.

"You went there to save someone you loved, not a world full of strangers you have no connection to! Life *is* sacrifice. It's not about the individual, it's about the whole!" Quasar looked down, seemed to notice the waves of heat shimmering from Tolen's hands and apologized. "Forgive me. I didn't mean to get carried away. Duty, trust, and selflessness are so rare in this world now. It's possible I have judged you unfairly. Time will tell." He nodded his head once. "I do not say this to boast, but you need my help. Leaving will only get you killed, or worse."

Tolen took a deep breath and focused on calming the Kuna. "I can't guarantee I won't lose control. You could get hurt because of me. The people you are taking me to could get hurt because of me."

"I know." The elf turned and walked ahead. He didn't motion for Tolen to follow and he didn't turn to see if he would. He was giving Tolen a choice.

Tolen stared after him. He knew the elf was right, deep down he knew. He couldn't live with himself if he were responsible for the destruction of another Hidden settlement, or death or injury to this elf who was so willing to sacrifice everything to see Tolen succeed. But if he went on his own into the unknown, he would fail. There were no visions to support this, just plain gut instinct. He had to make a decision right now, a deep unchanging, uninfluenced decision, a promise to himself that would keep him focused.

I am the master of my fate.

Hefting his pack higher on his shoulder, he fell back into step behind Quasar, and vowed to stay alert, focus on his gifts, the life forces around him, and *never* be a burden or threat to anyone—except the Dark—ever again.

12 MEMORIES

C*AN YOU SHOW me again, daddy?"*

Max Burdow chuckled, the laugh-lines crinkling beside his green eyes. "Okay, McLacy. Watch closely."

Max took the tiny key and slid it into the even tinier keyhole at the bottom of the old chest. On first inspection, the keyhole looked like another small knot in the wood—unless you knew what to look for. The lock clicked and the bottom of the chest popped up. Max removed the false bottom and Macy's eyes widened at the treasures inside. There were sheaves of papers—she ignored those—and dozens of beautiful trinkets; these she wiggled her chubby little fingers at.

"Please, Daddy. Can I hold just one?"

Max smiled, lifted out a piece of old leather and an intricately beaded bracelet, and handed them to his daughter.

She placed the leather in her lap and tried to put on the bracelet. Her father took over and latched the bracelet on her wrist. She twisted it this way and that. Some of the beads were silver and they glimmered in the light.

Max picked up the piece of leather and tried to interest Macy in the pictures painted on it, but she was too focused on the bracelet. "Can I keep it, Daddy?"

Max took a deep breath. "Someday, sweetheart."

"Ah, why can't I have it now? Is it because it's Grandma's?"

"No, baby. It's not the right time yet. But soon, I promise."

Macy nodded her little head. She knew her daddy didn't lie. She would get the bracelet soon.

"Soon everything in this chest will be yours," he said softly.

Macy blinked and stared up at the blue sky above her. Maybe a nap hadn't been such a good idea. She could still see her father's eyes. So much like her own, and filled with pain. A tear rolled down her cheek, but she didn't let it get any worse than that.

The first dream about her parents had come after she and Tolen had reached the citadel. She'd sobbed on Tolen's shoulder for hours afterward. It hadn't been a bad dream, but a beautiful one. More a memory than a dream. A single moment from her past, infused with sheer joy. Her father pushing her on the tire swing in their yard while her mother watched and laughed.

She took a deep breath. As she went in search of her past the memories were bound to come back from the place within her where she'd locked them all those years ago. She needed to learn to appreciate their return, not just hurt from them.

She pulled out the empty notebook Bastian had stuck in her pack and wrote down her latest dream/memory. The chest must be the hiding place her father talked about in his letter, but she had no idea where it could be.

She tucked the notebook back in her pack and nibbled on a piece of jerky as she looked over the map. She was twenty miles from *home*. A strange ache settled in her chest. It would only be the second time she'd set foot in her hometown since she'd been chosen. Thankfully, the Light had never required her return since. She wondered if the Light was okay with what she was doing now. Bastian said he'd followed his heart in giving her this information, and Macy didn't believe in coincidence. There was something she needed to learn, something her father knew, and it would help her on her mission, she was sure of it. She just hoped that she would know where to look once she got there.

Two hours and one smelly ride in the back of a farmer's feed truck later, Macy stepped onto Main Street in Whisper, West Virginia. It was busier than she remembered, and it took her a minute to be sure she was in the right place. There were a few new strip malls and restaurants. She was debating on trying to figure out which storage shed company would fit the key in her pocket and get her hands on a car, when she spotted the old library a couple of blocks down—the creepy stone lions that terrified her as a child still stood guard out front. She crossed the street and ducked into a McDonald's. She would use the restroom and clean up a little, and she desperately wanted a cheeseburger.

Ten minutes later, she stuffed the remainder of the burger into her mouth and tossed the wrapper in the trash bin beside the guard lions. She looked at their chipped, gaping maws, the graffiti across their backs, and wondered how she'd ever found them frightening. They looked positively cute compared to DéHool. She patted one on the head before walking up the steep steps to the doors.

An extremely old lady sat at the reception desk, a pair of reading glasses perched on the bridge of her nose. A crooked name-tag said her name was Ruth. She looked up with a kind smile as Macy approached. "How can I help you, young lady?" she asked in a gravelly whisper.

"Oh, um, I'd like to look up old newspaper articles for a school report."

Ruth's eyebrows rose and too late Macy realized school usually didn't start until fall for humans—Bastian held lessons all year. Even when she was only six, and brand new to the world of the Hidden, she'd never had a break from lessons. "Summer school," she added sheepishly.

"Hmm." Ruth shook her head with the look of a scolding grandma. "Back there and to the right." She pointed over her shoulder. "Most of the articles from the local papers have been transferred to the computer so they're easy to find. But there are still some books with the originals in them if you prefer."

"Thank you."

Ruth nodded as Macy walked away.

The back of the library smelled of old paper and dust. A handwritten sign pointed her to the bound newspaper articles. She skipped past these and sat down at the computer. A list was taped to the table telling the user how to access the old files, but Macy fished the tiny flash-drive out of her pocket and stuck it in the side. Years ago, she remembered Bastian bargaining with a Movan to get the tiny drive. As technological geniuses and the main reason for all the world's advances, Movan were great to have on your side—if you had the means to bargain with them. Movan didn't need money. Their bargains cost much more. Bastian never told her what he had to do to get the tiny drive, but she knew they would have failed many a mission without it.

Within seconds, the drive had done its work—scanned everything on the computer and synchronized to the Internet. A tiny search bar with the Movan symbol—a sun, half-black, half-white—appeared in the center of the screen. She tapped the desk and thought before entering her search. She could be extremely specific and probably get the precise info she needed, but the Movan weren't exactly loyal to the Light and she didn't want to send up any flags.

"Newspaper articles, Whisper Gazette, from January-December 2003"

Instantly files filled the screen. As she clicked on each one, it jumped to the front. She skimmed quickly until October of that year. Finally, on the front page of the paper dated October twenty-fourth she saw something that sent her heart galloping.

RECORD STORM CAN'T COMPETE WITH RECENT TRAGEDY

WHISPER — Two adults are dead and a six-year-old child is missing and presumed dead after an apparent explosion just after 10 pm last evening in a family home in the West Pine Subdivision.

While members of the community hunkered down from a violent storm, as wind, rain and lightning lashed irrepressibly above the town, one family was about to lose everything. The explosion almost completely leveled the home on Walnut Street in the tiny West Pine Subdivision, remains recovered inside suggest 34-year-old Maximus Burdow and his wife, 32-year-old Alison were killed in the explosion. The couple's six-year-old daughter, McLacy Burdow, is still missing. An open back door led investigators to the riverbank that runs behind the family's home.

Searchers have been combing the river and surrounding area for signs of the child.

"The explosion destroyed half the house, but the girl's bedroom and playroom were unharmed. It is believed she may have run outside when she heard the explosion, fell into the river, and was swept away," said Fire Chief George Pullard.

While the investigation into the explosion continues, plans to dredge the river are underway. However, the cold temperatures and the river's strong currents do not give searchers much hope in recovering the little girl's body.

So far, no foul play is suspected.

Maximus's grandmother, 96-year-old Mary Lightfoot, survives the family.

Macy glanced at the date of the memorial service planned and wondered idly how many people had attended. She knew her great-grandmother had lived in a retirement home. Surely she hadn't attended. Bastian had taken her to Grandma Mary's burial two years later—they'd hidden behind trees at the Whisper Cemetery. She remembered he'd been worried that she didn't cry, but by then Macy had taught herself not to feel. She shook her head at the memory and went back to skimming.

It wasn't until two weeks later that another article caught her eye.

Burdow estate auction to be held Saturday, November 7, from 2–4 pm at the Whisper library.

Items to be sold:

Macy skipped over the list until her eyes caught "antique German chest, approx., early 1800s."

She went back to the search bar and typed in her request. Within seconds, she learned that the chest was bought by a man who donated it to the town museum.

She jotted down the man's name and her heart nearly jumped out of her chest. She quickly deleted the search, ejected the flash-drive, and rushed out of the library.

She knew where the museum was. She'd stake it out later, find out where the chest was displayed, and then break in after dark to access it.

But first she needed the key, and she was pretty sure she knew where her father had hidden it.

A game her father played with her had flashed through her mind when she read the buyer's name. Max Burdow loved codes, and he used to pass Macy notes at dinner, much to her mother's annoyance, written in his own special system. Random words written in random order with random capital letters. It took a while for her to learn it—she'd been a good reader early on, but she was still very young.

It was a simple code—silly, really. All the capital letters formed words. Simple enough for a six year old to learn and never forget.

As she ran she looked once again at the name she'd copied of the man who'd donated the chest to the musuem.

"Finneus Icareous Nathaniel Drummond, Master Electrician."

FIND ME.

13 THE CRIES OF THE DEAD

Tolen shoved his thumbs under the straps of his pack and lifted it off his raw shoulders. His muscles ached and his mouth seemed determined to stay dry no matter how many times he sipped from his canteen. They had stopped only once since their argument, barely long enough to refill their canteens in a small spring. They'd snacked on pieces of dried fruit and jerky throughout the day as they'd hiked, not wanting to waste any time cooking a real meal.

A gathering of fluffy white clouds obscured the sun and cast their path in shadow. Tolen started to wonder where they planned to hide for the night. They were only a few hours from sunset.

The elf paused and Tolen stopped beside him. Quasar's eyes flashed silver again, pain shot across his features, and he stumbled sideways into a tree.

Quasar's knees wobbled and Tolen helped him sit down.

"Hey, are you okay?"

Quasar pressed a fist to the side of his head and looked up into Tolen's face, but it was if he were looking through him not at him.

"They're gone," Quasar whispered.

"Who's gone?"

"Dead. All dead."

Tolen's palms tingled and a chill ran up his spine. He searched the life forces around them, but all was calm. "Who? Quasar," he fought the urge to shake the elf, "Who's dead?"

Quasar shook his head side to side and rubbed his eyes roughly with his fists. "The entire colony. M-my *friends*. He slaughtered them all." The elf dropped his head into his hands.

The colony they were headed for? But how could Quasar know they'd been killed? He waited at the elf's side, focusing on any shifts in the Balance as sunset loomed closer.

Only the tiniest bit of light tinged the sky when Quasar finally spoke. "I apologize."

Tolen tossed the stick he'd been twiddling nervously between his fingers to the ground. "What happened?"

Quasar looked up into the sky and a slight shiver ran across his shoulders. "We must get moving." He stood up and started back on the path, his footsteps quick, almost agitated.

Tolen waited for him to explain, but after a half-mile Quasar still hadn't elaborated.

Fifteen minutes later, the first stars began to sparkle in the sky and he knew he could no longer wait. His worry affected his thoughts, which in turn filtered down to his gifts, and he couldn't allow himself to become overwhelmed. "The people you were talking about, was it the colony we were headed to?" he asked softly.

"We need to hurry. I paused too long." Quasar glanced back over his shoulder and something in Tolen's face must have convinced him to explain. He took a deep breath. "Keep up. I'll speak as we walk."

Quasar stared straight ahead, focused only on the path. His voice sounded hollow as he explained. "No, a different colony, but not far from where we are headed. An ancient people. Gifted, but not as powerful as they once were. They managed to stay hidden for centuries. Centuries!" He pushed a branch out of his way with unnecessary force and it slapped back into place with a resounding *snap*. "Daemon slaughtered them all."

Daemon. Heat rushed to Tolen's palms and he had to count to ten to calm down.

Daemon was on a killing spree. His hands started to shake and he shoved them in his armpits. "How do you know it happened?" He couldn't doubt the elf believed what he said, but he wasn't a Watcher.

Quasar took a deep breath. "How much of the old legends do you know?"

Tolen kicked a stone from their path. "Not nearly enough."

Quasar nodded as if he suspected as much and Tolen clenched his jaw shut.

"What I am about to tell you is a secret I guard with my life. It is the real reason Jonas was not entirely comfortable with my presence in his camp. It is why, aside from just being a Lafar, I deal with great persecution and fear when people discover what I am."

Tolen quickened his pace until he was close behind the elf.

"The Balance punishes those who crave a power they did not earn," Quasar began in a whisper, his reluctance to share this secret evident in his tone. "You see it in the deformities of those who follow the Dark. But some curses are not so easily recognized. Curses of the mind, not the physical body."

Quasar shuddered. "When I was still a boy, about your age in human years, I began to be curious about the Dark. I know most Hidden-kind see my race as vain and selfish, and for that time in my life, that stereotype was true, although I disagree that it applies to all Lafar. I convinced a group of my friends to go with me in search of a crazy adventure. Unfortunately, we found it." Quasar paused, lost in the memory. They walked several paces before he went on. "I alone survived the encounter, but at a great price. A Seraph—one of the highest servants of Light—found me where I lay dying in the forest. I could choose to live, she said, but I would carry a curse for the remainder of my days. A curse that would cause others to fear me, make me an outcast, but could one day save the lives of many and possibly change my fate in the next world. If I could not handle the cursed life, then she would take me to my place on the other side."

His eyebrows drew together as he recalled the painful memory. "I knew my mistakes had cost the lives of my friends, and up to that point I had led a very selfish life. If I were to die right then, I would not like my place in the next life. I chose to stay and the Seraph delivered the curse."

Tolen swallowed. "Curse?"

Quasar glanced back into Tolen's eyes. For a moment, the scar on his face seemed to glow fiery red. "The curse of the Seer." His next words erased any warmth Tolen felt from the fading sun. "Seers bear the weight of a million souls. They only see what they cannot change, forever shadowed by the cries of the dead."

The light dimmed further and Tolen swore he could hear strange whispers carried on the wind. He rubbed the goosebumps from his arms.

"The blood of those whose lives have been taken by evil cries from the earth and fills my mind with their final moments."

Tolen stumbled over a tree root and nearly collided with Quasar's back. He remembered how it felt to see the future—Macy's future that showed her dead in the Phantom tree's branches. The image had nearly killed him. But it was only a *possible* future. He'd changed the outcome. What would it be like to see death after it happened—when you could do nothing about it? No wonder Quasar was so touchy about what he saw as selfishness from Tolen. "I'm sorry, Quasar."

Quasar stopped at the base of a steep, rocky ridge with peaks a good hundred feet above. "It is a curse I deserve and it has come in handy at times. It is how I knew exactly where to find you."

He nodded tersely at Tolen's confused look. "The murder of your guards. It is how I have been able to find and destroy many Dark servants. Yes, it has been after their heinous crimes, but they received justice."

Tolen could see the desire to avenge the deaths of his friends in the colony burning in the elf's eyes. His heart pounded as a recent memory rushed forward—a faded piece of parchment containing the Hidden Hierarchy—and he realized just who this elf was. "You're a Reckoner, one of the Third Realm."

14 THE HONITAHAI

QUASAR POINTED TO the nearest peak. "We must climb to the top." But rather than start climbing he rested his foot on a knee-high stone. "I am a *cursed* Reckoner, Tolen. I did not receive my call because I was unfailingly loyal to the Light, although I chose from that day on to follow the Light completely. If I am to destroy a creature for its crimes, I do so with the Light's permission. As much as I want to avenge all the deaths I see, it is not always the case, but never again will I intentionally fail the Light."

"Is that why people fear you?"

Quasar looked up at the darkening sky and sighed. "I am a bringer of terrible news. I am guided vengeance and righteous anger. I am…*sorrow*."

Of course people feared him. If people knew he was a Seer, they would be afraid either for the news he could bring, or the vengeance he was about to deliver. A tremor of respect began to grow within Tolen. The elf before him had not lived a happy life. The choices of his ancestors— the Daklafar—had led him and his family to suffer unfair persecution. His own choices had given him a terrible curse of seeing what he could not change. He'd lost someone he'd loved as a daughter and yet was determined to protect the boy who played a part in her death, indirectly yes, but it was still partially Tolen's fault. It was getting harder for Tolen to not at least trust Quasar's motives.

With a new determination to try to see Quasar for who he truly was, Tolen cleared his throat and asked, "What does the Light wish you to do? Will we hunt Daemon?" This idea sent waves of hope through him and his muscles tensed in anticipation. To destroy Daemon before he could hurt anyone else, before he could hurt Macy, was crazy appealing.

Quasar shoved his foot into a gap in the rock and glanced over his shoulder. "Follow me. We don't have much time. The settlement is on the other side of this peak." And like a skilled mountaineer, Quasar began to scale the rocky cliffside.

Tolen buried his disappointment. He looked up at the steep wall of dirt and rock, and tried to ignore the worry for Macy that felt like ever-increasing weight on his shoulders. His hands shook and he clenched them into fists. *Don't think about it. Focus.* He squeezed his eyes shut once, forced his huge foot into a narrow crack, whispered, "*Mig'nata,*" and slowly followed Quasar upward as strength surged to his limbs.

By the time they reached the top, Tolen's arms and legs were shaking and his fingers and toes ached despite his enhanced strength, but the elf didn't seem the slightest bit tired. Night had fallen around them.

"Where are we?" He ran a hand through his sweaty hair and enhanced his eyes in order to look around. A little valley filled with trees rested between this peak and the next. Quiet in human sound, but teeming with plant and animal life, it felt old, wise, and gave him a strange feeling of familiarity.

"Canada." Quasar pointed to the tiny valley. "Waterton Lakes National Park, to be exact. The settlement is hidden in there."

"How far are we from the Zenith?" Tolen wondered.

"It's further northwest. Deep within the Canadian Rockies."

A low howl cut through the night and Tolen looked down at the valley. "How long will it take us to get down there?"

Quasar stepped right to the edge of the ridge. "Not long."

At least this side wasn't as vertical. Rocks poked out of the side, forming a natural staircase, and the occasional tree growing sideways from the stone provided balance points, keeping them from pitching forward head over heels.

Finally they reached a point where Tolen saw the ground begin to level out below them. His muscles were tired and shaky, but enhancing his strength hadn't seemed to drain his life force as much as it did when he used his gifts. He wondered if it was because they were near the settlement and he was already feeling the effects of their Sphere.

The closer they got to the valley, the more he swore he could see the tops of thatched roofs with crooked stone chimneys sending tiny plumes of smoke skyward. It was hard to be sure. Unless he really focused, the image would shimmer with each blink and return to nothing but forest.

Near the rim of the settlement, Quasar held up his hand. "You must wait here. The guards are just up ahead. I'll announce us."

"Why can't I come with you?"

Quasar turned and looked Tolen in the eye. "Their Sphere will sense the danger behind your unharnessed power. They would kill you rather than take a chance with you."

Tolen stopped mid-step and leaned against a tree. "I'll wait."

Quasar nodded and silently began to pick his way through the trees.

Tolen shook his head in frustration. The elf had said nothing about these supposed allies wanting to kill him. "*Konsh'la*," he whispered, and Quasar's previously silent footfalls became barely audible. Within a minute or two he could make out voices.

"Stop!" a deep voice shouted.

"I am Quasar Ladonré of the Western Lafar, Seer, and friend of Hunsí. I bring news."

Soft, frantic whispers that Tolen couldn't make out followed this declaration.

"What business does a Seer have with us?" a different voice asked with a trace of fear.

"My news is for Hunsí alone." Irritation leaked into Quasar's tone.

"Janz, stay with the elf. I'll speak with Hunsí," the first voice said.

Tolen heard the shift of bracken and was about to turn around before a vine strapped his arms to his sides and a knife was pressed to his throat. "Who are you?"

It was a woman's voice.

Tolen swallowed and the knife scratched his skin. "My name is Tolen. I'm here with an elf, Quasar, he says he knows your leader."

"Why are you not with him then? A spy?" The knife pushed deeper and he gasped.

"He told me to wait here." Tolen resisted the impulse to fight his way free.

"Not very wise on his part. He must not care if you die."

"He probably doesn't."

The knife twitched. "Tell me why I shouldn't kill you now."

"Because you need me." He focused on the vine, asking it to let him go.

It twisted away from him and the woman spun Tolen around, pointing her knife at his chest. "I feel your power, Honitahai child. Who are you?" A strange glowing satchel tied around her waist illuminated her face with yellow light. She was beautiful, her stance tall—nearly as tall as Tolen's 6'2"—and powerful. Her blonde hair fell over her shoulder in a long braid. The tips of her ears were barely pointed—smaller than Quasar's—maybe part Lafar? Her eyes were dark blue in the light from her satchel. Her no-nonsense attitude, the confidence in her voice, and the way she was beautiful even in anger reminded him of Macy. He swallowed hard and turned his attention to the grouping behind her of four equally savage men, their faces apprehensive.

They all wore the same type of clothing—a colorful mixture of tanned animal skins, tall lace-up moccasins, and glowing satchels at their waists. Two held longbows, one a sword, the last a knife like the one pushed to Tolen's chest.

He closed his eyes and sought for guidance. What should he tell them? What *could* he tell them?

The truth. Bastian's voice was just a whisper, but he trusted his Watcher.

He took a deep breath. *"Y'na To'Conchla Mindra." I am the Ninth Chosen.*

The woman jumped back, but kept the knife pointed at Tolen. The men shared shocked glances.

A heavyset man with a vine-like crown sitting atop his thick, gray hair, and leafy vines twisting into his dreadlocked beard appeared between them. "Calm, Sienn. He is the Ninth Chosen."

Quasar and three more warriors holding swords followed closely behind.

The young woman, Sienn, looked back at Tolen and the knife shook as she placed it back in its sheath. The five lowered their weapons and placed fists over their hearts. The men looked awestruck, Sienn angry.

Quasar motioned for Tolen to copy their movements. He awkwardly put his fist over his heart and tipped his head, meeting Sienn's angry glare until she looked away.

The gray-haired man touched Tolen's arm. "*Mindra*, I am Hunsí. Quasar tells me you seek the help of my humble band of Honitahai Nature Speakers?"

Tolen glanced at Quasar and nodded. "That's what he told me."

Hunsí's eyes narrowed. "You don't know why you are here? Why you put my family in danger?"

Tolen swallowed. He *did* know, and he hated it. "The Guardians wanted me to train and transcend at the Zenith, but minutes after I left the Light Realm my guards were murdered by a band of Kezgani."

A hiss ran through the group, but Tolen kept his eyes on Hunsí.

"If they knew where I was, it made sense they would know where I was headed. I could no longer go to the Zenith. Quasar found me. He said I needed an army if I am to succeed in my mission to unite the Chosen. That's why I am here." Out of the corner of his eye, he saw the group exchange glances, but he forced himself to maintain eye contact with Hunsí.

Hunsí scratched his massive belly. "It is dangerous to trust anyone but my own. Ninth Chosen or not, why should I risk the safety of my tribe to help you?"

Tolen cringed at the challenge behind the question. The minds around him were blocking him, just as Quasar had. He couldn't feel their thoughts, but he could read them on their faces. By helping him, they would be risking everything—their homes, their lives—exactly what he hadn't wanted to ask anyone to do for him ever again.

It's not for me. I will keep my promise. I won't be a threat to them. I won't. He focused on shielding his vibrations from affecting the Balance as he opened his mind, allowing his gifts to gently flow from his body. He called to the trees, the animals, the water he could hear nearby, the wind shifting through the leaves. He held Hunsí's gaze, ignoring the gasps from the others, as the trees wrapped around each other covering them in a leafy dome. Purple and pink flowers sprouted across the ground at their feet, their petals softly glowing with white light. Rain began a gentle tap on the leaves above.

Tolen called warmth to his palms and the heat burst forth into a ball of fire he held in front of him. He twisted his fingers until the ball transformed into a long flaming sword. He gripped the sword hilt in his right hand, directed the point to the earth, and knelt at Hunsí's feet. He placed his other hand on the ground and it trembled beneath his fingers.

"I do not ask help for myself alone, but for the sake of all creatures of Light." He held Hunsí's gaze. "I need your help, but know this, I *will* use my gifts to defeat the Dark, or die trying."

Tolen finally glanced into the faces of those surrounding him. They stared back, eyes wide. Hunsí's eyes were calculating, but he scratched his belly again and nodded once. As the flames dissipated, and the trees returned to their former positions, he motioned for Tolen and the others to follow as he led the way into the village.

15 THE WIZARD AND THE OAK

Macy watched the Ohio river flow by in swirling currents while waiting for the sun to go down. It was risky sitting here at the edge of the forest while the Dark was out there, but she couldn't scrounge around in someone's backyard in broad daylight, and she wouldn't be able to break into the museum until after it closed. After a few questions to the curator, and a quick peek around while on a supposed trip to the bathroom, she had a good idea where to start her search for the chest—she just needed the key. She was certain she could pick the lock, but something told her this was how her father wanted her to do it.

She glanced at the sun's position in the sky and started tapping her foot, almost regretting her earlier decision not to go searching through the three storage companies in town to find and stash Bastian's car somewhere outside the museum. It would have made for a quick getaway and been a good way to waste more time, but she'd enjoyed walking the streets of Whisper, discovering she had a lot more pleasant memories than she'd realized.

Her eyes rested on the old oak tree across the river, its branches wider and thicker than she remembered. A new wooden swing had replaced the old tire, but she still felt the same when she looked at it. Warm, safe, and happy. How much she'd loved her family! How desperately she missed them! She shook her head, took a deep breath and shifted her position, turning her attention to the little yellow house—different than she remembered. Whoever had bought the place added more rooms and a patio to the side destroyed by the fire. She could barely see the seam where the old portion met the new. They'd also added a chain-link fence.

Probably hoping to avoid the fate of the little girl they believed swept away by the river so many years ago.

Up until she'd fallen for Tolen and finally come to terms with her past, she'd hardly thought about her human life at all. Now memories had swarmed the past few days. But the memories didn't send her into a panic the way they used to. She no longer curled into a ball and begged for the pain to disappear. Now it was like remembering an old friend, and she felt sorry for all the good memories she'd repressed with the bad.

She no longer wanted to avoid thinking of her parents. She wanted to focus on the good memories, the lessons they taught her, instead of the final memory of their murder.

She turned her thoughts to the memory that had brought her to this place. She was probably four, maybe five years old. It was a gentle memory of her father pushing her on the old tire swing while he repeated a story he'd told her at least a hundred times. She often begged him to tell her something else, but now she understood. Repetition sticks. He told it over and over because he wanted her never to forget.

"Once upon a time there was an old oak tree—"

"Daddy, you tell me this story every time I swing. Can't you tell me a new story?"

"But this story is special, Macy."

"Why?"

"Because it's true."

Macy pumped her feet higher and watched her pink sandals point into the oak tree's heavy branches. She smiled. "Okay, you can tell it again."

Max tickled Macy's side. "Once upon a time there was an old oak tree—"

"In an old oak forest," Macy added and Max smiled.

Macy opened her eyes and continued the tale in a whisper. "But this one oak tree was special. A wizard had placed a spell on the tree so it would guard his most precious secret."

She looked at the tree and imagined for a moment another tree, a guardian to the one she loved. *Ardia.* Was the old oak tree another guardian, a guardian of her father's secrets?

"In the heart of the tree the wizard placed a key, a key that would unlock the source of all his powers. He knew he must hide the key so that if anything ever happened to him, the wrong people couldn't take the key, unlock his secrets, and use them for evil.

"One day when the wizard was very old and knew he was about to die, he told the only person he could trust about the tree and its treasure."

Macy's hands curled into fists at her side as she could almost hear her father finishing the story.

"He took his beautiful daughter, with hair like gold and a kind heart to the forest and stood in front of the tree. He took her hand and placed it upon the center of the tree. When she took her hand away a golden symbol glowed in the bark, two hearts entwined—one representing the old wizard, the other his daughter. The hearts split apart and there, in a tiny hole, lay the key."

Macy turned her face toward her father and grinned. "And to this day the beautiful daughter wears the key around her neck to protect her father's secrets."

Max chuckled. "Very good."

"Am I the daughter in the story, Daddy?"

Max's face turned serious. "Yes, Macy. You are."

"Then you're the wizard, but I haven't ever seen you do any magic." Macy giggled and jumped off the swing.

Macy rubbed a hand over her eyes. Her fingers tingled in anticipation. She could almost feel the rough bark under her fingers.

Finally, the sun dropped behind the trees, casting the tiny yellow house in shadow. She increased her hearing and strength before she leapt across the river. She vaulted the short chain-link fence and dropped soundlessly to the ground. Keeping to the darkest shadows, she crept to the back of the old oak. The story said the center, but the center of which side?

She ran her fingers along the bark, listening for sounds of discovery from the house. A soft blue light began to glow beneath her shirt. She looked down to see her Radia shard glowing brighter and brighter the further she moved to the front of the tree. She was fully exposed now. If anyone looked out the window, she'd be seen for sure. She moved quickly, her shard glowing. The tree became warmer beneath her fingers.

Her shard glowed so brightly she had to cover its light with one hand. At the same time, the tree grew feverishly hot and golden light streamed from beneath her fingers. She pulled her hand away to see a beautiful symbol, two hearts entwined, glow in the bark for a split second before a tiny fissure opened in the tree.

"*To' inreedo,*" Macy whispered and she could just make out the outline of a tiny tarnished gold key—half the length of her pinky—within the hole, and something else. Fingers shaking, she plucked the items from the hole. She didn't have time to look before a man's shout sent her scrambling back over the fence.

"Hey!" She heard him run into the yard, the door slam behind him, but she was already across the river, a triumphant smile spreading across her face.

Macy crouched behind the smelly dumpster near the back door of the museum. She took a huge risk wandering around in the shadows. Evil lurked nearby, so close she could almost taste it on her tongue. She'd felt it growing since she'd pulled the items from the tree, but it hadn't shown itself. The closer she'd gotten to town, the stronger it became. She was running out of time. She still hadn't looked at what her father had stashed with the key. The constant pulsating warning from her shard had her on edge, wondering if it was the right decision to come here and not just flee, but that chest held something she needed. She knew it did.

She allowed her thoughts to feel for the vibrations of evil moving nearby. It didn't seem like Raksasha—the skeletal, demon blood trackers—so she hoped that meant she could avoid meeting whatever it was before finding a safe place to crash for the night. She now wished she'd gotten the car, but if it came to that she'd "borrow" one. There were plenty lining the street.

But she wasn't ready to leave Whisper. She needed to find the Finneus guy who'd bought and donated her grandmother's chest. The clues to his whereabouts had to be somewhere in this tiny town.

The last worker finally came through the door and turned to lock up. Macy waited five minutes before leaving her hiding spot.

She pulled from her pocket the tool for picking locks she'd fashioned years ago and set to work on the door. She hadn't seen her grandmother's chest while on the tour earlier, which she hoped just meant it was being stored somewhere. On her little bathroom trip she'd discovered three separate storage rooms, one per floor. Each room was near the stairwell, which meant as long as she managed to avoid any night security she should be able to slip in and out easily.

The lock clicked. She slid inside and relocked the door behind her. Dull orange safety lights barely lit the hallways. "*To' konsh'la, inreedo.*" Her hearing intensified and soft footfalls sounded on the floor above. She quickly skirted the hall and found the stairwell. Sweat poured down her face as she worked at the lock on the storage door. Whoever was upstairs began making their way down and was very close by the time the lock clicked and she stepped into the dark, cramped space. She was met by rows of dusty boxes. She'd never be able to look through them all in time! She glanced over her shoulder, noticed an inventory list taped to the door, and her heart leapt.

A quick scan showed nothing of interest. She put her ear to the door and listened. She heard the night guard shuffle to the front of the museum. She left quickly and sprinted up to the next floor.

No luck there either. Unease crawled up her spine as she broke into the third floor storage room. What if it wasn't here anymore? Donated or sold to someone else?

Heart hammering, palms sweating, she slid her finger down the inventory list. Please, please be here! She paused on the second to the last item listed. *Antique German chest.*

Yes! It took her nearly thirty minutes of quietly sliding boxes and other junk out of the way before she glimpsed a corner of a familiar trunk. It took almost another ten minutes to uncover it enough to lift the lid. The museum had filled the trunk with old patchwork quilts. She stifled a sneeze as she lifted out the dusty fabric. She ran her fingers along the bottom, feeling for the miniscule keyhole. Her hair fell in her eyes and she shoved it back. Her heart skidded to a stop when her finger bumped across a small indentation.

She gently pushed the tiny key into the old wood, her pulse quickened as the lock clicked, and the false floor popped up. She lifted the wood to see the same strange assortment of baubles and papers she remembered. Just as her fingers closed around the first item in the box, an unearthly sound met her ears: a shriek, followed by a strange guttural moaning. Dogs throughout the city began to bark and the hair on the back of her neck stood up.

She ran to the small window in the room and looked at the street below. Dark figures rushed toward the museum, their evil pushing against her heart.

She was surrounded.

16 MAX'S SECRET

MACY SHOVED THE contents of the chest into her bag. More dogs howled, the sound becoming increasingly louder. Her hands tingled and her heart pounded. She remembered the fire escape the tour-guide had droned about earlier; there should be a door just outside this room that led to the roof. She didn't necessarily like the idea of scaling down the side of the museum, but the roof would at least give her a view of the street below and hopefully a weakness in the Dark's offense.

The back door rattled below. The security guard shouted into his walkie-talkie, his voice echoing through the wall. "Just send someone over, Jan! I don't know what's out there! I can't—Just send me some backup!"

Macy wondered what the guard thought he was facing as she ran across the room and flung open the door. She caught sight of him as he rounded the corner, heading for the stairs. A second later the alarms sounded, the loud wail drowning out the sound of footsteps.

She glanced left and saw the door marked Fire Escape. A few tries and she had the lock open. Three short steps later, she was on the roof. The warm summer wind carried a strange scent as it whipped across her face—a mixture of moist dirt and moldy old house. She crept silently to the edge and risked a glance down. For a moment she saw nothing, and then a dark form leapt from behind a dumpster and crouched beside the same side door she'd used to break in. The creature was humanoid in form, but its gait was catlike, stealthy. She racked her memory for something to tell her what these creatures were. In the past ten years of fighting the Dark, she couldn't remember seeing anything like it.

After a few seconds, she could see more forms moving in and the horrible smell increased. She circled the roof to see creatures lurking in the shadows the whole way around. For now, it appeared they were waiting for her to come out. She looked at the rickety fire escape stairs. If the rusted metal could even hold her weight, she'd be too exposed. How was she going to climb down the building without being seen?

Sirens in the distance joined the din from the building and the creatures shifted in their hiding spots. As a protector of the human race, it wasn't right to be relieved that the police might provide enough of a distraction for her to escape, but she had to believe the importance of the items she carried would help them in the long run.

She clutched the straps of her heavy bag where they cut into her shoulders and moved to the spot where the fewest creatures lurked. The reason there were fewer was obvious. The wall was solid with no windows or doors. A wide metal vent went from the ground up to the roof. If she could climb down the narrow space between the vent and the building, it should provide cover. She waited until she could hear tires skidding on pavement, the pounding of boots, and the squawk of police radios before she began her descent.

"*Mig'nata*," she whispered. She tugged the bag around so it was pressed against her stomach and gripped the metal, digging her fingers into the seams along the edge. As long as the vent held, she should be able to use her back as a brace against the building and shimmy down. Sweat gathered on her palms making it difficult to get a firm grip, but she held on.

Something screeched, different from the cry of the Raksasha but just as blood curdling. She'd been spotted. Soon more shrieks joined in, mixed with the surprised shouts of police officers who couldn't see what was making all the noise.

Macy pulled her Kuna to her palms, but maintained her focus on getting down. The ground was at least twenty feet away, and two creatures were climbing the vent beneath her. They glared upward with white eyes that glowed softly in the darkness. They were bald and their skin so coated with grime it looked like muddy scales. Each wore a filthy loincloth around their waists and carried long daggers strapped to their backs. As several more creatures rounded the corner, she noticed their long ears and something clicked in her memory.

No way. Daklafar? Lafar elves who'd joined the Dark!

Daklafar were supposed to be so evil that they couldn't exist in this realm. The Balance really *was* tipping too far to the Dark if Daklafar could be here.

Holding onto the vent with one hand, she aimed her other palm at the Daklafar climbing below. "*Mi'no ha!*" she shouted and a fireball shot from her hand into the face of the closest elf. He shrieked and let go. She twisted her fingers and tossed another at the next one. His eyes mirrored the light of the firebomb for a split second before he fell to the ground engulfed in flame.

Macy jumped the remaining ten feet to the ground and rolled. When she came upright, the Daklafar closed in. She picked up the pack and shoved it back over her shoulders. She could see out of the corner of her eye a group of police officers hiding behind their cars trying to figure out what to do. They might not be able to see the Daklafar, but the security guard had heard something try to break into the museum and now they would have seen her firebomb.

Macy's attention was drawn back to the Daklafar when more shrieks told her they'd moved into positions in nearly every direction. She didn't know how many there were, but as the nearest ones began to unsheathe their knives, she knew she would be lucky to take them, let alone the others she couldn't see.

The tallest of the Daklafar stepped forward and began to speak, revealing pointed yellow teeth. His voice was raspy and full of malice. "Give us the Claver, Chosen one."

Macy's nose burned from the smell of mold and decay. *Claver?* "I'm not giving you anything."

He began to pace in front of her and she called her Kuna once again. "*Mi'no ha!*" she twisted her fingers until the fireball erupted into a wall of flame which she directed at the surrounding Daklafar.

More sirens split the air.

Fire trucks. Some of the nearby buildings had succumbed to her bombs.

The cops spotted her and were shouting at what they probably thought was some pyromaniac. It wouldn't be long before they started shooting. She needed to draw the fight away from the humans.

"*Mig'nata!*" she pushed the power to her legs, used the cement wall as leverage to vault three Dak's who'd escaped the flames, landed on her feet, and ran toward the Monongahela National Forest where it encroached upon the town, hoping to draw them out and then lose them in the trees.

The night sky glowed red. She could feel the Daklafar closing in behind her. She was feet from where the buildings ended and the forest began when something grabbed her from behind, twisting her arms behind her back. Its hot putrid breath blew across her neck.

She dropped to one knee and rolled left, taking the Dak with her and pinning him between her pack and the ground, but his grip didn't lessen. Her arms screamed in protest.

"*Mi'no ha!*" a burst of fire shot from her palms, the creature shrieked and let go as the smell of singed flesh filled the air. She twisted away from him, whipped her knife from the sheath on her thigh and stabbed him in the chest.

A cold voice grated through the night. "You die, now!"

She rolled to the side just as a Daklafar stabbed his long knife into the ground, barely missing her stomach. He raised his knife again, but a gleaming silver sword with glowing symbols cut off the creature's hand and stabbed it in the back. She looked up to see a young man standing above her with shoulder-length blond hair, a blue shard glowing around his neck. Another Chosen one? Her own shard warmed to confirm it.

"Get up!" he shouted, his sword dripping black blood on the pavement.

Macy rolled out of the way and jumped to her feet. She caught sight of four other newcomers shooting arrows or swinging gleaming swords at the army of Daklafar. They moved too quickly for her to discern if they were male or female, young or old.

"When I give the word," the blond shouted, "send a firebomb to your exact left, understand?"

Macy nodded, pulling the heat from her chest and pushing it to her hands, ready.

They were cornered. The heat of her Kuna was ready, but there wasn't much room to maneuver if the Daklafar avoided her fireballs. Suddenly the blond sprinted to the building closest them, flipped himself off the wall and over the two Daklafar moving in, and in one fast swipe relieved them of their heads. "*Now!*"

"*Mi'no ha!*" Macy turned and aimed left without checking to see what she was aiming at. Her fireball hit a propane truck she was sure hadn't been there before. Blondie grabbed her arm and they dove for cover next to the building just before the tank exploded. The cops hid behind their cars, covering their heads as asphalt rained down in chunks and smoke blocked Macy and Blondie from view.

"Come on!" He jumped up and she followed him toward the forest.

Once in the safety of the trees, they were joined by the four others Macy had glimpsed fighting. There were two females and two males. Three of them also wore Chosen shards.

Gasping for breath, the redheaded girl reached out to shake Macy's arm, but the sound of bodies crashing through dry bracken stopped any introductions.

"Run!" Blondie shouted.

Macy pushed her feet forward, but something slammed into her neck, shooting pain down her spine. She heard a shouted oath before the ground came rushing up to meet her face.

Macy could feel warmth on one side of her body and see a flickering light behind her closed eyelids.

"She's wakin' up," a gentle female voice said.

Macy sat up and noticed a small fire burning beside her before it felt as if someone split her skull. "Crap!" She grabbed her head and tried to look around. The faces looking down at her swam. She closed her eyes and waited for the spinning to stop and the pain to lessen.

"You might not want to sit up just yet," the gentle voice spoke again with a soft Irish accent. Macy slowly opened her eyes and the face belonging to the voice slowly came into focus. It was the pretty redhead—probably right around Macy's own age of sixteen—with a smattering of freckles across her nose. Her bright, hazel eyes were curious, kind, and full of genuine concern.

When she could see Macy wasn't about to lie down again, she held out her arm. "I'm Keelyn."

Macy gripped the top of her arm in the traditional Hidden welcome. "Macy."

Keelyn motioned behind her to the people standing around watching. "The other redhead is my twin brother, Connell."

Connell knelt down and shook Macy's arm as well, but with less warmth and more suspicion in his hazel-brown eyes than his sister. His freckles were thicker than his sister's, covering his skin until he looked almost tan. Keelyn's red hair fell in gentle waves down her back, but his curled from his head in tight ringlets to his ears and brushed his collar. They did have the same high cheekbones, long forehead, and tiny dimple in their chins. A beautiful white-faced owl slept on his shoulder.

"Rune." Keelyn pointed to Macy's blond rescuer.

Blondie tipped his head, his dark blue eyes full of mistrust. He was tall, probably about the same height as Tolen's 6'2". His broad shoulders, and the muscles straining against his tee-shirt, gave him the look of an NFL linebacker. He'd tied his blond hair back into a tight ponytail, highlighting a single jagged white scar that scuttled across his left cheek. He didn't kneel down to greet her.

"Rune carried you here after the Daklafar shot you with one of their Deganista."

"Huh?"

"Poisoned darts. I took this out of your neck once we could stop running." Keelyn lifted a tiny dart off the ground and held it up for Macy to see. It sported a short wooden shaft with a gleaming silver tip on one end and a spray of downy feathers on the other. "It should have killed you. We think the only reason it didn't was because you were pushing so much strength to your Kuna it couldn't do the intended damage to your vital organs. At least that's what we're guessing."

Macy took the dart with shaking fingers.

"I'm Brina."

Macy looked up to see the other female, Brina. She had to be the tallest of the group, beating Rune by at least two inches. Her long hair curled and twisted into dozens of tiny braids she had tied back away from her face, revealing the beauty of her creamy chocolate skin and wideset brown eyes. Eyes that radiated kindness. She had a strong, no-nonsense grip when she knelt down to greet Macy properly.

The last member of the group, the one who was not a Chosen, came forward slowly, cautiously, almost as though unsure how he would be accepted. Macy's eyes narrowed when he came into the firelight. He was very small, if Macy were standing their eyes would probably be level, with a short, spiky, purple Mohawk, extremely pale skin—that even in the yellow light of the fire still seemed colorless—and the tips of his ears were slightly pointed. He could have been very old or very young—it was impossible to tell. His eyes were a strange brownish orange that seemed to shimmer like a cat's at night. But none of this is what made Macy pause. It was the small tattoo beside his right eye of a sun—half-white, half-black. The corner of his mouth lifted when he saw Macy's expression.

"You're Movan." She'd never actually met one. They were very secretive and kept to themselves. Those in Jonas's camp never mingled with anyone, and even when she'd ordered Tolen's watch in the Light Realm, it was a non-Movan emissary she'd dealt with.

He knelt down and offered her the warmest smile yet, showing bright-white teeth. "My name is Tokharian, but everyone calls me Toke." He took her arm and Macy felt a strange shock move up her arm and at the same moment Toke's eyes seemed to glow. He smirked and dropped her arm.

"Okay, that's enough with the introductions." Rune eyed Macy's pack on the ground beside her. "Don't even try to leave during the night—unless you want to die. We have traps set up all the way around us."

For the first time Macy noticed her surroundings. Several tiny bark huts encircled their little fire pit. The shrubbery and grasses encroached upon each of the huts, suggesting that this little settlement had been here a long time. The trees were so tightly packed it was hard to tell where they ended and the tiny homes began. It was so perfectly disguised a person could walk right past in broad daylight and not even notice.

Rune pointed to the hut nearest Macy. "You'll sleep in there with Brina. Tomorrow we'll start answering questions."

The look on his face said he thought he had more questions for her than she for him. He might be surprised. She wouldn't be trying to leave. Whatever was in that dart combined with the use of so much Kuna had left her weak and her head feeling like it was in a vice. If she tried to go anywhere just yet, she'd be easy pickins for the Dark. Besides, she was curious. Who were these people? How did they know to come to her aid? Her gut instinct was to trust them. They were Chosen after all.

But why were all these under-age Chosen and one Movan out here alone, without a single Watcher?

17 THE PLAN

TOLEN RAN OUT of Hunsí's hut and clenched his heated palms at his sides. The image of Macy fighting a large group of strange Dark creatures played over and over in his mind. She had managed to escape—he could feel it—but he didn't know where she was now or how she was doing. He couldn't get a read on her thoughts or her future.

The Kuna's heat in his chest pushed toward his palms again. His entire body tingled with energy as his life force sought to connect with the elements surrounding him. He pushed his fists into his eyes and breathed in deep and slow.

Wan. Nune. Yemn. One. Two. Three. *Tope. Zapan.* Four. Five. He could feel his control returning with each Hidden number he spoke gently in his mind.

He needed to go back into the meeting. The tenor of the conversation taking place—Sienn arguing with Quasar and demeaning Tolen for his inexperience and weakness at every turn—hadn't helped. He'd been trying so hard not to allow his anger to affect his gifts, but the vision had taken him completely by surprise and he'd lost the tenuous control he'd been holding onto. Thankfully, he'd been able to aim the flames shooting from his palms into Hunsí's fire pit, but it could have been so much worse. He hadn't been able to stop the reaction. The vision came, and with it the loss of control. He must have faith in Macy and stop worrying constantly. He had his own mission to focus on. He couldn't keep his promise if he kept letting this happen.

Minutes later he'd felt a stinging pain in his neck and knew she'd been injured. Without thinking, he'd placed his fingers on his own neck and whispered *"Ion'adras,"* to heal, his focus entirely on Macy. The pain had subsided, but he had no idea if it had worked, if it was even possible.

He heard Quasar explaining inside about his lack of control and put his hands over his ears.

Wan. Nune. Yemn. His body was slowly relaxing, but his hands still tingled. He tried to connect with Macy's thoughts just to know if she was okay, but he couldn't get a read on them.

He leaned against the tree nearest him, closed his eyes, and rubbed the back of his neck. He needed to go back in and apologize.

Macy was strong, smart, and an amazing fighter. She'd survived the Hidden world for the last ten years without him. She knew how to handle herself.

An owl hooted and Tolen looked up to see the ghostly white face of a barn owl staring down at him. Bastian said the Light used owls for their wisdom and boldness. A nocturnal creature, yet a follower of Light. Quasar trusted them with the task of warning the Zenith. The eyes of this particular owl were bright and in them Tolen could see wisdom, bravery, and something more.

Tolen whispered, *"Ma'sha."* Instantly the owl's thoughts were synced with his. His mind was just as clear and easy to understand as the owl he'd asked to warn the Zenith. As clear as when he talked to Ardia. Almost human.

I am Skyborne, the owl spoke softly in Tolen's mind. *I come with a message for To'Conchla Mindra.*

Tolen's heart jumped to his stomach, *I am the Ninth Chosen.*

The owl's head twisted to the side. *The Light knows your desire. A silent companion will watch over McLacy Allicandra. She will alert the Guardians as necessary. Focus on your task, Conchla Mindra, and allow Light's Aid to fulfill hers.*

A weight lifted from Tolen's shoulders. *I'm struggling to hear her. Why?*

The growing darkness is veiling your gift. It will be increasingly difficult for you to use your Second Sight in this realm. Skyborne dipped his head, spread his huge wings, and disappeared into the night sky.

Relief, mingled with apprehension, flowed through Tolen. Of course they were watching over him. Of course they were watching over Macy. Could he have the dedication to remember this and focus on his task? It scared him to feel so unsure.

Tolen heard the door open behind him and took a deep breath. "I'm coming. I…just needed some air," he spoke to whoever it was without turning around.

"Quasar explained. You are powerful and weak at the same time."

Tolen turned to see Sienn, her lips turned up in an obnoxious sneer, Hunsí and Quasar standing beside her, their faces unreadable.

He shoved his fists in his pockets and looked at the forest floor. He felt their eyes on him, but kept his gaze down and spoke through his teeth, "Yes, I am powerful." It wasn't arrogance. It was a frightening truth. "And weak. I lose control when my emotions are overwhelmed, when I'm scared, angry, or afraid for those I love." He glanced up into Sienn's face to see the sneer falter.

"I apologize for losing control." He met Hunsí's eyes. "I meant no disrespect. I had a vision. Someone I care for was in danger. It's hard to not be there to help and my gifts reacted." He looked back at Sienn. "But I *am* trying. I may not have complete control, or be as prepared as I should be, but what would you have me do?" He pointed into the night. "Face the Dark alone? Try to win the Final Battle alone? I may be the Ninth, but even those with extra gifts I can't last long alone.

"To defeat the Dark, all creatures who follow the Light will have to come together, not just the Chosen. We don't have much time. I know you sense it. Anyone with a connection to the Balance senses it—even if they don't completely understand what they feel. Whether you have faith in me or not isn't the point." His voice raised. "The point is whether you want to defeat the Dark or not, and unfortunately, you need me just as much as I need you in order to do that. I will stand here and let you humiliate me—I'll do whatever it takes." His breath came in short bursts and his head throbbed. "Will you?" He folded his arms across his chest.

Sienn looked away, but not before he saw the shame in her eyes. It was Hunsí who responded, hope and pain warring in his voice. "Yes *Mindra*, we are willing, but what do you want us to do?"

Quasar spoke before Tolen could come up with a response. "The boy's gifts are strong—you all sensed it when we came here—but he has yet to fully recognize and harness his strength. He will turn eighteen in less than three days and will then reach the fullness of his gifts. He has only known the human world up to now. He does not know his own kind. I fear that if he does not truly understand his heritage, his *birthright*, his strengthened gifts will rule him. Only living among the Hidden can teach him who he really is. Here he will have access to one of the most powerful Capkas in the world for his Transcendence. And you, Hunsí, there is so much you can teach him, you are the Keeper of the Book—"

Hunsí waved him down. "You want us to try and teach a Hidden-born, who was raised human, how to be his own kind and harness his gifts in less than three days? We may be too late." His pale-green eyes were focused on Tolen.

Quasar touched Hunsí's shoulder and the old man turned back to him. "I know it's not possible to learn everything, but we have no choice, and you know your tribe is the best suited for this. The dawning of his birthday will shift the Balance enough that the Dark will know exactly where to find him—unless we help him. Your Capka is the strongest chance he has. The Dark will stop at nothing. They are more actively seeking the Chosen ones. They are slaughtering colonies of Hidden as we speak. I have seen it." Quasar's eyes flashed silver again and Hunsí stepped back. "The more the boy accepts who he truly is, the more powerful he will become. The Dark will eventually realize they can no longer afford to send creatures to try to kill him. They will switch to plotting battle strategies. Once their focus shifts and we can begin making our own plans, our chance of saving this world from eternal darkness will significantly increase."

The exchange was barely less than a complete insult, but Tolen didn't argue. The fact that they were speaking about him like this—right in front of him—told him that they only said what they believed to be true. Tolen stood at a critical point on the path to his destiny and whatever Hunsí decided, it would considerably affect his chances of success. What Quasar said made perfect sense. He did not want to lead the Dark to another innocent settlement and he would do all he could not to, but what choice did he have? They needed the Ninth and the Ninth was not yet who he should be. He stifled a surge of anger toward his parents that did no good—their deception was in the past. It was the future he must focus on.

They needed the Dark to shift its plans and give him the chance to come up with his own strategies for fighting back—and he had to learn how to do that. He had to learn how to *be* the Ninth, to lead a people that until a few weeks ago he had no idea he belonged to, and he had to learn how to embrace his true heritage. He held his breath as Hunsí turned to him and looked Tolen up and down.

"I am not ready to place the fate of my loved ones in your hands, *Mindra*."

Tolen's heart sank to the pit of his stomach.

"But I suppose it's because I feel this way that I owe it to them to help you become exactly what we need in order to defeat the Dark once and for all." His eyes hardened. "You will take your place in this tribe honorably. You will do as you are instructed and do all you must to learn our ways."

Tolen nodded once and swallowed hard, keeping his determined eyes locked with Hunsí's. "I will earn your trust Hunsí. I promise."

"See that you do." Hunsí turned to Sienn. Anger twisted her features, making her appear much less beautiful and far more ferocious. "We have no time to waste. Wake the others. We start immediately."

18 THE WAYS OF THE HIDDEN

Hᴜɴsí ʟᴇᴅ Tᴏʟᴇɴ to a knee-deep circular impression in the ground about thirty feet in diameter and directed him to sit in the center. One of Sienn's companions lit the torches lining the circle, casting dancing shadows over Tolen's lap. Sienn walked back toward the main settlement and began knocking on doors.

Hunsí cleared his throat and Tolen looked back at the old man standing above him.

"A Watcher and a Seer. I do not think it an accident. Fate brought the two of you together."

Quasar tipped his head. But Tolen just continued to stare.

Hunsí poked at a vine sticking out of his matted beard. "We have many skilled warriors here for you to train with. You will stay with Sienn's family, not as a guest, but as a member of the family. You will do all that Mother Tashta asks of you. Our teacher will help you in your gifts and the Hidden way. Sashan will help you develop your Watcher abilities."

Quasar's head whipped up. "Sashan is here?"

Hunsí met the elf's gaze. "He arrived yesterday." He looked at Tolen again. "As I said. It is not an accident that brought the two of you together, nor that you, Quasar, chose to bring the boy here of all places."

Sweat beaded on Tolen's upper lip. Stay with Sienn? Great. She hated him. Learn the Hidden way, how to block his mind, and hone his Watcher ability—all in three days? Impossible. He couldn't stay here once he turned eighteen to continue learning. It would be too dangerous. But three days?

Quasar looked toward the village where a dozen or so people were gathering and heading this way. "What is your plan?"

Hunsí followed his gaze. "As you said. I am the Keeper of the Book. Before he can be a member of the tribe, he must be initiated."

Tolen watched the people as they slowly gathered around him. There was no pattern to the group—old, middle-aged, young, teenagers, even one small boy probably no more than ten or twelve years old. This couldn't be the whole tribe. Tolen wondered if initiation would be a test like the one the Dominants had given him back in Jonas's camp. He flexed his fingers. He was ready to show them what he could do, but could he control it, as nervous as he was?

The flickering light from the torches deepened the expressions on the villager's faces. Curiosity warring with frustration. They expected more from the Ninth Chosen—much more. He squared his shoulders and tried to appear unaffected by their scrutiny. He could do this. He *had* to do this.

Sienn stepped out of the crowd, still looking angry, and moved to stand beside Hunsí as the others sat down around the circle.

Quasar gave Tolen an uneasy look.

Hunsí began to walk around Tolen in a slow circle. Tolen held still and kept his chin up. He allowed his gifts to build within him, preparing. He felt the tingle in his palms, the heat rising in his fingertips, the breath of wind on his face, the gentle whispers of the trees surrounding him, and the warmth of the earth beneath his feet. He counted in his head and focused.

Hunsí stood in front of him once more and motioned for someone from the crowd to come over. Tolen's eyes narrowed with determination.

Two people came forward. The oldest man in the group and the young child. The old man held a huge, ancient book bound in what looked like animal skin. The writing on the cover was faded, nearly illegible, and written in the Hidden tongue. *To' P'pek to' Ladon Heche*—The Book of Light's Decree. A band of cracked leather containing a single small lock held the book closed.

The atmosphere shifted around him. Something was at work here. A force he couldn't quite pinpoint—but was sure he'd felt before. It wasn't evil, but it was extremely powerful. It felt similar to being under the protection of the Light Realm.

A big wooden chair was brought to an empty space in the circle on Tolen's right. The old man with the book sat in it, the small boy stood beside the chair, his blue eyes practically glowing in the firelight. A Watcher?

Another chair was brought to a space in the circle at Tolen's left and Hunsí moved over to occupy it.

Once Hunsí was seated, the boy walked over to Tolen and knelt down in front of him. His features were young, but his bright sapphire eyes were filled with wisdom and depth beyond his years. He tugged a cord from his neck, and held out a tiny, rusted brass key.

The boy began to speak in a gentle whisper, but his words pounded through Tolen's ears as if he were shouting. "*Arwah… Animashta… Leenwa… Télora… Lóklana… Kunamin… Honitahai… Dicernan… Dembashi… To'Conchla Mindra… Degani… Ladonradi…*

Wind rushed through the circle and the torches went out. The boy's voice turned sad, desperate, afraid. He continued to speak in the Hidden tongue but Tolen understood every word.

"*Darkness veils the Sight,*
Those with Power lose their Might.
Shields to heal left to die,
Unending Night; a fallen Sky."

The stars disappeared. The wind sounded like distant screams. Fear crawled up Tolen's spine.

"*A failed Trust; Balance broken,*
A Single Hope; a simple Token."

Despair seized Tolen's mind. His breath came in pants. He was losing control.

The boy's voice changed. Hope colored his tone and the heat in Tolen's chest cooled.

"*But lo, Eight remain,*
United under a Banner of pain.
One shall lead with Might and Shield,
With the breath of Radia, so nature will yield.
Water, animal, earth, light, unseen, fire, wind, and Sight,
The Chosen will save this world from endless Night." The child's voice rose, filled with courage.

"The Ninth shall lead them with Light's Aid beside,
To death or victory within the coming Tide. "

Tolen realized he'd just heard the prophecy in its entirety. Warmth bathed him from head to toe. As terrifying as it was, it also brought him hope.

His shard pulsed with energy. White light burst from it, brightening the faces of everyone in the circle. He placed his hand over it until the heat became so great he could no longer try to cover it. The boy stood up and walked over to the old man, slipped the key, now also glowing with white light, into the lock, and slowly opened the cover.

The old man's voice was thin and raspy as he began to speak, but soon it changed to something deeper and more powerful—his words seemed to touch Tolen's very soul. "A circle has no beginning and yet still we say, 'In the beginning.'"

Tolen's head started to pound and the man's voice slowly faded. His body began to feel light as if he were floating. The crowd around him faded into thick, suffocating, darkness. He started to panic. He couldn't see anything. There was no sound, no light. Just when he thought the darkness would swallow him whole, a tiny light appeared far in the distance, and Bastian's voice echoed in the void.

Where the Light is Darkness cannot be.

Suddenly a vast, starry universe appeared around him. The light from the stars pierced the darkness and brought a sense of wonder. He blinked, and when he opened his eyes planets appeared, circling a gigantic ball of fire. It was the most beautiful thing he'd ever seen.

A dark, cold shadow passed over him and he watched gratefully as it moved away from him. His gratitude turned to horror as he found his body moving, beyond his control, toward the black mass as it swirled and twisted around the planets. His body halted as it paused over one, the bluest one, the most beautiful one.

Earth. *Home.*

Never before had he felt such a sheer love for the place of his birth. He wanted to protect it, shield it from the darkness hovering above.

He watched, sickened, as the darkness split into a million clots of thick, black mist and layered itself across the surface of the Earth's atmosphere. The light from the sun seemed to bother the mist. It followed the path of the sun around the Earth, always staying in the night, avoiding the light. But as more rotations continued, Tolen began to notice the darkest patches of mist stayed in place, even when the sun was at its brightest point on the Earth.

Dread encased his heart.

19 FUTURES PAST

Tolen's eyes were covered in darkness for a split second, then he was hovering above a battlefield. Below him, a bloody war raged. Thick, heavy darkness covered one-half while the other side glowed fiery yellow. The creatures of the Dark were more horrible than he ever could have imagined—the Raksasha, the Shadows, the creatures he'd glimpsed in the Shadow Realm, paled in comparison to the bleak forms of evil raging below him. The ground was saturated with death and carnage. Tolen's hands trembled and strength surged to his gifts, but he knew he wasn't really a part of what was going on. He could do nothing.

Nothing.

Quasar's lecture came back to his mind. *"Imagine for a moment that you are standing atop a great building and below you a fierce battle rages. People are dying, men, women, children. Do you think for one second that you would turn your back on them? Do you think you would not wish to join the battle and offer everything you can? You knew. You chose your destiny. You were not a coward."* But never had his imagination dreamed up something this horrifying.

He saw a man—no, it couldn't be a man—a mammoth *creature* with only vaguely human features. Shiny black scales stretched tight over the sharp planes of his face like snake skin, three long silver horns pointed straight up out of his head like a grisly crown while a trail of smaller silver spikes ran in a straight line down the center of his forehead to the tip of his nose. But it was his eyes that instilled the most fear—blood red with black pupils that leapt and twisted like fire. He rode out of the black mist on a flaming chariot pulled by winged creatures with horse heads and sleek dragon bodies. He towered above his fighters by several feet, his lips curled back over silver fangs into a disgusting sneer. He opened his mouth wide and let out a howl so deep and bloodcurdling that Tolen covered his ears and wished for somewhere to hide.

The fighting stopped as those on the side of Light fell to their knees. The creature laughed and with a jolt of horror, Tolen knew who it was—Darsapean, most high servant of the Dark, epitome of evil. Tolen had felt the effects of Darsapean's power while trapped in the Shadow's veil and again as the master of evil threatened the fighters in the Shadow Realm. But both times it was just his voice. Just his voice, but still so powerful, so terrifying. If this monster were to escape Misery?

He watched the events unfold beneath him with helpless despair.

The creatures of the Dark—DéHool, Daklafar, Raksasha, and a hundred other creatures he couldn't name—rushed forward led by one Tolen knew all too well. Daemon, the Demon Master. They moved swiftly to take advantage of their enemy's moment of weakness. Daemon's skill was unsurpassed. The first line of Light followers went down without a fight, hewn where they knelt.

The enemy moved forward unchecked, the darkness covering them as they slaughtered their way through the army.

A burst of light and Tolen shielded his eyes. A group of Lóklana wielding pure light energy caused the creatures to skid to a halt, screeching. But the light faded quickly, and he saw that the Lóklana were covered in blood. It was obvious they'd fought long and their gifts were affected by their exhaustion. Just when the last bit of brightness faded, and Tolen was sure he was about to witness their slaughter, a hundred men flanked in from the sides to join the battle. He recognized some to be Radia Warriors, but his eyes were drawn to the man leading the group—he was dressed differently than the Radia Warriors, in glowing, silver armor. He was extremely tall, powerfully built, with dark-chocolate hair falling out of a ponytail at the base of his neck, and wide, fierce brown eyes.

Daedal Téloran.

His father.

The Daklafar fired arrows that bounced off some sort of invisible force field protecting the men. That's when Tolen noticed a woman standing in the air above the Lóklana, her long red hair and white robe billowing out behind her. Her eyes were closed and her arms spread wide. In one hand, she held a long staff made of the same glowing silver material as his father's armor and topped with a bright red stone. Her head swiveled toward a spot, and Tolen noticed the force field seemed to follow her look, protecting the fighters. The Dark creatures were now falling with the same speed the followers of Light had fallen. Darsapean howled again, but this time the fighters seemed unaffected by his power.

Daemon rushed forward and met Daedal's sword with his own. The strain of fighting against the force field was taking its toll and Daedal laughed in his brother's twisted, evil face. Daemon dropped to the ground and knocked Daedal's feet from under him. Roots snaked up from the ground and held Daedal fast. Daemon lifted his sword and brought it down toward Daedal's throat. His arms froze in midair and began to shake. He looked up at the woman in the sky, "The Key!" His features curled with pure hatred. "You'll pay for this treachery, Areen!"

Tolen looked at the woman—his mother! Her eyes opened for a fraction of a second before she shouted something he couldn't understand. Incredibly, a dozen more Spheres appeared at her sides, along with a dozen more Protectors, who rushed into the battle wearing glowing silver armor. The force field grew and the light slowly pushed the darkness back.

Dark creatures were falling back, retreating.

Darsapean's scream was cut off when his mother shot a thick beam of silver light from the staff—what Daemon had called the Key. He disappeared as it fell over him. More columns of silver light appeared and Dark creatures began disappearing everywhere. Daemon twisted out of the way of one of the columns and shouted something at the ground. A hole opened up, and the Demon Master escaped inside it. In the chaos no one but Daedal noticed him disappear. He ripped free of the roots, jumped to his feet and began chasing after the retreating dark creatures.

The scene shifted and Tolen was once again surrounded by stars. In the distance, a heavy, gray haze blocked all light and radiated anger. Somehow, he knew he was looking at Misery, the prison created by the Guardians to hold Darsapean and his minions and that it was his mother wielding "the Key" that had sent them there.

It shifted again and he stood in the citadel watching the Guardians counsel together, but this time there were humans present. They were dressed in ancient attire and Tolen knew this must have been shortly after the war he'd just witnessed that would become known as the Radia Revolution.

Sorrow and grief filled the room like a stifling cloud of dust. Tolen leaned forward to hear what was being said.

"We understand your position, Thaer Candra, but creating change within the Balance is not an easy thing to achieve, and could be very dangerous." Tolen recognized Zarin, the leader of the Guardians—looking exactly the same as he remembered him.

"We are prepared to accept the consequences, whatever they may be." The human called Thaer was vaguely familiar, although Tolen couldn't pinpoint exactly why. The deep-red scars running across his jaw and down his arms were distracting. He wasn't angry, just resolute, weary. The group of eight men with him seemed to share his state of mind.

Zarin nodded sadly. "To effect the change in the Balance you desire— to create a shroud that will block the Hidden from human sight—a Pact must be made between us. You ,and all the leaders you have brought with you, must agree and then it must be accepted by the Light. If the Light accepts your request, the Pact will be sealed. The current adult human generation will not be able to experience the change—their belief is too strong, too real, and the Light will want the knowledge to remain in your history to thwart a repeat of the mistakes of the past.

"But your posterity, your children, and your children's children will be under the new law from this day forward. The *Eché-mah Ladon* will become the Hidden, a race of legend, of mystery," Zarin's voice broke, "a myth. We will no longer be able to fight together, no longer can we partner against the Dark."

The humans all bowed their heads. "Understood."

"To seal your end, the Relics must be returned."

The men stepped forward, heads still down, and placed nine objects at Zarin's feet. Only Thaer Candra cast a regretful look back.

The room started to spin, colors flashed before Tolen's eyes, and the scene changed once again. He was in the same room with the same men, but obviously a lot of time had passed. The men were older and grayer, Thaer's scars had faded to white. Despite the healed wounds, the men looked worse.

Defeated. Desperate. Broken.

The doors opened to the throne room and Zarin came in, followed by the other Guardians. They looked exhausted as they took their places on their crystal thrones. Zarin remained standing and walked over to the group.

"We have summoned you here today to bring you news that will hopefully give you a measure of peace."

A hesitant look of hope registered on Thaer's face. The other men continued to stare at their feet, shoulders bent.

Zarin reached over to touch the top of Thaer's head. "The Light has heard your pleas, as well as ours for your sake. You need not fear that our Pact has caused the Light to abandon you. You have not been alone as the Dark has continued to attack your race. Your young may not be able to see the Dark as you do, but they can feel its effects. Teach them to recognize the good from the bad, the Light from the Dark. The Light will never forsake you."

The men started to sob and fall to their knees. Thaer looked up at Zarin with a tortured expression. "Why? Why would the Light continue to protect us after what we've done? We've denounced our ways, ignored the truth, lied to our children."

Zarin took a deep breath and moved his hand to Thaer's shoulder. "It is hard for us to understand unconditional love, being as imperfect as we are, but the love of the Light for its creations is without condition."

Thaer shook his head sadly. Tolen could feel Thaer's guilt and sorrow. He felt unworthy of such devotion.

Eight other Guardians stepped forward and placed their hands on the men's shoulders until they all looked up. The room brightened and the Guardians seemed to be glowing.

The voice Tolen heard was the same voice he'd heard before leaving the citadel. The voice of the Light.

"Fear not, and do not doubt. The Light is always with you."

The voice trailed off and the men's countenances brightened. They rose to one knee, their tears glistening on their cheeks, as the Guardians moved back to their thrones.

Zarin continued gently. "One of our oldest and wisest Watchers has revealed a prophecy. We are still unraveling its full meaning, but we feel it is good news. It has given us a warning concerning the Final Battle previously prophesied to take place between the Light and the Dark—as well as hope for humankind. The Light, through the Balance, is selecting human children with pure hearts. The Radia shards worn and protected by our Watchers have split in two. One-half of each shard is seeking out these children. Once in possession of the shards, the children are given a single Hidden gift, along with the ability to see the Dark. The Watchers have been assigned to protect the children who carry the other half of their shards. The Light gave them a charge and so their gifts are bound to that child. They can sense their thoughts and therefore are the perfect protection. These selected children will train in our ways, but their true identity will remain secret from humankind so as to protect the Pact. They will be the Chosen ones, silent guardians of their own race and hope for their redemption."

The scene faded and Tolen's strength went with it. It was as if he himself had participated in every scene he had watched.

Fear not. The Light is always with you.

Tolen opened his eyes to see that the fire was nearly out and the night sky had dissolved into a pale purple dawn.

Hunsí stood and held out his arms. "Welcome, Tolen Daedal Téloran, to the *Hinkta* Northern Honitahai tribe."

July 8

Two Days Until Transcendence

20 REBELS AND REASONS

MACY WOKE BEFORE the sun with her skin prickling. She kept her eyes closed and listened. Someone moved nearby, their nervousness sending slight tremors through the Balance. It wasn't Brina—she was still snoring softly on Macy's other side. Whoever it was didn't want to be discovered. When she felt the first gentle pressure on the pack beside her, she sprung. Before Rune had time to react, she jumped onto his back, held her knife to his throat, and forced him, cursing, out of the hut. She could feel a slight drain on her life force from the Deganista, but her strength was returning.

She pressed the knife deeper into Rune's skin and he winced.

"Looking for something?"

The others began pouring out of their huts and surrounded Macy and Rune.

"What are you doing?" Brina stepped toward them with her sword drawn.

"Stay back or I'll slit his throat." Macy allowed her Kuna to heat the blade until Rune winced.

"Stop!" Keelyn cried.

Macy tightened her grip as Rune tried to throw her off. She knew the move and countered with one of her own. Her knife grazed his throat and he gasped.

"What the—!"

"I told you not to move. Try that again and I *will* kill you."

Macy's nerves tingled. She felt the Balance shift slightly behind her and knew someone was there before Brina spoke.

"You won't touch him." The point of a sword pushed against Macy's back. Brina was Dicernan—an Unseen.

Macy ignored the pain of the blade and allowed her Kuna to rush to the surface. Smoke furled from her fingers and the smell of eucalyptus and roses floated around them. "I don't have a problem taking you all down with me. All I want to know is why Blondie was trying to search my things. Answer me that and I'll let you live."

Someone laughed and Macy glanced up to see a smirk on Toke's face. "You don't believe me?" Macy held her other palm up beside Rune's face, her arm still tight around his neck, and allowed the fire barely away from her hand, where it twisted and curled, casting an ominous glow across all their faces. Rune winced from the heat, but didn't try to throw her off.

Toke's smile faded as he stepped ahead of the crowd. "Brina ease up. She's not kidding."

Brina hesitated for a few seconds before she reappeared and lowered her sword.

Toke continued to walk forward slowly. "Rune, tell her what you were doing."

Rune took a frustrated breath and Macy pulled the knife back slightly. A thin trickle of blood ran down Blondie's neck. She kept the fire burning low and waited.

Rune's ego was more injured than his neck. Macy could hear it in the angry tone of his voice. "The Daklafar were after something. Something they thought she had. I want to know what it was."

"What?" Macy jumped off Rune's back and pushed him away from her. He twisted away quickly and Macy poised to fight, but he only glared down at her.

"What were they after?" he shouted.

Macy released the fire from her palms into the smoldering remains of the fire, it exploded and ash and sparks rained down on their heads. "I have no idea what you're talking about!"

"Rune, what *are* you talking about?" Keelyn put a hand on Rune's arm and the anger on his face melted slightly.

"The Dark elf wanted something and he thought she had it. What was so important that an entire band of Daklafar—creatures that shouldn't even be in this realm—would be after a single Chosen? And you," he pointed a finger at Toke. "You wanted us to go there, not because you 'sensed something moving',"he made little air quotes with his fingers, "but because you knew she'd be there. I'm sure of it." He looked back at Macy. "There's something weird about you. I can feel it and I want the truth." He poked his chin out and folded his arms across his chest.

Macy wasn't sure what she wanted to do more, yell back at Blondie for being a snoop, or demand to know what he meant about the Movan guy. She opened her mouth but Toke cut her off.

"What did the Daklafar say he wanted? Did you hear him?" The Movan's eyes were anxious and he'd started twisting his hands.

Rune shook his head. "I didn't hear exactly. It sounded like *cleaver* or something."

"The Claver?" Toke's voice dropped to a whisper and Macy remembered the Dark elf who was about to kill her had told her to give him the Claver. She'd forgotten all about it until now. She had no idea what the elf meant, but apparently Toke did. "Rune, Brina, relax. We have a lot to discuss. Let's make some breakfast." Everyone backed down as fast as they'd jumped up and moved away to sit on log benches surrounding the fire pit. Macy stared after them with her mouth open.

"Macy, do you mind?" Toke tossed a few logs onto the remains of the fire with a gleam in his eye.

While Macy pondered the man in front of her, the sun's rays scattered across the tops of the trees. Its warmth spilled across the mountainside and turned the morning dew into a thousand shiny crystals. Macy felt the shards hanging around her neck pulse with a strange, anxious energy. She had enough strength to leave, but a feeling told her she needed to understand this strange group, needed the information they had. Daklafar could be close, but she'd survived the night. There was something about these people and this place that repelled the Dark. A few more answers couldn't hurt. She glanced around at the motley group, shook her head in exasperation, and sent a smaller fireball into the logs. The soft crackle of burning wood brought familiar comfort.

Macy waited until everyone else was seated before she sat down on the dirt. She scooted back far enough so she could keep everyone in her peripheral vision as her eyes focused on Toke.

Toke nodded and Keelyn and Connell went into one of the huts and came back carrying armfuls of food and cooking utensils, the owl still on

Connell's shoulder. They then set to cooking a breakfast of what looked like fried ham and biscuits.

Macy gestured toward the twins. "I'm sorry, but as great as a cozy breakfast sounds I really don't have unlimited time. I'd appreciate it if you'd just tell me what you know so I can get out of here."

Rune's scowl deepened, but once again it was Toke who spoke. "And where exactly do you plan to go?"

Macy's mouth closed with a snap. She planned to see if there was really something to that Finneus guy—if it was really a clue. Although heading back into Whisper probably wasn't the best idea.

Toke's eyes narrowed. "Mmhm. That's what I thought. We're safe here. Our home is sheltered with ancient power. We will be well protected from the Dark as we decide our next steps."

"We?" Rune looked around the group. "What do you mean we?"

"We will be leaving here. Together." Toke looked at Macy as he spoke. "All of us."

Macy flipped her hair over her shoulder. "Excuse me? I don't think—"

"Do you want to know about the Claver or not?" Toke interrupted.

"I do," Rune grumbled.

Macy stared into the Movan's eyes, weighing her options. Bastian's instructions were as simple as they were hard to understand. The Light had a mission for her to complete. A mission of faith.

Her gut told her she was on the right track. The only explanation behind the Daklafar's attack so quickly after her arrival in Whisper was that they knew something about her past that she didn't. Something that apparently this guy knew as well.

"Okay. Tell me what you know." Macy leaned back against a fallen tree, pulled a purple sucker from her bag, unwrapped it, and stuck it in her mouth. The others gave her funny looks but she kept her focus on Toke.

The Movan's smirk was back. His eyebrow lifted. Macy wondered if he thought her confidence was a façade. He'd be surprised. His smirk became more pronounced and Macy felt the strange zing of electricity jolt up her arms again, the way she had when he'd first touched her. She looked at his hands to see that he was touching the log she leaned on. She sat forward and the zing disappeared. He tipped his chin and she wondered what in the heck that was all about. She knew Movan shared some sort of weird connection to electricity, that's why they were so adept at creating technology out of nothing, but she had no clue what he was up to.

"It has been a very long time since I have heard anyone speak of the Claver," Toke spoke softly. "It is an ancient and powerful tool created by Eamun Woodlore, the Spheres, and my fifth-great-grandfather San-harian long ago. It is one of nine Relics from a time when humans and Hidden coexisted together." He looked up at the sky.

"Why would the Dark want it?" Rune asked.

Toke ran a hand over his chin. "It's an extremely powerful artifact, but until it is united with the other eight its power is limited."

"What does it do?" Keelyn scooted forward, her eyes lit with curiosity.

"The Relics work much like your Radia Shards. It gives a gift to its bearer. The Claver gives the gift of Second Sight, it mirrors the Watcher ability."

"What do the other Relics do? What happens when they're united?" Brina folded her long legs beneath her and Macy was reminded of the times when Bastian would start into tales of the past—not history lessons, but real battle stories—and she would sit the same way, drinking in the tension of the moment.

Toke was like a father to them.

He continued, unaware of her scrutiny. "It is a long story, dating back to the earliest peoples of this world. The Hidden were not from this realm originally, but a far distant realm, from a far distant universe. When their star died the Light led them here—but it wasn't only the good Hidden that found the gates and passed to this realm. As a gift to the race that already populated this planet, nine Relics were created from the rarest elements of this earth that would give the pure hearted leaders mirrored gifts of the *Eché-mah Ladon*. Like the Guardians protect the Hidden, the Nine were given eight elemental gifts and one Watcher relic that would allow them to better rule and protect *their* race from the evils that had followed from the first realm."

Macy only vaguely remembered this story. She'd never liked the stories that related to humans—she'd wanted too much to forget her human life. "Why would the Daklafar think I had something like that?"

Rune grunted.

Macy flipped a stick and hit him in the face. He stood up with his fists clenched and she raised a challenging eyebrow.

"You little—"

Toke raised his hand.

Rune sat back down with his jaw clenched, but his eyes continued to hurl the profanities he wanted to say.

Macy resisted the urge to do something rude, deciding she needed to hear what Toke had to say more than she wanted to provoke Blondie.

Toke shook his head. "That's a very good question. The Claver hasn't been seen since the Revolution. The Relics were supposed to have been hidden with powerful protection. What are they up to?"

Macy still felt like the bigger question was why they thought she had it, how they knew to look for her or it in Whisper, but Toke was drawing in the dirt with his finger, lost in thought.

"Look, I don't know anything about the Claver, or why the Daklafar were after me, so don't bother asking. Thank you for helping me last night. I, uh, I appreciate it. I need to get moving now, though."

Toke looked up and shook his head. "We eat and plan first."

"There is no 'we.' I don't need babysitters." Macy stood up and pulled her pack over her shoulders.

"No, just people to show up and save your life."

Macy rounded on Rune. "You know what, Blondie, you're a real pain in the butt and I'm sick of listening to you, so before I go, how about we settle this like real Chosen—gift against gift?"

Rune's face burned scarlet and Macy bit back a satisfied smirk. She'd sensed he was Kunamin when she held her hand at his throat, but it was underdeveloped, weak.

"Macy, that's enough." Toke was standing now, and the power in his voice almost made her falter, but she swallowed and stood taller.

"*You* are not my Watcher." Her palms tingled.

"No, I'm not. Your Watcher is no longer a part of this world. But if he *were* here now, he'd be disgusted."

Macy's fingers trembled and heat built in her chest.

Macy. Bastian's voice was only slightly reproving. She didn't understand it. He wouldn't offer any advice, or warnings, but he could scold her? Whatever. "How do you know?"

"Because I know Forrest Bastian." His glare could have burned a hole in her face. "Chosen do *not* treat each other as enemies. Don't you understand who you are? The promise you have made? If you don't, your loyalties are sadly misplaced."

Toke knew Bastian, not just by legend. The way he spoke his name, the respect, the admiration—that wouldn't come from only hearing legends. She glowered. Not only would goading Rune bother Bastian, it would have bothered Tolen too. He didn't like bullies. Her stomach wriggled with guilt. She bit her lip and fought against her ego. "I'm sorry," she mumbled. "That was rude of me." She risked a glance at Rune, but he no longer looked at her; he stared at Toke with a calculating expression.

She didn't have time to wonder what it meant. "But I *am* leaving. If you know Bastian then you understand that if he sent me somewhere alone, there was a reason behind it." She turned to leave.

Toke spoke to her back, "And how do you know that we are not part of that reason?"

She paused in mid-step and turned around to face Toke, not liking the way he seemed to be in line with her own thoughts. He looked around at the others. "Brina, make sure everyone eats and then pack up what travel food we have available and enough supplies to last a few weeks. Close up camp and then all of you meet Macy and me at Gray Rock in one hour."

Rune threw them one last murderous look before Toke led the way through a slight break in the trees. Holding out a piece of ham, Toke beckoned Macy to follow.

She lingered for only a moment before curiosity and her rumbling stomach got the better of her. She accepted the meat and followed him deeper into the forest.

21 ACCEPTED

A welcome breeze blew through the cracks of the lone hut, caressing Tolen's face with its gentle fragrance. The air inside the hut—long since abandoned at the edge of the village—was damp and smelled of mildew and moist earth. A single glassless window stared out into the forest, but the trees grew so thick here the only light came in small shafts that broke through the gaps in the grassy roof and cast interesting shadows over the bare cracked walls. The reason for bringing him here was obvious. They'd thought this peaceful little place would relax him and allow him to rest. But his mind would not allow it.

He still couldn't believe that his strange vision had been the entire initiation. According to Hunsí, to be accepted as a member of the tribe, one must complete a vision given to the initiate's mind as the Book of Light's Decree was read—a vision that gives them insight to their purpose within the tribe and the world itself. Each vision was unique to the receiver. The people on the outside of the circle were there not to judge or test, but to help contain and control the power Hunsí needed to access the Share.

Once the Share was completed, the listeners knew their purpose and the tribe accepted them as family. End of initiation.

Despite Hunsí's announcement, the cursory glances cast his way as he'd left the circle didn't seem to be as accepting. They'd been taught their entire lives the legend of the Ninth Chosen. They were not expecting him to show up an untrained, unskilled, highly unsure of himself teenager. They'd expected a warrior.

His heart ached as he'd followed Hunsí here, barely acknowledging his suggestion of resting for a bit before meeting his tribe "family".

But rest was not an option. Tolen had *seen* the final battle of the Radia Revolution, felt in every piece of his life force, the drastic difference between the Light and the Dark. He squeezed his eyes shut. His parents, so strong, so powerful…Neither resembled the broken people they were now. His mother had been so tenacious and determined. His father had been a king in battle. It enthralled him almost as much as it confused him. If he hadn't known with every fiber of his being that what he'd seen was real, he'd never have believed it.

He had witnessed so much pain, loss, and sacrifice of his kind. The suffering yet determination of their human allies—no wonder Thaer and his companions sought to be free of the knowledge of the Dark. Knowledge could be a huge burden. Tolen had only been a witness, yet he knew he'd never be the same again.

The history of his lineage was no longer a story he'd been told and tried to accept and understand. Not anymore. It was a part of him—body, mind, heart.

He drew a shuddering breath and watched the dust motes dancing in the light from the roof. Before, he had *believed* he was doing the right thing. But now he *knew*—doing all he could to fulfill the prophecy as the Ninth *was* the right thing to do. For the first time since he'd learned who he really was he *wanted* his destiny.

He *wanted* to succeed.

The problem? After seeing the Radia Revolution and the strength of those evil creatures, he realized he was even less prepared than he'd imagined. He'd known he had a long way to go, and not near enough time to get there, but now he completely understood the fears of Quasar and all these people. They needed him, and he wasn't ready.

The light brightened through the roof and he pushed up to his knees, stood, and left the hut. He didn't know how long it would be before they came for him, but he couldn't stare at the walls any longer.

Silence greeted him outside the hut and he was grateful to be alone for this brief moment. He took a breath of the sweet mountain air and climbed the small grassy knoll just outside the door. Birds chirping and the soft tinkle of a nearby stream added music to the deep stirring magic of the moment. He stopped once he reached the top of the knoll and faced the bright rays of the rising sun with his eyes closed. He breathed deep, allowing the light to caress his face and arms, relishing its warmth as it passed through his body into his soul—or, in the more direct *Eché-mah* or Hidden term, his life force. He turned his palms towards the light and felt his skin drink the energy and vitality that came from the light.

The *Light*.

So much more than the absence of darkness, so much more than simple illumination. So much more powerful than anything he had ever dreamed.

Even in the human realm, he'd always believed in some sort of Higher Power. Some Being out there somewhere who created all this. In all his studies of science, philosophy, physics, and all the world's theories, he himself couldn't deny what he felt whenever he thought of someone out there planning it all. There had to be. At times, he'd wondered if whoever it was had exercised a cruel sense of humor to give him all these weird abilities and then stick him in a place where those abilities could get him locked up in a loony bin.

If he'd only known. The Light was much, much bigger than that.

Eché-mah Ladon—Light Messengers. The true name of the Hidden race.

His race.

For only the third time in his life, he felt fierce loyalty toward something. His first loyalty came as a child to his mother, the second as he'd fallen for Macy, and now he felt the same powerful desire to protect his race and the humans who shared this world.

When Quasar asked him if he would sit back and let innocent blood be shed, he'd known he never would. It was wrong, obviously. But now that he'd actually seen his people fighting, seen the horrible cruelty of the Dark, he truly wanted to be enough.

The image of his young and healthy parents doing all in their power to protect people they loved would be a strength and a boon to him for the road ahead.

Daemon's last words to his mother on the battlefield forced him to reflect on what had taken place in the dungeons of the Shadow Prison. Daemon had said, *"Your mother is not the person she made you think she is."* When his mother finally told him about her past, he'd been slightly disgusted with her. Seeing her on the battlefield fighting, doing all she could to save those on her side, his respect for her grew. But as he thought of the road ahead and how unprepared he was because of his parents' choices, he couldn't stop the resentment that had been taking root in his heart from digging in a little deeper. The entire world was at greater risk because of their choices. He loved them, he respected their roles in the Radia Revolution, but forgiving them for the predicament they put him in—intentional or not—was going to take time.

"How are you feeling?"

Tolen opened his eyes and turned to see Quasar standing behind him. It was as if the elf glided above ground as he moved. He never made a whisper of sound.

Tolen shrugged, turned back to the sunlight, and pushed his hands into his pockets.

Quasar moved to his side. "It's a lot to take in."

Tolen nodded.

"Hunsí is ready for you."

Tolen nodded again and started down the hill. He felt rather than heard Quasar fall in behind him. He didn't know what to say to the elf. He felt so strange in this moment. He wondered if this was how kids who'd been adopted felt when they found their birth parents. Did they feel as if they'd lost a part of themselves? That the person they believed they were was only just a figment, a dream, unreal? Were they overwhelmed by the shoes they must fill, the role they were to play in their new life?

Hunsí waited at the base of the hill, his dark eyes calculating as he looked Tolen up and down again. He must have been satisfied by what he saw, because his eyes softened slightly as he motioned for Tolen to follow.

"We have a lot to accomplish in the next few days."

Right. His dreaded eighteenth birthday. Tolen looked down at his watch, touched the face and thought of Macy, then cast a quick glance up at the sky before following Hunsí and Quasar back into the heart of the camp.

When they reached the village, Tolen was once again reminded of his stay with Jonas. People were outside their homes practicing their gifts and testing their skills with various weapons. But one thing was very different. Jonas's camp was a training camp, a specific place to go and learn the best ways to fight the Dark. A place you left once you'd received your training. This was a settlement, a village, a home. This is where Hidden-kind *lived*.

Chickens pecked their way along the dusty streets searching for bugs. Pigs snuffled and snorted in pens, while cows grazed in small fenced fields. Crops blossomed in tiny gardens, flowers bloomed in boxes, over trellises, and along walkways.

These people were not warriors. This was where the warriors came *after* battle. Their refuge. A place they believed to be safe.

The looks cast toward Tolen and Quasar said they were not entirely happy with their arrival or the news they'd brought with them.

They were frightened.

Guilt wriggled in Tolen's stomach like a poisonous worm.

Hunsí paused outside a small rock house. "This is where you will stay while you are here."

The home's exterior consisted of beautiful smooth stones in a variety of grays and subtle oranges, held together with an earthy brown cement. A tall stone chimney billowing plumes of white smoke poked its head from the far left side of the thatched roof. A box of fragrant multi-hued wildflowers hung outside a single small window. A heavy wooden door, painted a cheery apple red, stood ajar. The mouthwatering scent of eggs and frying meat made Tolen's stomach rumble.

Hunsí knocked on the open door. "Mother Tashta?"

"Come in!" a woman's voice called from inside.

Hunsí motioned for Tolen and Quasar to go in ahead of him. The inside was roomier than Tolen expected.

They stood in an inviting informal living room, its creaky wood floors covered with a brightly colored braided rug, a roughly carved rocking chair sat in one corner flanked by a low crackling fire. Opposite the fire rested two more log chairs draped with thick, crocheted afghans. Fluffy cushions and more knitted blankets filled the in-between spaces on the floor, and everywhere there were books. Stacks and stacks of books. Filling the shelves on the walls, piled on the floor, on the mantel, and on the single spindly-legged table that looked barely strong enough to bear the weight of the books and a tall oil lamp.

The right side of the room opened up to a spacious kitchen and dining area. A very large woman stood beside an ancient cook stove, flipping pieces of meat in a big black pan. Warm bread and a giant bowl of scrambled eggs steamed on the center of a long log table surrounded by a half-dozen mismatched chairs. Fresh fruit hung in baskets beside a heavy cast-iron sink.

The huge woman turned around and the wrinkles on her weathered face nearly hid her eyes when she smiled. She had to be ancient, but her bright eyes were youthful and filled with genuine happiness. She'd tied her long gray hair back from her cheerful face in an intricate braid. She radiated kindness.

Tolen liked her immediately.

"You must be Tolen, *to' Conchla Mindra*." Her voice sounded much younger than she looked. She dusted her hands on her apron and walked forward to shake Tolen's arm.

Tolen couldn't help but smile back. "Yes, ma'am."

She laughed and released his arm. "*Ma'am.* You're sweet." She pinched his cheek. "You may call me Tashta, or Mother, whichever you prefer."

Tolen nodded as Quasar stepped forward to greet her as well. "It's good to see you again." He bowed after she released his arm.

Tashta's eyes turned stern. "I only wish we could see one another under pleasant circumstances, Quasar. Cursed or not, you could visit me just because you like the idea."

Quasar chuckled humbly. "I'm sorry, Mother Tashta. Maybe when the Dark is destroyed and the world is normal, yes?"

Tashta smiled again. "Normal, bah." She waved her thick arm above her head. "No such thing as normal." She motioned to the table. "Come. Sit and eat. The others have already eaten breakfast. It'll just be the four of us."

Tashta waited for them to be seated before handing everyone a plate bearing a thick piece of ham, a pile of eggs, and slices of fresh bread smothered in strawberry jam. Tolen tried to help but she refused. "For this meal you are my guest, *Mindra.* Then you will be family and share in the duties of the household."

She spoke a gentle blessing on the food that included a plea for Tolen's wellbeing. Her thoughtfulness warmed him in ways he'd never experienced before. Maybe this was what it felt like to have a grandmother. He mostly concentrated on his plate while the others talked of the past. It was obvious Quasar had known Hunsí and Tashta for a very long time.

Before long the eggs were gone, the last piece of meat had disappeared, all that remained of the bread and jam were a few crumbs, it was time to talk about the hard stuff.

Hunsí cleared his throat and wiped his hands on his huge stomach. "Thank you, Tashta. You are an excellent cook."

Quasar and Tolen both murmured in agreement and Tashta smiled.

"Thank you for allowing Tolen to stay with you." Quasar touched her wrinkled hand. "You are the best Mother I know. He will learn much under your care."

"We all play a part in what is to come, whether we want to or not." Tashta smiled sadly and the guilt squirmed in Tolen's gut.

"I'm sorry to be so much trouble." He looked Tashta in the eye. "I will work hard. I promise." He wished he could promise her more—that he wouldn't be a danger to her family, that he was strong enough to protect them, that he would be everything they needed. He clenched his teeth.

Tashta stood up and put her arms around him. "I believe you, *Mindra*." She leaned back, gripping the tops of his arms, and met his eyes with warmth and acceptance. "Welcome to my family."

22 THE MASTER ELECTRICIAN

Macy pulled her Kuna just to the surface as Toke led the way farther into the dark forest, leaving the others behind.

"That won't be necessary," Toke said without turning around.

"What won't be necessary?"

"Your gifts."

She continued to let the Kuna build. This was getting too weird. "How do you know if I'm about to use my gifts?"

"I'm a Movan. Didn't you study your history? I can sense the electrical charge from your Kuna as it increases the energy flowing through your body. Now please, relax. If I wanted to hurt you, I wouldn't have sent my insurgents to save you. I would have let the Daklafar kill you."

"Your *insurgents?*"

"Or rebels, whichever you prefer." He continued walking, oblivious to the red flags going off in Macy's brain.

"Then you're not on the side of Light?" She placed her hand on her knife. Traces of darkness were a part of all Beings in this world, and she'd felt nothing overly sinister from this group, but something else could be at work here.

He paused beside a huge tree and glanced back with a smile. "Oh, we're on the side of Light. Our methods are just a little different than most, which often creates unacceptance and persecution from *some* followers of Light." He pointed to the center of the tree. "After you."

Macy looked at the tree and back at Toke. He was so short their eyes were level. "Excuse me?"

"Please step inside." He met her nervous gaze—his eyes softened and she saw something there, something familiar.

"Do I—do I know you?"

His eyes crinkled and she was sure she'd seen him before. He glanced around. "There are too many ears out here. Come inside. You'll be perfectly safe, I promise." He touched the center of the tree and the bark glowed gold for a single moment before a crack appeared, slowly widening until it was big enough for a person to step through.

It was just like the oak tree in Whisper that hid the key. Something stronger than curiosity propelled her forward. She stepped into the tree and found herself standing at the top of a steep wooden staircase. Midway down, a faint light flickered on below, revealing the end of the stairs. When she reached the bottom, she was standing in a huge underground room that reminded her of the pictures of libraries in old English mansions. The walls were paneled in dark wood, lined floor-to-ceiling with bookshelves and several closed doors. Heavy, wrought iron sconces held electric candles, and hanging between the doors was the occasional faded painting depicting extinct creatures of light she'd only ever heard of in stories—bright silver unicorns, Thunder Eagles the size of elephants, golden lions with the faces of beautiful men and women.

Two long velvet sofas with thick clawed feet sat facing each other in the center of the room. A dusty red and gold mosaic carpet covered the cracked wooden floor. Lopsided stacks of books and papers rested on a short wooden table between them. Small rickety tables throughout the room held various ancient looking silver and gold instruments. She'd have thought she'd stepped into a C. S. Lewis novel if not for the single wall of out-of-place computer equipment and a huge television.

When Toke came in behind her the equipment lit up, the TV switched on, and so did a radio from somewhere Macy couldn't see. He stepped around her, picked up a remote from the table, and shut off the TV.

"I keep meaning to throw that out. But Rune loves movies."

Macy tried to focus, but she couldn't stop looking around. When she finally glanced back at Toke, he was watching her with a tender expression. "What?"

"You look like your mother."

She stepped back and bumped into one of the tables, the instruments sitting on it wobbled. "Who are you?"

"It's a long story and there isn't enough time to tell it."

Macy swallowed. "I do know you then?"

He nodded slowly. "I have seen you twice before now. I was at your naming ceremony when you were a week old, and your father summoned me again when you were about four."

"Who are you, really?"

His lip twitched. "I am Tokharian, former member of the Southern Movan tribe."

"Former member?"

"Sit down. I have something I'd like to show you." He pointed to the nearest couch.

Macy realized her knees were shaking and she had to concentrate on where to put her feet. This man knew her mother. And she was sure she recognized him. She dropped onto the couch, raising a puff of dust.

Toke walked to a dusty bookshelf and pulled down an old paperback book, lifting it up for her to see. *The Master Electrician's Guide to Circuitry.* Chills moved down her spine.

He walked over and held the book toward her. "Open it."

She hesitantly reached out to take the book. It was thick and heavy. The plastic-coated cover was grimy and curled with age. She opened the first page to see a name scrawled in black ink at the top:

Finneus Icareous Nathaniel Drummond, Master Electrician.

Macy's pulse thrummed. She dropped the book in her lap and looked up at Toke. "You?"

"He is the only person who can tell you the truth of your parents past, *your* past."

Heat flooded Macy's chest, but she held it in. She looked up at the strange man standing above her. His odd appearance—the purple Mohawk, the rocker clothes—was both a disguise and a symbol. They allowed him to be approachable by rebellious Chosen, and reflected his need to be separate from the crowd. But more than that, it disguised his role, his importance, his truth. Tokharian was much more than he appeared. "You're Finneus?"

Toke grinned. "The one and only. Your father made up the name. I would have preferred something simpler, cooler—like Falkner."

She raised her eyebrow and he shrugged.

Macy shook her head as Toke sat down beside her, lifted the book off her lap, and tapped the scrawled name. "It was a code name your father came up with in the event you should ever need to FIND ME. He hoped that day would never come, but he had me help him create the living hideaway within the tree just in case. After his death, I knew it was only a matter of time. I bought the chest and donated it to the museum. I'd encoded the tree with your specific bio-electricity so the moment you touched it I'd know you were back. I travel a lot in my duties, but I make a point to come back here as often as I can. A few weeks ago, I felt the Shadows' reappearance. Since the last time they were released was your sixth birthday, I brought my insurgents here just in case." His eyes closed and he pinched the bridge of his nose. "I felt the Daklafar moving toward the town. If I had been faster we would have reached the museum before they did, but I was waiting for the tree to notify me to be certain it was you. I'm sorry. I nearly failed in my promise to your father."

Macy shook her head. It was too much to take in. The concern in his voice, on his face, was genuine. He knew her father, he knew Bastian. "How did they know? How did those Daklafar know to come looking for me in Whisper? I didn't even decide to come here until yesterday morning."

"They're after the Claver."

"But I don't have it!"

Toke sighed. "Just a few months before his death your father contacted me, said he'd found something. He'd been researching the Fall of the Watchers and the danger they posed to the Chosen, as well as the prophecy of the Ninth for years. I assumed it was something related to that, but it must have been for this." He met her eyes. "He must have found the Claver and somehow the Dark figured it out. In his searching, he had to have talked to many people—with the growth of darkness in the world, we just don't know who may have turned, or was tortured into revealing what they knew. Someone knew he had it, and they told the Dark where to find him. Whether they have connected him to you is uncertain, but one thing seems certain, the Dark is very interested in you." His eyebrows rose but she looked away, not quite ready to confide in him her involvement with the Ninth, or her place within the prophecy as Light's Aid.

"But how? How did my father know so much? Was it all stories he'd heard from my grandmother?"

Toke shook his head. "Your father was once one of the Chosen."

It felt like someone punched her in the gut. Max's vast knowledge, his knowing Bastian was a Watcher—the look in his eyes as he'd told him to take Macy as they were being tortured by the Shadows, not complete trust but resignation. Her voice scratched against her throat as she asked, "Was?"

"He fell in love with your mother and chose to give back his shard."

Macy swallowed. "The others?" She couldn't quite form a coherent sentence, but Toke seemed to know what she wanted.

"As I noted earlier, you obviously didn't study your history very well, but I assume you know that most of my kind are loyal to neither the Light nor the Dark."

Macy nodded.

"There are those who *have* chosen sides. Once a Movan gives allegiance to either Light or Dark, it changes them completely. They can never go back to a life of indifference. I sided with the Light when I was very young." He paused and Macy wondered what had happened to change him. "When I pledged myself to the Light, a Seraph gave me a job, or what I like to think of as a privilege. There would be many Chosen, as well as Hidden, who would lose their way, forget who they are, and turn their back on the Light. Not join the Dark," he added at Macy's look, "just give up believing that the Light cared about them, give up fighting for it."

One of Bastian's many lessons tickled in her memory. "The Lost Ones?"

He nodded and his eyes got a faraway look in them. "It's my duty to find the Lost Ones and help them find their way again. I am to teach, protect, and care for them, so long as they'll let me, without pressure or control over their free will."

"My father was a Lost One?"

Toke took a slow breath. "Yes."

Macy shook her head. The ham seemed to be turning in her stomach. Her father was a Chosen, a Lost One, someone who wanted to fight the Dark, but didn't fully follow the Light. It hurt more than she thought it should. "I don't see how you can hate the Dark and not be on the side of Light."

Toke rubbed his stubbly chin. "There are many people in this world who are good, pure people but have yet to find the Light. And even when they do, true conversion to the Light is deeply personal and comes at different times to everyone. Sometimes they think they believe, but once that belief is tested, they falter. True believers find strength in their challenges and accept that the Light knows best."

Macy shrugged. "If you say so." She fiddled with the curled cover of the book. "But if you work for the Light, why are you persecuted by other followers of Light?"

Toke sighed. "It's difficult to explain the reasons why people do the things they do, but I think one reason is that those who persecute do not understand what it means to be a *true* follower of Light."

Macy rubbed her forehead.

"Don't worry. The more time you spend with us, the more you will come to understand."

He took the book and put it back on the shelf. Macy watched him carefully and a memory rushed to the surface.

"I remember!" Her eyes widened. "I went outside to swing and you were there talking to my dad. When you noticed me, my dad turned around, picked me up, and introduced us. Your head was shaved back then. I asked you about your tattoo. You told me it was the mark of your people. That's why the Movan symbol always seemed familiar to me. It was because of you!"

Toke fingered the mark beside his eye.

"This feels so strange," Macy said, mostly to herself. To remember and yet not understand.

Toke touched her shoulder. "I'm sorry. We don't have a lot of time to go over everything right now, Macy, but I promise that as we travel together I will tell you everything. It is not a short story, and it is not all happy, but I want you to know that your father and I were once very close friends. He saved my life on more than one occasion. He was one of the bravest men I knew. You must trust me. I know what you took from the museum and only I can help you make sense of it."

Macy dropped her head in her hands. She thought of the item in her pocket that rested right next to the key. The item she'd yet to look at but now feared what it was. *Bastian, what should I do? Can Toke be trusted?*

Nothing. She felt nothing. Not even a single hint that Bastian was listening.

She took a deep breath and tried a different tactic. *Please, give me some indication that Toke really is on your side, the Light side, the right side. You sent me on this mission blind, please give me at least* some *guidance.* It felt strange talking to the Light this way; she'd always just gone with her gut, or followed Bastian's lead. The only other times she'd even tried to speak with the Light she'd been shouting, once when Bastian was dying and then again when Tolen nearly died.

She looked up to see Toke watching her expectantly. A tiny whisper in her heart seemed to say he was with the Light, but to remain cautious. She wasn't sure if it was really the Light she felt, or her own instincts. "Okay, we'll travel together. But if I feel you are threatening my mission in any way, deal's off."

Toke nodded once. "Fair enough."

Macy slapped her knees and stood up, ignoring the new painful ache that had settled in her heart. "Just one problem—you were right. I have no idea where I'm heading. I felt like coming to Whisper was the right thing to do. After I read about the chest, my plan was to find Finneus. And well," she pointed at Toke, "here you are. I didn't have much to go on after that."

"I think there will be something of your father's that can help us. Let's take a look." He looked up and the skepticism must have shown on her face because he added, "Macy, I'm the one who helped him uncover and put together most of what you'll find in there. I'm on your side and I want to help you in whatever mission the Light has for you. I mean that." The tenderness was in his eyes again, reminiscent of the look her father had often given her, that Bastian regularly gave her. She sighed, sat back on the couch, opened her pack, and started placing the notebooks and letters and the items from the trunk onto the table in front of her, for the first time getting a good look at it all. But the item with the key stayed in her pocket. She didn't want to know if it really was the Claver, not yet.

The maps and papers, the cup, and the bracelet she remembered. She didn't remember the piece of strange silver stone the size of a large marble, similar to the one she'd handed over to Jonas from the Doogar slave in the Shadow Prison. Among the papers from the chest, an old and battered copy of the prophecy caught her eye, but Toke went straight to the notes from the envelope with the letter.

He pushed a couple stacks of papers and books further aside and spread the papers out on the cleared space. Macy pointed to the penciled numbers at the bottom. "Some of the pages are missing."

Toke looked over the pages greedily. "No they're not. It's a clue."

"What?"

Toke put the papers in order, leaving a gap between the pages that were missing. "Look."

Macy shrugged. "I don't see what you're talking about."

"There are drawings before each of the missing pages. But each drawing is incomplete." He took the pages with the drawings out of the pile. There were ten altogether. Toke shuffled the pages around, turning them this way and that. At first, Macy couldn't see what he was doing until two pages matched up.

"Look for this symbol." Toke pointed to a tiny white sun with twisted beams. "The sun must always be on the east side."

Macy stared at the intricate drawings covered with symbols, and tried to find the tiny sun. It took several eye-straining minutes, but finally all the pages were turned in the right direction. Toke took another five minutes lining them up. When he was finished, Macy could tell it was a map. It didn't look like a normal geography map from her lessons with Bastian; it looked like the ancient maps she'd see him studying from time to time, covered with symbols and words she couldn't read.

"By the Light, he did it. No wonder they were after him. No wonder they are after you!" Toke put his hand over his eyes and collapsed back into the couch.

Macy looked at the map and felt tears prick the back of her eyes. What had her father known? What path was she on that had brought them back together? She traced a line on the map with her finger and at the same moment felt Bastian's shard pulse with energy—a clash of dread and excitement. She absently placed her hand over the shard, refusing to connect to it and have it overwhelm her again. "What did he do?"

Toke took a deep breath and placed both hands on the table. "Your father may have found the way to tip the odds in the Light's favor. It's crazy, risky, but with your father gone you might be the only one who can find them." His eyes were shining, and his voice trembled with something that sounded like excitement mingled with fear. "It's not going to be the slightest bit easy, the Relics will be vastly protected, and the Dark is going to be seeking us the entire time, but I know where we need to go first."

23 LESSONS FROM A NAIAD

Hunsí and Quasar headed into the heart of the village, deep in conversation. Tashta clutched Tolen's elbow and led him the opposite direction.

"The children have lessons every morning," she explained. "You will attend with them. You'll come home for lunch, and then attend a meeting with the Honitahai council. After that, Hunsí wishes you to train with the guard. Sienn is the captain. She'll lead you to the arena when your meeting ends." She paused and touched his cheek, likely sensing his growing nervousness. "Your welcome dinner will take place this evening in the courtyard. A great way to end a busy day." She pointed toward the center of the village, near the same spot Tolen completed the Share.

"You are one of us, Tolen. You have a grand heritage. Dark times these may be, but there is still much goodness and light worth celebrating." She pointed left to a broad, many limbed tree covered in lacy green vines and white flowers. "Lessons take place in there." She squeezed his elbow once, turned and walked away.

Tolen followed a group of children ranging in age, maybe ten to early teens. Someone tapped his shoulder and he turned to see the young boy from the Share. The Watcher.

"I am Sashan." The boy touched his fist to his chest.

Tolen cleared his throat. "Tolen."

Sashan nodded, his pale eyes shifting. He motioned to the tree. "Come." He walked forward and disappeared.

Tolen took the last few steps to the tree and the vines curled away from the bark to reveal a gaping hole. He stepped through into one of the most amazing places he'd ever seen.

What he'd originally thought was a single, huge tree was actually many trees growing side by side, branches intertwined, roots twisting one over the other. There was unity and love between them. Tolen could literally feel the Honitahai Nature Speak within him reacting to the pure love of its kind. Once inside the linked trees, he felt protected, safe, loved, and accepted.

Instead of desks or chairs, multi-colored hammock-style seats swung from low hanging branches. Fluffy cushions, like those in Tashta's house, filled spaces on the grassy floor. Flowers of every kind bloomed everywhere, the fragrance intoxicating. The trees opened to the sky in the center, letting the light from the sun turn the classroom into a living atrium.

Sashan led Tolen to a red hammock and then climbed into the blue one hanging beside it.

Tolen lowered himself onto the sturdy material and leaned back. The chair seemed to mold around him, cushioning every part of his body. A thin vine trailed down the handles, sprouted flowers, and continued to curl longer and longer until it reached the floor.

"Amladra recognizes you as Honitahai," a girl's voice said from behind Tolen. "They are welcoming you."

She walked around Tolen's seat and fingered one of the bright-blue blossoms on the vine. She was young, probably fourteen or fifteen. Her curly, white-blonde hair seemed to reflect the sun. Her eyes were a strange shade of bluish green, like spring grass. Her skin sparkled with a pearlescent sheen. There was a presence to her Tolen couldn't quite pinpoint— almost as if she were a part of the forest itself.

"Amladra?" Tolen raised his eyebrows.

We are Amladra. A chorus of female voices filled his mind and the trees surrounding him glowed fiery gold. *Welcome, Tolen, Conchla Mindra.*

Tolen looked back at the girl. A wry smile pulled at the corner of her lips. "Who are you?" He thought it would be rude to ask, *What are you?*

The girl's grin stretched into a wide smile. "I am one of the *Ahn-Kah-Chan,* a guardian of the forest." Her gentle voice reminded him of the tinkle of water falling over small stones in a stream. "My name is Kah-tahaka. My students call me Tahaka."

"Your students?" Tolen noticed the other children were all watching the exchange between the Ninth and their *teacher.*

"I am not as young as I look." She pushed a shimmering strand of hair off her forehead. "I age with the forest I am sent to protect. This forest is young." She winked and turned back to the rest of the class.

Tolen tried to imagine growing up like this—the way the children who stared at him curiously had—but he couldn't. Trees for school buildings instead of crowded classrooms. A naiad for a teacher, and fellow students that could speak to nature. It was as if he'd stepped into a storybook.

"Good morning, everyone." Tahaka waved her hands in the air and a pile of fallen leaves swirled up into her palm. "We have a visitor today." Tolen could feel eyes on him, but he kept his focus on Tahaka. "He comes to us from far away—from the land of humans."

Muted whispers.

"He is going to stay with us for a short time. We will teach him the Hidden way." She blew on the leaves in her hand and they curled into a flowing vortex that she sent spinning around each person in the room. As the leaves swirled around a child's head they closed their eyes. The leaves came to him and as they twisted around him, his mind was filled with chatter. He too closed his eyes and the chatter became the soft, clear voice of Tahaka.

"Each student is unique, Tolen. As they connect their mind to their gift, they hear and see what is taught in the way that is best for them to learn. Your first birthright is that of the Honitahai. Had you not been chosen to be the Ninth, you would have been raised in the ways of the Honitahai. Your parents would have found the closest Honitahai tribe and brought you to the Honitahai Council of Elders. You would have attended lessons, learned their histories, the origin of your gift, and the purpose of this life. You would have learned to master your strength."

Tolen squirmed, grateful that everyone was getting a private lesson of their own.

"Do not blame your parents for their choices, Tolen. Love is rational and irrational. Your fate is twisted, but your destiny is firm. You are accepting your role in this world, but you still have much to learn."

A vivid landscape appeared behind Tolen's closed lids. Vast mountain ranges were divided by sparkling ribbons of water and sprawling valleys.

The clear blues and greens were the vibrant, rich, living color of the Light Realm, but this was not the Light Realm that he saw. It was Earth as it was meant to be. Pure, perfect, unspoiled.

He saw villages of humans and Hidden-kind living and working together. Light's gifts were used to enhance and beautify the world around them. There was no envy or fear, no arrogance or pride. Just love and beauty. The air of peace and serenity was so alluring Tolen's heart ached to be a part of such contentment and acceptance.

Tahaka showed him many more things pertaining to the history of his race. He saw hundreds of colonies and tribes. He saw children sitting in various tribal councils where they were blessed and accepted into the tribe pertaining to their gift. Parents chose whether to live within the tribe or not. If they chose to live elsewhere, they would bring the children to spend summers with their tribe where they learned to enhance their gifts with others like them.

He saw the humans and Hidden grow and advance together as they shared their knowledge, talents, and gifts with one another.

He saw the Dark come in and subtly change their way of life by introducing greed and selfishness. He saw again the Pact with Thaer and the Guardians. But this time as Thaer turned to leave the citadel, Tolen knew why he looked familiar. It was his eyes. They were Macy's eyes—sparkling emerald, fiercely intelligent. For a moment, the realization pulled him from the lesson and he looked around to see the others all sitting back in their hammocks or resting on cushions looking as if they were asleep.

Tahaka raised her eyebrows at him, he closed his eyes, and the vision held him once more. He saw many Lafar choose darkness and become the Daklafar.

It seemed to go on for hours. By the time the visions left and the children began to stir, the sun was directly overhead and Tolen's stomach was rumbling. He found himself looking forward to seeing Tashta again and sharing what he'd learned. He was even looking forward to the Council of Elders, wondering where his parents would have taken him if his life had been normal—well, normal for Hidden-kind anyway.

Tahaka smiled at him as he walked outside.

24 PART OF A FAMILY

TOLEN WALKED QUICKLY along the dirt path that led to Tashta's home. Tashta was the Village Mother. There were so many terms in the Hidden world that he hadn't understood until his lesson with Tahaka. The Village Mother was so called because she took in the orphans, those without families of their own.

He saw Sienn walk into the house and paused before following. Tolen hadn't thought much about Sienn after their last confrontation. As much as he'd looked forward to seeing Tashta again, he didn't want to bring contention into her home because of Sienn's animosity. He was just about to skip lunch and head back to the courtyard when someone called his name.

He turned to see Sashan walking his way and waited for the boy to catch up. "Come. Tashta will be waiting and we all must help with the meal."

Tolen looked at the young boy. If he also stayed with Tashta that meant both he and Sienn were orphans. Pity swelled inside him. He took a deep breath and followed Sashan into the house.

Two males about Tolen's age were setting the table. Sienn stood next to the sink cutting fresh vegetables. Sashan went to her side and started helping. She nudged his shoulder in acknowledgment but didn't turn to look at Tolen. Unsure what to do, Tolen walked over to where Tashta stood beside the stove and tapped her shoulder. "What can I do?"

Tashta flashed him one of her warm smiles and handed him a spoon. "You can finish the soup while I slice up the bread and glaze the cake." She waved toward a faded piece of paper, and a handful of chopped herbs on the counter by the stove. "The ingredients are all added except the final herbs. Just follow the recipe."

Tolen looked at the recipe and the corner of his mouth twitched. It was written in the Hidden tongue. Funny how the fact that he could read the old, faded recipe made him feel more a part of this world. The world he truly belonged in.

Before long, the tiny house was filled with the aroma of vegetable soup, fresh bread, and spice cake.

Once the food was finished and on the table they each took a seat, Tashta at the head. She closed her eyes and they all bowed their heads. She once again offered a prayer over the food and included special requests for the health and safety of each of her "children." When she finished her lips curled into her crinkly smile.

"We have a new member of the family. Let's introduce ourselves to Tolen properly, shall we?" Tashta looked to the boy at her left. Tolen recognized him as one of the warriors who'd been with Sienn when he and Quasar first arrived.

The big boy leaned across the table and gripped arms with Tolen. "I'm Mahto, guard in training." He presented a firm grip, a warm smile with very white teeth, and shoulder-length blue-black hair tied back in a ponytail. His bright hazel eyes danced with humor. He was taller than Tolen, his shoulders so thick and broad that when he sat back down they brushed Tashta on his right and Sienn on his left. His name meant "bear" in Hidden language. Fitting.

Tolen smiled.

Sienn leaned over and barely squeezed Tolen's arm before dropping it and sitting back down. "We've met." She still didn't trust him.

"Sienn is the Captain of the Guard," Tashta supplied.

Sienn's eyes were a deep bluish-green. Not the bright emerald of Macy's eyes—more blue—but still, too close.

He gratefully looked away when the brown-haired boy to his right leaned over and gripped his arm. "Belahee'chay. Blacksmith." The skin of his hands was stained black and covered in calluses. He wasn't as tall and broad as Mahto, but still wider than Tolen and almost as tall, his smile shyer. The gentle giant.

"Your name means courage?" Tolen asked as he sat down again.

"Yes," Mahto said with a mouthful of soup, "but it takes too long to say so we just call him Belch."

"Belch?" Tolen leaned back in his chair.

Belch nodded. "It *is* easier to say. I won't tell you what we call Mahto behind his back." Tashta threw her napkin at him. He grinned and stuffed half a slice of bread into his mouth.

Sashan turned to grip Tolen's arm. His sapphire eyes were shifting again. "Sashan Woodlore. Son of Eamun." He held Tolen's arm for a second longer than the others and Tolen's blue Watcher's eye started to water. Sashan was here with Tashta, the village Mother, the keeper of orphans. That meant Eamun Woodlore, speaker of the prophecy of the Ninth and Guardian of the Last shard, was dead?

Tashta sighed. "Eat. Before it gets cold."

It was silent for a while aside from the clink of spoons and sounds of chewing. Everything was delicious—even better than the food at the citadel.

"So you are nearing your eighteenth birthday, Tolen," Tashta commented between bites.

Tolen nodded and wiped his hands on his napkin.

The others around the table shared surprised looks.

"You're not eighteen yet?" Mahto blurted and Sienn punched his arm. She and Macy would get along.

Tolen shook his head.

"Wow, you're in for a treat." Mahto ducked away from Sienn's next punch.

"No one's given me any specifics," Tolen shrugged, "but what I have heard doesn't sound like a treat."

"What? It's awesome man!" Mahto grinned.

"It's not all bad." Belch scratched his ear with his handle of his spoon. "I only flattened my own hut. When Mahto transcended they had to practically rebuild the whole Capka."

Tolen's eyebrows scrunched together. "Capka?" He remembered Quasar saying something about a Capka to Hunsí when they'd first arrived.

Mahto flicked a pea at Belch who caught it in his mouth. "It's the area of our village where the almost-eighteens go for their Transcendence. It's been blessed by the Spheres with extra protection so that we don't affect the Balance and endanger the village."

Tolen tried to look like he got it. "How old are you guys?"

Mahto flashed his bright smile. "I just turned thirty-seven in human years."

Tolen's eyes bugged. "Seriously?"

Mahto nodded. "Yep. Belch is twenty-nine, but Sienn's the oldest. She's *forty*." This time he jumped out of his chair to avoid her fist. "Hey, no one else can look as good as you at forty. That's a compliment!" She glared but let him sit back down before pulling his hair.

Tashta clicked her tongue. "Yes, but none of you *act* your human age, now do you?" She held back a smile as Mahto and Sienn went back to eating, their cheeks a little pink.

She looked at Tolen, seemed to sense his growing anxiety, and hurried to explain—having no idea her words would only make things worse. "Once Hidden reach the human age of eighteen, their gifts fully unite with their physical body. We call this Transcendence, as you are moving into another stage, a higher phase of your life. This immensely powerful connection of body and life force can be difficult to control, so they go to the Capka for help with the transition. When the change takes place within the body, the growth cycle slows down, and continues to slow down, until eventually you will age only one year for about every twenty human years. Once Watchers transcend they age even slower. Sashan is twenty human years old."

The ugly thought that had blossomed into being began to take solid shape in Tolen's mind and the room started to spin. "Excuse me." He jumped from his chair and stumbled out the front door. He broke into a run and didn't stop until he'd slammed the door on the old hut he'd stayed in the night before. His breath came in short bursts, his fingers tingled, and heat surged to his chest. He leaned over and gripped his head with both hands. Why had he never seen it before?

He pushed his hands against his eyes.

He knew why—he'd refused to *allow* himself to see it.

That was the real reason it was so hard to leave his human life behind, why he so desperately *wanted* to be human. He'd first thought of it in the Binithan when he'd found out Macy was human—when he became aware that they were different. But he hadn't let himself think any more deeply about it.

Sienn was forty and looked barely twenty.

His father said he was nearly two hundred human years old when he met Tolen's mother. He'd been too preoccupied with his concerns for Macy's mission to let that sink in.

He lowered his hands and closed his eyes. Macy was sixteen, he was seventeen—and they looked it. But in two days Tolen would stop aging normally. In twenty years he would still look like a teenager, in sixty years he'd barely look a day over twenty, and Macy…

Hot, blinding light burst from his body and singed the grassy roof of the hut, which started smoking. The ground trembled and quaked; distant screams came from the village. A fissure opened in the earth beside him and he fell to his back. An owl swooped in through the window and hovered over his head. The energy drained out of him as the wind picked up, shrieking through the trees, picking up leaves and other debris and covering everything with dust.

Believe, Tolen. Trust in the Light. The words seemed to be carried on the wind. Tolen closed his eyes and the world disappeared.

"Is he dead?" Mahto whispered.

"Mahto, stop," Tashta scolded. "He's experienced an overload. Would you like me to remind everyone what happened to the courtyard when Sienn first kissed you?"

Belch snickered. "That was a mess."

"Shh," Tashta soothed when Tolen stirred. "This boy has been through much. Each of you has been raised to know our world. Tolen was raised to believe he was human."

Tolen opened his eyes and pushed himself into a sitting position. "A human freak anyway."

They were back in Tashta's home. He was on the floor covered in a soft blanket. He recognized the smell of Lucid coming off the wet rag in Tashta's hand. Sienn, Mahto, Belch, and Sashan were all kneeling on the floor around him, along with a man Tolen didn't recognize. He cleared his throat. "I'm really sorry. I didn't hurt anyone, did I?"

Tashta shook her head. "No. Everyone is fine. You did well. You may have lost control of your gifts, but you maintained your shield." She pointed to the man beside her. "Bren is our Sphere. He came right away. He said you didn't affect our protection at all. He wants you to rest awhile longer. You drained much of your strength."

The unfamiliar man, Bren, leaned over, put one hand on Tolen's head, the other on his chest, and closed his eyes. Tolen felt the same warmth he'd felt when his mother had soothed his hurts as a child. Not relief from the physical pain, but the emotional pain in his heart and mind as he'd struggled to fit in.

Trust in the Light. Bastian's voice sounded in his mind again. There had to be a purpose for all of this. Loving Macy was right—it must be! He would deal with what was in front of him. He wouldn't think about life span right now, when there was a good chance neither of them would survive the Final Battle anyway. He shuddered and turned away from that thought as well. Trust. Okay. He could try. He swallowed back the pain and forced his thoughts back to the moment.

It took a while for Tashta to believe that Tolen felt well enough to go to the meeting with the Elders. She made him eat more spice cake and drink a cupful of the horrible Lucid tea before she let him leave. Mahto seemed to think it was hilarious and kept snickering behind his hand. Sashan, Belch, and Sienn had left shortly after he'd come to. Apparently Mahto would take Tolen to the meeting, so he had to endure his teasing.

"I feel great, Tashta, honest." He didn't really feel *great*, but he needed to leave. He needed the distraction.

Mahto turned a laugh into a cough when Tashta gave him a dirty look.

She clicked her tongue and shook her head. "You're so powerful, Tolen. Just do what the Elders tell you and you will be fine." The laugh lines beside her eyes crinkled and she patted his hand.

He stood up from the table and joined Mahto, who waited in the opening to the living room.

"Don't worry, Tashta. I'll keep an eye on him." Mahto winked at Tolen.

Tolen waved at Tashta and followed Mahto out the door, forcing his thoughts away from the heavy weight that had settled in his chest just over the crack in his heart.

25 DECISIONS

MACY WATCHED TOKE sweep around the room, gathering supplies while talking to himself. "Yes, I'll need that… No, that can stay… Dangerous, risky, no one else would have ever attempted it…" Occasionally he would shake his head.

"Hey, I still have some questions."

He didn't seem to hear her. He kept moving about the room, muttering to himself.

She stepped in his path. "Hey! What does all this mean?"

He paused with his hand on a doorknob and turned to face her. "I'm sorry, Macy." He looked around. "Repack your things and I'll tell you what I can on the way back to the others, okay? I'm just going to grab some more supplies." He opened a door that led into a huge closet.

Macy nodded, not trusting her voice. She shoved the notes and trinkets back in her bag while Toke stuffed a strange assortment of gadgets, metal, wire, books, ancient-looking scrolls, and notebooks—*stacks* of notebooks—into his bag. She wondered how he planned to lift it all.

"Okay, that should do it." He pulled the pack over his shoulders with a grunt. "Hmm, that's going to be a bit inconvenient." He shrugged. "Oh, well. Let's go."

He led the way back to the stairs. As soon as they left the room, everything shut down and the stairway was bathed in darkness. Once outside, Toke took the lead again. "Okay, would you like to know a little about the trinkets in the chest?" He glanced back and waited for her nod before continuing. "The bracelet works as a sort of dark detector. It's very rare, made by ancient Movan, likely traded to one of your distant Algonquin relatives. I think your father kept it on the chance that you might need it one day. I think he always suspected the Balance would select you as one of the Chosen, but he wanted a way to protect you just in case. My guess is the cup is another bauble that depicts your heritage. I don't remember seeing it in your father's possession when I was with him. And the strange silver stone—"

"I've seen one before."

He glanced back. "You have? Where?"

"It'll take too long to explain."

His eyes narrowed.

"I'll answer your questions when you've answered mine."

He paused mid-step and nodded. "Fair enough."

"Why was my father one of the Lost?"

Toke's eyes were calculating and unsure. He was clearly wondering if she could take it.

"After everything I've been through in my life do you really think I can't handle a scary story?"

"It's not scary, it's sad."

The ache in her heart fluttered. "All the same. I can take it."

He tipped his head and started to walk again. "How much do you know about your parents' families?"

She kept pace beside him, not wanting to miss anything. "Not much. I only remember ever visiting my great-grandma Mary on a few occasions. I never met any of my other relatives. Bastian offered to help me learn more of my family history, but I…I didn't like thinking about my human life."

Toke held a branch out of the way and touched her shoulder as she passed. "I understand. Tragic events are far harder to process as children, you dealt with your loss the only way you could. It's nothing to be ashamed of." She nodded and looked away. He continued once they were walking again. "Your great-grandmother was the only one who accepted your parents' union. Your mother's family were devout Catholics. They were furious when she changed her plans to take her vows in order to marry Max. They disowned her. Your father's parents were another story altogether. His parents were both Chosen—"

Macy stopped walking. "What?"

Toke waited for her to catch back up. "Yes. Legendary in fact. As I said, you are a descendant of the Algonquin, some of this land's earliest peoples. Many of your ancestors were Chosen. When your father was born, they raised him with all the knowledge of the Hidden world passed down to them for generations. They took him on missions, trained him. He never fit in with the human world, but he wanted to. He really, really wanted to. He envied the human's ignorance, their pretend safety. He couldn't see the Dark yet, but his parents taught him to recognize it in feelings, to avoid it, to fight against it. He envied the freedom of the humans to go about their lives as they chose, without conscious fear of the Dark.

"It was no surprise that he was Chosen. He was already a formidable fighter, a fierce opponent to a force he couldn't even see, even at just six years old." He walked ahead not realizing what this revelation was doing to her. Macy's feet felt heavy. Her brain couldn't seem to process what Toke said. How many of her ancestors were Chosen ones? How far back did the line go? Back to the Revolution? Back to the first Chosen ones? Did her mother understand what she was getting herself into when she married Max?

"He was barely twelve the day I found him. He ran away from his parents when he was eleven. He believed in the Light and the purpose of the Chosen, but he was tired of fighting and death. He grew tired of watching the humans go about their lives while he hid and lived in a constant state of stress. He knew they still needed his protection but he wanted to do it in his own way. He wanted to live among them, be one of them, and keep his real identity a secret. I think he nursed a little bit of a Superman complex back then." He chuckled, but Macy didn't see the humor. How many times had she wanted the same thing? Her jealousy for the human life he'd lived had been her biggest reason for not accepting Tolen in the beginning.

"I found Max hiding in an abandoned apartment building in Chicago. He'd actually made a pretty nice place for himself. He went out at night, fought the Dark, and then went to school during the day. He'd learned how to blend in from his parents, so no one suspected he was different. He swept floors at a local restaurant and it paid enough for food and supplies. He was content. At least he thought he was.

"The Light eventually led me to him. When I arrived outside his building, a group of ten Raksasha had him surrounded. He fought really well, but he was injured and weak from the poison in his wound. I jumped into the fight, and between the two of us, we managed to finish off the Raksasha. I took him inside and cleaned him up. Eventually I convinced him to come with me here to my home. He helped me find more Lost Ones and stayed with me until he met your mother."

"How old was he when he met my mom?"

"Seventeen. I'd never been able to convince him to give up his super-hero lifestyle completely. He still chose to live among the humans and fight the Dark like Batman. He was attending a private Catholic high school in Whisper when he met Alison. He was completely taken from the first moment he saw her. No amount of chatter from me could convince him to stay away from her. With time she fell for him, too." He paused and Macy remembered that Toke had said the story was sad.

"Your father knew that when he turned eighteen he would have to choose whether or not to make his duty as a Chosen a life-long commitment. It was something that, up to now, he'd been looking forward to. Now, a big decision loomed on the horizon. Continue the life of a superhero, or give up his gifts and assume the life of a normal human being." He tugged his pack higher on his shoulders. "You know what he chose. He severed ties with me, gave his shard back to the Guardians, and went on to live a human life with your mother. At least for a time. He couldn't deny what was going on around him, even though he couldn't see it in the physical sense. He began to research. He became obsessed when you were born. He wanted to find a way to make a safer world for his daughter. Looking for nontraditional, unthought-of ways to defeat the Dark was something he had focused on in his youth. I didn't know he was actively doing it again until he used an old method of ours to contact me, to invite me to your naming ceremony."

"The ancient custom was performed by your great-grandmother. It was such a privilege to be there." He paused to look at her. "McLacy Alli-candra, helper of light." He started walking again. "As I said, I think your father somehow knew you would be important to the cause. We talked and then parted ways again until I returned when you were four to help him set up the tree. I was halfway across the continent when I sensed the

Shadows' movement on your sixth birthday. By the time I arrived back in Whisper it was too late." His voice caught. "I've been waiting for you ever since."

Macy took a slow breath. The others were close. She could feel it. But she wanted one more answer before they reached them. "Toke?"

He stopped and turned around.

"What was my father? I mean, what was his Chosen gift?"

A sad smile touched his lips. "Animashta."

She nodded once trying to ignore the ache in her chest. "What did you mean since my father's gone I'm the only one who can find them? Find what?"

Toke tugged his pack higher on his shoulders. "We're close to the others. I'm sorry, the answer will have to wait."

"Why?"

He took a deep breath. "I trust them, but a few of them are still on the cusp of their decision to fully follow the Light, I want nothing to sway them. I don't want them overhearing something that will lead to confusion and doubt."

Macy nodded, her thoughts so muddled she barely listened as Toke rejoined the others and explained where they were headed. Something about "old ones" and the need for more information. Her head spun with all she had learned. Strange how it all rang so true. It fit in with some of her memories, the stories her father used to tell her, the way he had with animals. Her memories of her mother were not as vivid and it made her sad.

The others fell into step ahead of her; she didn't care about their curious looks or Rune's irritated scowl. For the millionth time, she wished Tolen were here. To be able to talk to the one person she could be totally honest with, to have him comfort her and counsel with her. Being alone and making decisions by the seat of her pants hadn't been a big deal before, but now that she understood what true companionship was, she missed him more every day.

She shook her head. Whatever she was supposed to do, this was a part of it. She wasn't sure if she should fully trust Toke, or his rebels, but she would welcome their help for the time being, and she wanted to hear all he knew of her parents.

An hour later, she was pulled out of her musings by raised voices. Toke and Rune were arguing.

Rune's voice carried back to her. "Why are we expected to follow you without an explanation?" He planted his feet in their path and tossed his pack underneath a tilted pine.

Toke set his pack down and motioned for everyone to stop. He turned back to Rune. "I told you where I am going and that it is of vital importance. I *asked* you come with me. No one is making you do anything, Rune. I want to visit the old ones. I need to know if my thoughts are correct before I act on them. You are free to leave if you choose."

Rune threw a disgusted look at Macy. A look she recognized. Rune was jealous.

He looked back at Toke. "Why won't you just tell us what your thoughts are then? Don't you trust us?"

Toke sighed and ran his hand across the stubble on the side of his head. "I offer you a choice, Rune. Stay with me until nightfall, when we reach the next stage of our journey, and I will explain to you all that I can. Or choose to leave me and go out on your own. You know I've never forced you to stay. Time is not on our side. I don't want to wait to explain, but I can't do it while we're walking. It's something I need to show you. You know I want you with me, but that has to be your decision."

Keelyn walked up to Rune and touched his back. "Rune, please."

Rune pinched the bridge of his nose. Macy wondered at his story. Why was he so volatile? He shouldered much of the same anger she'd harbored before loving Tolen had erased it. A tiny glimmer of concern tried to override her irritation with Rune. She knew what Tolen would do. She moved up the line, stepping around the others, until she was face to face with Rune.

"I know you have no reason to trust me. I can't tell you my mission because even I don't know exactly what it is. I came to Whisper in search of my past. I was trying to follow my heart and now my heart tells me to follow Toke. To trust him. I may not know why I'm here or what I'm supposed to do, but I can feel it's big; something bigger than any of us has brought us together here and now. I honestly believe that."

Rune looked up, his eyes suspicious as she plowed on, going with the feeling in her heart that it was the right thing to do. She wasn't sure if she would be going against the Guardians by telling the rebels what she knew about Tolen. But thinking about Tolen, about his friendship, his guidance, his love, she realized she needed this group, and maybe they needed her too. She glanced at Toke and he gave a small nod. "When it's safe to stop, I'll tell you what I do know." She held up her hand when Rune opened his mouth. "I don't know much, but I promise I won't keep anything from you that's mine to tell."

A spark of curiosity replaced most of the suspicion in Rune's eyes. Macy could feel the curious stares of the others, but she kept her eyes on Rune. Somehow, she knew his decision would affect the decisions of the others as well. Toke might be the silent guardian, but Rune was the ringleader.

Rune turned his gaze to Keelyn and the slightest softening appeared in the hard lines around his mouth. She gave him a tiny nod and his stance relaxed. "Fine."

Toke stepped around the two and led the way again. Keelyn stayed beside Rune, Connell and Brina passed on either side of Macy without a glance in her direction. She followed behind the rebels, her thoughts swirling so much that within minutes she had a monster of a headache.

26 MEETING THE ELDER

Tolen followed Mahto past the main section of the village onto a shadowy path leading deeper into the forest.

Mahto paused beside an old tree covered with tangled branches and vines. Upon closer inspection, Tolen noticed it wasn't a tree at all, but an ancient stone house so overgrown with plant life that it blended into its surroundings.

The wavy glass in the single window beside the rotting door was so thickly coated with grime that it blocked any ability to see in or out.

"It looks abandoned." Tolen looked at the weathered door that hung loosely in its frame from faded leather hinges.

"I know, right?" Mahto nudged a pair of scuffed rubber boots with his foot and scared out a mouse. "The Elders don't like change, or cleaning for that matter." Mahto wrinkled his nose as he knocked on the dusty door.

"I resent that, Mahto." An ancient woman with more wrinkles than a piece of cracked leather opened the door. Her back was so hunched that her head appeared to be sprouting from the front of her body. She wore a patched and frayed brown dress the texture of cheesecloth, and her dirty feet were bare. Her gnarled fingers wrapped around a long, spindly, wooden staff and when she opened her crinkled lips she revealed a mouth devoid of teeth. Her hair stood out from her head in bushy gray waves that spilled down her back to the ground where it had collected several dead leaves and twigs. Her eyes were a strange brownish-green and when she looked at Tolen, it was as if she was looking straight into his soul.

Mahto chuckled and the corners of the old woman's mouth lifted slightly. "I meant no disrespect, Kichaya."

She lifted a bushy white eyebrow. "Maybe, maybe not." She smacked her gums and looked back at Tolen. "Come in."

Tolen looked at Mahto and he shook his head. "Just you, man." He wiggled his eyebrows. "Have fun."

Kichaya swatted Mahto's shoulder. "Get back to your chores, you naughty boy."

Her voice was vaguely familiar. Where had he heard it before?

"Yes, ma'am." Mahto gave her a mock bow, winked at Tolen, and walked away.

Kichaya stood blocking the doorway. She studied Tolen with a stony expression, stuck a bony finger in her mouth, and smacked her gums against a yellowed fingernail. "Such a tangled path—"

"It was you!"

Her gaze turned quizzical.

"It's your voice I've been hearing in my dreams! Calling to me…" he trailed off, realizing how crazy he sounded.

But she nodded and then began thumping the side of his head with her knobby knuckles. "What were your parents thinking?"

Tolen stepped away from her and opened his mouth to respond, but she waved her hand.

"No matter. What's done is done." She took a noisy breath. "Come in, come in." She stepped back and motioned him inside.

Tolen took a deep breath and ducked through the doorframe.

As she closed the door behind him, layers of vines and branches twisted over the door and tiny window. He felt a strange sort of power blanket over the home. It was different from the shield cast by the Spheres at the citadel. It felt heavier, denser. More as if the strength of the Light was trapped in some sort of bubble that would eventually run out of air.

Tolen looked around the tiny stone room. It was cleaner than he had expected from the outside. Warm embers burned low in the fireplace, next to which sat an old rocking chair with a basket of colorful yarn and what looked like the beginnings of an afghan. A small roughly cut wooden table surrounded by five low stools seemed to be the main focal point in the room. An array of dried herbs, rocks, glimmering crystals, and bits of old leather were strewn across it. A stack of faded papers, on the top of which sat a map that looked very much like the one Quasar carried, rested to the side of the mess.

"Sit, sit." The woman sat on the stool closest to the papers and motioned for Tolen to take the seat to her right.

Tolen was so tall that when he sat down his knees bumped the underside of the table. Fearing he looked as ridiculous as he felt, he turned and stretched his legs out to the side.

"I am Kichaya. In the earthen tongue, it means Leading Light. I am a commune, gifted…or cursed," she added with a flicker of a grin, "with the ability to speak for the Light, as they choose me to."

The small stool creaked as Tolen shifted his position.

Kichaya tapped her staff on the ground. "The others are coming."

Swirls of golden light twisted from the ceiling, curling and dancing around the room until they separated into two glittering forms that sat on the stools opposite Kichaya and Tolen. Their forms slowly filled out with transparent color, although the edges of each form still glowed gold. The men turned their see-through faces toward Tolen, their clear eyes curious.

Kichaya tapped her staff on the ground again and the candlelight seemed to brighten until the home was filled with golden light. The men turned their attention to her.

"Father," she said, motioning to the man on her left. "Brother." She nodded at the man closest to Tolen. "As the Elders of this tribe we have been called together to discuss this boy." She nodded at Tolen. Her voice had a gravelly quality to it, like stones crunching under tires. "The Ninth Chosen's destiny is in danger; his parents' meddling with fate has far-reaching consequences. We can try to teach him in the little time we have with him, we can protect him through his Transcendence, but there is a deeper, more problematic issue at work that could make all efforts for naught."

The golden figures looked at Tolen again. Their curiosity turned to concern.

The man on Kichaya's left spoke in a soft melodic voice, "Has he accepted his role and the sacrifices necessary to succeed?"

"We shall see."

Her father and brother nodded.

Tolen's chair creaked and he tried to stop fidgeting.

"Let's begin." Kichaya pushed a small maple leaf in front of her, and next to it she sprinkled a tiny pile of dirt. She continued adding things to the row in front of her until, beside the dirt and leaf, sat a piece of animal fur, a vial of water, a Fire Stone, a piece of crystal that glowed with warm light, and a small cracked mirror. She flicked her wrist and a gentle breeze seemed to come from nowhere to swirl over the objects. She then closed her eyes and began to snore. He cast a quick glance at the ghost men, but they too had their eyes closed.

Tolen listened to the old woman's snore for what felt like forever, and was just debating whether or not to shake her awake, when suddenly the leaf changed to a vibrant green and vines began shooting out of it. The vines reached out and began to touch the other items. First the Fire Stone—tiny flames erupted from its surface. Next, the crystal. Its warm light brightened to a brilliant white—too bright to look at. It illuminated the other objects as one by one the vines touched them and they took on a life of their own. The animal skin took the form of a tiny field mouse, his nose twitching, his eyes darting around. The vial broke and the water lifted up into a small shimmering ball. The mirror began to spin in the air until it seemed to disappear, its only indication that it was still there from a slight distortion of the objects behind it. The pile of dirt reformed into the shape of a tiny eagle. The breeze picked up to a fierce wind that blew against Tolen's face, but the items themselves seemed unaffected.

Each one of the items, along with the swirling wind, represented a gift of the Light.

"You have accepted you are the Ninth." Kichaya spoke with her eyes closed, her voice monotone, deep. "But accepted the sacrifices necessary to succeed you have not."

Kichaya opened her eyes. They were no longer the strange greenish brown. They were bright green, the color of emeralds, the color of Macy's eyes—they *were* Macy's eyes. The old woman's features faded to be replaced with Macy's. Tolen's hands began to shake. It was an illusion. Just an illusion. But he couldn't stop himself from reaching out, his fingers aching to trace the curve of her lips, the tiny dimple beside her mouth.

Just as his hand passed through the wind, Macy's face disappeared and he was looking into the weathered, unsmiling face of Kichaya. Her eyes were back to muddy green, and all of her earlier humor was gone.

Tolen dropped his hands to his lap and felt his face go red. He didn't dare meet the eyes he felt focused on him.

Kichaya cleared her throat, but Tolen kept his eyes down. His heart raced and his fingers tingled. The surge of desire that flowed through him at seeing Macy's face scared him. He knew he loved her with an intensity that he'd never felt before, and it was this intense love that fueled his gifts, but this power was different. This longing to see her, to feel her in his arms again, was so incredibly dominant it overruled every other thought, desire, and need. Nothing mattered in that moment. Nothing but being with her.

His hands trembled and he squeezed them together. His mind and heart waged a painful war. Logic told him to stay where he was, but *love* urged him to run out the door and find Macy. Find her and forget everything else. His chest started to constrict, heat flooded his palms, and he started panting. No. She had a mission, and so did he.

Who cares about our duty?

He squeezed his hands so tight he could feel the blood pulsing through his fingers. *We care. We both care. It matters to us.*

Does it? Or did he want more than anything else, more than duty, more than the lives of everyone around him, to be with her? To hold her. To make her his own in every way possible? Yes, *yes.* That is what he really wanted. That was his deepest desire.

No. No. There's more. His legs started to bounce up and down. It was taking all his control to stay seated. He grabbed the sides of his head.

"Please stop doing this to me." Tolen's voice shook. "Please."

He could barely hear Kichaya's gravelly voice over the fight taking place inside his body. "It does not come from me. The ritual shows me what the *Light* decrees, what others see is a reflection of their own truest desires. You are battling between the man you want to be and the man you are *meant* to be." She shifted in her seat to face her family.

Tolen dropped his head to the table as his energy drained completely out of him. Agony ripped through the crack in his heart and he bit back the sob that burned in his throat. "The Light told me our relationship mattered. I thought this meant it was okay for me to love her." His earlier pain about Hidden aging came back like a punch in the stomach. Was he to love Macy, but never truly have her? He knew his role as the Ninth Chosen. He'd accepted it. He wanted to fight for the Light, for what was right. Is that what his fears were trying to tell him—that a human and a Hidden—that a future with her wasn't even possible? Would he have to sacrifice love for duty in order to succeed, just as Macy had warned?

Kichaya touched the back of Tolen's head and he felt a measure of warmth surge into his body. He lifted his head to meet her eyes. "You have chosen the direction you are headed based on duty to help the good peoples of this world." This reminded him of Quasar's accusation that he'd risked his life to enter into the Shadow Realm to save his father, but he didn't truly understand what kind of love it would take to risk everything for a world of people he did not know. But that *had* changed. He'd felt so much compassion for the people he saw in his visions with Hunsí and Tahaka.

"Tolen, this is a good desire, but your heart remains divided, your deepest desire still lies with the girl. She clouds your thoughts—"

"How can I not think of her? She's my trigger, the strength behind my gifts."

Kichaya shook her head and moved her hand to his cheek. "*Mindra.* So much you misunderstand. You took care of your mother out of responsibility and regret for past actions, and you are seeking out the other Chosen to fulfill your destiny out of duty and responsibility to the Light. Yet, you are missing the real reason you exist. The real reason behind everything." She dropped her hand and sat back.

"What? What am I missing? I am trying to be everything everyone needs. I'm doing my best. I'm here, aren't I? I left her!" He slapped his palms on the table.

Kichaya didn't flinch, but the two ghost figures did.

"Your body is here, but your heart is not!" Kichaya's chin quivered. "Until you are whole in purpose *and* place, *Mindra*, you will never truly be anywhere."

Tolen shook his head. So what was he supposed to do? Ignore his feelings for Macy? Let her go so he could be the man he was meant to be? The thought burned like acid. No. It wasn't fair. His relationship with Macy mattered to the Light. He must believe that. They'd sent Skyborne to comfort him!

Lunch churned in his stomach. What if Macy had been right in her fears that their relationship was only meant to be temporary, long enough to bring the Hidden and the humans back together to fight for a joint cause? To defeat the Dark.

Acid rose in his throat and he raised anguished eyes to Kichaya.

27 DISTRACTION

Tolen could see the sympathy in Kichaya's eyes but it brought him no comfort. His chest filled with painful heat as the agony threatened to consume him.

Kichaya leaned forward and grasped hands with her father and brother. They leaned close, heads touching. Warmth filled the room and the auras around the ghosts brightened.

Kichaya sat back and sighed. "The Light has allowed you a choice, *Mindra*." She took a shaky breath.

"All human Chosen are given a choice when they turn eighteen—the amount of human years it takes for all Hidden to reach the apex of their gifts. It is not an easy choice and they have many years to decide. You have not had many years. The Chosen are given the option, once they are old enough to fully understand their calling, to remain Chosen and have their gifts become a forever part of them, continue the battle against the Dark for the remainder of their lives, or to denounce their duty, give back their shard and return to human life."

The division in Tolen's heart shuddered and his mouth went dry.

"You told your Watcher in the deep places of the Binithan that you wanted to be a Chosen and that you wanted to fight. But your main reason was you wanted the power to save your father. You have saved him. The strength behind your original choice is no longer there." Kichaya placed her gnarled hands on the table. "The Light is giving you a choice. You can choose to remain the Ninth Chosen and fulfill your place in the fate of this world. Or you can forsake the life of the *Eché-mah Ladon*, return your extra gifts, and resume your years free from your complicated destiny."

Tolen's throat constricted. "My age?"

Kichaya's eyes filled with moisture. "You can choose to age as the humans do."

He was Hidden-kind. Macy was human. Even if he stayed with Macy and they survived the Final Battle, he would only have her for the brief human years of her life and then he would continue for who knows how long without her. Bastian, his parents—they were all over a thousand years old. How could he survive the pain of thousands of years without Macy when being apart for a few days twisted his heart in knots? He'd done all he could not to think too much about her, but his subconscious had kept her close.

For a moment, the prospect of giving up his duty felt exhilarating, freeing. The idea of going somewhere with Macy to live out their lives together was so tempting he broke out in a sweat as he fought the internal battle over what he wanted most and what he knew he was supposed to do.

If he gave up his destiny, he was denouncing the prophecy that also affected Macy's destiny. Whether by love or destiny they were intertwined. And as long as the Dark continued to thrive unrecognized by humans, as long as the Chosen were not gathered together to bring both races together, there wouldn't be a world for them to be together in for very long.

Thinking this way, did he really have a choice?

The Light is offering you a choice.

Tolen fingered his Radia shard. His thoughts turned to his conversation with Bastian in the Binithan.

"I have no choice but to be a member of the Chosen, because the Balance selected me. Even though I have no idea if I can, or want to?"

"Tolen, fate, and destiny are more than what you have been taught to understand. There is choice in everything, and with every choice there is a consequence, good or bad. Whatever you choose now will still affect your destiny.

"It does not matter how much it might seem that your path is decided for you, choice will always play a role and help determine the outcome. No matter what the Balance decides, you choose where you will go, what you will do, and how you will deal with it."

"But you said the Balance had already shifted, fate was already in motion. Doesn't that sort of imply I'm kinda stuck?"

"No, Tolen, every choice you make from here on out will affect your final destiny in unfathomable ways. There are events in this world that must happen—it is the law of survival—but the ways in which things come about changes day by day, choice by choice."

"So I can choose whether or not to be a Chosen?"

"Yes."

Tolen's body trembled. He couldn't decide right now. He needed more time. He looked Kichaya in the eye. "How long do I have before I have to decide?"

Kichaya sighed. "The decision must be made before the last hour of your Transcendence. I must warn you, your decision will be solidified by the Balance and cannot be undone. Once the choice is made, you must follow that path to its end and never look back."

Tolen swallowed. "Okay." He looked away from her intense gaze wondering. If he chose a human life, would anyone ever forgive him? Could he forgive himself?

Tolen was looking forward to the distraction of training with the Guard the rest of the day. Mahto was waiting when he walked out Kichaya's door.

He walked silently beside Mahto, his thoughts chaotic. Tomorrow he would be taken to the Capka to prepare for his birthday. Two days spent with the village. Two days to understand his race. Two days to become who he was born to be, *or* two days to decide to leave it all behind and abandon these people to their fate.

To become whole in purpose and place.

Purpose? To save the world.

Place? Tolen looked at the arena several steps ahead. It was a large, open meadow filled with tall wooden stands holding various forms of weaponry—swords, axes, bow and arrows, knives of every size, clubs, spears, and dozens more he couldn't name glowing pale shades of green and blue or emitting soft yellow light. Several people chatted as they milled about, cleaning swords and armor, filling quivers with arrows, setting up misshapen targets.

Sienn waved him over. He took a deep breath and squared his shoulders. Purpose and place. Purpose and place. He was here, but where was his heart?

He shook his head when Macy's face swam across his vision. *Focus.*

An arrow zinged by his head and he dropped to the ground.

Mahto's laugh echoed across the arena. "Good reflexes, man!" He rushed over to help Tolen up. "You might want to watch where you're going, though." He dusted off Tolen's back.

Tolen looked over to see that he had wandered right in front of the archery range. So much for focus. What had Kichaya done to him?

Her ritual had brought Macy to the forefront of his thoughts where she refused to leave—and now he knew deep down that he didn't want her to.

"You all right, man?" Mahto tipped his head to the side.

"Great. Thanks."

"It's okay, man." Mahto slapped his shoulder. "Everyone gets freaked out when they meet Kichaya for the first time. She's a little loony, spending all that time alone talking to ghosts. Make anyone a little weird, I think." He pointed to Sienn standing off to the side, lacing a quiver across her back. "Come on, a little guard practice will help you take your mind off it."

They walked side by side to the archery weapons stand; Tolen very much hoping the huge boy was right.

Training with the Guard wasn't much different from training with the Radia Warriors, except for the fact that most of them here were young and their training seemed more focused on fun than hard work.

For the first hour, Sienn worked with him using a bow and arrow while Mahto made obnoxious comments every time Tolen missed the target. Sienn eventually got irritated and ended up making Mahto finish Tolen's archery instruction. As much as Tolen feared this would only give Mahto more opportunities to make fun of him, he actually found the big bear to be quite a good teacher. He was a skilled bowman with flawless technique. He showed Tolen a few tricks that greatly improved his aim at various distances. By the end of the lesson, Tolen was laughing so hard at Mahto's antics they were distracting the other archers. Eventually Sienn came over and told Mahto to take Tolen to practice somewhere else.

"Yes, my lady!" Mahto slapped Tolen on the shoulder again—he was sure to have a bruise—and laughed. "I'll remove him from your presence immediately."

A smile fought its way onto Sienn's face but she still slugged him. "Just remove yourself while you're at it, all right?"

Mahto bowed and nudged Tolen toward the other side of the arena. He wiggled his eyebrows. "How can I argue with someone that beautiful?"

Tolen chuckled but his stomach did an uncomfortable flip. Mahto and Sienn were free to love—they were one and the same. He shoved his fists in his pockets. It wasn't fair.

Hasn't anyone ever told you? Life isn't fair. He clenched his teeth as Macy's voice filled his head.

"Movan-made." Mahto paused beside the stand containing the glowing weapons. "Freaking awesome, man."

The weapons looked incredibly cool and for the moment distracted Tolen. He reached out to touch a long sword, carved with ancient runes that glowed a soft blue, the hilt wrapped in worn braided leather. "What kind of sword is this?"

Mahto laughed and lifted the sword off the rack. "I knew you'd like it over here. This stuff is my favorite." He laid the sword across his hands holding it out for Tolen to see. "This is a Kamud. They're forged specifically to harness the light energy within the carrier. It's the sweetest blade you'll ever handle. Once your energy is directed into the blade, your aim is more true than possible on your own. It becomes a part of your body, an extension of yourself. You become one. It reads the battle, your moves, and the moves of your enemy."

"Really?" Tolen's eyes widened.

"Yeah. Totally cool, huh?"

"Totally." Tolen grinned. "Can I try?"

"You have experience with a blade?" Mahto's eyes narrowed mockingly.

Tolen shrugged. "I practiced a little with some Doogar and Radia Warriors."

Mahto chuckled, looking impressed. "Well, all right then. Let's see what ya got." He handed Tolen the sword and grabbed another one from the rack. As they walked toward the center of the arena, several guards stopped practicing and moved over to watch.

Tolen could feel the strength within the blade. The more he thought of it, the brighter it became.

"The sword is trying to connect with you, Tolen." Mahto paused and turned to face Tolen, his own sword too bright to look at directly.

"Allow your gifts to flow into it."

Focused on the warm hilt he could feel in his hands, Tolen closed his eyes. He visualized light and warmth moving from his hand into the sword. He opened his eyes and the light blinded him. Reflexes had him trying to drop the sword but it felt welded to his hand.

"Whoa, whoa, ease up man!" Mahto ran over, shoved Tolen's sword toward the ground, and pushed a fist into Tolen's chest, making him step back. "Pull back. You're sending too much!"

Tolen was sure his hand was going to melt off. He fought against the heat, pulling it out of the sword back into his body, and the sword fell to the dirt with a *thud*. He cradled his burned hand against his stomach. "What was that?" His gifts fought for release—tempting him to pick up the sword again and allow them freedom from his body.

Mahto picked up the sword and then dropped it when it singed his fingers. "Ow!" He stepped away. "You got some power, man!" Tolen waited for him to walk off in shock, or at least look at him in fear the way those at the citadel had, but Mahto surprised him when he burst out laughing. His boisterous laugh filled the arena and soon others were joining in. Tolen looked around and even though his hand stung, he too began laughing. His gifts relaxed as the laughter cleansed away the worry and stress.

"That was the coolest thing I've ever seen." Mahto wiped the tears that streamed from his eyes and leaned over gasping for air. "You should have seen your face, man!" He stood up, widened his eyes, opened his mouth, and pretended to be staring at his hand in shock. Then he started dancing around holding his hand.

"Ha ha. Very funny," Tolen chided but couldn't keep from smiling. Mahto went to slap Tolen's arm, but he ducked out of the way. Mahto grinned. "Meant no disrespect. I didn't think about the fact that you're the *Ninth* and have a lot more power than the rest of us." He looked Tolen up and down and held back another laugh. "But I'm going to be telling that one at dinner tonight." He reached down and picked up the now-cool sword. "How about we try it again, but this time, maybe you should only allow one gift to join with the sword." He chuckled. "This is great. No one would know to look at you, this scrawny kid, the kind of power you've got. That's a great asset in a fight, man."

"Okay, one gift." Tolen wriggled his eyebrows. "And then we see if my scrawny butt can kick your humongous one."

Mahto laughed loudly and smacked his thighs. "Sounds good, little boy."

Grinning, Tolen took the sword. This time he let his Kuna warm from his palm into the blade. It was a gift he felt comfortable with—he wouldn't let himself think of the other reason he wanted to use it.

The energy passed into the blade, and although it was still brighter than Mahto's, he was in control. He could feel the Balance as it surrounded the blade, as the Kamud became a part of him—mind and matter. He lifted the sword and Mahto met his strike with a resounding *clang*.

28 A SAFE PLACE

T HEY TRAVELED MOST of the day through thick forest. Macy kept track of their direction from the occasional peek of the sun through the treetops. Once it dropped past midday, she used Bastian's compass from time to time, just for a sense of direction. About an hour before dusk Toke slowed his pace and they entered a wide clearing, in the center of which stood a broken-down house probably built by early settlers and abandoned at the turn of the century. She could hear a brook somewhere nearby.

As Toke headed toward the front door, Macy was reminded of the last place she'd lived with Bastian. The ramshackle house in Nevada had been in better shape than this one, but the seclusion, the quiet beauty of a forgotten time was the same.

Once he'd ushered everyone inside, Toke placed a metal instrument in the doorframe that tickled something in her memory. It matched the one Bastian had put in her pack. When she felt a heaviness settle over the small house, she finally remembered exactly what it was. A Treasta, a Movan made *shield*! Bastian used it from time to time when she'd been young and had had a hard time shielding her life force from disrupting the Balance. Its power didn't last long, about six hours or so, but it helped. After training all day, it proved even more difficult to maintain her shield. The Treasta allowed her to rest and know that they wouldn't be attacked for the next six hours. She remembered the day it *mysteriously* disappeared—right after a long lecture from Bastian about how she was holding herself back, relying on the Treasta more than her own strength.

She couldn't imagine why a group of fully capable Chosen and a skilled Movan would need one though, or why Bastian had felt the need to give her his.

Toke seemed to notice her curiosity and explained. "The Treasta does more than just shield the young and unexperienced. It also works as a warning system to the Movan. It allows me to know when someone is moving toward us with intent—meaning the person or creature knows where we are—and gives us time to find out who it is and what they are after."

"How does it do that?"

"Even thoughts produce electrical energy. The Movan developed the Treasta as a means to recognize direct thought energy. If thought energy is being pushed in the direction of the Treasta, it sends out a warning signal that only a Movan can pick up on."

"That explains how the Movan manage to stay one step ahead of everyone." Macy's tone only reflected slight envy. It also offered one more reason why they weren't readily trusted.

Toke allowed the comment with a dip of his head.

Macy turned away with a smirk to face the room. Almost the entire backside of the house had completely collapsed on itself. The roof planks settled over the dirty floor like the rib bones of a giant skeleton, and the darkening sky glowed blue-gray, barely visible, through the remaining fingers of wood. The rebels settled in around what was left of the stone fireplace. Brina got a small fire blazing as Keelyn pulled food out of different packs and put together their nightly meal.

Rune was the only one who didn't help with the meal preparations. He sat off to the side, poking Keelyn every time she walked by. His smile completely transformed his face and Macy admitted silently that he was fairly good looking—although nothing compared to Tolen. He looked over to see Macy watching and the smile quickly collapsed back into his usual scowl. Connell remained the quietest of the group. Whenever Macy caught him looking at her he would quickly look away. The snowy owl never left his shoulder.

Toke walked around her and set his bags on the dirty floor. "We should be safe for a few hours. We'll eat and get some sleep, then we'll head out just after dawn."

"I thought you were going to tell us what's going on?" Rune's face was too angry to look like a pout but Macy felt like that was exactly what he was doing, and it took a lot of self-control not to make a sarcastic remark.

Toke cleared his throat. "We'll talk while we eat." His tone said enough and the others fell back to work in silence. Macy was grateful for a few minutes to decide what she should actually tell these guys. Was it right to bring them into the dangers of her mission—especially when she didn't even know exactly what she was in for? But, that being said, something had brought her to them, something that went beyond searching out her past.

It was a lot scarier than she'd thought it would be, making decisions and following her heart.

A plate appeared in front of her face and she looked up to see Keelyn standing there smiling. "Oh, thank you. I um…could have got it myself."

Keelyn shrugged and sat down beside Macy, holding her own tin plate. "No biggy. You can make breakfast and serve it to me."

Macy grinned, drawn to Keelyn's easy manner. She'd never had a friend before Tolen, but she could picture being friends with Keelyn. She guessed Keelyn to be Lóklana—her kind nature just radiated light. She'd heard all the positive light energy Lóklana held had a way of making people want to be around them. Keelyn was the first Lóklana Macy'd ever met, and she was starting to believe the rumors.

She chanced a look at Rune. A scowl still twisted his features and he hadn't touched the food in front of him. Macy couldn't help herself. She stuffed a piece of dry meat into her mouth and made a huge production of chewing slowly. He scoffed and looked away, his fingers drumming out an irritating rhythm on his crossed arms. Keelyn looked from Macy to Rune and stifled a laugh behind her hand. Rune looked back and his eyes darkened for a second before he stood up and stalked to the back of the room near the broken pile of beams.

Macy swallowed and gestured toward Rune. "Is he always like that?"

Keelyn nodded but her eyes were gentle. Tolen gave her the same look when she was being obnoxious and he thought it was endearing. Her heart clenched and her appetite vanished. She sat her plate beside her.

Toke looked over at her and set his own plate down. Connell, Brina, and Keelyn kept eating but their eyes were darting back and forth between

Macy and Toke. Rune seemed to sense the change in atmosphere and turned around to face them, but stayed standing at the back.

Toke cleared his throat. "I know there is much I should have told you all before now—"

Rune snorted.

Macy's fists clenched in her lap. Now he was just being a disrespectful jerk. If he kept it up, she was going to show him how hard it was to talk with his lips melted together.

Toke raised his eyebrow. "*But…*" He tipped his head at Rune, "there was a lot I didn't know, and considering the fact that I am adamant about you making your own choices, I was afraid to tell you the real reason that I chose to stay so close to Whisper these past few years. I wanted you to stay there because you wanted to be there—not because it was where the Light needed us to be." His disheveled purple hair was drained of color in the darkening room and the flickering light from the fire cast dark shadows around his odd eyes. For a moment, he looked old, really old.

"I never meant to keep anything from you." He looked at his hands and started twisting a thick silver band on his middle finger. "I told you when I found you that I would never ask you to do something you did not want to do. I did not take your shards when you left your Watchers and chose to keep your gifts but no longer adhere to the Chosen code. I told you I was on your side, your advocate, a guide, a teacher, a friend, but not your leader. You all were agents to yourselves." He looked up and met the rebels' eyes one by one. "And to that I hold, but there is another reason I came looking for you."

The rebels looked at each other. Macy pushed her hands into the dirt. Toke had already told her this. It made sense, though, why he hadn't told them. If they were rebelling against the Chosen code, but still using their shards, the idea of the Guardians being aware of them kinda made their rebellion pointless.

"Yes, I knew who you were and where you were before I found you. Whether you have chosen to side with the Light and follow the Guardians or not, the Light still cares about you and wanted to make sure you were safe through your rebellion. When I left my tribe, I pledged myself to the Light. A Seraph gave me a charge. I would have a gift that would allow me to find the Lost Chosen and watch over them—even if they chose never to return to their duty."

"Why? To make sure we didn't turn our shards over to the Dark?" Rune's voice shook, his face a mixture of anger and hurt.

Toke sighed. "That may have been a part of it, but I believe it was more because the Light never stopped caring about you, even if you had stopped caring about them."

Rune shook his head and turned away.

A flicker of pain crossed Toke's face.

Brina pushed her plate across the dirty floor away from her. "Okay, so now we know the real reason you *came* for us, but what does it have to do with Whisper and little miss fireball over there?" Her tone was indignant, but Macy recognized the familiar cover for the pain of betrayal.

Toke tugged his bag closer to him and started rummaging through it. He pulled out one of the many notebooks and looked at Keelyn. "A little light please."

29 HISTORY LESSONS

KEELYN GLANCED AROUND until her eyes landed on an old vine twisted around what was left of the remaining rafters. She raised her palms above her head and whispered. "*Radi'non.*"

Macy watched as tiny spots on the vine began to shimmer like polished silver and then raced across the vine, following its path between the beams and down the walls. As the silver lights passed along its surface, it brightened to a warm, beautiful shade of green. The now vibrant vine gave off light the color of a buttercup sunrise, illuminating their faces with a fuller spectrum of light than that of the fire. The effects of the light called into being by Keelyn filled Macy with more peace and contentment than she'd ever felt from Serenity Stones. The tense mood surrounding the group shifted and Macy suspected Toke had asked Keelyn to do it more for that reason than because he actually needed more light.

He smiled at Keelyn. "Thank you."

She grinned and placed her hands in her lap.

Macy nudged her shoulder and whispered, "That was awesome."

Keelyn shrugged and her eyes flicked to Rune. Macy followed her gaze to see his scowl was less pronounced, but he hadn't moved any closer.

Toke opened the well-used notebook. The metal coils were bent and the cover falling off, the edges of the pages frayed and slightly discolored. He tapped the faded green cover. "You have seen me writing in many notebooks in the time we have spent together. Sometimes I have shared with you what is in them—if you wanted to know. I have not opened *this* notebook for nearly seventeen years." He threw a meaningful look at Macy. "In these notes I once recorded a hope, a dream, an incredible possibility—and until recently, very recently, I believed that all hope was lost in ever seeing it happen."

"Macy, can you get me the stone?"

Macy took a deep breath and rummaged through her pack, forcing her head to reconcile with her heart the decision to share her secrets. She needed whatever information this strange Movan had, she knew she did. It was just accepting help from perfect strangers—whether one of them knew her parents or not—went against everything she had ever done growing up. Bastian had introduced her to other Watchers and Chosen at times, but they were so spread out, their missions so clandestine, she'd never worked together with them on anything. She hadn't ever had to place her trust in anyone other than Bastian—until she'd met Tolen.

Her hand twisted around the piece of silver stone. She needed to know what this man knew. She took another deep breath before she pulled it from the bag and placed the stone in Toke's palm. The group leaned in to see and Rune took a few steps closer.

Toke's fingers trembled as he closed his fist around the stone. "This stone is called Clenadium. It is a rare metal found in very few places on Earth. It is the *only* material found on every planet in every galaxy in the universe. It is the residue, or what is left from the first materials gathered together to form a world. I told you of Sanharian—he was a master at reading the electrical impulses in the world around him. He could always find the most powerful natural elements based on their bioelectricity. The Movan were already using their gifts to create formidable weaponry—for both sides." He scowled. "Sanharian came across Clenadium; this stone held the most bioelectricity of anything he'd ever seen." He pinched the stone between his fingers and it started to glow, much as when Jonas had touched the piece she'd given him.

"Sanharian created a type of armor out of the Clenadium that could block the gifts of the Dark and strengthened the wearer beyond imagining—something that came in very handy later during the Radia Revolution. The metal was so rare, however, that only a handful of the suits were made. Then he, along with a small group of Spheres, other gifted Hidden, and Watchers, created the Relics." He paused and tapped the stone on his leg. "Later, one other item was created, one far more dangerous yet necessary.

When the Hidden were first brought here by the Light, the ability to cross to other worlds was lost. But the great minds of long ago recognized the necessity of finding a way to open the 'gate' so to speak. Which meant they needed a key that could open the space between worlds."

"So they could send Dark creatures to Misery." Rune's whisper barely carried across the room.

Macy's skin prickled.

Toke nodded. "The netherworld of Misery had been there on the fringes as the Hidden traveled through the bridges of space. It was the perfect place to banish the evils that had followed them here. The Key was forged by the gifts of Sanharian, strengthened by a very specific Radia shard guarded by Eamun Woodlore himself, and wielded by an extremely powerful Sphere. Near the end of the Radia Revolution, the Key was brought into battle. A Sphere called Areen—,"

"What?" Macy exclaimed, making everyone jump. She shook her head. "Areen? The same Areen who ran off and had a forbidden relationship with the famous Protector Daedal Téloran?" Her palms were sweating.

Toke lifted his eyebrows. "How do you know about that?"

Macy jumped up from her spot on the floor, waved off the question, and started pacing. "Sorry for interrupting…go on." She absently pulled a sucker from her pocket, tugged off the mangled wrapper, shoved the sweet in her mouth, and started twisting her hair around her pinky finger—ignoring the confused stares from everyone.

Areen?

Tolen's mother? *Whoa.*

"Areen was able to manipulate the vibrations surrounding the battlefield to create a literal break in the fabric of reality, opening a door to Misery. With her wielding the Key, Darsapean and thousands of other creatures of evil were removed from this world."

Macy shook her head. *Areen?* The same Areen that was sitting in a wheelchair in the Citadel of Light? The same Areen that had accused Macy of being a deluded *child?* Unbelievable. "That was never part of my history lessons."

Toke handed the stone back to Macy. "Those who knew of the Key were sworn to secrecy. An item of that power could be used for very dangerous purposes. After the Revolution, it was said the Key was destroyed, along with all the suits made from Clenadium, and the Last returned to Eamun's care. The suits were supposedly melted down and returned to the earth. No one has seen any of the metal since."

"Okay, then how do *you* know about it, and how did she get a piece of it?" Brina's voice trembled with something that sounded close to fear.

Toke looked at Macy. "Her father."

Macy stopped pacing and turned to Toke as all eyes found her.

Toke looked at his rebels, his family. "Macy's father was once like all of you. I found him when he was eleven years old." His eyes flicked to Macy. "He'd been taught by his parents the history. It took some time, but eventually he began to trust me and he told me of his ancestry. Max's family can be traced back to before the Revolution. He is a descendant of the human, Thaer Candra, the Chief of the humans during the war. He was one of the Nine."

"When you say *nine* you mean he was one of the humans who controlled a Relic?" Connell's soft voice asked.

A chill seemed to move through the room. "Yes. But his role was even greater. It was when Thaer was a part of the Nine that the Pact—the *Shroud*, that blocked the Dark from human sight—was created."

Macy dropped back down beside Keelyn. "Why didn't Bastian ever tell me?"

"He may not have known." He shrugged. "It is not a widely shared piece of our history."

Macy thought back to when they'd first found Tolen and his mother. Bastian had showed no indication that he'd known Areen, or her place in history.

"This is all fine and interesting, but I still don't get what it has to do with us saving her skin and now going with *her*." Rune stepped forward and pointed a finger at Macy.

"Hey, I didn't ask you to come!" Macy turned and shouted.

"Rune, Macy, please. I am trying to explain, but there are things you need to know before we can even begin to make sense of what is really going on."

Keelyn reached back and tugged Rune's arm until he sat beside her with a huff. She grabbed his hand and smoothed out his fist, entwining her fingers through his. Macy looked away, her throat feeling tight.

Toke took a deep breath. "As I was saying. Macy's father was a direct descendant of one of the leaders of the humans. An even lesser known legend, that could be simply a rumor, is that the descendants of those early leaders could choose to sever the Pact and destroy the Shroud within the Balance that blocks the Dark from the eyes of the humans."

30 THE PROPHECY

OLY CRAP," BRINA whispered.

Connell twitched, and the owl on his shoulder opened one eye.

Macy's stomach started turning. The idea that she was Light's Aid was starting to make scary sense. She thought she would simply be Tolen's sidekick, but this was a lot bigger than that.

"I'm so confused." Keelyn rubbed her forehead.

"Join the club," Macy whispered and Keelyn giggled. "So if the legend is real, that means I can sever the Pact. But why? Why sever the Pact?"

Keelyn leaned closer to Rune and he put a protective arm around her shoulders. "Do *you* think it's just a rumor?" he asked Toke.

"I'm not sure, but Max Burdow, Macy's father, believed it. He had been taught by his parents the secrets surrounding the Relics, the Hidden-Human Pact, and what really happened when Darsapean was sentenced to Misery." Toke tapped the notebook. "As for your question Macy, we can only guess. I think, and now this is just speculation, that severing the Pact could be a strategic move."

"A fail safe." Rune rubbed his temple.

Toke shrugged. "The Guardians are not known for taking chances."

"And severing the Pact has absolutely no chance of backfiring." Brina rolled her eyes. "Can you imagine what will happen when humans can suddenly *see* creatures of darkness?"

A look passed around the group and Toke shook his head. "Like I said, speculation and rumors, neither of which are worth giving merit until we know more."

"Hence our little excursion." A tiny grin lifted Brina's mouth when Toke nodded.

"We need to see if there is truth to the rumors. If there is, Macy will need our help."

"But why would the Dark want the Relics?" Macy leaned forward, her mind reeling, trying to make sense of the puzzle before them. "Only humans can use them. The Dark hates humans."

"Think strategically," Toke answered. "Just as the Hidden will need human numbers help to defeat the Dark, the Dark will see the same need in order to defeat the Light. Many of their strongest warriors were killed or locked in Misery after the Revolution. They need an army, and what race has the highest numbers? Dark, Hidden, or human? They want a way to create more Darkened, they want to control the human race."

Macy leaned back with a huff. The others shared a nervous look, but no one could argue Toke's logic. It made too much sense. "Do you think the Guardians have figured it out?"

"We can hope so, but hope isn't enough. We need to act. Now." Toke met each of their eyes in turn and Macy felt a shimmer of pride as she saw each of them nod. This little band of Chosen *would* rise against the Dark despite their wavering loyalties to the Guardians—they did *not* favor the Dark.

Slowly the entire group turned to look at Rune, but he had eyes only for Toke. "Okay, so it's up to us to save the day." A light chuckle came from the group. "And a visit to the Old Ones is where you want to start?"

Toke's eyes reflected his relief. "Yes. The Old Ones should be able to confirm or deny the rumors surrounding Macy's ancestor, Thaer Candra. Then we need to go after the Relics. We need to get them before the Dark. My instincts say their arrival in Whisper had more purpose than just *thinking* Macy had the Claver. The Dark knows her history and they, at least, are giving the rumors merit. They will want her dead before she can wake up the humans to the evils of the Dark."

Macy swallowed, but didn't meet the sympathetic eyes she could feel watching her. The object in her pocket seemed to burn against her leg.

"How do you know where to look for the Relics?" Brina pulled her knee up to her chest and started twisting one of her braids between her fingers. "And even if we find them—they've got to be seriously protected."

Toke pointed to a page in his notebook. "Max. He was obsessed with the prophecy of the Ninth. He spent years picking through it, studying it.

"He fixated on the idea that there was more to it. He believed that the only way to rid the world of the Dark once and for all was to sever the Pact and reunite humans and Hidden. When he left his calling at eighteen to marry Macy's mother I assumed he'd given up his obsession, but when he found me and invited me to Macy's naming ceremony, I knew I'd been mistaken." He motioned to Macy. "In your father's papers he has a copy of the prophecy. Would you mind getting it out?"

Macy's fingers felt as shaky as her mind as she pulled the stack of papers out of her pack and rifled through them. This mission was getting more complicated and dangerous by the minute. The page containing the prophecy was severely wrinkled and creased—the letters almost too faded to read—with so many notes in the margin it was impossible to decipher. It shook as she handed it to him.

He placed it on the ground in front of him. "Can I have the pages we decoded earlier?"

Macy paused. The time to decide had come. Should she put all her cards on the table and trust this band she barely knew with everything? The idea of heading off on her own just didn't make sense anymore. She'd learned too much from Toke. And the road ahead would be impossible without help. It was all happening so fast.

Toke looked up and met her eyes. "Macy?"

She took a deep breath.

"Macy, it's unfair of me to ask you to trust me without the time to prove myself. But there simply *isn't* enough time. I can only ask you to follow your heart. If it honestly tells you to stay away, then I will not push you, you are free to leave."

"But you said—" Rune sputtered but Toke held up his hand.

Macy ignored the others and closed her eyes. Bastian had also told her to follow her heart. And she trusted him. She also trusted her father. And he trusted Toke.

She opened her eyes, pulled out the pages, and handed them over.

Toke spread them out. "Each one of these pages corresponds to a certain piece of the prophecy. Can you see it?"

The group leaned forward and started looking at the symbols, but no one seemed to see what Toke was talking about.

"Look here." He pointed at the first line. "Darkness veils the Sight. See the symbol of the faded eye on this page?"

This time they all nodded and Toke became more animated. "He's figured out the location of each of the Relics based on clues he deciphered in the Prophecy. He hid the map within his notes by encoding it with the symbols. Look here, he's written: *Sight refers to the Watchers, possibly those within the Guardians.*" Toke shook his head. "He was right. My sources tell me that Eamun Woodlore, the Keeper of the Last, was murdered just a short time ago. Since then the *Sight* of the Watchers—who are members of the Guardians—hasn't been reliable. Their ability to watch the future has become dimmed."

"What about the Last?" Connell asked.

Toke sighed. "My source tells me Eamun hid it before he died. It's waiting for a new Keeper."

"One more thing the Dark is after then." Brina added.

Toke nodded.

"This is crazy." Rune looked back at the prophecy and tapped the page. "Why are only certain words capitalized?"

"I'm glad you brought that up." Toke pulled out a sheet of blank paper from one of his notebooks and started writing down the capitalized words with Max's theory of its meaning beside it. Macy leaned over his shoulder.

Darkness: *Dark*

Sight: *Watchers within the Guardians*

Power: *Guardians, the head of the Second Realm of Three*

Might: *Protectors*

Shields: *Spheres*

Unending Night: *the literal end*

Sky: *citadel*

Trust: *likely relates to a future event, possibly involving a betrayal*

Balance: *the Shroud*

Single, Token: *the Key containing the Last shard*

Eight: *?*

United: *the linked Hidden and human races*

Banner: *a cause to fight for*

One: *the Ninth*

Might, Shield, Radia, Sight: *The Ninth's strongest most vital gifts*

Chosen: *the Chosen humans*

Night: *Light's destruction*

The Ninth: *this title is significant. It is a representation of the Order of the Nine Realms, a representation of the order of the Hidden. The order of all things. I feel there is more. I'll keep searching.*

Light's Aid: *a helpmeet, or partner to the Ninth. Someone of great power and importance*

Tide: *The Final Battle*

Toke then drew a line up to *Single, Token*, matching Max's notes. "Okay, now listen to what Max says here. 'According to old legends and histories I have been able to find, the Last will always have a Keeper. The Keeper will hide the Last when its power informs him his time to die is near. Upon hiding it, the Keeper invokes a special protection that allows a Seeker to not only find the Last, but also confer its power to the new Keeper.

"The Light chooses the Seeker, a person of great power and strong will (so as to not be overcome with temptation to use the Last for themselves), the Seeker will be led to the Last, and then the Last will lead the Seeker to who it has chosen to be the new Keeper.

"This protection is Hidden power at its oldest. The Keeper is the only one who can be gifted full range of its power. So even if the Seeker loses, has the Last stolen from them, or somehow it ends up in the hands of the wrong person, it will still be a formidable weapon, enhancing the bearer beyond imagining, but its full use cannot be accessed until the Seeker puts it in the hands of the new Keeper—'"

Macy leaned back and put her hand over her mouth, stifling a gasp. Her fingers trembled and she could feel the heat of her Kuna building in her chest as the puzzle pieces suddenly clicked into place. This was why Bastian had felt it was time for her to know the truth about her father. Without realizing it, by giving her these letters, he'd inspired her to go in search of her past, which in turn had given her the one thing she needed to understand everything.

Eamun Woodlore was dead. The Last was in need of a new Keeper. This was her mission. She was the Seeker. The truth of the declared thought ran through her veins like wildfire, heating the Kuna, but in a powerful, encouraging way. *A failed Trust.* It means Eamun's death—the

Last shard waiting for a new Keeper to entrust with its care. *Balance broken. The severing of the Pact. The collapse of the Shroud…*"

All eyes turned to her, but she was lost in a flood of revelation.

According to Jonas, Daemon was searching for way to release Darsapean from Misery. The Key would do just that. But to make it work they needed the Last. What if being the Seeker had shifted the Balance enough that they'd been following her since she'd left the Light Realm, and Bastian couldn't warn her because his Watchers Sight had dimmed? She had just become a triple threat to the Dark—Seeker, Light's Aid, *and* descendant of Thaer Candra. No wonder they wanted her dead.

And all that rock they were mining? The Clenadium? The heat inside clawed its way up her throat. Smoke began to rise from her fingers. If they couldn't find the Key, they would attempt to forge another one. It was all starting to make scary sense. Why Daemon was so bent on kidnapping Areen—it wasn't just some past vendetta, he needed a Sphere, and he would want it to be one he had power over. Her eyes fell on the line, *a fallen Sky*—the fall of the Citadel of Light. This was the real reason Daemon had been torturing Daedal in order to tell him how to get into the Light Realm. If the deciphered map was correct, and she had no reason to doubt her father, there was another map, the original map, leading to the Relics somewhere within the Citadel of Light.

"Macy?" Toke touched her arm. "Macy, are you all right?"

Macy took a deep, shuddering breath, fighting to bring the heat back into her body. The smoke stopped but she didn't lift her eyes from the paper as she reached into her pocket. Her fist curled around the object next to the ring of keys—it was warm to the touch. "I do need your help, whether I like it or not. I wasn't sure if I should tell you, but you have to know…" She stabbed her finger at the second to the last line in the prophecy. "The Ninth has been chosen. My Watcher and I found him just more than a month ago. His name is Tolen. He is the son of Daedal and Areen. He's almost eighteen. We have so much less time than you think. The Dark has already tried to break into the Citadel. They want the real map. The prophecy is so freaking far in motion it's insane."

She looked up, met Toke's fierce expression, pulled her hand out of her pocket and opened her palm. "I am the Seeker. The Last Shard, the Relics, the Pact. This mission is going to cost us everything."

31 INTERRUPTED WELCOME

THE SUN HAD passed below the horizon and the first stars were just beginning to appear when Sienn declared a draw in Mahto and Tolen's sword fight.

Tolen slapped Mahto on the back. "I still say I won."

"Nah, it's a draw." Mahto reached for Tolen but he ducked out of the way. "Sienn called it. Neither one of us was on the ground."

"I came close to winning more times than you did."

"No way, man." Mahto waved his hand in the air. "I never yielded. It's a draw."

"If you say so." Tolen laughed.

Mahto shook his hairy head. Sweat poured down his face and his ponytail was a knotted mess.

Tolen was covered with dust and sweat, but he felt energized, excited even.

"Go help Belch with dinner." Mahto pushed Tolen's shoulder. "Sienn and I have to check in with the night patrol."

The corner of Tolen's mouth twitched. "Uh-huh. Sure you do." He wiggled his eyebrows.

Mahto aimed a kick at Tolen's backside, but Tolen ran ahead toward Tashta's house, chuckling. He was still laughing to himself when he walked through the door.

Tashta smiled when she saw him. "Ah, Tolen. You bring light with you. I take it you enjoyed a pleasant day with Mahto and Sienn."

"Mahto's great." Tolen took off his dusty shoes by the door and moved to the sink to wash his hands. "I don't think I've laughed that hard in my life."

"Yes, he is quite silly." She clicked her tongue. "Sometimes a little too silly. I don't know if that boy can ever be serious." Her tone was full of endearment. She loved her children. "Sashan is meeting with Kichaya tonight. I'm taking them some food to eat while they visit. Belch is in the square bartering for some venison that was just brought in this morning. He'll be back in a few minutes, giving you plenty of time to shower." She threw him a towel and showed him to the bathroom.

A hose stretched from the window down to a metal barrel and then back up, where it hung from a rusty metal hook above a steel washtub.

"I heated the barrel for you, but it only gets lukewarm and won't last long. Get wet, turn off the hose, wash, and then turn it back on to rinse off. Soap's in the tray, shampoo's in the bottle on the sink." She pointed at a tall glass bottle filled with blue liquid and patted his hand before she left.

Tolen picked up the bar of soap. It was coarse and grainy, but teased his nose with a smell of vanilla and spices. He took the cork out of the bottle of shampoo; it smelled like blueberries.

He wasn't about to complain about hot water. He'd take a cold shower just to feel totally clean again. This would be his first time to really wash up since he'd left the citadel. Rinsing in rivers didn't count.

Ten minutes later, he walked barefoot into the kitchen wearing a pair of old shorts and a t-shirt. He used his fingers to pull his damp hair into a short ponytail and tied it at the base of his neck with a string ripped from his frayed backpack.

Belch stood beside the sink preparing the meat he'd brought home. Tashta hadn't yet returned.

"What can I do?" Tolen stood beside Belch as he tenderized the steaks.

"Cut those up," Belch pointed with the mallet to the fresh vegetables beside the sink, "and toss them in the soup."

Grabbing a knife from the block, Tolen started cutting up potatoes, carrots, celery, and onions. Eyes stinging, he asked, "How long have you been with Tashta?"

Belch shrugged. "I don't remember ever being with anyone else. My parents were killed when a band of Raksasha attacked our village. One of the survivors brought me to Tashta. I was three months old."

"I'm sorry."

"Don't be. Aren't most orphan stories sad?" He tossed the steaks onto the skillet where they began to sizzle and pop. "I'm lucky. I survived and I couldn't ask for a better mother in Tashta. I love it here."

The guilt twisted in Tolen's stomach. So many lives lost to the evil of the Dark. He could do something about it. Should do something about it. Macy's face flashed across his vision. He turned to easier topics. "Is everyone in this village Honitahai?"

Belch poured a spicy smelling liquid over the steaks. "No, not all, just most. Hunsí has been chief for about two hundred years. His great-grandfather first settled here so it began as a Honitahai tribe. As time went on, children were born with other gifts, but our Honitahai skills are legendary, and that tends to draw in those wishing to learn from us—or from Tahaka anyway."

Tolen nodded. "She's incredible."

"Yes she is." Belch cleared his throat. "Even Ras'met, Dominant over Honitahai, isn't as skilled as Tahaka. He came once to be tutored by her. It was fun to watch them." Belch laughed as he flipped the steaks.

Tolen might not have been here long, but already this village felt more like home to him than anywhere else. "Thanks for letting me crash in on your family like this. It's nice to be accepted for who I am instead of pretending to be something I'm not."

Belch paused his steak flipping and patted Tolen's shoulder. He didn't say anything, just smiled and went back to cooking.

The tantalizing aroma of tomatoes, blended herbs and spices made Tolen's mouth water as he carried the bowl of chopped vegetables to the stove and tipped them into the simmering pot of soup. "I've never tasted such delicious food. You guys are amazing."

"We do take pride in our food here." Belch laughed. "Maybe it comes from growing and caring for it yourselves. I dunno. But everyone in this village likes to eat." He moved the skillet off the burner and covered it with a lid. "Come on. Everyone else is going to meet us there."

"There?"

"Your welcome dinner. Everyone brings their favorite dishes. You'll love it."

Tolen had completely forgotten about the welcome dinner. His nervousness began to return. "Um, maybe I should hurry and change clothes."

Belch shook his head. "Nah, nobody will care what you look like. It's the food that gets the attention around here."

Tolen smiled to himself as he slipped on his tennis shoes and helped Belch carry the meal and cutlery to the square. Several families also carried in plates and bowls of food, organizing it all into colorful arrangements along the tables.

Belch led the way to a long wooden table set toward the edge of the open space and began setting the food down at one end. "This is a good spot." He straightened up and smiled. "Ah, here comes Tashta now."

Tolen set the plates and utensils on the table and turned to see Tashta walking toward them, carrying a huge basket of fresh fruit. He hurried over and lifted the basket for her.

"Oh, thank you, Tolen." She wiped her sweaty face on her apron. "I noticed the merchant in the square when I was on my way back from Kichaya's. I thought some fresh fruit with dinner would be a nice treat."

"Will Sashan and Kichaya be joining us tonight?" Belch asked as he began inspecting the fruit.

"Unlikely. They have much to discuss." She pointed at the orange Belch was rolling around in his hands. "I looked for the best ones. He said crops weren't as plentiful this year. Much of his stock spoiled before he made it to the village. He's thinking of moving a few of their Lóklana up here. See if they can help us grow our own."

Belch examined the skin. "The seasons are changing. The shorter growing cycles are affecting the crops. It would help a lot if some Lóklana chose to live here. I have a hard time imagining them enjoying our winters though." He closed his eyes and rubbed the fruit in his hand. The skin brightened to a more vibrant shade of orange and the few wrinkles disappeared. Tolen had never thought about Honitahai and growing crops before.

Tashta kissed Belch on the cheek and walked around the table to inspect. "Everything looks delicious you two."

"It's all Belch. I just provided manual labor. He's amazing." Tolen's stomach growled, proving his point.

Tashta and Belch laughed.

"Yes, every time I cook with him my stomach gets impatient," Tashta said. "Come. I'll help you finish setting our table. Mahto and Sienn are taking the long way home. I told them not to be late." She shook her head with a smile.

Just as Belch, Tashta, and Tolen were taking their seats, Sienn and Mahto arrived—a little pink in the cheeks. Belch coughed to cover a laugh. Tolen met Mahto's eyes and held back a grin. Mahto's eyes twinkled. They sat down as Hunsí stood at the head of the table and began to address the group.

"It has long been the tradition in our tribe to welcome guests and newcomers with a feast." He waved his hand toward Tolen and then to his right where Quasar sat looking up at him. "Tonight we honor the return of my old friend, Quasar, and the arrival of a child of prophecy. Tolen Daedal Téloran, we welcome you to our home and hope you find great comfort here." He lifted his glass, and waited until every adult present did the same before taking a long drink.

Tolen lifted his cup to his lips feeling slightly ashamed at such a kind welcome when everyone here knew his presence was a danger to them all.

Before long, he was laughing so hard at Mahto and Belch's antics that he could no longer wallow in guilt.

Mahto had just begun a brilliant reenactment of Tolen's mishap with the sword, jumping around and holding his hand, when one of the guards Tolen recognized from practice came over and whispered in Sienn's ear.

Sienn met Mahto's eye and he paused mid hop. It would have been hilarious if it weren't for the look on Sienn's face. Sienn got up and she and Mahto followed the guard out of earshot.

"I take it dinner interruptions are not normal," Tolen whispered.

Belch shook his head. "Meal time is family time. Only the night guard would ever dare interrupt, and only then if it was something they couldn't handle."

Heat rushed to Tolen's palms as he pushed away from the table.

"Tolen, wait." Tashta put a hand on his arm. "They will tell us."

Tolen paused and a few seconds later Mahto and Sienn returned, wearing matching looks of concern.

"What is it?" Tashta's voice trembled.

Mahto grabbed Tashta's hand. "Daklafar."

"*Ibi'ta!* Daklafar! You're certain?" Tashta grabbed her throat.

Mahto nodded. "Fifty or more. The rumors are true. Creatures are escaping Misery. The Daks haven't found the village, but they're searching. Gayne thinks they may have been tracking the merchants. It's a good tactic, if you think about it." He rubbed his forehead. "Even trade is being affected by the growth of evil."

Tashta looked around at the villagers, her eyes worried, her fingers trembling.

The heat increased in Tolen's palms. Daklafar. Dark elves. He cast a quick look at Quasar to see him gripping the table so hard his knuckles were white.

"What's the plan?" Belch stood up and began clearing the table. Tolen moved to help, needing to keep his hands busy and avoid an outburst of power.

Sienn pulled her quiver and bow off the back of her chair. "The Guard is assembling. We're meeting in the weapons gallery. We're going to destroy those creatures before they get any closer to the village."

Mahto cast a look her direction that Tolen knew all too well. As brave and strong as Mahto knew Sienn was, he still feared for her.

"Can I help?" Tolen asked.

Mahto shared a look with Sienn and they both turned to Tashta. "If Tashta agrees."

Tolen looked at Tashta and she met his eyes. "You're not fully prepared Tolen, but according to Quasar your compassion for others makes you a formidable fighter, even if your emotions affect your gifts." She sighed. "You will go, but you will listen to your siblings. You will do as Sienn directs, understood?" Her tone was that of a mother—firm, but filled with love and concern.

How had this little family managed to take a place in his own heart in a single day? "Yes. I promise."

"Hurry and change. You've got five minutes." Sienn motioned to Tolen's shorts and t-shirt. "Mahto will go with you."

32 UNINTENDED RESCUE

Tolen ran back to Tashta's, not waiting for Mahto to catch up. He threw on his jeans, a long-sleeved shirt, and shoved his feet back into his sneakers. He pulled the weapons belt out of his pack that Macy made before they went into the Shadow Realm and tied it around his waist. He quickly checked the pouches Macy refilled at the citadel. Sleep Dust, Camouflage, and a handful of Glockshaw along with the herbs to make more—if he could remember how she'd taught him to do it.

He rushed back to the living room to see Mahto waiting. He followed the boy's urgent steps out the door. "How come Belch didn't want to be part of the Guard?"

"Belch has a willing heart but a soft one," Sienn answered from up ahead. "He's part of the home front. He protects the village while the Guard is away. He and a group of others like him—strong and powerful, yet gentle—comfort and protect from within."

They entered the weapons gallery and Mahto started loading up beside Sienn and other guards.

"Choose your weapon, Tolen." Mahto gestured to the wall.

Tolen looked at the array of swords, Kamuds, bows, knives, and other strange weapons he couldn't name but looked deadly. How to choose? "I haven't practiced with anything besides a sword and bow."

Mahto strapped his sword on his back, took Tolen by the elbow, and whispered in his ear. "Walk along the wall and pay attention to what you feel. The weapon that will best serve you will call out." Tolen looked at him with his eyebrow raised.

Mahto nodded with no hint of humor in his eyes. "Trust me."

"Okay."

Mahto let go of Tolen's arm and went back to help Sienn fill quivers.

Tolen walked along the wall, not sure what to do other than look. A long table stretched the width of the wall. Weapon upon weapon hung from the wall and more were laid along the table. He knew what he was most comfortable using. He even felt more confident with a bow after today's lesson, but he tried not to let that sway him. What weapon would best serve him?

As he neared the end of the wall, a trickle of warmth seemed to be reaching toward him, moving toward his chest, igniting the Kuna within. He kept walking and the feeling got stronger. There on the table, buried beneath an assortment of old tools, was the weapon that called to him. He moved the greasy tools aside to see a faded leather pouch, about the size of a large grapefruit. When he picked it up warmth zinged his fingers. With the pouch in hand, he tugged the old strings to loosen the top. He jumped when Mahto spoke from over his shoulder.

"Good choice. Do you know what they are?"

Tolen looked in the bag to see shiny silver disks, about the size of his palm. His throat tightened. "Yes."

"Have you ever used them before?"

Tolen shook his head not trusting his voice. Macy used them. Bastian called them Shakra.

"Do you know how to use them?"

Tolen shook his head again.

Mahto lifted the pouch from Tolen's hand and pulled out one of the shiny silver disks. "Like the Kamud, these are of Movan design and so they react with your gifts. It takes a tremendous amount of willpower. As with the sword, you send your strength to the Shakra but once they leave your hand they are guided by your will. If you don't stay focused, they can't do your bidding. Very few can control them. Most prefer the sword." He put the disk back in the pouch and pulled the strings tight before he handed them back to Tolen. "Okay man, remember to be careful as you send in your strength. You don't want one welded to your hand." Mahto pushed Tolen's arm and motioned for him to follow.

Tolen tied the pouch onto his weapons belt.

"You might want a new belt. That one looks ready to fall apart."

"It's fine."

Mahto tipped his head.

"Sorry, it has sentimental value."

"I understand, but you might want to save it for special occasions. You don't want to lose a battle over sentiment."

Tolen nodded, but didn't select a new belt.

Mahto shrugged and tied a sheath holding a normal sword onto Tolen's back. "Just in case. It never hurts to have more than one weapon on hand. Let's go. The others are waiting."

Sienn was at the front of the Guard, Mahto and Tolen brought up the rear. The only sound came from the subtle clank of gear and armor bumping against each other as they ran. The village had been warned. Lights were doused, children shushed, chickens penned. The tension in the air was tangible. Home front protectors stood ready around the borders, both old and young.

Near the edge of the village, Quasar fell into a jog beside Tolen. "Can you use one more?"

Mahto grinned. "Definitely. I've heard of your skills, elf. I can't wait to see you in action."

Quasar nodded and stared ahead. Tolen wasn't sure why, but it bothered him when Mahto referred to Quasar as "elf." He too used the term in conversation and thought, but until now, he hadn't realized how derogatory it sounded. Shame clouded Tolen's thoughts. He'd given Quasar little thought since he'd been swept into Tashta's family and the ways of the village. But if it weren't for Quasar, he never would have even known of this place, learned to love and appreciate members of his own race, or have a safe place to face his eighteenth birthday. He owed a lot to Quasar, the Lafar elf he hadn't trusted. He fell back a little and was glad when Quasar slowed and Mahto kept going.

"Thank you Quasar, for bringing me here. I nearly killed you and yet you did what you had to do. I'm truly grateful and I'm sorry for not telling you so before now. I hope you can forgive me."

Quasar paused and Tolen stopped to face him. "I have watched you from the shadows as you have made your way into the hearts of those around you. You have become a part of the village in a single day. You have managed to control your emotions without even realizing it. You have made hope blossom within me and increased my desire to do all I can to see you succeed."

Tolen opened and closed his mouth. "Thank you."

Quasar tipped his chin and hurried to catch up with Mahto.

Tolen matched his pace and soon they were at the very edge of the forest surrounding the village. The company slowed down. Whispered messages carried back through the guards giving instruction. They were breaking off into four groups with the intention of surrounding the area where the scouts had first seen the Daklafar.

Tolen, Mahto, Quasar, and three others were directed east. A guard, with blond hair and dark eyes led their group deeper into the forest.

He held up a hand to signal them to stop and whispered to the guard next to him. The message filtered back and Mahto repeated it to Tolen and Quasar, who leaned in close to hear.

"The Daks are just ahead," Mahto whispered. "They've broken off into groups. They're setting up for an attack. It's going to be harder to surround them. We're going to climb the trees and try to see the others." Mahto pointed up and Tolen started to climb behind Mahto, with Quasar the caboose. The other guards were in the trees ahead. Tolen could just see their outlines if he focused hard enough.

Mahto tapped his eyes and ears. Tolen nodded that he understood and spoke the words to enhance his sight and hearing.

It was a few seconds before he heard the Daklafar. They spoke in a strange guttural language, consisting of grunts and odd shrieks. It was a full minute before he saw them. They were so filthy and ugly it was hard to imagine they were once beautiful and flawless Lafar.

He heard the guards in the other tree explain the plan. Both groups would count how many creatures they could see and coordinate an attack.

Tolen began counting. Ten, no twelve. He wasn't sure. Even with his enhanced sight, the Daklafar blended so well with the darkness that he couldn't be positive that he wasn't counting the same one twice. Mahto whispered twelve and Quasar nodded. The other guard's whisper carried over. He agreed. There were twelve.

"We'll stay in two groups, each group taking six. We'll draw the attention of those closest. You run around to the front and kill the creatures ahead when they try to double-back."

"Agreed." Mahto whispered back.

"On my word, drop."

Tolen shifted his position to the edge of the branch and balanced on the balls of his feet.

"Three, two, one, DROP!" The guard's yell earned a startled yelp from the closest Dak. He shrieked at his brothers and soon they were turning to fight.

Mahto led the way around the battle. They stuck to the trees until they were between the fighters and the Dak running back toward them. Tolen pulled a Shakra out of his pouch and waited.

When Tolen could just see their outlines Mahto yelled and jumped into their path. A tall Dak released an arrow, but Mahto deflected it with his sword. He ran ahead but Tolen couldn't watch what happened next as another Dak rushed toward him, curved dagger brandished high above his head.

Tolen sent his will to the Shakra and threw. The disk blazed with light and shot like a bullet through the Daks head and into the chest of the one running behind. It pulled free and launched back into Tolen's hand, still blazing and so hot he could barely hold onto it.

The other Daks were dead and Mahto was motioning for them to hurry. Screeches and screams mixed with the clinking of blades echoed all around.

Tolen caught up with Mahto and Quasar and they rushed into a small clearing where the rest of the Guard was fighting a lot more than fifty Daklafar. Their estimate had been wrong. Sienn was fighting two at once. Two of the Guard were on the ground beside her. Alive or dead Tolen couldn't tell. Mahto flew to her side and began swinging. Quasar took off toward a large group. Tolen followed, pulling Shakra out of the pouch. This time he sent all three, asking them to search out the darkest, most evil fighters.

He fought as many as he could with the sword while the Shakra zinged through the crowd taking out targets. It was hard, just as Mahto said it would be. He had to think about directing the Shakra at the same time as he fought the battle right in front of him.

The Daks began to fall quickly and soon they were retreating. Tolen followed the guards who were chasing them. The Shakra zoomed back into his hand at the same moment a thought that was not his own, filled with agony and fear, ripped through his mind.

No! No! Please, don't let them find me. Please!

Tolen skidded to a stop and looked around. He heard the other guards catch up to the retreating Daklafar. He heard the *thwack, thwack,* as arrows met their backs.

Please. Please. The voice began to cry.

Tolen settled the Balance around him until he felt himself disappear. He couldn't tell where the voice was coming from, but it was close. He moved slowly across the ground, careful not to step on a twig or rustle too many leaves. He pushed out with his Sphere ability. If the creature was injured, maybe he could sense its life force even if it was shielding.

A whimper and Tolen looked up. In between the dead branches of a lightening cracked tree, a tiny Dak lay trembling, his arms wrapped over his head. Tolen walked over slowly. He was badly injured. Dark red blood gushed from an arrow embedded in his thigh.

Tolen paused beside the dark elf and debated. Could this creature really be who he'd heard? He wasn't supposed to be able to hear Dark creatures. He called to the vines growing around the dead tree and slowly they crept up and wrapped around the Dak's arms and uninjured leg. The creature was so weak, he didn't even notice.

Tolen let go of the Balance, reappeared, and tapped the creature's arm. The Daklafar started, tried to curl tighter into the tree, and gasped when the effort jostled his leg. He cried out in the strange tongue of the Daklafar.

Tolen's confusion grew. Maybe this wasn't the creature he'd heard. He looked around. But when the voice pierced his thoughts again, this time in defeat, he knew without a doubt it came from the creature in front of him.

I'm so sorry, mother. I've failed. The Dak's eyes closed, a whimper escaped his throat, and he passed out.

Tolen called the vines back and lifted the Dak into his arms, trying not to disturb his wound. He was so tiny, maybe four feet tall, and bone thin.

The other guards had already piled carcasses and kindling in the center of the clearing so when Tolen walked in carrying a body they thought nothing of it—until he walked past the growing pile and turned toward the area where he could see medics working on some of the Guard.

Quasar put a hand on his arm. "Where are you going?"

"This one isn't dead."

Quasar lifted his knife. "Then let me kill it if you cannot."

"No!" Tolen held out his hand. "He's different."

"Tolen, look at him! He is no different from his bloodthirsty brothers. His choice is plain in his features!"

Quasar's shout brought over more guards, including Mahto and Sienn.

"What's going on?" Sienn looked at the creature in Tolen's arms. "Throw that thing in the pyre," she growled.

"No." Tolen stood firm. "He's different."

Quasar threw his hands in the air. "How can you be certain?"

"Because I can hear him."

"What?" Sienn, Mahto, and Quasar asked together.

"I heard his thoughts. He's not one of them. I don't know how and I don't know why, but I heard him. We need to save him."

Mahto opened his mouth and closed it like a fish. "You're insane, man."

"I'm not. Please. I can heal him, but we need to get this arrow out." He hurried toward the medic area, gently laid the Dak on the ground and moved his leg. The creature trembled, but didn't wake. "We need to hurry. He's lost a lot of blood."

"You're crazy, man!" Mahto shook his head at Tolen but his eyes were resigned. "If he wakes up and makes a move for any of us, I kill first and ask questions after, agreed?"

Tolen nodded. "Just help him."

Mahto whistled a loud three-trilled tune. "Day, bring the medicine bag!"

A burly redheaded medic ran over carrying a bulging pack.

Day knelt beside the creature and gasped. "His blood ain't black. It's red! This isn't a Daklafar!" He set to work, resentment wiped from his face, and had the arrow out within seconds.

Tolen ignored the shocked gasps of the others and followed behind Day whispering, "*Lon'adras*" as he trailed his fingers around the wound, stopping the blood flow and sealing the edges. He pushed warmth into the boy, trying to heal him further, but he shuddered as if it caused more pain and Tolen stopped.

Sienn glared down at them. "Get him up. We think we've got them all, but it won't be long before they send someone searching." She whistled a less complicated tune than Mahto had and two guards appeared at her elbow. "Fief, blast that pyre to ashes, and Gayne, you and the others hide our tracks."

The two nodded and went to the pile of creatures. Fief lifted his hands and shot a fireball into the black mass and twisted his fingers until it exploded into a stifling cloud of ash. Gayne and a group of ten or so walked over and began regrowing the grasses around the area until the evidence of the fight was completely gone, the clearing filled with new vines and flowers. Not a single burned blade of grass remained.

Sienn gestured again to Tolen. "Carry him to Kichaya, but if you fall behind, you stay behind."

Tolen stood up and balanced the boy in his arms. The guards gave him baffled looks as they passed. Quasar shook his head in disgust and jogged ahead. Only Mahto stayed at the back with Tolen, but Tolen was sure it was only to be close enough to make good on his threat if the boy woke up and tried to escape.

JULY 9

ONE DAY UNTIL TRANSCENDENCE

33 A FRACTION OF LIGHT

R INGING SILENCE FOLLOWED Macy's statement, everyone's eyes locked on the object in her palm. It was small, about the size and weight of a tangerine. Beautiful. The silvery Clenadium ran in veins through the ball like smoky marble. The coloring beneath the veins was a soft orange with hazy swirls of sunset red and pale yellow.

"The Claver?" Keelyn whispered.

Toke gingerly lifted the object from Macy's palm. "There's only one way to find out. You are the humans. Each of you take a turn holding it. Clear your mind and see if it speaks to you." He sat the ball back in Macy's palm and she closed her eyes.

She tried to focus on only the ball, but the weight of new knowledge kept distracting her. She took a deep slow breath and called her Kuna back into her palms. The smell of eucalyptus and roses slowly calmed her and she felt the ball warm in her hand. But after several minutes nothing else happened. Disappointed she opened her eyes.

Toke shrugged. "Maybe it's not a Relic after all."

The ball was passed around until it reached the last person, Keelyn.

Rune dropped the ball into her open palm. It lit up at once and Keelyn gasped and burst into tears. Rune knocked the ball out of her hand where it rolled to a stop at Toke's feet.

Rune's arms were wrapped around Keelyn's shoulders but his whisper still carried. "What happened?"

Keelyn whimpered as Toke picked the now dark ball back up.

"Toke? What did it do to her?" Connell moved to stand beside Rune and patted his sister on the back.

"If it's the Claver, and she was able to connect to it, then it showed her a vision."

"Keelyn?" Rune stroked her hair.

She took a quick breath. "I saw a village," a sob hitched in her throat. "Nearly everyone dead…Crying…" She broke down again and Rune soothed her with whispers.

Toke met each of their eyes. "It is the Claver. Macy keep it safe." His lips turned down. "We won't use it again unless we feel we have no choice."

It was a few hours before everyone finally dozed off—except Macy, and a glance at Toke said he couldn't sleep either.

He motioned for her to follow him to the back of the house beside the crumbled rafters.

"Well?" The side of Macy's lip was raw from chewing it.

Toke looked at his sleeping children and sighed. "I hope this isn't too big for them."

"I hope it's not too big for me!" Macy fought to keep her voice low.

"The Light picked you for this mission, Macy. You are far more powerful than you realize."

His comment did little to comfort her. She'd never been more afraid of a mission in her life. If she failed this, it meant the end before the fight even began. "If they picked me, then the Light picked them too." She looked to where Keelyn slept in Rune's arms, her face still not quite peaceful.

Toke turned his orangey eyes to the night sky. "Because of my Calling, visions are not foreign to me. I've always trusted them to lead me where the Light wishes me to go. I must confess. I did not come back to Whisper because I had a vision, nor simply because I felt the Shadows' movement—although that was part. I came back because I had a strong feeling Max's daughter was going to need my help and I refused to ignore that feeling. It was only after we fought with you at the museum did the Light confirm the rightness of my decision. Because I chose you, the Light chose us. We are to go with you."

Chills rushed up Macy's arms. Because Toke chose to bring his family to Whisper in the chance Macy needed help, now they were a part of her scary mission, and he was afraid for them. She tried to ignore the guilt and tiny beads of jealousy this triggered.

Everything happens for a reason. Bastian's voice was just a whisper.

She looked back around the group. " Do you really think it's a good idea to go after the Relics? Isn't it better if they stay hidden? I mean look what happened to Keelyn. You really think it's smart for us to be carrying those things around?"

Toke twisted the ring on his finger and looked back at her. "The Dark knew your father had the Claver. They somehow knew where to find Eamun. I am afraid the powers that have protected the Relics all these years are weakening. Your father's map is not the original. And if somehow the Dark gets their hands on the real one…I just don't think it's a risk we can take."

"If ancient power can't protect them, how are we supposed to?"

He looked back at the room. "I don't know. I just know what I feel."

"Which is?"

"Our main goal must be finding the Last Shard and getting it to the new Keeper. The fact that it chose us convinces me that there's a connection between it and the legend surrounding the Pact. Hopefully we'll know more once we speak to the Old Ones. And then we *must* go after the Relics."

○○○

Streaks of soft pink and yellow lit the eastern sky as Tolen continued to pace the length of Kichaya's strange home, doing his best to ignore the crowd that had formed just after dawn. He'd helped the medics heal the rest of the injured guards and then had begun his vigil outside Kichaya's door.

Unearthly moans echoed through the heavy door every few minutes. Bright shafts of colored light shot out the window, between the door and the threshold, and out the chimney in between screams.

Tolen tugged on his ponytail. Tashta had begged him to sleep, but he couldn't bear to leave the young Dak alone. He was afraid something might happen and they would kill him despite their word.

When he'd first carried the creature into the village he'd feared the people would try to stop him, but no one did. Their faces were a mixture of confusion and sorrow. They felt bad for the battle that had taken place. Dark creatures or not, they respected life. Tolen's affection for these people had risen greatly in that moment.

Even now, as he paced, several villagers paced with him, their expressions wary yet also curious. Only Quasar sat off to the side, his face a hard, bitter mask.

The front door opened after a particularly loud, drawn out, and pain-filled scream.

Tolen rushed forward when Bren motioned to him. "Kichaya wishes for you and Quasar to join us."

Tolen looked at Quasar. His stony expression didn't change, but he stood up and met them at the door.

Bren looked at the others and shook his head. "You might as well go back to your homes and get some rest. If there is any change, I'll send word."

They gave him solemn nods. As they each turned back to the village they either patted or shook Tolen's arm, lending their support, and amazing him with their kindness.

Bren opened the door. "Come." He stepped aside and waited for Tolen and Quasar to move into the shadow of the house before closing the door behind them.

Tolen moved toward the moans but Bren held him back.

"Wait." He looked back and forth between Tolen and Quasar.

He paused at the look on Quasar's face. "Say what you must."

Quasar let out a loud breath, as if he'd been holding it for a long time. "Why? That creature deserves death!"

The harshness of Quasar's tone made Bren take a step back. "Only Kichaya can answer your question. Whether or not that creature should be allowed to die is not up to us."

Tolen bit his lip. "What's going on in there?"

Bren shook his head again. "The Light has granted Kichaya the chance to try and pull the darkness from the boy. You are right. He is different from the others. The darkness has not completely taken his heart. There remains the tiniest fraction of light within him."

Quasar scoffed and spun away from them.

Bren glanced from Quasar back to Tolen. "We have seen it in the very youngest of Daklafar—the change is not complete. We have tried this once before, many, many years ago, but without success. The creature did not survive. The Dark is powerful, once it has that firm of a hold on someone it does not like to relinquish that hold; it would rather that its host dies."

Tolen was reminded of the poisoned darkness he'd received when under the power of the Shadows, how when he'd tried to heal himself he'd felt more pain and agony than from any physical injury—he'd felt the darkness trying to stay inside, content to let him die rather than let go. It made no sense.

It does not make sense because your heart is pure, Tolen. Bastian's voice whispered. *Darkness cannot comprehend Light, nor can Light fully understand the Dark without becoming darkness.*

Bren put his hand on Tolen's shoulder. "The prognosis is not good, but Kichaya still has hope. She feels that the two of you may be able to help save him."

Tolen nodded. Quasar didn't turn. Tolen touched Quasar's arm. "Quasar?"

Quasar rubbed a hand over his face and turned to follow Bren. He wouldn't meet Tolen's eyes, and Tolen wondered why he was so upset. Given what happened to his people, Tolen thought that Quasar would be happy at the idea that there was hope for at least some. But the older Lafar quivered with barely contained rage.

Bren's pace quickened when another scream echoed through the house. He tapped a back wall in the kitchen and the vines covering it curled away to reveal a dark, narrow corridor. Up and to the right colored light spilled into the passageway, shifting through pale shades of blue, red, and yellow. Bren rushed into the room.

Quasar paused at the door and his face drained of color. Tolen stepped through the opening and as he took in the scene before him, he knew the image would be burned in his memory forever.

34 REBEL FRIENDSHIPS

MACY STUFFED A slice of jerky into her mouth. Despite going to bed later than everyone she'd woke up with the sun and decided to use the quiet morning to look over her father's notes. She'd built a fire and surprisingly, Rune helped her put together a quick breakfast for everyone. She wasn't sure if he was better or worse being quiet and thoughtful instead of rude and sarcastic.

She'd taken her breakfast to sit beside a slender tree and continue reading where she'd left off. *The Fall of the Watchers*. Bastian had mentioned them in his letter and they were obviously something that greatly concerned her father. The idea that they could be somehow watching her through Bastian's shard made her skin crawl.

"Some of the Fallen are believed to have married human women, their mutated offspring revered by Darsapean as his best secret weapon. Human in appearance, these creatures are the only known beings of the Hidden race with the ability to hide their darkness. They have co-existed with humans for centuries. They are responsible for the Darkened and for leading many Chosen into the clutches of the Dark."

"Hey." Brina sat down beside Macy and offered her an apple.

Macy's eyebrow rose. "Um, thanks."

Brina shrugged.

Macy finished her apple before Brina cleared her throat. "So, the Ninth. He's really been chosen?"

"Yep."

"Wow, and you met him. Is he way powerful then?"

"He's amazing." Macy felt a blush creep into her cheeks and kicked at a pile of sticks by her foot.

Brina gave her a sideways look. "You like him."

Macy cleared her throat and went back to looking at the notes.

Brina took the hint, changed the subject, and Macy could see they would get along. Brina was just as backward and shy with friendship as Macy was. "So, your Dad, he was a Chosen?"

"Yeah," Macy nodded, "I didn't know until Toke told me."

"Your family history seems pretty cool."

"I guess." Macy shrugged. "It feels more confusing than cool right now."

"That makes sense."

Macy glanced at Brina out the corner of her eye. "How old are you?"

"Seventeen." Brina gave her a half smile. "My height makes people think I'm a lot older."

"My lack of height gets me the under-twelve discount at restaurants."

Brina laughed.

Macy leaned back against the tree. "How long have you guys been with Toke?"

"Rune's been with him the longest, since he was nine. Keelyn and Connell have been with us three years." Brina glanced back at the little shack where Toke and Rune rested against the weathered outer wall having a quiet, but animated, discussion over some of Toke's notebooks. Keelyn and Connell sat off to the side, grinning at the antics of the squirrel Connell was tempting with pieces of his breakfast. "Four for me. Since my mom died and my dad disappeared."

Macy tossed the apple core into the trees. "You didn't have a Watcher?"

Brina shook her head. "I did. But my parents were both high-ranking military and fully aware of the Hidden world, so I was allowed to stay with them during their leave. I spent summers with my Watcher, and whenever my parents were on tour."

Macy chewed her thumbnail. "I didn't know that was allowed."

Brina pointed to the page Macy was reading. "I don't think it was. Toke has talked to me about the Fallen. He thinks my Watcher may have been one of them, or at least worked for them."

Macy swallowed. "So the stories are true?"

Brina lifted her shoulder. "Toke thinks so."

"What about the offspring of the Fallen and humans?" Macy glanced back at the last paragraph she'd read.

"He thinks that's true too. He thinks that's why the numbers of Darkened are increasing so quickly."

Macy shivered despite the warm summer air. "I wonder if that's what my Dad meant."

"What?"

"He wondered if the Fallen were somehow connected to the Guardians' loss of Sight. Bastian told me that all the Watchers are connected, and if they let each other in, they can see what other Watchers see."

Brina nodded thoughtfully. "I guess it makes sense."

"Right." She paused before adding her next thought. "But what if whatever they are doing is weakening all Sight? What if our shards become too dangerous to wear?"

Brina folded her arms across her chest. "I don't even want to think about that."

Macy absently fingered her shards. "How did you discover your Watcher was bad?"

"It wasn't until my mother died and my father went MIA that I started to see him for what he really was. He'd always been controlling and bossy, but after he gained complete guardianship, he became downright mean. Toke found me about a month after I'd run away. He followed my Watcher for a while and discovered he'd been using my parents' military connections to take out human targets."

"What?"

"Just because humans can't see the Dark doesn't mean they can't do damage to their plans. When humans choose good they weaken the Dark. It's always been this way. That's why the Dark hates them so much."

Macy bit her lip. "Your parents…?"

Brina looked away and nodded. "They were a threat to the Dark, so the Dark eliminated them."

"I'm so sorry."

Brina crushed her apple core under her foot. "I think my dad figured it out before they got him. I think he's still hiding somewhere. Toke and I searched for him, but the trail went cold."

Macy thought about Bastian. He in no way fit the description of Brina's Watcher. Bastian had been firm but kind, and always tried to get

Macy to spread her wings and make her own decisions. It had always been her choice to let Bastian make all the decisions and guide her actions. Bastian may have kept things from her, but it was to protect her, not control her. Every mission they ever completed was in the name of the Light. Bastian was a Guardian. He was *not* one of the Fallen. He was a good man. End of story.

But…*could* some of the Chosen be brainwashed slaves controlled by Fallen Watchers? She looked around at the other rebels. Toke must believe it, and Rune probably thought so too. Keelyn and Connell seemed to embody Light in their natures. They might be with the Lost Ones, but they were good. You couldn't be near them and not know that. Brina held no love for the Dark, but to be double-crossed by her Watcher must have felt like the ultimate betrayal by the one thing that was supposed to be so sure, so perfect—the love of the Light.

She ran her finger over her father's written words. His fingers had swept across this page, pencil pushing into paper immortalizing the thoughts that plagued him, so important he wished to preserve them for his daughter so she could have the whole picture and then decide for herself what to do with the knowledge.

She thought back to Bastian's letter.

If there be truth to your father's discoveries, do not let it sour your opinion of the Light. There are frailties in Hidden kind and men, even in those entrusted to lead, but there is no frailty in the Light. Please, please remember this.

Toke looked past Rune's shoulder and met her eyes with a solemn dip of his head.

After breakfast, Toke declared that some practice time was in order before they moved on. A route to the village was planned and Toke felt they had plenty of time to take a short breather from walking. Macy suspected he was trying to distract them all from the situation and didn't want them brooding and stressed for the entire trip.

In truth, she was grateful for the distraction.

Toke led them to a small, perfectly round clearing just behind the shack and Rune started placing several different weapons on the ground.

Movan weaponry. *Sweet!*

She recognized Shakra and the Shupata bow, but some she'd never seen before.

"This is a Kamud." Toke handed her a long sword by the carved stone hilt. "Its name means invincible or unparalleled."

"I've heard of those! This is what you guys were using when you found me in Whisper. Are they really invincible?" Macy's fingers tingled from her excitement.

"Invincible, no. Unparalleled, yes."

Macy raised her eyebrows.

Toke turned to the others. "Rune?"

Rune stepped up beside Toke with a smirk and unsheathed his sword. It was longer and more curved than the one Toke handed to Macy, but the stone hilts were the same, as were the symbols carved into the blade.

He gripped the sword in both hands and after a brief look of concentration, the blade began to glow, the symbols burning bright blue. It reminded her of using Shakra. Rune had sent his will to the blade.

Toke leaned over and picked up a normal sword off the ground, like those she had used to practice with the Radia Warriors. He bowed to Rune and the two began swordplay. It was over in seconds with Toke on the ground and Rune's blade at his throat.

"Impossible." Macy snorted.

Toke stood up and traded Macy the Kamud with the normal blade. "You try."

Macy took the sword and bowed quickly to Rune. "Gimme your best shot, Blondie."

Rune smirked and moved in for a jab. Macy blocked and the slash of Rune's blade made her arms burn and her ears ring from the clang. Normal sword fighting didn't weaken like this. You used technique to move just right, allowing the blade to take the force and push your moves, allowing your arms to stay strong. But each time Macy's blade met Rune's her arms felt weaker as if it were drawing her strength. Within seconds she was sweating, and before she realized it she was on the ground with Rune's blade pointed at her heart.

Macy jumped to her feet. She charged Toke, took the Kamud from his hands, and rushed Rune. He met her swipe with a block.

She sent her will to the blade, but the connection was far more powerful than when she used Shakra. The blade warmed in her fingers and she felt her Kuna zing into the metal, combining itself with the blade, so that the blade became an extension of her gifts, drawing power from her opponent and strengthening hers with every contact.

Rune's gloating disappeared, replaced by determined focus. Macy's palms tingled and her chest heated up with each slash of the blade. It was exhilarating. She knew she should be exhausted, but she felt empowered, *invincible.*

She knocked Rune to his back. "Ha!" she laughed as she placed the sword at his throat.

The others stood off to the side silently waiting to see Rune's reaction.

Macy couldn't wipe the smile from her face. "That was awesome!"

Rune's face split into a shocking smile. "I know, right?" He dropped his sword and reached up for Macy's hand.

Macy tried to drop her sword to help him up, but she couldn't let it go. Heat surged through her fingertips getting uncomfortable.

Rune's grin became more pronounced. He jumped to his feet and leaned forward. "What's the matter? A little power hungry, are we?"

Toke came over and touched Macy's shoulder. "You have to *want* to let go Macy. Pull the power back in. Control it."

Macy took several deep breaths and stared at her hands, fighting for control. It was so hard! It felt so good to release this way, no flame, no explosions, just sheer power. She looked up to see Rune still grinning and she pulled the Kuna back into her body. It hurt, but she wasn't about to let Rune see how much.

He walked over and leaned on his sword. "Not bad, kid. Not bad at all." Then he turned and walked off laughing, and Macy wasn't sure, but she thought she might have just made herself another friend.

Weird world.

35 HEALING

THE YOUNG DAKLAFAR writhed and moaned from a small wooden table under a shaft of sunlight coming through a hole in the ceiling. A crackling fire blazed in the hearth, which should have made the tiny room stifling hot, but the cold coming off the Daklafar's body seemed to be blocking the heat. His skin was a blotchy mess of churning color—purple, blue, black, pale white—as if a swirling bruise covered his whole body. He wore nothing but a filthy black loincloth. The wound on his leg had healed—the only spot on his battered body that was the color of healthy skin. Every few seconds his back would arch off the table, a pain-filled moan would escape his dark lips, and his black eyes would roll back in his head. The sight was horrifying.

Kichaya dipped rags in pots filled with bubbling liquid and draped them over the boy's forehead. She dabbed her fingers in bowls of green salve and massaged it into his blackened feet. She tossed various herbs from large sacks into the air, muttering under her breath, sweat dripping from her nose and chin. She looked exhausted but determined. "Just when I think the boy is fighting back, the Dark overwhelms him again!"

She motioned to Tolen. "Come. Help me!" She pointed at Quasar who still stood in the doorway looking like he was about to throw up. "You too. I need you both."

Bren took over rubbing the salve into the boy's feet, while Kichaya moved Tolen to the boy's middle and put Quasar at his head. She squeezed Quasar's hand. "Speak to him the words of the Lafar, Quasar. Coax him back to the Light. He is a strong boy. His heart is good. Please!" Quasar clenched his teeth but nodded. She sat him on a stool and Quasar leaned in toward the boy's ear. Tolen couldn't make out what he said.

She grabbed Tolen's arm. "You must use your Lóklana. Direct it at his heart. The strength of the sunlight is not enough. We must hurry!"

Tolen balked at her request. The last time he'd used his Lóklana he'd fried the creature he'd directed it at. "Kichaya, I don't know how!"

Kichaya paused with her hand in the air. Herbs trickled from her fist. "You must balance the Lóklana with your Sphere ability. The Sphere in you will know how much light to give to help him without hurting him."

Frustration crippled Tolen's thoughts. "I don't know how to do that!"

"Figure it out!" Quasar shouted. "Accept who you are! Let your gifts work together!" His violet eyes flashed with longing. "Please Tolen, we must save him." The hope warring with the pain and fear in Quasar's eyes pierced Tolen like a knife. He looked at the writhing boy and his heart welled with pity. No creature should have to suffer like this. *If we cannot save him, please, take him quickly. Let him suffer no more, whether by our hands or by the Dark.*

Tolen thought of the love the Light showed for its creations, he thought of his love for his parents, Macy, the love he felt for his new family, this village—his people—and the warmth swelled from his heart down to his fingers. For the first time could feel his Sphere ability as a separate entity. He held the healing power there in his fingers, just above the boy's heart while he searched for the Lóklana inside him. It was strange looking for specifics. He'd always just willed them into appearance before.

Tolen closed his eyes. *Please, help me to find myself, help me save this child.*

Across the dark backdrop of his closed lids all the lights of the spectrum burst into being. It was the most beautiful thing he'd ever seen. Each crystalline color represented one of his gifts and resonated with its power, allowing him to individually recognize it.

The Sphere's light was the soft blue of a summer sky, the Kunamin a vibrant orange, the Honitahai a glowing emerald, the Animashta a deep red, the colors continued, mixing, changing hue, until Tolen realized there was much more depth to his gifts than he had realized.

Finally, brightest of them all, pure white light, the Lóklana showed itself. Its light washed over all the other lights blending them perfectly together. Tolen felt a power with this gift unlike any he had felt before.

He called forward the pale blue light of the Sphere's and watched it join the white light until the two melded together, creating a brighter, white-blue light.

Tolen's heart sped up with his breathing. It was difficult holding the two gifts together, each strength complimenting, yet unintentionally trying to outdo the other. *Control. Focus.*

He opened his eyes and looked down at the boy. Only seconds had passed, yet time seemed to have slowed down. The forms of those around him appeared as if in a haze, only the boy beneath his hands stayed in focus, his ravaged body convulsing. Somewhere through the haze Kichaya's voice echoed.

"We're losing him!"

Tolen looked down at his hands and allowed the warmth, the cool blue, mingled with pure white, to surge into his palms. He rested them over the boy's heart and a force beyond him welded his hands to the boy's chest. It was just as with the sword, but this time Tolen felt in control of the power. He could feel a literal war going on inside the young boy's body. The Light in his heart, small but resilient, fought desperately against the Dark that poisoned his outer shell. At the same moment that Tolen sent the Lóklana Light in to strengthen the boy's spirit, the boy's entire life flashed through Tolen's mind.

Tears coursed down Tolen's cheeks and he struggled to breathe as he saw the boy's birth to a beautiful young Lafar with charcoal colored hair. She smiled as her husband handed her the healthy baby boy. The scene flashed through the next five years until Tolen saw another child, a little girl, running behind the boy through a plowed field under a dreary gray sky, a sky so opaque and lifeless it could only be the sky above the Shadow Realm.

Celeste, the boy whispered in Tolen's mind through a pain filled moan. *Celeste!*

The Dak's memories of his sister became clearer and the creature began to sob painful, gut wrenching sobs. The boy had hoped to save them. His mother, his sister. Tolen watched five more years pass as the boy and his sister grew up under the hand of Daklafar masters too cruel to be seen as anything other than slave drivers.

The family were slaves.

Tolen saw other families and elderly all working for the Daklafar. Beatings, brutal executions, starvation; these poor Lafar were but a remnant of their former greatness. It broke Tolen's heart.

A few more years passed and Tolen saw the young Lafar being carried away screaming after his father was executed for rebellion. The Daklafar gave him a choice: Join, or watch the rest of his family be executed. The boy took the oath out of a desire to protect his family—he felt no loyalty to them. It was all he could do to save what was left of his family.

He knew those that offered up their children as volunteers were given certain freedoms, more provisions, nicer homes—if you could call a bark hut a home, but it was better than the ground. Celeste was malnourished and weak; his mother was torn with grief. He felt he had no choice. He was barely fourteen years old.

Tolen waited for the scene to change and show him what happened next, but something changed. It was quiet. The boy was no longer screaming or crying and the room felt hot. He opened his eyes to see that everything was back in focus. The others weren't moving; they were staring at the boy.

Tolen looked down and felt his hands release themselves from the boy's pale chest.

His breathing had steadied and under the filth his skin had brightened to soft healthy pink. His charcoal hair had turned the same color as his mother's, with soft blue highlights.

His pale lids flickered and he slowly opened his bright violet eyes.

Kichaya placed her hand on his cheek. "Welcome back to the Light, young one. Do you know your name?"

New tears spilled over the boy's cheeks following the dirty tracks on his face. "Blaze." He took a shuddering breath. "My name is Blaze."

36 SECOND BIRTHRIGHT

Tolen opened his eyes to gentle light melting in through the window of the room he shared with Mahto, Belch, and Sashan. The rays turned the faded yellow quilt he lay under to brilliant gold. He'd never really thought about how beautiful the light was before. So many things in the last few days would change the way Tolen looked at light forever.

Blaze had passed out again shortly after telling them his name. Kichaya told both Quasar and Tolen to get some rest and she would send for them when the boy woke.

They didn't speak as they'd walked back to the village together. The experience seemed too sacred, too miraculous to discuss just yet. But an idea had formed in Tolen's mind through the early morning hours and he wanted to discuss it with Quasar before they visited the boy again, and before he was locked up in the Capka.

Tolen stretched, yawned, looked at his watch, and sat up with a start. It was almost noon! He was supposed to go to class with Tahaka. Crap!

Soft laughter and quiet conversation came from the kitchen. The smell of bacon and fresh bread tickled his taste buds. He jumped up, made his bed, threw on his clothes, and rushed to the kitchen.

"He's alive!" Mahto threw a hand to his mouth in mock shock.

"Ha, ha." Tolen looked around. It seemed that only Mahto and Sienn were home. "Where're the others?" he asked as he folded several pieces of bacon in a slice of bread.

"Sashan is already at Tahaka's. Belch and Tashta are in the square helping the rest of the village prepare the welcome feast for Blaze," Sienn said softly.

Tolen stepped back, not sure what to make of her tone. "Well…Um, that's good. Awesome. Well, I'd better get to class. I've…got a lot to learn." He spun toward the door where his sneakers sat waiting, but a hand on his arm stopped him.

"Tolen, wait." Sienn stood up and Tolen looked from her to Mahto.

Mahto shrugged, holding back a grin. Sienn's cheeks went slightly pink. "I need to apologize to you."

Tolen started to shake his head, but she interrupted.

"No. I've been a real jerk. I didn't want to trust you. I was angry that you weren't what we expected."

Tolen glanced down and Sienn touched his chin. "You are different than we expected, but also much more than we expected."

He looked up to see genuine warmth in her eyes. "What you did for the Daklafar reminded us all of the real reason we choose the Light and fight the Dark. No matter what happens tomorrow, you can count on the Guard for any help you need." She bowed and sat back down.

Tolen stammered out a thank you and stumbled over to slip on his shoes. As he rushed out the door he heard Mahto teasing Sienn.

"You sure are hot when you're embarrassed." The sound of a short scuffle followed by a drawn out theatrical smooch followed.

Tolen laughed as he ran the short distance to Tahaka's school.

Tolen skidded to a stop just outside the strange door of the school and saw Sashan waiting with a wry smile on his face.

"Tahaka told me I should have woken you so you would be on time, but you were snoring so loudly I do not think you could have heard me."

Tolen shook his head. "I don't snore." Sashan lifted an eyebrow.

"Okay. I don't snore that often. Only when I'm really tired."

Sashan chuckled. "If you say so." He waited for Tolen to follow him inside. It was quiet, the students already involved in their lessons. "Tahaka wishes us to work together today." He pointed to a gap in the trees and led Tolen to a small area with only two hammocks.

Tahaka appeared as they took their seats. She touched Tolen's forehead and he heard her voice in his mind. *"You have learned about the Hidden past, about the way we live now, and you have learned certain truths. Your experience with the Daklafar opened your eyes to the diversity of your gifts. You can now recognize and tap into them individually. You can combine them in different ways. But only two of your gifts are your birthright, a literal part of who you are and would still be yours had you not been selected to become the Ninth Chosen. The rest of your gifts must be developed, honed, and appreciated or they will leave you.*"

Tolen thought about Kichaya's promise. He would go back to who he would have been, a Honitahai, if he chose to forsake his destiny. He would lose all his other gifts.

"*Today you must understand your second birthright, for it is this gift that is necessary to enable you to control, use* all *your gifts correctly, and know* when *to use them.*"

Tolen shifted in his seat as she continued.

"*Your second birthright is that of the Dembashi, the Watchers. Far, far back in your distant past, you are linked to the Dembashi; you are one of their descendants.*" She stepped back and Tolen opened his eyes. Tahaka's eyes were sparkling. She stepped over to Sashan and touched his head. A few moments later she faced both of them and lifted her hands in the air.

The leaves blew around them again and the chatter started. Tolen closed his eyes and her voice was clear once more, but this time, in his mind's eye he could see Sashan sitting beside him, watching him.

"*Sashan will teach you the history of the Dembashi. Before you leave today you will understand your second birthright, and you will control it.*" Tahaka's voice trailed off and Tolen trembled.

A thought crossed his mind that made breakfast turn in his stomach. If being a Watcher was as much his birthright as a Honitahai, if he chose to live a normal Hidden life, he would still see the future. He would still be plagued with visions of all those lives he was supposed to protect—*watching* the horrible future before it happened and be helpless to do anything about it. New empathy for Quasar welled within him.

Why was it so hard to do what he knew he must? Why?

Sashan began to speak quietly, pulling Tolen back into the lesson.

"I am Sashan Woodlore son of Eamun, son of Laird. My father lived many centuries, had many wives and many children—but only *one* wife was not a Watcher. She was a Honitahai by the name of Syn'ca. She was his third wife in his third cycle, a marriage of prophecy and filled with great love. They parented many, many children. It is from this wife that you descend, Tolen Daedal Téloran."

Tolen sucked in a breath. He was related to Eamun Woodlore? Which meant he was also related to the boy beside him. A feeling of kinship and loyalty fell over him.

"I learned much at my father's hand. I know all the prophecies of the Hidden. I have taken my father's place as head of the Watcher race. I see what all Watchers see. This is a great burden that I fully accept. As long as I live we all remain connected. I now receive the prophecies the Light wishes all of Hidden and humankind to heed.

"The Watcher's duty is a sacred one. Since our Creation, we have seen glimpses of future events, past lives, thoughts of intent—but until Radia, we enjoyed no direction, no purpose to our gifts. When she sent us her shards she also sent us our purpose. We are meant to be servants, protectors of those the Light loves. Our gifts were not intended for our own selfish desires, but to bring to pass the goals of the Light: Peace on this earth between all its peoples and protection from the evil that would try to take it from them.

"It is no accident that Eamun's descendant was selected to be the Ninth Chosen. It is no accident that he is a descendant of the third wife of the third cycle. We have entered the last age of mankind. The first, peace between the races; the second, war and dissonance; this—the third age—has yet to be determined. Will this be another age of death and destruction, or can peace be restored again?"

Tolen's Watcher eye flashed with color. Images blurred past his vision.

"Control it!" Sashan shouted.

"How?"

"Look!"

That's all it took and he was there, watching *her*, watching Macy. She sat among a group of young people and one purple-haired, short adult, plotting with them. She'd discovered the point of her mission. Eamun Woodlore was dead. When he'd first thought of this as Sashan introduced himself, he hadn't given much thought to the Last Shard. But now? Daemon was after the Last. Macy was the Seeker, part of two-fold protection for the Last Shard and she was planning to search for the Relics to end the Pact. A burst of pain shot through his chest. This was why she was being hunted.

She told them about Tolen, about his destiny, how much she believed in him. She didn't say she loved him, but he could see it in her eyes, hear it in her voice.

He pulled himself out of her thoughts. He could feel the weight of his destiny literally resting on his shoulders, almost suffocating him. He thought of her mission, her importance, and her solid determination to see her path to its end, despite the danger she faced. He wasn't like her. He over-thought everything.

Could he live with himself if he left the current path to his destiny and lived a human life? Could Macy?

As soon as this thought completed, new images gathered in his mind. But this time, instead of blurred, they appeared as clear groups of images, like a wall of TVs showing different programs on an oversized screen in his mind. Each "screen" showed different events taking place around the world, like a newscast. When he focused on one screen, the people and events moved to the front and became extremely clear. He didn't even have to whisper the Hidden words "to watch". Their thoughts—if they weren't guarded or blocked—were as clear as if spoken aloud.

Tolen scanned screen after screen—or rather life after life, culture after culture. It was overwhelming, but *not*. So much to see and under-stand, yet as he needed to know he knew, as he needed to hear he heard. Just as the Light had said—he was beginning to understand about seeing the need in the moment when it was needed. He could see now why pointless visions of future didn't appear. Only when a choice triggered, or was about to trigger, a large shift in the Balance did the future register to the Watcher's Second Sight. He could choose to concentrate on one indi-vidual's immediate future and possibly see more, but the visions would not come unless there was a ripple in the Balance.

As each future flashed before him, he began to notice a pattern, the images of people with greater need were brighter, louder, and clearer.

He concentrated on bringing the brightest image to the forefront. The other pictures faded to fuzzy color, and then he could see in clarity so perfect he would have thought he was standing in the Shadow Realm right in front of Blaze's family and friends. There was unrest and fear in the slaves. Something big was about to happen in the Realm. Daklafar were demanding more work and giving less food and supplies.

He let the image snap back beside the others and called up the next brightest. It was Macy again, sitting with the group. Something was about to happen that could cause her to fail in her mission. Blaze needed him. Macy needed him.

His gut twisted. This was the real choice. Not whether or not he would take up the mantle of the Ninth, but whether or not he would do the right thing at the right time.

He opened his eyes to see at some point he had fallen out of his hammock and rolled onto his back. The sun's light no longer shone directly above. The school was silent and bathed in shadow. Sashan stood over him with his arms folded.

"You have control?"

Tolen nodded, not trusting his voice.

Sashan's pale eyes shifted slowly. "Come. Dusk is nearly upon us. You must meet with Kichaya before you enter the Capka."

"Blaze?" Tolen's voice cracked.

"He is awake. Quasar is waiting for you there."

37 LOVE AND LOYALTIES

Kichaya's door opened without his touch. Tolen walked into the tiny kitchen to see her staring at him, her eyes expectant.

Quasar sat beside her nervously tapping a steaming mug. When he saw Tolen he stood up, but Kichaya waved him back down.

"Sit. Tolen has something he wishes to discuss before you visit the boy." She looked back at Tolen. "Correct?"

Tolen nodded. Kichaya pointed to the chair beside her. "Come. Have some Lucid. You look exhausted."

Tolen sat down as she filled a mug and placed it in front of him. He wrapped his hand around the warmth, trying to figure out the best way to say what he needed to say.

Quasar looked impatient and Kichaya put a hand over his. "Blaze is fine, Quasar. Bren is with him. This is important."

Tolen fingered the clay handle and lifted the cup to his lips. He hated Lucid, but he couldn't deny he needed a pick me up. He took a nervous sip and was pleasantly surprised. It was warm, sweet, and far better than any Lucid he'd ever tasted. He'd have to get the recipe and make sure his mother switched. The liquid rolled down his throat and seemed to warm his entire body, relaxing him and clearing his thoughts. "Kichaya's right. I've got something I want to discuss with you both."

Quasar took a deep breath and a tiny smile started at the corners of Kichaya's mouth.

"Something Bastian taught me about fate keeps coming back to me."

The two seemed glued to their seats, their expressions frozen as they waited.

"Bastian told me that because of decisions made by others before me, some things have already been set in motion concerning the future that cannot be controlled or stopped—but my current choices affect the future as it relates to my own destiny.

"I accept the fact that the Balance selected me to be the Ninth Chosen, that it was the will of the Light. But when my parents chose to hide me from that destiny, it changed the course of my future. If Bastian had trained me from birth, if Macy and I had met when she was six years old, maybe we wouldn't have fallen in love the way we did."

He ignored Quasar's sharp intake of breath and met both their eyes evenly. "But that *is* what happened. I am the Ninth, and Macy is Light's Aid. Our destinies are intertwined whether we are in love or not. She is human." A lump started in his throat but he worked past it and kept his voice even. "My heritage points to a distant future that she will not be a part of. I accept that we each have a role to play in the prophecy. You don't believe Macy is my trigger." He met Kichaya's gaze. "But you don't understand. Macy means everything to me.

"*Love* is my trigger and my love for her is the reason I want to make this world a better place, the reason I try so hard to fulfill the depth of who I am. I am *not* lessening the importance of any other life on this planet or saying that I care more for her life than the lives of everyone I am responsible for. But she is *my* personal reason. The reason *I* want to exist. The reason I *will* do everything I can to succeed.

"My parents twisted my future from the way everyone thought it should be, but my feelings for Macy straightened it back out. It's because of her that I understand the importance of loyalty and stability. Because of her, I realized there are things worth fighting for, worth dying for. I guess you could even say the light I have seen in her has helped me understand the Light all that better." He sat the mug down, squared his shoulders, and leveled his gaze at them both. "I'm sorry I'm not the hero you expected. I'm sorry I won't do this the way you want, but this is who I am. I may be the Ninth Chosen but I am also Tolen Parks, a kid who grew up thinking he was a freak and only learned a little over a month ago that he was supposed to save the world." He paused and looked out Kichaya's dirty window.

"I can't save a world that doesn't know it needs to be saved." He turned back and met Quasar's eyes. "There's something I must do after I transcend."

"You have decided to be a Chosen?" Kichaya asked, her eyes hopeful.

Her face fell when Tolen shook his head. "I'm afraid I can't answer that yet. But whether I choose to follow that destiny or not my next steps will be the same. Even if I choose to give back my shard I will still see the future and there are two things I want to change about the future I've seen."

Quasar cleared his throat. "What is that?"

"I'm going to the Shadow Realm. I'm going to rescue Blaze's family—and any other Lafar I can." Quasar opened his mouth but Tolen lifted his hand up to stop any argument. "After that, I'm going after Macy. She needs my help. I will go where I need to go, when the time is right." He couldn't stop the tiny smile at their shocked faces.

Warmth swelled in his chest and he knew he was on the right track.

Quasar pushed out of his chair and stood up. "I'm sorry Tolen, but I don't think you've thought this through. You cannot face the entire Daklafar army *in* the Shadow Realm alone, Ninth Chosen or not."

"I won't be alone," Tolen whispered, his eyes never wavering from Quasar's.

Quasar shook his head, but his eyes had turned calculating.

A blossom of relief and anticipation caused Tolen's smile to grow more pronounced.

"How do you expect us to get in?"

Tolen looked toward the back where Blaze rested.

"You would drag him back in there after all he's been through?"

"Quasar, Bastian taught me nothing ever happens without a reason. There are no such things as coincidences. My path has been guided my entire life—I never realized just how much until recently, but it has. You were meant to bring me here. I was meant to save Blaze. His role is bigger than we realize. I cannot see the distant future as it relates to him, but I feel his importance." Quasar's expression turned angry. "And so have you."

Quasar said nothing and Tolen sighed.

"You said you felt it was your duty to right the wrong committed by Nova, but it was more than that—you were led to me. You brought me here. Why? Because you felt like it was the right thing to do. I saved Blaze because it felt right. Every time I follow what *feels right* it leads me down the right path, not always the easiest one, but the right one."

"Tolen, you are attempting something that many of my people have already tried at and failed. The Daklafar have made their choices, and it's something my entire race has paid for for centuries. The world would not be happy if the Ninth died trying to save a bunch of *elves*." Quasar spat out the last word, letting the derogatory remark cut through the air.

Tolen placed a gentle hand on Quasar's arm, pausing his pacing. "Then it's time we show the world the truth."

"Which is?" Quasar's chest heaved, but hope blazed in his eyes.

"That the Light loves the Lafar. If They didn't, if They had forgotten them, the Ninth would not be led to save them. It's time for this prejudice to end. The Light desires this. It is the right thing to do. I know it, just as I knew going after my father was the right thing to do. By saving him, I weakened the Dark. I uncovered a plot that gave the Guardians more time to prepare. By rescuing the Lafar imprisoned in the Shadow Realm, we can cause significant hurt to their forces. We take away their slaves; show them they can be attacked in their own realm. What better way to get them to back off me and start strategics? We enter the realm with Blaze, someone who knows their way around, knows their ways, knows their *weaknesses*. You have to admit," Tolen swallowed, "if Nova's parents had had such an advantage, their chances would have been that much better."

Quasar turned toward the window, arms folded across his chest. "I won't deny I greatly desire this. I want to succeed where so many of my friends have failed, but am I willing to go along with you just because of my own desires? I'm not sure. You need to issue the Call. We need to gather our armies. The Dark is taking us out one small village at a time. It knows you are a formidable foe. I am certain they are devising a plan to annihilate you."

If this was supposed to be a pep talk, he could use a few lessons in optimism.

Quasar slowly turned back around. "It stands to reason, then, that the last thing they would expect would be for you to go into their own realm to rescue creatures they believe to be under their control. But how can we possibly succeed?"

Tolen glanced to Kichaya for reassurance. Her face was impassive, but her eyes were twinkling. He took it as a good sign. "The Light will guide us."

Quasar shook his head, but he hadn't seen what Tolen had seen, what he had felt. He stood up and gripped Quasar's shoulder. "We have to trust the Light will show us the way it is to be done. I won't rush into anything. We'll follow the steps in the order the Light directs."

Kichaya had remained silent during the whole exchange, but now she stood up and put one hand on Tolen's arm and the other on Quasar's clenched fist. "We have to let go of our assumptions Quasar. The prophecy never told us how the Ninth would behave; it just said he would be our only hope. The future is not set. The Final Battle was prophesied because the actions of the Dark made it an absolute. The Light, through the Balance, has provided us with the chance we need to defeat it."

She lifted her chin toward Tolen, her muddy eyes shining. "The time has come for stronger faith. Faith in the choice of the Light, and faith in the child who works his fate with his own hands."

Quasar ran his hands over his scarred face, closed his eyes, and spoke firmly. "You honestly feel this is the course you must take?" He kept his eyes closed.

Tolen took a deep breath. "I *know* this is the course I must take."

Quasar drew in a shaky breath. "Then I will go with you." He turned, Kichaya and Tolen stepped back as Quasar resumed his pacing. "One minor problem. We're going to have everything imaginable on our tails in the next few hours."

Kichaya squeezed Tolen's fingers. "Tolen will succeed in the Capka. He will control it." She smiled, showing her shiny pink gums. "Of this I have no doubt."

Hope swelled in Tolen's chest, overtaking the fear of what tomorrow might bring.

The corner of Kichaya's crinkly mouth lifted. Tolen could see the hope and faith in her eyes. At least two people believed in him. Well, three. Bastian believed in him too.

He looked up at Quasar to see skepticism in his eyes. He met his gaze until Quasar looked away.

Tolen didn't know what it would take to get Quasar to believe in him. Probably the same thing it was going to take for everyone else.

A miracle.

ooo

Macy stopped in the center of the path and Keelyn bumped into her. "Macy?"

Macy waited for the others to catch up. "Toke, I just realized. Today is July 9th."

"Yes it is. And?"

"Tol—the Ninth turns eighteen tomorrow."

"What?" Brina shifted from foot to foot and her hands blurred.

Rune put his hand on Keelyn's back. "What's going to happen?"

"I don't know." Toke looked up at the sky. "But I imagine it will be something spectacular to behold."

38 THE STRENGTH OF A CHILD

TOLEN FOLLOWED QUASAR into Blaze's room.

Bren sat beside the young boy, helping him eat a bowl of soup. He was clean and his thick, blue-black shoulder-length hair was tied in a sleek ponytail. He wore a pair of leather trousers and a white cotton top. He sat propped up against the wall, his weakened body trembling slightly, his eyes moving nervously back and forth from Tolen to Quasar.

Bren held out the spoon to regain the boy's attention. "It's okay, Blaze. These are the men who helped save you." Blaze still looked afraid.

Tolen's heart clenched as he thought of all this child had suffered in his short life. He walked over and pointed to another chair beside the bed. "May I?"

Blaze slowly nodded. He glanced at Quasar, and Tolen followed his gaze. The older Lafar remained in the doorway, his face impassive.

Tolen rested his elbows on his knees and dropped his chin on top of his laced fingers. "Please eat. You need your strength."

Bren lifted the spoon and this time the boy turned his head and opened his mouth, but his eyes stayed on Tolen.

"Do you know why I saved you?"

Blaze tilted his head and nodded once.

"It's hard for him to speak," Bren whispered. "He remembers the language, but it's difficult for him to form the words. His mind is still healing. Memories create pathways in the brain that are hard to reroute."

Blaze frowned. His lips moved for several seconds before the words finally came out awkward and choppy. "Old woman…t-told me."

"You know that I heard your thoughts?"

He nodded again.

"Then you know who I am?"

"*Conchla…M-Mindra.*" Blaze croaked. "You are the Ninth."

Tolen took a deep breath. It was crucial that he get this out right. He'd sensed the boy's love for his family through his thoughts and memories. He knew Blaze would want to go back and try to save his people, but did it make it right to ask so much of one so young? Seeing him now, full of light, he looked much younger than fourteen and far more vulnerable. What had felt like such a good plan moments ago seemed less so now. Maybe Quasar was right, maybe they should try this without him. The boy continued to watch him, his expression quizzical.

"How are you feeling?"

Blaze raised his eyebrows. "B-better than I was after they shot me with that arrow." His lips turned up in a half smile.

Tolen chuckled once. "I bet."

"Wh-when you were h-healing me I-I saw m-my whole life pass by…" And his eyes said he knew, he knew Tolen had been there reliving those memories with him.

"Yes, I saw your past. I saw your family."

Blaze's eyes filled with tears. "I m-must save them. Please, *Conchla Mindra*, I know y-you can help me save them." He leaned forward, almost upsetting the bowl of soup in Bren's hands, and the color drained from his face.

Tolen laid a hand on his shoulder and gently pushed him back against the wall. "It's okay, I want to help them if I can."

Relief flooded the boy's face and Tolen's heart ached again for all he'd suffered.

"Wait, Tolen." Quasar stepped into the room and grasped Tolen's shoulder. "Are you sure about this?" Quasar worked hard to sound neutral, but his fear for the boy was obvious. He'd wanted to hate the child when he wore the features of the Daklafar, but now he wanted nothing more than to protect him, just as Tolen did. "He has already been through so much. Can he not stay here?"

Blaze shook his head. "No. My family. She—they need me. Celeste…" His breathing hitched and his trembling increased.

"It's okay, Blaze." Tolen touched the boy's forehead. "*Lon'adras. Pench Ni'yālo.*"

Blaze's trembling stopped and serenity softened the concern on his face.

"I need you to trust me." Tolen placed his hand on the Blaze's arm, coaxing more warmth and light into the boy's cells. "I have a plan and I'd like your help, but I'm not sure yet if that includes you going in there with me or just sharing your knowledge of the Shadow Realm with us. We need to see how quickly you heal, and weigh the risks, okay?"

The boy swallowed, and squeezed his eyes shut.

"But I promise Blaze, I will do all I can to help them."

Blaze opened his violet eyes, seemed to sense the truth of Tolen's proclamation, and nodded.

Quasar's sigh of relief reaffirmed Tolen's split second decision to alter his original plan.

Tolen knew there was a good chance they would all die, but it was like Macy told him hours before they stormed—well, sneaked into—the Shadow Prison:

"Is this really the best idea? Probably not. Is there a chance we could both die? Yeah, sure. But guess what, Tolen? This is the life of a Chosen. Every day is crazy and risky. Our destinies as Chosen were not meant to be easy, just worth everything we have to go through in the end."

They had nearly died as they tried to rescue his parents from the Shadow Realm, and probably would have if he hadn't somehow opened a link directly to the citadel, summoning the Guardians.

Never in a million years did he think he'd be going back to that place of horror, but this time he *was* stronger. He understood so much more. He knew he was nowhere near as comfortable with his gifts as he needed to be. But he felt more ready to do this now than ever before.

Blaze looked at Quasar. "If y-you succeed in saving our people you will have a great advantage in the battles with the Dark. We know much from living within that realm." The boy seemed to sense Quasar's reluctance to go in.

Quasar nodded once.

Blaze took a piece of bread from Bren's outstretched fingers and chewed absently. "W-what is the plan?"

"First, we need a way into the Shadow Realm." Tolen's heart lifted seeing the boy feed himself. "Can you open a link?"

Blaze shook his head. "O-only captains."

Tolen bit his lip.

Kichaya spoke from the doorway. "You can open a gateway, Tolen. I was told you have done so once already."

He turned in his seat. "Once, to the Light Realm, by accident. I have no idea how I did it."

Kichaya tilted her head. "I have a theory. Gatekeepers are always two, one Lóklana and one Sphere. During the Revolution, they used their power to open direct links, or what I prefer to call gateways, from field hospitals to the citadel in order to transport the severely injured." She tapped her temple. "Because you hold both Sphere and Lóklana gifts within you, I think this is why you could open a gateway. I heard you also have the curse of the Dreamers?"

"Curse describes it better than gift." His eyebrows rose and a grim smile stretched his lips. The Light giving him a single Dark gift was beginning to make even more sense. "You think because I am both Sphere and Dreamer, that's how I can open a link, I mean a gateway?"

She nodded slowly. "The Light will have given you this curse because only darkness can understand darkness. And the Dreamer Curse, though horrible, is the least likely of the Dark abilities to corrupt the Ninth. You are a formidable foe."

He didn't like carrying around anything from the Dark, but if he could use it against them. "I still don't know how I did it."

"I will consult with the Light. You must go to the Capka. Quasar is to go with you. You can plan there. I will care for Blaze. He will be accepted into the tribe this evening while you transcend. By this time tomorrow, Blaze will be well, and you will know what to do."

The boy's violet eyes lit up and a warm smile broke across his face.

39 THE CAPKA

THE CAPKA RESTED a fair distance from the main village, its existence camouflaged by dense foliage and uninviting prickly vines and bushes. Tolen thought it looked like nothing more than miles of weed patch—until he stepped inside the disguise.

Inside was a circle of ten grass, mud, and stone huts, all covered with bright flowers and tendrils of leafy, green vines. It was warm and inviting and held the same majesty and power as the Citadel of Light.

As they walked into the clearing in the middle of the circled huts, people in long deep green robes started coming out of them. Two from each hut, one man and one woman.

They came toward Tolen and Quasar until they were surrounded.

"Welcome, *Mindra*." A tall, thin man, with hair spilling over his shoulders the color of teak stepped forward and grasped Tolen's arm. "My name is Lynd. We prepared a hut for your transcendence. Come." He swept his arm to the left and waited for Tolen to fall into step beside him. Quasar and the others followed in a line behind.

Lynd continued to speak as he walked, his voice was gentle, soft, and reminded Tolen of a soft summer breeze. "Transcendence is the most momentous occasion in life, *Conchla Mindra*. It is a beautiful gift that should be cherished and not feared. Because you are the Ninth and your gifts are more numerous than most, your experience will differ than the rest of your kind, and so you have come to fear this sacred experience. I wish to change your perception."

He glanced over and gave Tolen a tiny smile and nod. "I have summoned some of the best Spheres to help you through this night, *Mindra*.

I do not believe Darkness shall touch this place tonight. Tomorrow the Dark may be able to sense you, but that remains to be seen. Tonight, you are safe in the Capka, protected by Spheres and great warriors." He paused outside the door of a particularly leafy hut.

"*Mindra*, there is something you must understand as you go forward. The person you are now will cease to exist in its current form. You will retain your memories, desires, loyalties, every feeling and experience you've ever had, but your perception of them will change, intensify.

"In a transcended, metaphysical body, your gifts will strengthen as will every emotion you've ever felt, every connection to every experience and person you've ever had. Your current body is incapable of withstanding such an emotional climate. Your new body brings an ability to love fuller, learn faster, see more clearly." He touched Tolen's arm and a zing of warmth passed into his heart. "Allow the change to come, *Mindra*. Do not fight it and it will be the greatest gift you'll ever receive."

He opened the door, motioned Tolen and Quasar inside, and followed behind them to stand just inside. The tiny hut barely fit the three of them. Tolen's head nearly brushed the ceiling. "Transcendence comes in three phases." Lynd placed his hands inside hidden pockets of his robe. "The Source, the Meridian, and the Crown. The Source will be the most unpredictable as it is unique to the individual. The Meridian will be the most dangerous as this is when the gifts reach their highest strength—the body will be tested as will the life force. With so many gifts it could be very painful," he looked at Quasar. "Do what you must to keep him inside these walls at that time."

Tolen looked nervously between the two as Lynd went on. "The final phase, the Crown, is the settling of the Balance around your new visage—the final stage of transcendence to your true self. Everything comes together with the Crowning. It is the longest phase. It takes time for the power and knowledge within the body to equalize." He sighed and looked around. "Eat. You will need your strength for what lies ahead. We will be concentrating too hard to hear you or speak, but I will know when each phase has ended, and I will come check on you." He gripped Quasar's arm, and a knowing look passed between them.

Tolen's stomach twisted. He glanced at his watch as the door closed. Five-thirty. If the change began on the anniversary of his birth hour, he had just over seven hours.

Tolen dropped his pack onto the floor and sat on one of the tightly woven mats that served as a bedroll. Quasar situated himself on the other bedroll and looked at Tolen with a somber expression.

All he could do now was wait.

Six-thirty. Tolen munched on a piece of bread hoping it would settle his turning stomach. Quasar stared out the window at the setting sun.

Seven-thirty. Tolen lay back counting the thin beams in the ceiling above him.

He dozed off and on, but by nine o'clock the anticipation threatened to drive him insane. He struck up a conversation with Quasar to keep from running away screaming. "Can I ask you something?"

Quasar looked up from sharpening his knife and nodded.

As the question formed on his lips he faltered. He really had no right to ask.

Quasar leaned forward slightly. "Yes?"

"It's about Nova."

Quasar sighed. "What would you like to know?"

"What was she like? She seemed so kind, but…" Tolen trailed off, feeling guilty for asking about something so painful.

"She *was* kind," he said defensively and sighed. "And funny, mischievous, and brave." He chuckled sadly. "She was a handful. My wife, Nebula, always complained about Nova's dirty feet. That child never wore shoes." He drew lines in the dirt. "Nebula and I lost our only child some years back. But Bolide and Nova always felt like our own flesh and blood. Their parents were our dearest friends."

"I'm sorry to bring up painful memories, Quasar. Just seeing Blaze's life, seeing the way his parents were good, even as prisoners in the Shadow Realm, I see how Daemon managed to tempt Nova. If he showed her truth, that her parents really are still alive and just prisoners…Seeing it firsthand, I can't blame her for what she did. She saw betrayal as her only option. I wish I could have known more about who I was—what I know now. I wish I could have understood. I wish I could have saved her." He met Quasar's gaze while offering only words, but hoping the man knew how much he meant them. "I truly am sorry."

Quasar nodded once and looked back at his knife. He glided the blade over the sharpening stone a few times and his voice trembled slightly when he spoke. "Curiosity about Nova and my race is understandable, Tolen. We have not given you much reason to trust us." He placed a hand on Tolen's foot. "Do not blame yourself for Nova's death." He took a slow breath. "Her choices determined her fate."

"My ignorance of my destiny didn't help the situation though."

Quasar inclined his head, allowing that. His eyes narrowed. "Tolen, you are aware of my negative feelings toward you when we first met. I admit there was a lot of bitterness in me. I was angry with your parents, with Jonas, with the Guardians, and with you." He slid his knife back in its sheath and crossed his long legs beneath him. "But I never blamed you for Nova's death. Being cursed as I am, I understand all too well fate and destiny. I accepted her mistakes as the cause of her death but I was still angry. Angry that the choices of others had skewed the prophecy, dampened hope, and given the Dark a head start." He held up a hand. "None of this is your fault. That is important for you to understand. I am impressed with you, Tolen Daedal Téloran." His thick scar pulled up in a gentle smile that transformed his face and lessened Tolen's guilt. "Selflessness doesn't come easy, but I see you try—consistently try—to fulfill your purpose. That is a rare quality."

His smile widened. "Watching you, I must admit I finally have hope. I may not always agree with how you do things. You are young and naive. But perhaps those of us who have lived for so long forget that the young see the world with fresh eyes. Wisdom comes with age, which stands to reason that it is the choices we made when we were young that brought us wisdom."

His gaze turned serious. "I will go with you, Tolen. Wherever your path leads."

Touched, and more grateful than he knew how to express, Tolen reached out to shake Quasar's arm. His previous reservations about this Lafar melted away, replaced with a respect and admiration as great as he felt for Incrah and the Radia Warriors, but also different, deeper. Possibly because like Tolen, Quasar also had to work hard to change the others' opinions that were based solely on who he was born to be.

"Thank you, Quasar. For everything." It didn't fully say how he felt, but when Quasar met his eyes he seemed to understand.

The next two hours passed in silence. Quasar dozed off shortly after their chat. Tolen tried to sleep, but every nerve in his body had begun to tingle. He didn't know if it was because it anticipated the change coming, or if it was just his own anxiety. It felt weird waiting for his birthday like this. As a young child he had stayed up late eagerly counting down the hours until he could open the present from his mother.

She always made a big deal of his birthday. She made the most delicious pie—never a cake like the other kids on their birthdays, with thick frosting and wax candles. She always said her triple-layered fruit pie and way of celebrating had been passed down in her family for centuries. Instead of games and silly songs, the whole family would gather for a big meal where they talked about you and your life accomplishments, and at the moment the clock chimed the hour of your birth, your parents handed over a gift that specially signified the new stage of life you were entering into.

It felt strange to see his past in a new light. His mother had bestowed Hidden traditions on him his entire life and he'd never realized it. So much he hadn't understood, so much he'd taken for granted, so much he'd resented being different. But here, living among his own kind, he felt nothing but gratitude for what made him different. He was becoming proud of his race and culture. He still wished Macy and he were the same, but he could no longer say he wished he were "normal". It was a nice feeling, freeing almost, to not only accept what made him different than those he'd spent his life comparing himself to, but to deeply care about and appreciate his uniqueness. It was also helping him more fully forgive his mother.

Despite her choices, despite giving in to her fears, she loved him. She only wanted what was best for him. And she had tried, hard, to give him as best of a life as she could. She wasn't human, yet she'd lived among them, giving up her traditions and family ties to protect him. She had been a brave warrior and a kind mother. His eyes pricked and he rubbed them with his fists.

"Are you afraid?" Quasar whispered.

Tolen jerked his eyes open and looked over to see Quasar watching him. "It is understandable to be afraid," he said gently.

Tolen shook his head and looked back at the ceiling. "I'm afraid, but not really about Transcendence. It makes me nervous, but not…"

"Not as nervous as your destiny as the Ninth Chosen." Quasar sat up and rested his chin on his knee. "It is a grand destiny Tolen, but you will not face it alone."

Tolen nodded. "I know, it's just the more I know about my destiny and my strengths, the more I see my weaknesses. You told me I didn't need to train, I needed to *become*. I am feeling that happen here as I bond with my kind, learn my culture. I feel my path shifting in the direction that will help me become the Ninth."

He took a deep breath. "I think I finally understand something that makes accepting who I am that much easier. This role, this destiny, it goes way beyond me. I'm meant to be a symbol, a captain, a blossom of hope. I'm a tool, an instrument—and I accept this. I welcome it even, because it means I'm not solely responsible for saving the world as I had first thought. I just need to lead the movement. Spur the action." Tolen ran a hand over his face. "It's just sometimes I feel like a tool who doesn't understand the instructions and an instrument who can't read the music."

"I think that is how we all feel from time to time, *Mindra*." Quasar pointed out the window. "I see visions I do not understand. I desire revenge, but the means of delivering retribution are often kept from me. I don't believe any of us ever know exactly what is expected of us *all* the time. But we are never alone in any moment of our lives. A voice will always guide you toward the next step to take and teach you the notes if you are listening." He pulled out his Fire Stone and sat it between them where it glowed softly, illuminating the tiny hut. "Trust in the Light, Tolen. Follow your heart. It has led you this far and has not been wrong."

Tolen nodded and closed his eyes. Quasar was right, but knowing what to do and having the courage to do it were two very different things.

Quasar sat up taller. "The time of your Transcendence is close."

Tolen knew this. He could feel it. At some point in their conversation the tingle in his nerves had increased to a slow burn—sort of like how he felt after hours of stacking shelves in Mr. Grange's store. He glanced at his watch. The face began to glow more brightly. If his Transcendence commenced at the exact hour he turned eighteen, 12:42 a.m., then there was only twenty minutes to go.

Uncomfortable heat started building in his toes.

"Quasar?" Tolen's tone had Quasar rolling up to his knees.

Quasar put a hand on Tolen's forehead. "Stay calm." Tolen tried to slow his breathing and not be afraid.

Ten minutes. The wind picked up and began to whirl around the hut.

Five minutes. The sky darkened to deep black outside the window.

Three minutes. Tolen put his hands over his eyes, as his surroundings seemed to pitch and sway. He could hear Quasar speaking but his head had become clouded with a million voices and he couldn't decipher what he was trying to say.

Two minutes. Colors swirled behind his closed lids, nauseating him.

One minute. Fire clawed through his veins and his body started to shake making his teeth rattle.

"Tolen, don't fight it!" Quasar's voice seemed far away, an echo.

Ten seconds. The colors continued to swirl, but a tiny pinprick of light appeared and Tolen felt drawn to its strength, its warmth, its truth.

Three seconds. White-hot light burst from Tolen's body knocking Quasar onto his back.

Two.

One.

Quasar shielded his eyes when another burst of light filled the hut.

He lowered his hands when the light faded and jumped to his feet.

Tolen had disappeared.

JULY 10

TRANSCENDENCE

40 THE MERIDIAN

Macy woke up not long after midnight with her body tingling. A strange power crackled in the air. She felt its strength and anticipation. Her shard started to glow and warm against her throat. She opened her eyes to see the others looking around—their shards also glowing. All at once the entire forest let loose. Birds chirped excitedly, wolves howled, owls hooted—Connell's owl took off and flew circles above their heads—the cricket song increased, the half-dead vines covering the trees they slept under sprouted leaves and giant white flowers until their little campsite became a beautiful hidden garden.

Toke sat up and a huge smile lit his face. "What did I tell you? Many will wake up with strengthened hope this day."

Rune snorted. "Or wake up screaming."

Keelyn slapped his arm.

"What? The humans who notice this are going to think they've gone loony. The Hidden who have paid attention to the signs have just learned the Ninth turned eighteen—when they might not even have realized that he'd been born—and now they have to face the fact that the Final Battle isn't far away. And the Chosen around the world are having panic attacks as they try to prepare to move when the Ninth issues the Call. Trust me, there are a lot of people screaming right now."

Toke sighed and lay back down. "Get some sleep. We'll head out early."

Macy's throat felt thick. She'd dreaded the arrival of Tolen's birthday for weeks. She knew it was going to be terrifying for him—the overwhelming emotions, the surge of power, the shifting flux in the Balance that would make him instantly visible to the Dark, drawing in any creature within a hundred miles. She prayed the Zenith was powerful enough to protect him.

Stay strong Tolen. She lay back on her blanket but couldn't get her eyes to close. *Stay strong, shield.*

ooo

"Tolen!" Quasar screamed and looked around. He couldn't feel the subtle vibrations he learned to attribute to the boy. The Ninth had disappeared.

Quasar's muscles tightened in rising panic.

An unearthly howl ripped through the darkness and Quasar ran out of the hut. Faint light glowed from the other buildings. He ran to them one by one, banging on the doors, but no one responded to his cries, too focused on maintaining the shield to hear him.

ooo

Tolen was flying.

Over the trees, their leaves passing beneath him in a long, green blur, beyond a wide rushing river, through clouds that covered his skin in icy mist, past vast cities dotted with huge skyscrapers shrouded in choking clouds of pollution, above the most impoverished settlements that turned his stomach, across rural towns and neighborhoods—both upper class and destitute.

In what felt like a single moment, he traversed every inch of the planet. But more than that, he *felt* the people below him. He felt their despair, loneliness, and fear. And just when he thought it would be too much, he sensed their hope and courage as they faced their challenges.

His mind flooded with their thoughts. His heart swelled and ached with their feelings. With each thought, with each bout of courage he witnessed, with every view of love and loyalty, his desire to protect and help these people grew.

His thoughts began to quiet as he rose higher and higher until he floated in space and looked down at the earth as a sphere. Countries became brown and green masses encircled by deep blue and wisps of soft fluffy white.

Beautiful.

As he watched, a new darkness dimmed the light of the sun and stars, and a growing dread filled his heart. Veils of darkness began to drape the earth the same way he'd seen it in the vision with Hunsí. The shrouds were so dense in places that the light could not get through. Evil grew alarmingly fast—humans and Hidden kind suffered from its effects.

Soon there would be more darkness than light. He felt it, saw it happening. If the humans didn't learn about their true past soon, about the truth of what happened beyond their physical sight, all would be lost. They would not recover from this.

A sense of urgency replaced his wonder and his body began to descend. Faster and faster he flew, until everything passed in a blur. The wind stung his cheeks. His eyes watered, but he did not try to figure out how to slow down. He must hurry! It was worse than anyone knew.

The hut appeared and Tolen squeezed his eyes shut before he crashed through the roof, but the crash never came. He blinked and looked up into the shocked faces of Quasar, Lynd, and a huge member of the Guard—he couldn't remember his name—illuminated by the light of the Fire Stone.

"You see. I told you he never really left." Lynd touched Tolen's forehead. "You did well in the first phase, *Mindra*. You will complete the two remaining phases over the next few hours. Try to rest. I must get back to the others. Your power has indeed increased, but you are shielding well. We should be able to maintain the extra protection necessary for the village until you finish." He stood up. "Good luck."

"I'll let the others know," the burly guard muttered and quickly left the hut, leaving Quasar staring at Tolen.

Tolen tried to stand but a feeling of vertigo seized him and he lay back down. It was still dark outside, he could see stars outside the window—millions of them.

The forest was alive with sound. He could feel the life forces of the trees, hear the thoughts of animals, along with distant whispers of people, but it wasn't at all overwhelming. He found he could think *around* the voices.

"What did Lynd mean I never really left? I saw the whole world. I could see it, smell it, feel it. I was not here." Tolen rubbed his eyes.

Quasar dropped down beside Tolen. "I've never seen anything like it. You disappeared in a blaze of light. I ran from the hut, I tried to raise Lynd and the others, and when I couldn't, I ran into the forest and questioned the guard. The Balance shifted. I'm certain the whole world felt it. No one outside the Capka saw anything. I ran back to the hut to see Lynd kneeling over your bed waving his hand in the air.

"He said the Balance shifted around you, that you were in the *between* world of the Dicernan—existing within the Balance, neither here nor there."

Tolen shook his head. That explained why he never felt himself crash through the roof. "So the next phase will be dangerous?"

Quasar sighed and stood up to put hot liquid into two mugs, his hands trembling. He passed Tolen one of the steaming cups. "Lucid." He waited for Tolen to prop himself up on one elbow before settling back to the ground with his own mug. "We don't really know what to expect. Many experience at the Meridian an outward push from their gifts. They burst forth without control."

Tolen thought of how Mahto said he'd flattened some of the Capka's huts and shivered. The hand holding the mug shook as he sipped the warm liquid.

Quasar drank from his cup and sounded calmer as he continued. "Lynd is not sure what you will do. You have already experienced many uncontrolled bursts of power in your life, which suggests you may know what to expect and therefore have more control."

"That's what you're hoping, you mean."

Quasar shrugged.

"Any idea how long before it starts?" Tolen ran a shaky hand through his hair. The sense of urgency hadn't left. He knew they needed to go forward with his plan, but he couldn't go anywhere until he finished transcending and they were able to plan with Blaze. Funny, a day ago he'd been dreading this, yet now, even at the prospect of pain and misery in the next phase, all he wanted was to get it over with and get back out there.

Quasar shook his head. "It's different—"

"For everyone." Tolen tipped his chin. "You'd think I'd quit asking by now." He took a deep breath. The Lucid had relaxed him some as well as given him a small burst of energy. He pulled Tashta's basket over and rummaged through the food. He passed over the fruit and unwrapped a thick piece of cured ham. While he chewed, he pulled out more and offered it to Quasar, who declined. Tolen continued to scarf down slices of ham, cheese, and bread, until his stomach felt like it would burst.

"Are you finished, or do you have room for dessert?" Quasar held back a grin as he tugged a small box out of his pack and lifted the lid to show Tolen what was inside.

Tolen's eyes widened. "Is that—?"

"Triple-layered berry pie?" Quasar chuckled. "Yes. Tashta made it for your birthday. She asked me to surprise you at the right moment." He looked at the crumbs in Tolen's lap. "You weren't in the mood to eat earlier, but it seems your appetite has returned."

Tolen grinned as Quasar put a slice of pie and a fork on two plates, handed Tolen one, and then lifted his plate up. "To your life, Tolen."

"Thank you." Tolen raised his plate in reply, sliced his wooden fork through the soft pie, and lifted a bite to his lips. When his teeth sank into the crispy crust and the juice flooded his mouth, a soft moan escaped his lips. "It's just like I remember." He looked down as he finished, thinking of his mother, wishing she and his father were here with him. He knew they'd be thinking of him in this moment. He hoped they knew how much he loved them.

"So *Mindra*. What are your life accomplishments? Who is Tolen Daedal Téloran?" Quasar wiped his mouth on a cotton napkin and leaned against the side of the hut.

Tolen scraped the last tiny crumbs of pie off his plate and set it on the ground beside him. He was grateful to Quasar for trying to make this a more special occasion for him, and maybe even distract him from the fact that his family wasn't here with him, but he wasn't sure he wanted to share about his life. Surely the human life he'd led would not seem like much of an accomplishment. "I really haven't done much."

"On the contrary, I've heard otherwise. But, aside from your recent exploits, I'm curious about *you* Tolen. What were you like as a child?"

Tolen shifted his position so he could also lean against the wall of the hut. "I was a turd."

"A what?"

"Turd." Tolen smiled. "It's just another name for stubborn and unpleasant."

Quasar's eyes widened.

"I liked adventure. I loved spending time outside and pretending I was some sort of storybook hero. I didn't like hiding who I was. My mom made me wear a contact in my blue eye to keep people from noticing me and I hated it. I'd take it out whenever she wasn't looking. After several odd looks from strangers I relented. It made me feel more like a villain than a hero when people looked at me that way." He shook his head at the memory.

"We moved around. A lot. Every time someone got suspicious or started asking too many questions we'd leave. Sometimes she'd change our names. It wasn't until we moved to Green River that she finally let me use my first name again. I never knew my real last name until the Guardians told me." Tolen put his hands behind his head and shrugged.

"That must have been hard." Quasar propped his leg up and clasped his hands over his knee. "Most children rebel when uncomfortable. They can sense when things are not as they should be, but they do not understand what is going on, or how to deal with it."

Tolen shrugged again. "I still feel guilty for making my mom put up with so much from me."

"Turd."

Tolen chuckled. "Yes. Turd."

Quasar smiled. "There must have been some accomplishments though. Some things about your former life you are proud of?"

Tolen glanced at the ceiling. "My mom would have a list."

"What would she have said?"

Something burned the bottom of Tolen's foot. He grabbed his toes and cringed. "I think it's time for phase two."

Quasar nodded. "Keep talking—it might distract you from the pain. Your mother?"

Tolen swallowed. "Okay…um." It felt as if he'd stuck his foot in a barbecue grill. "She—she would be listing off my grades and touting the fact that I would have graduated in the top ten percent of my class." He sucked in a breath as the fire moved to both feet. "Which really isn't saying much since my graduating class only had seventy-five students." He forced a laugh as the burn climbed up his legs. He was almost afraid to look down. He started panting and sweat began to drip into his eyes.

Quasar leaned forward. "I can feel the heat, Tolen. Kunamin is a very powerful gift. I'm not surprised it is manifesting first. Just keep breathing. It will be worse when it reaches your heart." He grabbed a rag off the table and dipped it in the pot of Lucid. "Hold that on your forehead."

Tolen put the rag on his head and tried to concentrate on its soothing effects.

"Tell me more," Quasar encouraged.

Tolen spoke through clenched teeth as the Kuna pushed upward. It was in his stomach, inches from his heart. "I—she'd probably have a list she compiled of all the books I've read." A tortured groan escaped his throat as the Kuna touched his heart. He lay down and clutched at his chest.

Quasar took the rag and dripped Lucid over Tolen's face. "You like to read?"

Tolen nodded, his chest getting hotter.

Quasar spoke louder trying to keep up the distraction. "What sorts of books?"

Tolen started panting. "Science, philosophy, mixed in with a lot of science fiction and fan-fantasy." The heat surged into his heart and he couldn't stop the scream that tore from him. Scalding heat slammed into his palms and he pushed them to the ground which instantly glowed red-hot.

"Tolen, aim out the window!"

Tolen sat up and tried to turn, but the flame shot from his hands before he could and he blasted out the side of the hut, the burst so hot and quick nothing remained but a few smoldering pieces of ceiling.

Tolen twisted over onto his hands and knees.

41 THE CROWN

A STRANGE SORT OF power hardened Tolen's muscles. The pain this time felt like the strain of trying to lift weights too heavy for him.

In his mind he saw the long, lithe body of a cheetah, a majestic golden lion, a towering Grizzly, an eagle soaring through the sky with its wings spread wide—and he knew he was gaining the blessing of the Animashta. His muscles understood how the animals moved, his mind understood how they thought, his instincts linked to their instincts. Being Animashta was more than being empathetic to the animal mind. As they accepted him, he became *one* with them. Their strengths became his strengths. And if he was not careful, their weaknesses his weakness. Outside, wolves began to howl, owls hooted, birds chirped, and a dozen other animals joined the call.

Quasar dripped more Lucid over Tolen's neck.

Tolen's body moved without his control, pulling him to his knees, chest out, arms splayed open. His muscles locked in place. He couldn't move. The pain changed. His body felt as if it was being turned to stone. The dirt beneath him rumbled and loosened, wind rushed in through the broken wall, whirling the dirt into a cloud around him. Vines grew in through the window. The dirt and the vines shrouded him in a cocoon that tightened around his frozen body until he could no longer see.

"Tolen!" Quasar shouted just before the last little bit of light from the hut disappeared and the howling wind cut off to frightening silence. He still couldn't move. There was so much pain as he fought against the invisible bonds restraining him.

Tolen, do not fight it! Bastian's voice called through the silence. *Relax. It hurts.*

I know. Hold on. You are almost finished.

Tolen's eyes rolled back in his head and his body started to convulse.

Let go. You are ready.

Tolen took a deep shuddering breath. *Am I?* More pain at the question. Agony.

Yes, Tolen. You are ready. Accept who you are. Transcend.

The pain was blinding, consuming, crushing. His life began to flash before his eyes. Colors and images speeding past, emotions overwhelming his senses. *Macy…*

There she was. Her face in front of the blur of life behind. She reached out her hand, her eyes filled with love and trust. *Stay strong, Tolen. I believe in you. I love you.*

A beautiful yet terrifying future began to play out before his eyes. Macy stood outside a stone house, much like Tashta's home, a small, auburn haired boy by her side and a tiny blond baby girl in her arms. He saw an older version of himself lift the baby out of her arms and nuzzle his face into her neck. A thick scar ran down the length of his right arm, red and puckered. He shared a worried look with Macy as they both looked up toward the sky. Heavy darkness rolled in from every direction, completely obscuring the blue sky and blocking the light from the sun.

She squeezed his hand, not in encouragement, but in defeat. In that moment he realized the future he saw. The future where he chose to give back his shard and the gifts of the Ninth, live a human life-span, with the gifts of the Honitahai and Dembashi as his only ties to his true race. They would have some beauty; they would have a family. His heart clenched. But they would also have horror. Darkness would continue. If the rolling blackness in the sky gave any indication, the Light was losing. Macy's children, *his* children would be raised in a world of Dark—if they survived at all.

Tolen. Macy's frightened voice pulled him from one possible future and dumped him into another. This future was fuzzier, still hazy with indecision, but some things were clear. Macy would be a part of his life, no matter which way he chose. He saw Blaze, Quasar, and himself enter the Shadow Realm. He saw Macy standing in the same strange place he'd seen in the vision he'd had at the citadel, surrounded by Dark creatures—being hunted by Daemon.

"Tolen." Her voice was so clear. The future before his eyes began to fade and once again he could feel his stony muscles cramped in the cocoon.

"Tolen." A soft touch on his hand made him squeeze his eyes shut.

It's not real. It's just an illusion. She's not here.

Fingers traced his jaw and a shiver ran through his locked limbs.

"Tolen? Is this real? Am I really here?"

His eyes snapped open. Macy was sitting in front of him, her beautiful green eyes full of question and awe.

It took every ounce of strength to stretch his stone hand toward her. Their fingers met and fire burst from both their palms, sealing them together. His skin became soft, and he could move his fingers. The flame faded but the light remained.

Macy's face split into a huge grin. "Holy crap! It *is* real! You're real!" And then she was kissing him and it was fire and pleasure and aching joy. Her kiss released the rest of his body from its stony prison and he wrapped his arms around her, relishing in her nearness. He'd missed her beautiful face, but until this moment he had no idea how much he missed the gentleness in her eyes that reflected the beauty within.

She buried her face in his neck. "How is this possible?" Her voice was thick with emotion. "One minute I was staring up at the night sky thinking about you and the next, here I am." She leaned away and bit her lip. "Where are we?"

Tolen shifted into a more comfortable position and pulled her closer to his side. The cocoon was gone, but so was everything else. They sat in a sphere of soft yellow light. If he focused, he could swear he could see stars outside the sphere. He tightened his arms around Macy, almost afraid to speak. His thoughts were becoming all too clear, he understood where they were, and even a little bit of the why, but this knowledge also meant they didn't have long. He took a deep breath. "We're *between*."

She looked up at him and touched his cheek. She looked at his lips and he kissed her again before explaining. "I pulled you into the space between spaces. We're juxtaposed between where you were and where I am."

Her eyebrows drew together. "So we're not really together? How can I feel you then?" She was so beautiful, her green eyes filled with love and joy mingled with confusion.

He cleared his throat, trying to not get distracted by the overwhelming peace and contentment he felt holding her again, and determined to help her understand. "We *are* together, but metaphysically, not physically. We're connected through love and destiny. It's this connection, this link that allows us to be together."

"You sound so sure, so confident, so…*smart*."

Tolen chuckled and traced his finger over her cheek. "Should I be insulted by that?"

"No. You're just different. More mature, I guess." Her brow puckered. "Is that okay?"

Macy feigned concern, but the grin gave her away. "More than okay. It's *very* attractive."

Tolen shook his head and kissed the end of her nose. His arms started to tingle and he knew the sphere was shifting.

"So, how's the Zenith?" She laid her head on his shoulder.

"I'm not in the Zenith."

She leaned her head back to look up.

"It's a long story and we don't have time to get into it."

"How much time do we have?" She bit her lip, and he shook his head.

"Five minutes, maybe less."

"Then let's not waste any time." She kissed his chin. "I've got so much to tell you!"

She spoke fast and used her hands the way he remembered, filling him in on her new friends. Tolen could feel her care for them in her words. She told him what he'd already seen, but he let her talk, just to hear her voice. The light in the sphere was beginning to fade when she finished.

"Our time is almost up." He pushed a lock of hair behind her ear. "There's something I need to ask. Remember when we were in Jonas's camp and you told me we couldn't be together because I am Hidden kind and you are human?"

He saw the grief enter her eyes and he knew she understood what had been plaguing him. "You still chose to be with me, even though I will outlive you by possibly," his voice cracked, "thousands of years?"

She pointed to his watch then touched his face, "Don't you remember what it says?" Moisture pooled in her eyes. "I love you *beyond* time."

Tears filled his own eyes as he reached up to hold her hand against his face. "Why?"

She cleared her throat, but emotion still laced every syllable. "Love rarely makes sense Tolen. All I know is I want to live however many years my life has left, whether it's ten or a hundred, with you."

His heart pounded a painful rhythm in his chest. "Macy, I've been given a choice. I can give back the powers of the Ninth, keep only the gifts in my blood of the Honitahai and Watcher, and live a human life-span…with you."

Her eyes widened and he saw a thousand emotions play across her face. Hope, desire, longing, fear, doubt, pain. "I know it's wrong to want it that way Tolen, but a big part of me does, it really, really does."

He ran his thumb across her lips and leaned forward to kiss her. The pain was returning to his body. They had only moments left. "You know I would. Despite the consequences. I would give up everything to have what I want. *You.*"

She grabbed his face with her hands and kissed him hard. "And that's enough. To know that I mean that much to you. That's more than enough. Your love for me will not stop when I pass through Light's door before you—"

"Don't." He dropped his head to her shoulder. "Please don't say it like that."

She tugged his chin up. "Love transcends death and time. This," she touched his lips, "will never truly end. We can't sacrifice the whole world. They need us."

He closed his eyes and nodded. "I love you Macy. With all that I am." He pulled her into his embrace, and as the light around them dissipated into nothingness he whispered in her ear a final warning and promise. "I can see where you're going, but I don't recognize the place. Macy, you must be careful. Stay focused on the guidance of the Light and Bastian's shard. My Watcher gift is strengthening. I will know when you need help, and I promise it will come. Trust in me. Trust in the Light."

Her image began to blur, he could barely feel her in his arms. "Macy, I love you. Be safe."

"Tolen!"

She faded completely and he was back in the cocoon, her last kiss still warm on his lips, her last words ringing in his ears, *I trust you. I love you.*

The smell of earth and rain filled his nose and everything became perfectly clear. Who he was, why he was here, and what he needed to do.

The crack in his heart was gone. He felt healed, whole, and finally ready.

He saw a vision of the path that began as a baby when he was selected to be the Ninth. It was clear, narrow, and straight. He saw the side road he'd ended up on when his parents tried to change his destiny. The first path was still there, a thin ribbon of white light. He saw how every choice he'd ever made affected his path. Some choices turned his new path back in line with the first, others twisted back out into the void. He saw the path of choice he'd been given for a human life with Macy. It was a different color, a soft gold, and although it ran parallel with the first he could see they were not the same. He realized that even though he could choose not to be the Ninth, the fate of the world would still affect his path. Still carry him toward a destiny partially determined by the fate of Light and Dark.

He could see a third, almost imperceptible path that mimicked the white light of the first path, not as vibrant or solid, more subtle, not yet set.

Possibility.

The less vibrant path intersected, passed over and through the first path, more solid and bright in some places than others. He could see how each side road that took him away taught him something that brought him back to the first path. Curious about what caused the brighter areas, he looked more closely at the choices that had changed the course of his path. As he caught glimpses of his life, he realized that the brightest spots were the points on the path that turned back to the first path—each an act of selfless love.

Your head and your heart were whole in purpose and place in those moments, Bastian whispered and Tolen's life force zinged with truth.

What had motivated him throughout his life? Love. What motivated him to be the Ninth? First, to save his father. Second, to avenge those taken by the Dark. But what would keep him on the path of the Ninth? What was it really that drove him? Made him willing to sacrifice everything?

Love, purpose, and place.

Love for *his* race—the *Eché-mah Ladon*—the Hidden, *and* the human race, and Macy, Bastian, and his parents.

Purpose. Every good creature on this planet deserved the right to happiness and peace and he had been chosen to make that possible. His purpose was to stop the Dark.

Place. His place was to stand between the Dark and the good people of this little blue planet.

His heart swelled with the desire to protect—not just Macy—but all the innocent people of this world from the Dark. He sensed his gifts burn within him, strengthening, combining, molding into him as his mind and his heart became one in purpose. Energy and vitality pushed through his muscles and he felt stronger than he ever had, but for the first time he felt in control of the power, one with it, complete—as if he were welcoming an old friend back into his heart.

The floating screens reappeared in his mind's eye, but they were even clearer than when he'd first envisioned them. The prism of gifts was there too in the background, the colors more vibrant, more alive, completely connected into a beam of white light—separate only when he needed them to be.

His hands began to glow soft yellow, filling the dark cocoon with more warm light. The light moved up his arms, slowly illuminating his body. The space remained tight and cramped, but it became strangely comforting.

Soon he literally glowed inside and out. A gentle calm filled him body and soul. A peace and an understanding, a culmination of the *who* he used to be becoming the *who* he was now. A balance between both worlds. He would still veer once and a while, he knew he was not perfect. But he would take with him what he'd learned and it would only make his path ahead even clearer and filled with even more purpose. He would never again question destiny. He would forge his own path, but it would always lead to the same destiny—and he would love Macy through every part of it for as long as he possibly could with her beside him in the flesh, and then forever after that. He would not have to sacrifice love for duty in order to succeed.

The light brightened further and Tolen swore he could hear the pit-ter-patter of rain hitting the outside of the cocoon.

A soft voice echoed from the walls of his shelter. *"Mindra, the time has come. What do you choose?"*

For the first time, Tolen felt not a single prick of doubt. Pain, yes, but he could survive it. Would survive it. "I accept my role. I choose to be the Ninth Chosen. I choose the path the Light has set." Euphoria such as he could only compare to how he felt when kissing Macy swept through the cocoon.

"Thank you Tolen Daedal Teloran. Your selfless choice will bring hope to the world and many blessings to you as well. Stay true to your heart. You are now ready to pave the path to your destiny."

The walls of the cocoon crumbled.

As the rain washed away what was left of the hut, Tolen stared up into the dawn of a new day with a heart that was whole and filled with purpose.

"You are affecting the Balance, but not in the way we expected." Lynd sat beside Tolen with a pleased expression. The other Spheres and Quasar also sat around him, their eyes weary, but hopeful. "It's strange. Surging. It's too powerful for us to shield one minute, then almost disappears the next, as if you are fully shielding yourself. Whether this is because you have not fully completed your Crown, or the result of some other form of power we have never before seen, we do not know for certain."

Tolen shrugged, unwilling to let the ominous comment affect the lightness he felt. "Well, let's hope it's a good thing."

Lynd tilted his head. "Yes, let's hope."

They all slowly stood up and Tolen shook all their arms. While he expressed his thanks, Quasar stuffed the last of their things into their packs.

Once they'd left the Capka and were far out of earshot of the Spheres, Quasar spoke. "Things are changing already. I can feel it. The forest has awakened around us. I'm certain the Dark knows you have transcended. Either they will aggressively hunt you or they have finally begun to fear you."

"I know."

"Are you ready?"

Tolen took a deep breath and nodded.

"Do you still wish to stick to your plan?"

Tolen nodded again. "Yes."

Quasar dipped his chin once. "Then let's go. I'm certain Kichaya will be waiting."

42 DARKNESS DEFIED

MACY WIPED THE tears from her eyes as she heard the others begin to stir. The ground was hard under her back, but she could still feel Tolen's warmth around her. He'd accepted his role. He was the Ninth body and soul now. This was a good thing, but she couldn't quiet the tiny part of her that grieved for a future lost. She'd never realized that Tolen hadn't put two and two together about their aging before. How hard it must have been for him. He really did love her.

She felt a hand on her shoulder and looked over to see Toke watching her with an understanding smile on his face. "Come on, Macy. It's time to go." She swallowed and nodded.

He squeezed her shoulder and then stood to help the others pack up.

Macy closed her eyes once, and took a deep breath, determined to follow this path, wherever it took them.

○○○

The sun's rays highlighted the roofs of the tiny homes in the village as Tolen and Quasar walked to Kichaya's home. The villagers stood in the streets smiling, and several came forward to shake Tolen's arm and congratulate him. He could feel their acceptance and see the hope in their eyes. They were beginning to believe in him. His heart felt double in size.

Mahto stepped out of the crowd, a grin spreading from ear to ear. He clapped Tolen hard on the back, making him stumble. "You only destroyed your own hut!" He laughed loudly. "I expected a lot more from you, man."

Tolen shrugged as Mahto fell into step beside him. "I couldn't break your record Mahto. What would it do to your reputation?"

Mahto pounded Tolen's back. "You're funny, man." He pointed ahead and his jovial tone disappeared. "You headed to Kichaya's?"

Tolen's smile faded. "Yeah."

"You leavin'?"

Tolen nodded and a lump formed in his throat. Caring for these people had come so quick, yet so powerful.

Mahto looked away and sighed.

Tolen paused and Mahto stopped walking. Quasar kept going, kindly giving them some privacy. "Mahto, thank you for your acceptance. These have been some of the best days of my life. I'll be forever grateful to you." He put a hand on Mahto's shoulder and met his eyes. "I'll be at Tashta's for lunch. Can you make sure everyone in the family comes? There's something I need to discuss with all of you before I leave."

Mahto grasped Tolen's shoulder in return. "We'll be there."

Kichaya's door was standing open when they arrived. Tolen heard her talking with Blaze. Quasar knocked on the open door.

"Come in you two." Kichaya called and they walked into the warm house.

Blaze was sitting at her tiny table, a mug of Lucid steaming in front of him. He looked healthier than he had just a day ago. His cheeks were healthy pink, his hair shiny, and his eyes sparkled. He tipped his head at Tolen.

"Good morning, Blaze." Tolen reached out and gripped the boy's thin arm. "It's so good to see you up and about."

Blaze nodded once. "It feels good to be myself again." He shook Quasar's arm.

Tolen and Quasar took two open seats around the table and Kichaya placed mugs of Lucid in front of them. They sipped quietly for a few minutes while Tolen tried to decide how to bring up what he needed to discuss. He wanted to hurry, but he knew everything must be handled in the right way and given the right amount of time.

"Lynd sent word that all went well with your transcendence." Kichaya's toothless grin stretched her face. "I can see the change in your visage, Tolen. You radiate peace and joy, despite the concerns that plague you. You are finally whole in purpose and place, are you not?"

Tolen reached over and squeezed the old woman's fingers. "Yes,

Kichaya. It'll take constant effort to keep my priorities in order, but I know I'll be strongest when they are."

Kichaya's eyes twinkled. "You have come far in the last few days, *Conchla Mindra*." Joy laced the title—so much more significant now that she knew he had accepted it body and soul.

Tolen smiled.

"I sense an urgency from you. I take it you are ready to initiate your plan? You still wish to enter the Shadow Realm?" Kichaya glanced at Blaze. He sat stiffly in his chair as if he were afraid Tolen had changed his mind.

"Yes, we're still going through with it."

Blaze relaxed. "I want to go with you."

Tolen nodded but Quasar lifted his hand. "If I may?" He looked at Kichaya who nodded. "I understand Tolen's plan, I even accept that he can see the path he needs to follow, but I still fear we're rushing into this. It's too dangerous. A siege like this should be planned months in advance."

Tolen took a deep breath. "Gathering forces, plotting for months, it's definitely the *best* way, but we're playing dice here. Every hour is a risk now. We don't have the time we thought we had. I've seen the growth of the Dark with my own eyes. Daemon is so close to achieving his goal. Timing is everything. We need to go to the Shadow Realm now, and we'll need Blaze's knowledge to succeed. It's not fair, and it's not easy, but it is *right*."

Quasar took a deep breath. "I know you want to follow your heart, Tolen. But are you truly certain you're not following your desire to move quickly just to get to the girl?"

Tolen didn't get angry. He hadn't proved yet that his heart was in the right place. "I'm certain. Please Quasar. I need you to trust me. I need you with me on this. I need your skill, your insight, but most of all I need your friendship."

Quasar shook his head. "We need more time!"

Tolen slapped the table, making Blaze jump. "We have none!"

Quasar grabbed Tolen's shoulder. "Tolen, I respect your desire. The Light knows I too desire to save my people, but it's too dangerous. You may be shielding yourself well enough now with the help of the Spheres here, but you heard what Lynd said, you are too powerful not to affect the Balance, no matter how much you focus on your shield. The moment we leave here they will mark you. If you enter the Shadow Realm they will know it. They will kill you before you get three feet inside."

Tolen opened his mouth, but before he could reply Kichaya put her hands up between the two of them.

"If you boys could stop arguing for a moment, Blaze and I have discussed this very problem, and I believe the boy has a solution."

Quasar leaned back and a warm feeling started in Tolen's chest—an indication of truth he was beginning to recognize.

"What's your idea?" Tolen turned in his seat to Blaze.

Blaze looked back and forth between Quasar and Tolen. His voice shook a little when he spoke. "I know a way we can hide your life force from the Dark that doesn't require using your shield."

Quasar looked at Kichaya who nodded. "It's been done by spies in the past. I had no idea it was still practiced. It is very dangerous. Although given the circumstances of the captured Lafar, it shouldn't be a surprise." She nodded to Blaze to go on.

The boy cleared his throat. "When the Daklafar killed my father and threatened to kill my mother and sister if I did not join their ranks, my mother knew I would be lost forever as soon as they forced the darkness upon me. She begged the eldest Lafar in the village to teach me how to hide my true self—to hide my light. My last night with my family he performed the ceremony. He warned me that if I wasn't careful I could become truly lost. He told me I would have to bury my light deep, guard it from the darkness that would take me. But I had to allow my selfishness, my own darkness, to come to the surface to change my appearance so they would believe their ritual had worked. I looked like one of them, but I never truly was one of them. You will not have to go that far."

"What must we do?" Quasar leaned forward and placed his elbows on the table. His voice rigid with grim acceptance.

"You have to become one with your fear."

Tolen shook his head. "I don't understand."

Blaze lifted his hands. "Fear is a weakness that triggers the vibrations in the Balance and draws evil toward you, like a lion stalks its prey. Only when you become one with your fear, accept it as a part of you—a part that can be controlled until it is overcome—can you truly hide from the Dark."

"But that means—?"

Blaze nodded. "It means accepting the darkness that already exists within you—instead of fighting against it, ignoring it."

Tolen was reminded of a conversation with Kiad, the Doogar. He'd been learning how to shield and Kiad had told him he should not try to recognize his own darkness. Quasar seemed to be on the same train of thought.

Quasar shifted. "That's not a good idea."

Kichaya lifted her shoulder. "A dangerous and difficult idea, but not necessarily a bad one."

"But that kind of thinking is exactly what gave our race the arrogance to believe they could go after the Daklafar in the first place. And we now know what happened. No one escaped. They were either killed or forced to become slaves!"

Tolen put his hand on Quasar's shoulder. Despite the advice from the Doogar, he knew what he had to do. "You don't need to do this Quasar, it's not your shield we need to worry about. But if we're going to succeed, we can't rely on the hope that I'll be able to hold my shield in place. I have to do this." A soft breeze passed through the house and Tolen could swear a warning came with it. Not a *don't do this* kind of warning, but rather a *tread carefully* kind of warning. He met Blaze's eyes. "Teach me."

Quasar placed his hand on the table. "Teach us both."

43 ONE WITH THE BALANCE

T HE THREE SAT in a triangle formation in the center of the same room where they had healed Blaze. The sun passed through the roof, bathing the floor in light. Kichaya stood in the doorway, ready to intervene if necessary. Blaze sat at the point, Tolen and Quasar on each side of him. Blaze arranged an array of multi-colored stones in two lines in front of each of them. "The stones represent your fears. The biggest ones that affect the Balance. Smaller, inconsequential fears don't have as much affect." Blaze ran a hand over his face and his eyes got a faraway look in them.

"Blaze?" Tolen touched his hand. "You okay?"

"It's still strange." Blaze looked back at Tolen. "My memories seem almost like dreams." He took a deep breath. "When I see them again it will be real once more." A gentle smile lifted his face for a fleeting moment. "I must warn you, as soon as you decide to truly face your fear— your own darkness—it will try to overwhelm you. It is…terrifying."

Tolen and Quasar nodded. Tolen's palms started to sweat, not from Kuna, from nerves. He felt totally in control of his gifts, for once.

"But if you succeed, if you can bring both sides of yourself together, you become one with the Balance—level. Whole. It is not easy to maintain. Circumstances shift, new fears can be introduced. It is a practice that must be honed continually."

"I understand." Tolen took a deep breath.

"There are three things you must remember as your fear tries to take you—this is key to your success." Blaze looked each of them in the eye.

"One—you are stronger than your fear. Two—you must accept your fear as a possibility. Three—your fears are only as real as you allow them to be."

Quasar cocked his head to the side and Blaze smirked.

"My mother taught me that the darkness within us—anger, hatred, jealousy—each of these are the byproduct of fear. Because that is true, it stands to reason that fear is a choice. Faith is the opposite of fear. Meaning when we choose to believe in the Light and Their ways, fear loses its power." He drew an imaginary line on the ground by his feet.

"Before you can try to face your fears you must decide you are stronger than them. You have to believe in yourself and the gifts the Light gave you. You must accept your fear—acknowledge that no matter what you do, bad things may happen. You may not control the situation, but you can control how you deal with it. It is our fear of the unknown that causes us to falter. We must accept the unknown with faith that we are strong enough to see the task through, move forward despite the pain, and rise when we fall. As we recognize our strength, and accept the possibility of failure, we realize that our fears are of our own making—they aren't real. We are only as strong as we are weak. Turn your weakness—your fears—into power, and nothing can stop you."

Tolen swallowed. "I'm ready."

"Close your eyes."

He closed his eyes.

"Reach out and grab the first rock you touch." Blaze lowered his voice to a whisper.

Tolen heard Quasar pick up a rock beside him. He felt across the ground until his fingers closed around a sharp stone about the size and shape of his thumb.

"Let your life force reach out to the shimmers in the Balance surrounding you. Once you feel it, concentrate on the balance within you."

Tolen felt for the Balance the way he did when he was trying to become unseen. Slowly he could pinpoint the shifts, almost like the slow rippling waves of the ocean, constantly moving without the aid of wind, but unstoppable. When he was practicing the art of the Dicernan, he allowed the waves to move around him until he became hidden inside them. Now he allowed himself to feel each shift and twist of the Balance surrounding him. The warmer, stronger pull of the Light that drew him in.

The colder, more foreboding waves of the Dark that he naturally pushed away from. The push and pull reminded him of trying to shove the same polar ends of a magnet together.

The Dark and the Light were part of the Balance, stuck in the same space, but they constantly repelled each other. The more he concentrated, the more he could feel the same war within himself. His faith in himself, his destiny, his people, warred with his self-doubt, his fear of losing Macy, and his fear of not being what the people needed.

As he became more aware of himself, the fears he fought to hide began to take clearer form.

"Your weakest fears will appear first. The ones you least dread facing. As it takes shape imagine yourself casting it into the rock in your hand." Blaze began to sing a low soft chant—much as Bastian had on occasion—with the firm cadences of the Native American speech, but in the language of the Hidden.

Quasar's breath quickened in the same moment his own did as the first fear hit him. He was standing in the middle of a wide street, his feet shackled to the ground, surrounded by crowds of people screaming and mocking him. Some of them he knew from the different places he'd lived. Some were strangers. He could see Hunsí's tribe, Quasar, and Blaze. They were all throwing rocks and garbage at him while calling him names. *Freak! Loser! Wimp!* He tried to push their leering faces into the rock in his hand, but the image shifted and his heart increased its rhythm. The people were now dead. Lying in the very streets where they'd mocked him. The people he knew mingled with the strangers. Quasar and Blaze, their last expression of betrayal was still visible on their lifeless faces. The gutters ran with blood. Cries of children echoed from broken buildings surrounding the streets.

He'd failed them.

His hands shook and he wished he could open his eyes, but the fear held him. He couldn't escape it, now that he'd let it free.

Blaze's voice seemed to echo past the cries of the children. His face flashed across the black sky of this nightmare. "Faith…"

I am stronger than my fear. Tolen reached down and broke the shackles from his feet.

He closed his inner eyes against the gruesome scene before him. *I accept my fear.* This could happen. Many people were going to die as they battled against the Dark. It was inevitable. But he knew Quasar, Blaze, and Macy would give it the best fight possible. He would not give up, and for every life the Dark took, he would revisit it upon them ten-fold.

Strength burned through his body.

My fear isn't real. The scene changed. Instead of being shackled to the street he was fighting beside Quasar, Blaze, Hunsí, and strangers. Many of their people had fallen, but even more creatures of darkness littered the ground. He felt this fear fall into the rock in his palm. It got heavier and sharper and it stung where it pricked his skin.

The second fear rolled in slower, building until it crushed him like a weight. Trapped in his mind, he felt his body collapse to the side. Blaze was shouting, but Tolen couldn't hear him. This picture was one he'd seen before, painted for him by the epitome of evil Darsapean himself. Only now, it was worse.

Magnified.

This time as Macy lay dead on the ground, Daemon stood above her. His huge sword gleamed red with her blood, the Last Shard dangled from his fist, a twisted grin revealed his black pointed teeth. His yellow eyes glowed in triumph. The walls of Misery crumbled and waves of darkness surrounded the earth. Dark creatures crawled over the planet in droves. The oceans turned red with blood. Darsapean sat on a black throne bathed in flame, Daemon standing at his side.

Tolen held Macy's lifeless body in his arms, and the guilt and the pain washed over him for not only failing her, but also failing the Light. Two failures that felt like one.

Broken sobs racked his body and some part of him knew it wasn't just in his mind this time.

One failure. One doom. The ultimate loss. He would let the Light down. He would not save anyone. Not Macy. No one.

You are stronger than your fear. Blaze's voice.

No. I am not strong enough.

You are.

No. Not for this. I am not who they need me to be. I cannot save them. I cannot protect Macy or anyone else.

Tolen, the Light trusts you, trust Their choice!

That time it was not Blaze's voice. It was Macy's. The sound of it cut him deep—and for a second woke him up. He remembered this wasn't real. It was in his head. As soon as he thought it, the image assaulted him again and he had to fight to hold on to the sound of her voice.

Tolen! Remember who you are!

Strength surged through him again, but this time his response was slower as he pushed against the darkness with every ounce of energy he had. *But if I fail the Light…all those people.*

You won't. Win or lose, you will give it all you've got, and that will count for something. You can't control the outcome Tolen—

But I can control how I deal with it.

Her approval carried to him, filling him with warmth and hope.

I accept my fear.

The image of Macy dead fought for a place at the forefront again, and he heard Blaze shout, "Let it go Tolen. Accept your fear and let it go! Now! Before the darkness changes you!"

Tolen fought against the darkness, pushing against the grisly image and instead picturing Macy whole and healthy and beautiful. He felt again the warmth of her lips as they'd kissed goodbye in the Capka. Warmth surged more powerfully through him and strength flew to his limbs. Yes, he did believe there was a life after this one, but he was going to give it his best to be sure they enjoyed a life together in this one.

My fear is NOT real. The weight fell completely from his shoulders and dropped into the rock in his hand. It was now so heavy and sharp he no longer desired to hold it. With this thought it dropped to the ground and he knew he'd just released so much more than a tiny rock.

Thank you, Macy.

The Balance settled around him and for the first time he felt himself move with it. Twisting effortlessly with the waves as if he were a part of it, rather than hiding inside it. He sensed each pull and ebb of the Light and Dark within it, but neither forced his direction. He was one with the Light inside the Balance, now a separate magnet from the Dark. It could not touch him, or even come near him. It was repelled by him. Incredible!

A wide smile broke across his face as he opened his eyes. This time he knew what he saw was real. Quasar sat with his head in his hands, his collar wet with sweat and tears. Tolen sat up and put his hand on his shoulder.

Blaze sat in front of them, his face a mask of pity and understanding.

Tolen's arms and legs felt shaky—not from weakness, but strength and joy he wasn't quite sure how to channel. He saw Blaze with new eyes.

Respect for this young boy blossomed in his chest until he felt awed just to be in his presence. "I can't believe you went through that so young."

Quasar looked up.

"It was not the easiest thing to do, but it worked." Blaze shrugged under their scrutiny. "I would do anything to protect my family." Tolen acknowledged the double meaning with a nod.

"Unbelievable." Quasar's voice shook. "That's why you were with the war party. They really thought you one of them?"

Blaze nodded. "A few of my friends and I have been trying to figure out a way to escape the Shadow Realm for a while. I hoped by being accepted into an attacking army, I would learn the way to do it. But I'd never been in this realm before. I had no idea how frightening it was. I could feel it trying to drain the Dark from me, but I thought it was trying to kill me. I still didn't believe the ways of the Dark were right, but I was beginning to wonder if some of the stories I'd been told my entire life about the human world were true—that if we didn't take over, their strange power would destroy us all. Once I was here, I got scared. I was going to go back and tell the others it was too dangerous. If we escaped to this world we would all die…then you captured me."

"This just keeps getting stranger and stranger," Quasar whispered. "Blaze, how many Lafar would you guess to be like you in their feelings?"

The boy lifted his shoulder. "Most of my village. A few families in the village south of us. A thousand maybe."

Tolen's head flew up. "A thousand?" He met Quasar's shocked look.

"How many of them would be able to fight?" Quasar's eyes were calculating.

Blaze cocked his head to the side. "Three hundred, maybe more. The old ones made an oath after a war broke out many years ago between the slaves who refused to join the Dark, and those Lafar who *had* been seduced and joined them. Many died. They did not like killing their own, even though the Daklafar are nothing like us." He sighed. "They made an oath never to raise arms against their own again."

Tolen rubbed his sweaty palms on his jeans. A feeling of anticipation, without the cloudiness of doubt, told him that the Light approved of his next course of action.

Kichaya held out a small scroll made of thin animal skin, faded and cracked with age. "The instructions for opening the gateway." She waited for him to take it and touched his hand. "The Light will allow it, and Sky-borne will guide you. Give him the scroll when you finish, he will take it back to its resting place. Send whomever you can save back here. We will take care of them." She moved her hand to his cheek. "Good luck, *Conchla Mindra*. I hope to see you again in this life."

44 REVELATIONS AND INVITATIONS

Macy followed behind the others slowly, relying on them to keep watch for anything dangerous. Her thoughts were consumed with other issues. Bastian's shard had been pulsing with strange energy ever since her visit with Tolen. She couldn't figure it out. It felt like an odd mixture of joy and trepidation. However, the two emotions were so contradictory that she couldn't be sure, and she wasn't about to connect to it to find out more. She worried about Tolen, and though she hated to admit it, she was worried about the danger ahead. Tolen said he would send help when it was needed. Just how bad were things going to get?

She twisted a lock of hair around her finger. What if the villagers didn't know anything? What if the rumors were just that, baseless, useless, rumors? What if this whole thing was a waste of time when they should be going straight after the Last Shard?

"Hey."

Macy's hand flashed to her knife.

Connell held up his hands. "Sorry. I didn't mean to scare you."

Macy shook her head and took a deep breath to calm her racing heart. "Occupational hazard. Sorry." She lifted her chin. "I thought you were up there with Keelyn and Rune."

"Yeah. They were getting a little mushy. It's annoying." He shrugged. "Brina's bickering with Toke. It seemed quieter back here."

Macy nodded. This was the first time Connell had actually spoken to her directly. She wondered if there was more behind it than just him wanting to get away from the others. He walked silently beside her for several minutes before he confirmed her suspicions.

"So, have you ever had any pets?" Connell scratched behind his ear.

"What?"

"Pets?" A tiny dimple appeared in his chin. "You know, furry little friends?"

Macy snorted. "No. Bastian didn't think it was fair to keep an animal with us, given our dangerous lifestyle." She pushed her hands into her pockets. "I always wanted one though."

Connell nodded and glanced up into the leaves. "I don't think you have to be Animashta to be drawn to animals. There exists a natural kinship between them and all Beings. It just has to be nurtured in the right way. I think people often believe it was only their idea to domesticate animals—they don't realize that the animals wanted to be with them, too." He lifted his shoulder. "So…if you could choose, what type of animal would you want as a pet?"

Macy flicked a ladybug off her arm, curious at Connell's sudden friendliness. Maybe it just took him longer to get used to new faces. She could relate to that. She shrugged. "I always thought it would be nice to have a big dog. One of those huge ones with the wrinkly faces that drool all the time."

"Ah, a Mastiff." He grinned. "Good dog. Very loyal. Good protector. The only downfall is they eat as much as a horse and poop just as big."

Macy chuckled. Connell turned out to be as easy to talk to as his sister was. His tone was quieter and his demeanor more subdued—much like the owl he carried—but easy just the same. "Your owl. What's its name?"

Connell raised his arm and the owl on his shoulder ruffled its feathers lightly. "This is Macdara. And she isn't my owl." He met Macy's eyes. "She's yours."

"I'm pretty sure I've never owned an owl."

"No, but your father did."

Macy looked at the beautiful white-faced owl on Connell's shoulder. Macdara opened one eye and looked back. "I don't understand."

Connell took a deep breath. "Macdara showed up at our home right after Rune carried you in. Someone who loves you asked the Light to watch over you and they sent Macdara. Although she tells me she's watched over you your entire life."

Macy looked at Macdara again, reminded of that dreaded night not so long ago when the Raksasha had chased her and Bastian from their little Nevada home. A Ghost Owl had appeared warning her and Bastian of the approaching Shadows. Could they be the same owl? "Have I seen her before?"

Macdara opened both eyes and rubbed her head against Connell's cheek.

"She said yes." Connell reached up to stroke the owl's head.

"How much has she told you?"

Connell shrugged again. "Only what she wants me to know. She wants you to trust Toke. She remembers his friendship with your father. She trusts him."

Macy looked ahead at the back of Toke's purple head. "You can tell her I do."

"She wants me to tell you that her brother, an owl by the name of Skyborne, was sent by the Light to watch over the Ninth. Neither of you have been as alone as you thought in your quest."

Macy's throat felt tight. "Tell her I said thank you."

Connell tilted his head. "She heard you."

Macy's fingers trembled. "Why have you waited until now to tell me this?"

Connell shrugged again. "Macdara told me to wait."

Macy's eyes narrowed. "Why?"

Connell took a deep breath. "Animals connect to their thoughts and feelings differently than we do. We rationalize or make excuses for how we feel or don't feel, and even deny our true feelings. Mankind calls an animal's reactions to the world around them instinct." He chuckled softly. "They have no idea. An animal *is* what it feels. It is genuine, pure, and perfect. They don't pretend." He stroked Macdara's wing.

"That's really cool, but it doesn't exactly answer my question."

"Humans pretend all the time. That's why the Hidden are afraid of us you know."

"What?" Macy wondered where this conversation was going.

"It's true. The Hidden are a lot like animals—I mean that in a good way—they are who they are. If they choose Light, they remain their beautiful selves. If they choose the Dark…"

"Their features change. They change. They are recognizable by what they have become." Macy could finally see where this was going.

"Exactly. But humans can be on the side of Light or Dark and still look like sweet innocent little grandmas."

"Except for the Darkened."

"True, but Darkened are pure evil. Humans can have evil intents and still look innocent. Macdara knows you hide things about yourself. She decided to wait to reveal herself until she had a chance to observe you for a while and make sure your loyalties remained with the Light, once you were away from the influence of your Watcher."

"And now she trusts me?"

"She does."

Macy nodded, unable to feel offended. It also explained why Connell was suddenly friendly.

"Are you okay?" Connell looked at her with concern.

Macy rolled her shoulders. "Yeah. Just thinking. Tell her thanks for deciding to trust me."

Connell's eyebrow rose. "She *can* hear you. We can't understand them, but they understand us."

Macdara flew off Connell's shoulder and perched on Macy's.

"Come on. We'd better catch up with the others." Connell smiled and lengthened his stride.

Macy took a deep breath and followed, the gentle weight of Macdara's talons resting on her shoulder bringing a measure of peace.

Toke called them to a halt just before four PM. It wasn't much farther to the village, but he wanted them to arrive in the morning to keep with proper visiting manners among the Hidden. In a village of old ones, they would receive a warmer welcome if they came with the proper respect.

They set up camp in a tight group of trees, refilled their canteens in a nearby stream and gathered native plants and herbs for dinner. Once back at camp, the other rebels settled in around the fire. Macdara had returned to being Connell's shoulder angel so Macy joined Toke in the shadow of a thick tree where he worked on the little silver Treasta he'd used at the house the night before. He twisted the top off and fiddled with the wiring and gadgetry inside.

"Is it broke?"

Toke shook his head. "No. I just wanted to increase its power. I'd like everyone to practice tonight and I want the extra protection."

Macy watched in fascination as each wire he touched glowed neon blue and followed his fingers, twisting and curling with his thoughts. He glanced up at her. "I take it you have never seen a Movan work before?"

She shook her head. "How do you do that?"

Toke tapped one of the purple spikes of his hair. "Just as you were born with the ability to receive the gift of the Kunamin, Movan were born with the ability to connect to the electrical impulses all around us. Your shard awakened in you the ways to manipulate fire and your Watcher taught you how to use it. Years of training and focus teach the Movan to manipulate the electricity they feel. I can feel the current through these wires and I can feel where they are strong and weak. That tells me where I need to put them, or fix them."

"Wild." She slid down onto her elbow for a better view. "The first time we met I felt something when you touched me. What was that?"

Toke paused what he was doing to look into her eyes. "I was sensing the strength of your gifts."

Macy's eyebrow rose. "How?"

"Each Hidden gift carries different measures of electricity, just as different thoughts and emotions produce different electrical impulses in the brain." He touched her cheek. "You are far more powerful than you realize, Macy—more powerful than any Kunamin I have met before."

Macy looked away. "You just sensed Bastian's shard."

Toke lifted a shoulder. "Maybe." She could tell he said this to appease her. "So…what's troubling you?"

Macy twisted her hair on her pinky. "Where do I start?"

Toke chuckled. "I imagine you feel slightly overwhelmed."

"Slightly?" Macy shook her head. "When I learned that I was Light's Aid I was totally freaked out, and now discovering the Last Shard has chosen me to be part of its three-fold protection, and trusts me to keep it out of the hands of the Dark…I think the Light has a lot more faith in my abilities than I do."

A tiny smile lifted Toke's mouth. "It's not your abilities alone that make the Light want you for their most sacred and important missions. It is your heart, Macy. It is *who* you are, not what you can do."

Macy squirmed and wouldn't meet Toke's eyes. "I'm not that good of a person."

"By whose standards?"

"Mine, I guess."

"Macy, I'm only going to say this once, so I want you to listen very carefully. The Light chose you, and the Light does not make mistakes."

She didn't know how to respond to this, but as it warmed her heart, she could see why the Lost loved Toke so much—he believed in them.

Slightly uncomfortable, she turned to a less troublesome, albeit annoying topic. "Do you think Rune will ever admit the way he feels about Keelyn?"

Toke turned back to the Treasta and for a minute didn't answer. Macy wondered if she'd stepped on a touchy subject when he finally replied. "Rune's past is even more tragic than yours, Macy. His heart is far more guarded than even your own." He looked up to where his family sat throwing leaves at each other.

A lump rose in Macy's throat. "I'm sorry. I guess it really is none of my business. I'm afraid to lose Tolen, but the love I have for him seems to overpower my fear." She glanced over to see him looking at her again, a curious expression on his face. She felt her face go red. "Okay, corny, I know."

Toke shook his head. "Not corny at all. Perfect love eradicates fear. The two emotions cannot coexist at the same time. Fear isn't real. Love is. The real emotion always wins over the false conceptions we create in our mind. True love is eternal, always growing, never changing. You will always fear losing him, but your love for him is stronger than your fear, because deep within, you know that *love* extends beyond this life."

Macy's eyes burned and she looked away. She'd told Tolen that only hours ago, but it still hurt.

Toke went back to his tinkering. "I was thinking that I'd like you to help Rune with his Kuna this evening. He can learn much from you about many things."

Macy looked at him, but he hid his smile. She couldn't hold back one of her own as she glanced up at Keelyn and Rune as they smeared each other with muddy leaves. You could almost see the love pouring from Keelyn's eyes. She adored Rune.

Maybe she *could* help. She stood up and dusted off her jeans. "Thanks, Toke."

Toke chuckled. "Any time."

Rune followed Macy's instructions, placing the last of the herbs on the patch of cheesecloth. He twisted it artfully just as she'd showed him. He was a good student.

"Perfect." She finished off her own and then showed him how to stow the Glockshaw in the pouch on his belt to protect them.

When they finished she handed him three of the smaller practice Glockshaw she'd made earlier. "Ready to throw?"

Rune nodded, an excited gleam back in his eyes. Macy had been afraid of his reaction when Toke suggested she train him, but with Keelyn's encouragement, he'd taken to the idea better than she'd expected. Macy knew Keelyn wanted to watch him throw, but it made him nervous to have an audience, so Toke kept them busy at camp practicing their own gifts while Rune and Macy worked.

"Okay, allow the Kuna to rise to your palms and hold it there. It's going to want to release like it did the first time, but you just have to focus on holding the heat in place. It'll get uncomfortable, especially since you're only used to calling it into your sword—releasing it into an object keeps it from building in your hands, but you'll get used to it." She held her palm out toward the wet leather target that hung between two trees across the river a hundred yards away, and let the heat roll through her body, down her arms, and into her hands. She pulled back slightly and held it in her palms. She remembered the first time she'd done this with Bastian. The heat in her hands had felt so foreign that she'd released too quickly and singed Bastian's eyebrows.

She allowed the fire to release from her hand but held it close, just a soft dance of flame from her palm. She twisted her fingers and the fire formed into a wide petal flower—reminding her of the one Tolen had made back in Jonas's camp. The task had taken years to master. Had she learned to focus her Kuna with love instead of anger as a child it might not have been so difficult. She hoped she could help Rune not make the same mistake.

She held the flower there for a moment longer before curling her fingers again until the flower turned into a small raging ball of fire—she kept it small, she didn't want to blow a hole in the target. She whispered, "*Mi'no ha.*" As the fireball shot toward the target, she kept her focus on its center then pulled the heat back just a bit before it hit, so only a shower of sparks hit the center red dot.

Rune stared in awe at the target for a moment before raising his palm.

"Concentrate first on just holding the heat in your palms. Rein in your anger and focus on something that makes you happy. It'll give you more control."

Rune closed his eyes. Macy sensed the heat build within him. Her own Kuna reacted to the nearness of its own kind. Sweat beaded on Rune's forehead and his breathing sped.

"Keep holding it. It's hard, I know, but the more you practice holding it in, the more control you'll have over it."

Rune grunted. His breath came out in short bursts through his teeth.

"Just a few more seconds," Macy encouraged. His fingers turned blistering red. "Now!"

Rune opened his eyes and released a fireball so large it melted the target before it even hit. He glanced at Macy with the look of a scolded child.

She held back a laugh as she pulled the heat from his flame back into her own body, killing the fire he'd started. "Well, with a fireball like that, who needs Glockshaw?"

He grinned. "Let's go again."

They practiced for nearly two hours until Keelyn brought them dinner. Rune watched her walk away with a look of longing that Macy knew all too well.

She didn't know if now was the right time, but she didn't know how much longer they would all be together. She ignored the pang of regret this thought stirred and cleared her throat. "I know what it's like to have something you can't live without."

She felt Rune whip around to look at her, but she kept her eyes on Keelyn's retreating figure. "I know we live a life where early death is highly possible—so yes, you may lose her. But you won't mourn her any less if you deny how you feel about her." She chanced a glance at Rune; he looked angry and embarrassed.

"If anything, you'll wish you'd taken advantage of the time you had. Believe me, I know." Her voice trembled.

The anger melted from Rune's face. He looked back toward the camp where Keelyn had disappeared. It sounded as if she and Connell were arguing about who was the best cook.

"You might be right, but the idea of it…" He trailed off.

"Terrifies you. Makes you feel weak."

His answering glare said she'd hit it on the mark. If he only understood how alike they were.

Macy held up her hands. "I'm not accusing. I'm speaking from experience. I lost Bastian before I had the chance to tell him how much I loved and appreciated him. I thought I'd lost Tolen before I'd told him how much he meant to me. But I got lucky. Bastian was allowed to join the Guardians, so I was able to see him again, and amazingly, Tolen survived the attack by the Shadows. Those experiences taught me to never take the time you have with those you love for granted. If anything, my pain was deeper because I hadn't told them how I felt." She bit her lip. "I can't tell you what to do here, Rune. It's your life. It's just…I can see how much you care for her and I know she feels the same for you. I hate seeing the two of you waste what time you might have with each other because of fear."

Rune took a deep breath and met Macy's eyes for one agonized second before looking back at the Glockshaw in his hands. "I'll think about it."

Macy held back her disappointment. He was stubborn, but he also knew she was right. It took a lot to change the instinct of self-protection. If Rune had suffered even worse than she had—having her parents murdered by the Shadows right in front of her—opening his heart would be unbelievably hard. Hopefully she'd given him enough to think about, and one day he'd decide Keelyn was worth the risk. "Okay. Enough mush, back to Kuna."

The corner of Rune's mouth twitched and his shoulders lifted slightly. "Right. Show me that thing you do with your fingers again."

45 PAINFUL GOODBYES

TOLEN PAUSED OUTSIDE Tashta's door. The soft voices of his family carried through the window. He couldn't hear what they said, but he felt the sadness as soon as he walked in—a sadness that showed on their faces when the three of them entered the kitchen.

The table was laid with the afternoon meal, but no one was eating. Their eyes all focused on Tolen. Emotion flooded his body and he took a deep breath to steady himself. He blinked several times as Tashta pointed to the two additional chairs for Blaze and Quasar and motioned for them to be seated. Tolen took his seat beside Sashan and looked around at their expectant faces. Tashta's eyes were wet. He looked away.

"I'm sure you all know I have to leave. I knew I wouldn't be here long, but I never would have guessed it would be so hard to leave. I want to thank you all for your kindness, for showing me why it matters so much to know where you come from—for teaching me the value of *family*. I understand now that the word is far bigger than blood status. I truly do feel that you are all my family and it hurts more than I ever could have guessed to leave you. But I must follow the path to my destiny. A path I would not have found or understood without your influence. I-I can never thank you enough." He cleared the lump from his throat and turned to Belch.

"Thank you for your friendship and kindness. It brings me much comfort to know the village has you here to protect them."

Belch leaned over and gripped Tolen's arm, his kind eyes gentle and sad. "It was an honor to meet you, Tolen."

Tolen patted his arm and turned to Mahto and Sienn. "I learned so much from both of you. Thank you for your patience with me." He ran a hand through his hair and tugged the ponytail at the base of his neck. "I know you meant what you said about helping me when I needed it. And well…I need your help." Sienn nodded and Mahto's cheek twitched as if he were holding back a grin. Tolen quickly told them of his plan to enter the Shadow Realm, of Macy's plight, and of the growth of the Dark from what he'd seen in the Capka. As he spoke, Mahto's grin faded and Sienn's expression hardened to a soldier's determination. "I can't see exactly where Macy will be, but it feels southeast of here. Sashan can guide you when the time comes."

Sienn stood up and gripped Tolen's shoulder. "We'll secure the front here, choose a select few of the Guard to protect you and the Spheres to your exit point, and wait for Sashan to tell us where to go from there."

Mahto stood and put his arm around her shoulders. "We won't fail you."

Tolen nodded, too overcome to speak.

A knock sounded at the door and Belch left to answer it. As the others' attention was turned to the door Tolen whispered to Sashan.

"Are you okay with this?"

Sashan nodded. "It is the right course."

Relief flooded through Tolen. "You know what I have *seen* so you can further explain the details to the others as they become clear when the time is right. I only know my next few steps; the rest is still hazy—still affected by the indecision of others. My path should remain clear, but I will need your help to guide them."

Sashan nodded. "As Mahto said, we will not fail you." He gripped Tolen's arm. "I have faith in you, *Mindra*."

"Thank you, Sashan. For everything." Tolen squeezed his shoulder.

Hunsí walked into the kitchen, followed by Tahaka. They too had come to give their farewells.

"I was afraid when I first met you, *Mindra*." Hunsí scratched his belly. "But I am no longer afraid. I now have hope." He shook Tolen's arm.

Tahaka placed her hand on Tolen's cheek and whispered a short blessing of peace and safety. "You have been chosen by the Light to be a beacon of hope for this world. Stay true to who you are and what you have learned. Your people will be a symbol of love and strength to you throughout your journey."

"Thank you." Tolen looked around at his family and back at Tahaka. He wished he could tell her how grateful he was, but his throat felt too thick, he couldn't form the words. Tahaka's gentle smile said she understood.

Tashta wrapped her arms around him and whispered in his ear. "You will always have a home here, Tolen. Promise me someday you will bring your sweetheart to meet me."

Tolen's throat tightened. "I promise."

Lynd led the way with six more Spheres to the sides and behind their company.

Blaze and Quasar walked quietly on either side of him. Mahto, Sienn, and a dozen other Guardsmen walked behind. Two scouts went ahead. Hunsí reported that a number of Dark creatures had been spotted in the area just before dawn. Whether it was because Tolen's transcendence led them here or not, no one knew for certain—but either way they decided to lead him a good distance away before they released him from the protection of the Spheres.

Tolen counted on the ceremony he'd performed with Blaze to help. If he could hold on to that flow he'd felt within the Balance, he might not shift it as much as they feared.

He wouldn't open the gateway until they were alone and far from the village. If the Dark became aware that a gateway had been opened, he didn't want it anywhere near his people. The plan was risky and full of holes, but they didn't have time to waste.

The sun was below the trees when Lynd signaled them to stop. The scouts waited near a tiny stream. They walked over and spoke quietly to Sienn. She glanced back at Tolen, worry creasing her brow.

"Wait here," Tolen said to Blaze and motioned Quasar to follow him.

The two moved quickly to Sienn's side.

She pointed to steep mountains several hundred yards to the north. "There is a narrow fissure between those cliffs. You will escape through there."

"Escape?" Tolen swallowed.

Sienn nodded gravely. "There are sentries posted along the top of the mountain. About fifty or so. Gungruin disguised as Punti, Animashta warriors from a village that was destroyed near here." She glanced at Quasar who nodded and looked at Tolen.

"The village I saw before we arrived."

Tolen sighed. "What are Gungruin?"

"Mimickers," Sienn answered. "They become whatever they touch. They are one of few creatures of darkness that can withstand limited sunlight. Daemon has posted them anywhere he thinks you might go. Our village is so well hidden that it is not known by many. The Punti village was not so lucky."

Tolen's stomach twisted at the thought of the innocent villagers being killed just in the chance they might harbor the Ninth, harbor *him*. He swallowed back the guilt and anger. He could end this. But only if he stopped the Dark. "How will we get by without them seeing us?"

"They *will* see you, but we'll take care of them." Sienn whistled the strange three-trilled tune. Mahto and the red-haired guard, Day, showed up at her side. She motioned toward the gathered Spheres. "Send Gafta and two others with the Spheres. Get them back to the village. Then you two lead the assault on the Gungruin." She turned back to Tolen. "Get the boy and follow me."

Sienn led them at a sprint deep into the trees. She didn't stop until they reached the base of the mountain. She pointed to the fissure between two steep rock faces. "Through there." She glanced up as the sound of arrows zinged through the air. She looked back at Tolen, murmured, "Be safe," hugged him quickly, and turned away.

Tolen watched with concern as his sister ran toward home—his heart felt heavy but determined, as he followed Quasar and Blaze into the fissure. They pulled off their packs and had to shuffle sideways in order to fit. At certain points, Tolen and Blaze had to help Quasar, who was slightly wider, push his way through. The fading sunlight barely illuminated the cramped space, so they couldn't see where it ended. Soon they heard shouts behind them and the whiz of arrows. If there was someone or something waiting for them on the other side, they'd be trapped, easy targets. He allowed his gifts to build and tried to use his Watcher's ability to look ahead. But for some reason he couldn't see what might happen when they stepped out of their escape route.

Minutes that felt like hours later the light got brighter and the fissure widened. Quasar picked up his pace and eventually Tolen and Blaze were jogging to keep up. When Quasar stopped abruptly they almost ran into him. Over Quasar's shoulder, Tolen could see the sky above a vast expanse of woods, and nothing else. There was nowhere to go, the mountainside dropped off into nothing.

"Now what?"

Quasar tipped his head and curling his hand over the edge, began shimmying his way outside to free climb his way down the mountain.

Tolen was about to follow when he had a thought. "*Tin'ruhl*," he whispered and sent his thoughts to the mountain. He heard a loud rumbling and Quasar lost his footing, but before he could plunge into the depths, a short ledge appeared under his feet. More rock ledges began to thrust out from the mountainside to form a natural staircase leading down to the ground. Quasar began to jump quickly down each step. Tolen motioned Blaze ahead, and as he followed he whispered again so that as soon as he jumped to the next stair, the one he'd left would move back into the mountain.

He didn't know how high they were, but he was sweating by the time they reached the shelter of the trees and the last stair rumbled back into the cliff face.

"Nice work." Quasar breathed heavily.

"Thanks."

"Where to?"

Tolen looked at Blaze, his sweaty hair plastered to his face. "Here is just as good a place as any." He glanced up at the sky and Skyborne swooped down to land on his shoulder. He pulled the scroll from his pack, and with the help of the owl began to read as he called his Dreamer gift and his Sphere ability to the forefront of his mind. The two gifts tried to battle each other, sky blue against deepest gray, and it was hard for Tolen to get them to link together. When they finally collided rather than joined, it felt as if someone hit him in the head with a hammer.

His voice twisted and darkened to the strange Dreamer quality, raspy and wild, as he spoke the final words on the scroll. A shimmer in the air in front of them was the only indication that it was working. Slow, painfully slow, the shimmer finally darkened and Tolen could see the lifeless sky of the Shadow Realm. He held out the scroll to Skyborne with a thought of thanks and then with a stroke of inspiration altered his plea. Within seconds another owl had the scroll, and Skyborne along with six more owls led the way through the gateway.

Tolen looked to his companions. Quasar's face was determined and focused, Blaze looked anxious and scared.

Quasar was the first to step through, followed by Blaze. Tolen cast one last look behind him as the gateway shimmered closed and he stood once again in the place of his nightmares.

46 DARK PLANS

THE SOUND OF dripping water echoed through the darkness. Something huge, black, and shiny coiled and twisted in the far corner of the room. Its putrid breath came out in loud puffs as it slept.

A long-fingered, scaly black hand slowly stroked its back.

"It won't be long now." The deep, cold voice spoke into the darkness, and tossed a handful of fermented maggots into his mouth. He chewed slowly and swallowed. "Soon we will have our freedom. It is all coming together as planned."

47 THE SHADOW REALM

TOLEN TAPPED HIS watch. The screen had darkened until it barely illuminated the numbers, as if it were storing energy. They hid in an ancient skeletal forest, surrounded by the burned remains of tall trees and the carcasses of creatures he couldn't name. Skyborne and the other owls hid in the dreary forest, ready to act on Tolen's command. The last twenty minutes had been spent going over his plan, while he tried to ignore the frightening scenery around them and the strange, depressing energy of the realm. The darkness tugged at him, but this time it felt apart from him, as if he were still repelling it. It was there, but it couldn't touch him.

Quasar looked doubtful. Blaze wanted to go for it, but he looked wary, as if he wasn't sure it would work.

"I still think our numbers will be too few." Quasar wove a loose piece of thread back into place on his quiver. "It will be a slaughter."

"I don't think so." Tolen rushed on before Quasar could interrupt. "Listen, it's not a question of numbers, it's figuring out a way to divert their larger numbers. All we need is enough chaos and distraction that we can move the women and children into the forest without being seen."

Tolen held up his hands when Quasar opened his mouth to retort. "Just listen. We know there is no way we can smuggle entire families out of the realm without getting caught, not unless we have a riot big enough that they call the sentries down to fight."

Blaze nodded, his eyes calculating. "It's a crazy plan, but maybe that's why it could work. This will be the last thing the Masters will expect. There hasn't been a revolt for a hundred years."

Quasar slipped the last of his arrows back into his quiver, checked his sword, and glanced from Tolen to Blaze. "Well, I guess that means it's about time for another one."

Tolen sucked in a deep breath. "Okay, Blaze, lead the way. We need to get to your village as quickly as possible. As soon as we're safe, gather everyone you can. We'll go over strategy tonight and prepare for battle tomorrow."

Blaze shifted his feet. A tremor crept into his voice. "All right. This way."

They ran at a crouch, dodging behind boulders and large, black spindly trees with drooping gray leaves. Not a hint of green or any other warm color touched this dreary place. *Where darkness is, light cannot be.* No light, no color. Tolen shivered and focused back on his feet.

Every once in a while Blaze would pause with a finger to his lips, other times he would stop and look around with a confused expression and when he did this, Tolen tried not to worry they had gotten lost.

Finally, after almost an hour of walking, Tolen could just make out hints of civilization. Rows of strange black crops grew in large, dusty gray fields. Abandoned equipment and hand tools were scattered between the fields. Blaze kept to the trees that rimmed the farm ground as he led them toward a small cluster of colorless grass huts. He pointed a finger to one of the smallest huts. "My sister," he whispered.

Tolen and Quasar shared a shocked look. A young girl stood outside feeding a strange assortment of animals from a sack slung over her shoulder. Her hair could have been red or brown; the Shadow Realm drained it of any real color. Her dress was ragged and dirty, as were her hands and face. She was painfully thin and obviously malnourished, but her hair was neatly combed back into a long braid, and her features still held the gentle beauty of the Lafar.

They edged closer and Tolen heard a sound he never would have expected to hear in the Shadow Realm. She was humming! Her voice was melodic, like bells. As she hummed, an inner light brightened her features. She was good, as good as anyone in the world of Light. Another confirmation that he was doing the right thing.

Blaze motioned for them to stay in the trees while he snuck down the side of the rickety fence, crept up behind his sister, and put his hand over her mouth. She struggled for a moment until she saw his face. Her eyes went wide and then filled with tears. Blaze dropped his hand, she threw her arms around him and sobbed. Blaze looked back at them, raised three fingers, and led his sister into the hut. A startled cry met their ears followed by the sound of more crying.

Affirming joy settled in Tolen's heart at the reunion. He cast a quick look at Quasar to see the elf's mouth in a hard line, his eyes like black onyx. Right there in front of them was proof that Daemon had shown Nova some piece of the truth. Tolen could understand perfectly now why she had betrayed him—and so did Quasar.

Three minutes later a back door of the hut opened, Blaze stuck his head out and motioned for them to come quickly.

Once inside, Blaze introduced his mother, Haven, and sister, Celeste. They wrapped their arms around him, shaking with sobs.

"My boy…" Haven hiccupped through her tears. "You saved my boy."

48 DANGEROUS MOVES

MACY TWISTED ONTO her side and tried to allow the sound of cricket song and wind in the trees to lull her to sleep, but her mind was running a million miles an hour and wouldn't slow down. What would they learn from the villagers tomorrow? How close was she to her goal? What kind of dangers was she going to face? Was she really strong enough to succeed in what the Light asked of her?

The Light doesn't make mistakes.

She swatted a fly away from her face. They'd chosen her for a reason. Jonas had told her that back in his camp, and she'd thought she'd figured out why, but it just seemed that the more she learned, the more she found out she hardly knew anything.

Someone tapped her on the shoulder and she turned to see Toke kneeling beside her with a finger to his lips. He motioned with his head for her to follow him.

She got up silently and followed him into the trees.

Toke looked over her shoulder before whispering, "This should be far enough."

"What's going on?"

Toke took a measured breath. "I value and appreciate your trust and honesty."

Macy's eyes narrowed. "I sense a *but* in there."

Toke inclined his head. "But these children are *lost*, and I fear the temptation of the Last Shard may be too great for them."

"What do you mean?"

"The Last is the most powerful shard left on the planet. The enhanced gifts of its bearer would be unsurpassed, except maybe by the Ninth himself. That is why *it* chooses its Keeper. My Chosen, at present, are not completely loyal to the Light. Their motives are currently very selfish. Their temptation will be too great."

"What do we do?"

He sighed and she could hear the weight he carried evident in his voice. "When the time comes to take the Last from its hiding place, they cannot be with us."

"We ditch them?"

He ran a hand over his eyes.

She bit her lip and nodded. "How much do you think it will it tempt me?"

Toke touched her shoulder. "It will be the greatest test of your life."

She swallowed and glanced out into the night.

He squeezed her hands. "Faith."

She took a deep breath. "Faith."

Toke touched her hand. "Do you know where your loyalties lie?"

Macy looked at the ground, over at her new friends, and back at Toke. "Yes."

Toke's eyes suddenly looked thousands of years old. "Then you know what you must do if we find the Last."

Macy nodded and turned to walk back to her bedroll. Of course she knew what she must do. As the Seeker she would be led to the hiding place of the Last Shard. She would retrieve it, then she would protect Toke's family—her friends—from the temptation and danger of the Last. She would leave, abandon them.

She lay back down and for a time stared at Toke's back as he stared off into the darkness, her heart feeling as if it were being ripped to shreds.

Macy jolted awake when someone put a hand over her mouth. Her hands fumbled for her knife until she looked up into Keelyn's face. Keelyn put her finger to her lips and slowly removed her hand. Macy looked around to see Toke waking the others. "What's going on?" She whispered.

"They're here," Keelyn breathed.

"What? Isn't the Treasta working?"

Keelyn nodded. "It's something else. Pack quick. We've gotta move."

Macy quickly packed her things, slung the bag over her shoulders, pulled out her knife, and let her Kuna build. She walked over to where Toke was supervising what to take and what to leave behind. He looked up at her with an expression that sent shivers down her spine. "What's the plan?" she whispered.

"I sent Brina to see what's coming." He tied his blanket to his bag. His eyes were puffy and red. "As soon as she gets back we'll come up with a plan."

"How close are they?"

"A mile or two."

Brina appeared at Toke's elbow, her face flushed, her hands shaking.

Toke put his hand on her arm. "What is it?"

"I've only ever seen pictures, but I think," she looked like she was about to puke. "Kezgani."

Macy's hand flew to her mouth. "Seriously?" How many more creatures that should have been in Misery were now on the loose?

Rune cursed.

Toke's hands curled into fists. "Were those the only creatures you saw?"

Brina's voice shook. "No. A DéHool was at the head, flanked by two Thrundoon, and a small army of Raksasha followed behind."

"How many would you guess?"

"Probably fifty Kezgani and about the same amount of Raksasha."

"At their speed how long would you guess it will take them to get here?"

"Five, maybe ten minutes tops."

Toke tugged his messy hair. "A war party."

A collective gasp passed through the camp.

49 BATTLE STRATEGIES

Toke lifted his hand. "They're not headed for us. The Treasta is showing their advancement, but their thoughts are not focused on us. We just happen to be in their way. They're headed for the village."

"What! Why?" Macy's fingers twitched and she gripped her knife more tightly in her fist.

Toke sighed. "Information. To send a message. It could be anything."

"Can we beat them there? Warn the people?" Keelyn asked.

"We will warn them, but it won't be enough. There's not enough time and the creatures are too many. It will be a slaughter." He looked at the group. "But we might be able to slow them down. Do enough damage to their numbers to give some of the villagers a chance."

"You mean offer ourselves as a sacrifice?" Rune muttered.

Toke shook his head. "Do not doubt your strength."

Keelyn put her hand on Rune's arm. "We can't leave them alone. It's not right." Rune pulled out from under her hand and Macy could see the fear in his eyes, not for himself, but for Keelyn. But her eyes were on Toke. "Do you have a plan?"

Toke rubbed his jaw. "If we can divide their numbers, get at least half the army to follow us, the village might stand a chance." He looked around at his family. Macy could see it wasn't something he wanted to risk, but whether or not his rebels accepted the Chosen code, they couldn't just sit here and hide while the Dark sought out and slaughtered innocent beings.

Connell came forward with his bow slung over his back and held out his sister's matching bow, Macdara was no longer with him but flying above them, watchful.

Keelyn took the bow without comment, slipped it over her shoulder, checked the arrows in her quiver, and looked at Rune. He shook his head, but proceeded to slide his sword into the sheath on his back. Toke put on his weapons belt and loaded it with various objects. Macy looked over her belt and checked her pouches and weapons. She should have made more Glockshaw when she practiced with Rune.

Toke motioned them closer to the dying light of the fire. "This is what we're going to do. Brina, enhance your strength and run ahead unseen, warn the village."

She nodded and disappeared, her invisible feet turning up dust and leaves as she ran.

"Keelyn, you run straight for the village as well, use your Lóklana to clear a path through the army, get to the village and protect as many women and children as you can." Keelyn paused long enough to touch Rune's shoulder before taking off after Brina. Rune's fists clenched.

"Macy, Rune, enhance your strength and run down the sides of the advancement. Use your Kuna and your swords. Draw the army toward you. Connell and I will use the Shupata from the rear." Connell threw an extra quiver over his shoulder and they all started running.

Macy veered left and Rune to the right. With enhanced strength in her legs, eyes, and ears, it didn't take long before she could hear the army approaching. She rubbed her hands together as she ran and called the Kuna to her palms. She wouldn't hold back. They needed to stop this army now; she couldn't worry about reserving her strength.

"*Mi'no ha!*" she twisted her fingers and pushed a ball of fire into the left flank of the invading army. Pain-filled shrieks said she'd hit the mark and the left side began to slow down and fan out. She caught sight of Keelyn trailing white light. A Raksasha raised a bow, an arrow notched and aimed for her back. Macy called up a fireball and tossed it at the Raksasha. He exploded in a shower of flame before the arrow released. Rune's terrified face met hers across the battlefield. He nodded in thanks, and they both started running full tilt into the throng amid flying arrows while tossing more fireballs. Far up ahead, white light lit the trees and she knew Keelyn had made it to the village. A grim smile lifted the corner of her mouth as she rushed, jabbed, and killed every dark creature in sight.

ooo

Tolen grabbed the side of his head and leaned against the wall of Blaze's hut. Macy was in a battle, fighting Kezgani and Raksasha. She wasn't alone—they were winning. Tolen pulled himself out of the vision. She was strong. She would be okay. The real danger was still ahead. He shivered, but reined in the fear. She would get help soon. He needed to focus on where he was needed right now.

He glanced around, but only Quasar seemed to notice Tolen's moment of distraction. Tolen met his concerned gaze with a tiny shake of his head. Now wasn't the time to discuss it.

In all, about thirty people made their way to Blaze's home. The group consisted of mostly the elderly, Blaze's mother and sister, and a few of his friends—two of which showed the Dark features of the Daklafar. They, too, had completed the ceremony that allowed them to look the part to protect their families. Such strong, brave children.

The rest all looked like the Lafar Tolen was familiar with, although their beauty was masked by years of slave labor and hard living conditions. The lack of true light in the Shadow Realm had drained their skin and hair of color, and their normally violet eyes appeared flat black.

In one way, it was good that only thirty people had showed up. They were all crammed so tightly into Blaze's tiny hut that there was barely enough room to move, let alone breathe. The small windows were sealed shut, making it even stuffier. The eerie blue lights dancing in the tiny lanterns cast deep shadows on everyone's faces, making the room look as if it was filled with talking corpses. Although no one was talking now. They all stared at Tolen with a mixture of expressions. Curiosity, anxiety, distrust, even fear.

He took a deep breath and looked around the room. Quasar gave him a reassuring half smile. It was obvious he was grieving for the loss of his friends, who Haven had informed them had been executed because of their daughter, Nova's treachery. But there was still a slight, though guilt riddled, amount of joy in his eyes from knowing that some of his people had survived, and he would possibly be able to save them.

The man who appeared to be the oldest Lafar in the room, his hair soft gray and lines edging his eyes and mouth, stood in the middle of the group and offered his arm to Tolen. "I am Astral, honorary leader of this village. Welcome."

Tolen nodded as the old man dropped his arm and turned to speak to the group.

"We come here tonight because of the change we see in Blaze." Astral looked at Blaze with a gentle smile. "He is the boy we once knew. He is free from the darkness that held him bound. He comes to us with another boy, a boy of legend." He looked at Tolen and his eyes narrowed slightly.

Tolen kept his chin up and met the man's eye while still trying to show respect. After a moment or two, Astral tilted his head and looked back at the group. "The Ninth believes we can be freed from our prison. At least those of us who never entered into the oath with the Dark— those of us who chose slavery over joining the Daklafar when we learned we could not save our friends." Everyone in the room bowed their head at the sad memory.

"For hundreds of years our kind have suffered here, kidnapped by those who should have been our kin. Twenty-five years ago a group came to try to turn the Daklafar. They learned of us and wanted to help. Few of them survived. We abandoned hope." A few sniffles could be heard throughout the room. "But now we can see hope rekindled in this pure child." He gestured for Blaze to stand beside him. "I know most of the old ones have entered an oath to never shed the blood of our brethren again, despite the evil they have become, but I come to ask you to break your oath and stand together once again." A few people started to stand.

Tolen stepped forward and faced the old Lafar. "Astral, wait." His heart thudded with apprehension, but his body was flooded with warmth. They were all looking at him in confusion. "You can't do this. You can't break your oath."

Astral shook his head. "There are not enough to fight if the old do not join."

Tolen shook his head. His palms started to sweat and he put his hands behind his back. "The Light would have known of your oath. It was a good deed. If you go against it now, you would be degrading the truths you have stood for all these years. Hold to your oath. Stay true to your promise.

"We hold Light within us. You have lived in the most horrible of circumstances in the most horrible place in existence and still managed to hold onto your light. I believe that part of the reason is because you turned your backs on everything associated with darkness. We have to trust that our plan is sound. If we are meant to succeed, the way will come to us, and we will succeed." The people stared at him in awe. Astral's eyes filled with tears.

Tolen turned to Blaze. "Blaze I want you to be a captain. I need you to choose another captain and four runners from this group."

Blaze selected his two Dak friends and three others from the crowd. Tolen nodded as they each came to stand beside him.

Tolen addressed everyone in the room. "I have a plan, but I'm going to need your help."

The people nodded and Tolen continued. "Blaze tells me there are four villages."

Astral nodded.

Tolen looked at the four runners. "Each of you will be responsible for going to a village and spreading the word. Get numbers of those willing and able to fight, as well as the number of women and children who wish to escape. Be careful who you speak to, in case there be any who might get scared and rat us out. Choose two more captains for each village and find a meeting place for the fighters within the village to receive instruction, as we can't all assemble here. Have the captains assemble volunteers to fashion weapons, and those good in medicine." Tolen turned to Astral. "We'll need to set up a field hospital at a central location to the battle where we can quickly help the wounded."

"I'll take care of it."

Tolen tugged his ponytail and went back to addressing the runners. "Inform the volunteers to get some rest and then be at their meeting place ready to receive the details of the plan in four hours. They should be ready for battle at dawn." He looked around the room. "Any further suggestions?"

The people all shook their heads, the anxiety on their faces replaced with determination.

Tolen took a deep breath. "All right, runners, meet me back here with your chosen captains in one hour with names and numbers of volunteers and families."

Astral and the four runners quickly left the hut.

Tolen looked around at the remaining crowd. "Thank you for coming. Go home and discuss what you have learned. I invite you all to return in an hour as well if you would like to be part of the planning."

His voice came out clear and strong and the others left voicing their acceptance of Tolen's plan to Blaze and his mother as they walked by.

Quasar moved through the crowd, sidled up to Tolen and whispered in his ear. "That was impressive. If I did not know better, I would believe you had much practice leading war parties."

"Do you think it will work?" Tolen whispered back.

Quasar shrugged. "We can only hope. How did you come up with a plan so quickly?"

"I didn't." Tolen admitted sheepishly. "Ever since we rescued Blaze I've been thinking about Mrs. Clancy's history class and how she loved the overused phrase, 'the enemy of my enemy is my friend.'"

"What?"

Tolen shrugged. "She was obsessed with *The Art of War* and dissecting and comparing Sun Tzu's battle tactics to various wars and their outcomes." Tolen waved his hand at Quasar's dubious look. "It doesn't matter."

Quasar's confidence in Tolen's plan seemed to be fading and he wished he hadn't said anything. "You read this plan in a book?"

"Sort of." Tolen took a deep breath. "Quasar, I'm open to other ideas if you've got them."

Quasar shook his head as Blaze walked back toward them. "There is always room for plans to go wrong, no matter how long you have to prepare them. It is good for us that battles are usually won by faith and heart. I just hope these people have both."

Tolen swallowed back nerves. Quasar was right to be leery of a battle plan based on high school history lessons and books.

Faith was a powerful and dangerous thing.

50 OUT OF DEVASTATION

The devastation seemed endless. The creatures that had beat them to the village had wreaked considerable damage before they'd been able to defeat them. Several huts still burned and the dead lying in the dirty street were far too many. Keelyn's Lóklana had faded, but luckily most of the women and children were safe. The old ones were all gone, killed or taken captive, and very few of the men had survived. It was a slaughter. Simply a means to an end for the Dark. Take what they needed. Destroy the rest.

Macy's legs trembled as she walked to where Toke was helping a young boy—no more than eight or nine years old—to the makeshift hospital they'd set up in one of the few huts still standing.

She helped him lower the boy onto the cot then followed Toke back out into the village to look for more injured. Rune and Brina were somewhere doing the same. Keelyn and Connell were gifted in natural medicine and were helping the wounded.

Once they were alone she kicked the ground. "We were too slow! We shouldn't have waited to come. We shouldn't have cared about stupid customs!"

"I didn't know the future Macy. If I'd known their fate, I wouldn't have hesitated, but I didn't, and we did all that we could."

She gritted her teeth, knowing that Toke felt just as guilty as she did, but she couldn't stop her anger. "It's not enough!"

"Control yourself. Many of these children are still frightened. We'll have our chance at vengeance, but right now you need to be calm."

She shoved her smoking palms into her back pockets as they stepped into a copse of trees near the edge of the village and she nearly tripped over a body. Toke leaned down, rolled the body over, and placed his ear on his chest. It was an old man, his entire body soaked in blood. There was no way he was alive.

Macy leaned down to help Toke lift him up and the man opened his eyes. He grabbed Macy's hand and when he spoke blood dribbled out the side of his mouth. "Eamun's Island…" He choked and Toke lifted his chin. "You must stop Daemon…Gateway almost finished…the Key…" his hand went limp and his head lolled to the side.

He was gone.

Macy's heart clenched. If he was saying what she thought he was saying, her earlier guesses were right on the mark.

Toke ran a hand over his sweaty face. "Let's get him back to the village and hope someone knows what he was talking about."

It took them until well past midnight to finish taking the bodies to a mass gravesite, and almost another full hour before Macy and Toke found someone who knew the old man. They found her, a young woman named Dreya, with a group of people planning the ceremony for the dead.

"Yes, I know him," Dreya said with quiet dignity. "He is my father."

"I'm so sorry," Toke whispered with his hand on her arm. "I wish we could have done more."

She wiped a tear from her cheek. "If you hadn't come, we'd all be dead."

"He told us something before he died. We were hoping you could help us." Toke told Dreya what her father had said.

She lifted her chin, grief stricken but clearly determined to help. "Eamun's Island is not far from here. The humans call it Poverty Island. It was a small settlement of Hidden kind. Eamun lived there for centuries until the Dark found him. The Guardians sent us word after Eamun's death; they believed he managed to hide the Last Shard before voluntarily passing into the Light.

"But a strange power was covering the island and the Guardians could no longer see anything on it. Three days ago they asked us to send spies onto the island to see what they could discover. My father and the other elders did so, at great risk. Only one spy returned, just hours ago. He saw Daemon. The Demon Master has been tearing the island apart looking for the Last and he's been using Clenadium to build a gateway. A gateway to the Shadow Realm. The old ones believed he reforged the Key and just needs the Last to make it work. We were preparing to send word to the Guardians when we were attacked."

"The spy. Did he make it?" Toke leaned forward.

Dreya shook her head.

"So the Guardians don't know?" Macy whispered.

"No."

Toke took Dreya's thin hands in his. "Just one more question and then we will leave you to grieve in peace." He took a deep breath. "There is a rumor, an old tale about the Final Battle. It says that the day would come when the descendants of the Nine would sever the Pact, and with the aid of the Relics raise an army of humans to fight against the Dark. Do you know if this is true?"

Dreya turned her eyes to Macy and nodded.

Macy paced up and down outside the tiny hut, working to control her Kuna. They'd helped the village as much as they could, they'd participated in the burial ceremony, and the kind villagers had provided them a tiny hut to rest in. But no one was resting. Toke was outside with her while she tried to stop her hands from smoking. The others spoke in whispers inside.

"I need to go now," she whispered fiercely.

"I spoke to Dreya. They're getting us boats and supplies. It's just a few hours walk to the shoreline."

"No, Toke. You can't come with me. The Last is there and so is Daemon. I need to get there now. I'll draw less attention alone. I'll find the Last and you can keep your family safe from temptation."

Toke stepped in front of her. "Macy, we have to try to destroy that gate. This village was slaughtered not because they knew where the Last was like we suspected, but because they knew what Daemon was up to. No one knows it's there besides us. Even if we send word, it will take too much time to get there. We have to try!"

"But—"

Toke lifted his hand. "We'll go in after the gate. You go in after the Last. Our attack on the gate may be just the distraction you need."

"I can't let you do that."

Keelyn stepped out of the hut. "You can't stop us either."

The others followed her out. Rune took her hand. "You didn't think we would figure out what you two are always whispering about?"

Toke twisted around to face his rebels. "How long have you known?"

"Since last night when you snuck away to talk to Macy when you thought we were all asleep and Connell sent Macdara to spy on you."

Toke ducked his head. "I'm sorry—"

"For not trusting us?" Rune asked. "It's not like we've given you a lot of reason to trust our motives. But we were talking in the hut and after what we saw tonight, whether we completely follow the Light or not, this was beyond wrong. We're not going to sit back and let Daemon allow millions of Dark creatures in through that gate. Not if we can stop it."

Toke's eyes filled with moisture and soon they were all hugging him. Macy stood off to the side, uncomfortable, until Keelyn opened her arms and beckoned her to join them. "Families stick together." Macy smiled as she joined the group hug.

Two hours later, Brina, Keelyn, and Connell slept fitfully on the floor of the hut. Toke was outside checking on supplies, and Macy and Rune sat talking quietly. Something had changed between them when Macy saved Keelyn and they'd fought together. A friendship forged out of appreciation and trust.

Rune watched Keelyn sleep, her head resting on Connell's stomach.

"How long until you turn eighteen?" Macy asked.

"Three months. October first. You?"

"Just over a year. October *third*."

His mouth lifted in a slight grin. "It's a good month."

She nodded. "Have you decided?"

He sighed and took a moment to answer, knowing full well what she meant. "It's so unfair if you think about it. They steal our childhood and then once we've experienced the Dark and all its evil for twelve years they say we have a choice to go back to our human lives—but our knowledge remains with us. We can live as humans, but we'll still know about the Dark, even though we'll no longer be able to see it. We'll live the rest of our lives knowing we had the power to fight it, but we selfishly chose not to. I never considered going back to human life, and once I met Keelyn my choice solidified. I can't leave this life because I know she never will."

Macy nodded, understanding more than he realized. "Do you really think they stole our childhood?"

"What would you call it?"

She shrugged. "Hope."

He tipped his head and flicked a stick across the short space between them. "Why go back anyway, right? Human teenagers are annoying. Self-absorbed, arrogant."

"Not all of them." Her thoughts turned to Tolen as they waited for the sun to rise and the moment to depart.

○○○

mother and sister push their meager furnishings against the thin walls of the hut to make room for the planning party. They left the small table in the center. Tolen, Blaze, and Quasar moved in around it. Behind them in more rows stood the eight new captains—six male and two female— beside Blaze and his friend, Erid. Most of the elderly who'd attended the first meeting had yet to return.

The number of fighters versus those who needed to be rescued worried Tolen, but even more than that, in his ignorance of the Hidden world he'd overlooked—or had never realized—one glaring fact.

Lafar weren't gifted with specific Light gifts.

Instead the Light had gifted their race with something else. Something they both revered and, in the case of the Daklafar, resented.

Lafar treasured superior insight, skill, and knowledge that far surpassed human and other Hidden intellect. They could connect with the world around them on a level unequaled by any race or gifted person. They could enhance their strength and natural senses without need of calling upon the Hidden tongue—but not one of them held any elemental or metaphysical gift. Some could be gifted, or cursed as in Quasar's situation, by a Seraph to do the Light's bidding, but those cases were very rare, and none of the Lafar trapped here were so gifted.

Tolen would be the only gifted fighter among a race of fighters who, although once were a level up on normal humans and Hidden, had been subdued and tortured for most of their lives. That meant that the most dangerous and difficult part of this mission would fall to him—a fact that he would have wanted anyway, but worried him nonetheless.

Haven brought over another pot of their tasteless version of Lucid tea and filled up their cups as they discussed the Dak's weaknesses.

Blaze pointed to a spot on the crudely drawn map. "This is the spot that holds the most guards." He moved his finger across to the other side. "This side has the least."

Tolen looked at the vague details that didn't explain much. "Why is this area more heavily guarded?"

One of the female captains, Skye—if Tolen remembered right—spoke up. "It's Darsapean's castle. Daemon lives there and we think it might be where he smuggles in creatures from Misery."

Tolen whipped around to look at the young woman. "What gives you that idea?"

She shrugged, looking uncomfortable under Tolen's scrutiny. He softened his expression in encouragement and she went on. "Several months ago, my sisters and I were part of the shift of slaves sent to clear an area within the castle grounds, and while we were there, my sister, Spire, came across some strange metal. When she picked it up one of the guards beat her with a rod until she could barely move. She died a few hours later." Anger clouded her features. "Later that night, I snuck back to kill the Dak responsible. I saw Daemon there giving direction to a group of Kreydawn. They were building something with the strange metal, a sort of gigantic arch. By the next day, the guard was doubled. Within a week there were more guards around the area than anywhere else—even the Shadow Prison. Within a short time creatures supposed to be locked in Misery began flowing into the realm. It seemed to fit."

Tolen gripped her arm. "I'm sorry for your loss."

She nodded her thanks. "I got my revenge. I slit the Dak's throat in his sleep, and for good measure finished off his entire guard."

One of the male captains chuckled humorlessly. "She's the reason they doubled the guard the next day."

Tolen was taken aback by the suffering of these people. He had to get them out of here and Skye had just given him an idea. "We've decided to separate the women and children into ten different groups and we've chosen their separate paths to the exit point. We know we need a diversion to get them out. We have to keep the Dak from anticipating our next move. We want to confuse them." The others around the table nodded.

Tolen's heart started to race as the ideas flowed into his mind. "We set up a series of perfectly timed attacks, beginning at each village work center. If we make them think it's a workers' revolt, that will draw all the local guards from their posts to deal with the uprising, giving the families time to escape, sneak to the exit point and get hidden."

"How will we know when to attack?" a tall thin captain asked.

Tolen nodded toward the window. "I've asked a good friend to help." A chorus of soft hooting met their ears and Skyborne landed on the windowsill.

The captain smiled. "I have only ever heard the old ones mimic that sound. It is grand to hear and see them for real."

Tolen went back to the developing plan and pointed to the dot representing the castle. "Once the local guards are distracted we set off a series of explosions at the storage facilities, here and here." He pointed to opposing grain silos. "The local guards will be too busy to go, they'll have to send some of the guards from the castle grounds. We'll already have some men in place around there." He looked at Skye. "Your platoon. You'll be spread out, so they won't know your numbers, and fighting from a distance. Arrows, fire, explosions, anything. Hopefully the Dak come running, thinking we're there to destroy the gate. Quasar and I will have broken into the grounds and be doing exactly that."

Murmurs hissed through the crowd and someone scoffed. "But you'll be captured or killed."

Tolen shook his head. "I hope not." He glanced at Skye. "This is where I'll need your knowledge." He turned to Blaze and his two Dak friends. "And yours as well. Will you come with Quasar and I?"

Skye looked at the other captains. "With honor."

Blaze smiled grimly. "I am with you, *Mindra*."

Tolen nodded. The others moved in closer as they picked apart the plan with more detail and put those with the most knowledge of specific areas over certain points in the mission. Hours later the rest of the elders returned with news of weapons, medicine, and more volunteers.

The plan was coming together.

51 AND INTO THE MIRE

I T WAS ABOUT an hour until sunrise as Macy and the others tugged their little boats the rest of the way onto the rocky shore of Eamun's Island. The villagers loaded them up on Lucid tea and she'd handed out the last of her sucker supply for energy, but they were so pumped about what they were about to attempt she didn't think sugar and calories would actually make a difference.

They worked silently, first anchoring the boats to the rocks and then covering them with the black blankets stowed inside. The villagers said this side of the island was the least guarded way since the waters here were extremely rocky and dangerous. An invading army would never use this route. Only a few reckless Chosen used to sneaking around would be crazy enough to try it.

Toke tapped his mouth and motioned for them to move forward slowly and quietly. It was difficult to do. The rocks shifted with each step, slowing them down as they had to pick where to place their feet.

The air felt thick, heavy, and filled with dread. The temperature was significantly colder on the island than on the water, like an icepack pressed over a wound.

Toke pointed to a crumbling lighthouse that was barely visible in the murky moonlight. They could just see movement in the shadows within and surrounding the abandoned building.

Raksasha.

Toke motioned them around him and whispered. "Macy, Camouflage?"

Macy nodded, opened a pouch on her belt, and walked around the group. Once everyone had taken a pinch, she did the same, and they sprinkled it over themselves.

The unnatural cloud cover above the island crackled with electricity that twisted and curled back on itself—a witch's cauldron. Toke pointed at the surrounding forest and they moved quickly, not daring to look around. The Dark would know they were here soon enough, and with the dense clouds it wouldn't matter if they waited for sunrise—the storm made it perfectly easy to work in daylight.

Once in the shelter of the trees they inspected their weapons. Keelyn and Connell helped each other strap on their restocked quivers. Brina's arsenal was small, just her sword, but being able to become invisible was her greatest weapon. Rune strapped his Kamud across his back and checked the pouch of Glockshaw Macy made for him. She hoped he was confident enough to use them. She went over her own weapons. Only one Shakra left from the battle with the DéHool outside the Binithan, three Glockshaw, some Sleep Dust, and a little of the Camouflage left. Her knife bounced comfortingly against her thigh.

Toke came behind her and laced a Kamud across her back that was very like Rune's. "Just do as we practiced and you'll be fine."

She nodded, not trusting her voice. He put his hand on her shoulder and looked in her eyes for a long moment before walking back around to the others and going over their individual jobs. Macy tried not to let the guilt pull her down. They'd all accepted the plan. They would go for the gate and she would go after the Last Shard. She might have accepted the plan, but that didn't mean she liked it.

Toke nodded at Brina and she disappeared to scout the area.

Brina was gone for nearly thirty minutes, long enough that Toke started pacing. When she finally returned, looking even more freaked out than when she'd discovered what was after the villagers, everyone jumped to their feet.

"Brina?" Toke asked.

"It's big. No, it's huge!" She paused to catch her breath. "It's the largest gathering of Dark I've ever seen. They've got hundreds of Kreydawn moving carts filled with those silver rocks toward the center of the island. I could just see what looked like a silver structure sticking out above the trees. It looked like about six DéHool controlled by Thrundoon are standing guard around the area."

Macy pictured the demonic wolves controlled by their pitiless gigantic masters and shivered.

"Raksasha are hiding in the trees." Brina started nervously twisting her braids. "There were other creatures running the perimeter. I-I've never seen anything like them before. Their tremors in the Balance were the coldest I've ever felt. It was difficult to remain unseen whenever I was near one." Her voice quivered.

Toke guided her to a broken bench and sat her down. "What did they look like?"

"They were fast—even faster than Raksasha. Some ran on all fours, using their arms as front legs. Their faces seemed to be constantly shifting so I couldn't tell exactly what they looked like."

Toke paled. "Grey skinned? Lean, with a thin covering of pale hair?"

"Yes."

"What are they?" Rune asked.

"Gungruin."

Macy's hand flew to her mouth. "Skin shifters?"

Toke nodded. "Were those the only creatures you saw?"

"Yes. I couldn't get close enough to see if there were others inside the compound, though."

"How many would you guess guard the perimeter?"

Brina's shoulders trembled. "It was hard to tell how many Gungruin." Her mouth twisted over their name. "They moved so fast—I'd guess fifty or more. There could be as many as a thousand Raksasha—the trees are full of them. Then there's the six DéHool and Thrundoon."

"Toke. We can't do this. It's too many." Macy stepped forward.

Toke looked around at his Chosen, his family.

"We're ready," Keelyn said, and Rune frowned.

"If we can even slow them down, we're giving the world hope right?" Connell asked.

Toke nodded.

Connell shrugged. "That's good enough for me."

Macy looked at the twins. They were so good, so pure. They naturally followed the Light, even if they didn't see it within themselves. Rune, too, as stubborn as he was, was fiercely loyal. He would do anything for his little family. Brina was hard on the outside, but her love for her little band was just as strong. Macy looked around at their scared but determined faces and her heart sank.

She'd never had friends until Tolen, and now she had five she couldn't stand to lose. Now that she had finally opened her heart again, it seemed determined to make up for years of being bottled up. It swelled and ached as she looked at her friends.

She clenched her teeth. She would have to move fast to get the Last. There was no way they could win against an army this big. They needed to get in and get out!

Toke moved to the center of the group and motioned them all forward. "We can't win an outward battle. We're too few. But we can cause chaos. Disrupt their work. We may be able to buy some time for the Guardians. I know none of you have pledged yourselves to the Light or to the service of the Guardians, but this is no longer about loyalties. It is about right and wrong. And what the Dark is trying to do is the essence of wrong. We cannot allow them to bring Darsapean back. It would be the end of everything."

He started pacing. "Connell has sent Macdara to get word to the Guardians, but we have no way of knowing how long it will take them to dispatch an army here, and by then it could be too late. Keelyn and Connell will take to the side and draw them out with arrows. Brina will lead Rune in toward the structure—see what you can do with the Glockshaw. I'll help Keelyn and Connell. Macy will clear the path for Rune and Brina." He looked at Macy and it felt as if someone was stabbing her in the chest. "Once you're through, run hard and don't stop. Follow the guidance you feel and you will be led to the Last."

He looked around the group and met their determined expressions one by one. "Whatever you do, do not let the Gungruin close enough to touch you. They can take on the appearance of anything they've ever touched. They can look like women or children. Friends. They are the reason the Dark won so many of the first battles in the Revolution. People were killing their own thinking they were Gungruin and protecting Gungruin who looked like their own men." A visible shudder passed throughout the group.

Brina stood up and squared her shoulders. "I'm ready."

Toke turned back and put his hand on her cheek. The others moved in, touched shoulders, and grasped hands. Macy stood off to the side and watched the emotional goodbye feeling sick. Toke opened his arms, she stepped forward hesitantly, and then everyone patted her back and shook her hands.

"Chosen?" Connell gave a tiny shrug and put his fist out. His eyes slightly embarrassed at the corny suggestion.

It took a moment, but finally they all smiled and put their fists together. "Chosen!"

ooo

Tolen glanced behind him from his crouched position. He couldn't see the others in their hiding spots, but he could feel them. He'd been practicing with his Watcher ability, trying to keep an eye out for each area of the battle while staying present in his own, but it was hard to do in this realm with the darkness like a veil over his sight.

Skye left them in a spot in the skeletal forest that gave them a bird's-eye view of the castle grounds. They could just see the top of the gate—which resembled a tall, glistening arch—where it pulsated with dark power and energy that was both compelling and terrifying. Tolen did his best not to stare at it for very long.

They hid in the scrubby black underbrush that dotted the outer rim of the dark forest. It wasn't much cover; he hoped the smelly, charcoal colored mud they'd slimed themselves in would keep them hidden from the Daklafar's eyes as long as possible. Luckily, he had some of the Camouflage Macy had restocked for him and he'd mixed it with the mud he'd plastered over his body. Raksasha would definitely be joining the battle at some point and he didn't want them discovering him. Lafar blood they would expect to smell, not that of a Chosen.

A signal from Skye would let them know that she'd seen a good portion of the guard heading toward the villages because of the revolt. Everything was in place. Now all they could do was pray everything would go according to plan. An annoying voice in the back of Tolen's mind couldn't stop going through all the things that could go wrong in a plan conceived in a matter of hours.

Faith. They must have faith and do their best. There was nothing more to be done.

The first round of revolts was to take place in just under three minutes. He'd set timers on his watch to let him know when each was to start.

They needed to be timed perfectly if the plan was to work. Each session designed to pattern after the first. Ten minutes after the bell tolled the second battle would begin, the third at eleven minutes, fourth at twelve minutes, and so on. Order, hidden beneath chaos. As long as things went as they should, he would break into the grounds in a little less than a half an hour.

Two minutes. Quasar gripped his shoulder and Tolen closed his eyes. The first battle area came into his mind's eye and he watched through misted sight as if he were there…

Two haggard-looking Lafar walked into the grain silo, bulging sacks of the dark, coarse grain on their backs—or at least what would appear to the Dak guards as grain—heads down, weak, broken looking. As they disappeared into the silo the tiniest of grins crossed the face of the last man.

Ten seconds. Nine. Eight. Tolen's muscles tightened in anticipation.

BOOM! Only the tiniest shudder could be felt from his vantage point, but in his mind he watched the destruction and reaction of the surrounding Daklafar Guard. First confusion, and then anger as the processing plant came alive and the Lafar slaves rushed out, brandishing wooden poles with nails sticking out, crude bows, and other makeshift weapons. Many of the slaves fell to the more advanced weaponry of the Guard, but numbers were in their favor.

Tolen's heart ached for the fallen as he opened his eyes. "The first battle is underway."

"The people?" Quasar murmured.

"We're losing some, but they're holding out and gaining ground. I saw the Dak calling for reinforcements."

Quasar nodded and looked at Tolen's watch. "Send word to the next group."

Tolen jumped, so caught up in *this* battle he hadn't been focused on the time. He had to pay better attention. He closed his eyes and concentrated on Skyborne's brother. Instantly the owl's mind was clear and open.

Give the alert. He watched as the owl gently squeezed the captain's shoulder.

This pattern continued through the six different battles and distractions that wrought chaos throughout the realm. Dak ran around everywhere trying to restore order. Crops and houses burned. People fought bravely. By the time the Dak thought to check the villages—to threaten the women and children—the families were gone, led to safety by their appointed guards and Skyborne's troops, to the creepy forest where they would hide until Tolen could get back to open the gateway.

Only minutes remained until Tolen, Quasar, Blaze, and his two friends would head for the castle.

Tolen nudged Quasar's arm. "Skyborne just sent word. The last of the families are safely hidden in the forest. He'll keep watch over them."

Quasar nodded and turned his eyes back to the castle.

Tolen closed his eyes and *watched* the guards surrounding the castle gates rush after a handful of other Dak heading back toward the village. He opened his eyes. "It's almost time."

A glimmer of light washed across their faces. Skye's signal.

Tolen looked back to see Blaze pop his head up once from his bush and nod. He'd seen it. His friends would follow.

As long as the first team planted the explosives in the carts of silver rock the Kreydawn rolled inside the castle gates, the next phase shouldn't be too hard to pull off. Tolen would use his Kunamin to lob fireballs over the wall and into the carts, then they could hunker down and wait for the explosions.

Skye signaled again.

"Now!" Tolen whispered and ran. Quasar shadowed him, and the light footfalls he could hear behind said the others were there as well.

They rushed as quickly as they could across the pitted ground toward the pile of boulders where they would mount their attack.

Tolen watched the Suppressors guide the mindless Kreydawn from various positions, their mouth-less faces hidden beneath their dark cowls.

They dropped down to their bellies behind the boulders out of eye-sight of the Suppressors. The first ten carts were the ones that were supposed to have the explosives. It might not be enough to bring down the gate, but they could hope.

The castle gates opened and the Kreydawn began to push the carts inside. Tolen stood up. As soon as the first of the ten were inside, he shot a huge fireball and at the last second twisted his fingers, dividing the bomb into ten, and sent them shooting into the carts. Before the Suppressors could figure out what was going on and try to stop the Kreydawn, the first five carts passed through the entrance. The Suppressors ran as soon as the explosions started, leaving the Kreydawn to die mindlessly in place.

Tolen heard a strange guttural shout right behind them and something sharp poked into his back. He turned slowly to see ten Daklafar guards standing around them, weapons pointed.

The nearest Dak slammed the butt of his spear into the side of Tolen's head and everything went black.

52 OBSTACLES

MACY WAITED IMPATIENTLY behind a thick tree. The swirling clouds blocked most of the light, so she enhanced her sight and hearing. She saw Rune's silhouette a few trees away. Brina waited just ahead of Rune. They were going to go on Toke's signal, timing their advance for the same moment Keelyn and Connell released their first arrows.

Her palms tingled in anticipation. This wasn't the first time she'd waited on the edge of battle, but it was the first time she'd ever faced an army this large—or Gungruin. Gungruin's mimicry could be undone with water, but the idea of trying to toss her canteen at one before it killed her was not very appealing. They must be fast and nimble and avoid being killed *or* touched.

A low whistle met her ears. Toke's signal. The first arrow zinged through the air, the blue light of Toke's protection dome lit the tree line, and Rune and Macy started running, following behind Brina.

Raksasha shrieks filled the night air along with the sound of the beating of huge wings. Shrieg. Macy's skin prickled at the sound as they ran. The Raksasha swung like gigantic apes above them, yet to notice their advance.

Macy hoped it would hold. They needed to make it to the gate without being spotted. It was a dim hope, but a hope all the same. With her enhanced hearing she could make out the sound of arrows pinging off Toke's dome, the whoosh of the twins' arrows as they returned fire, and the occasional thunk and grunt when they hit their mark.

A wall of twenty Raksasha jumped down from the trees to block their path. Macy and Rune shouted *"Mi'noha!"* and threw fire at the wall of enemies. The Raksasha burst into flames. Rune twisted his fingers and the creatures crumbled to ash.

The clearing was in sight. The strange, silvery rock gleamed threateningly—its strange pale light threw an eerie glow on the faces of the Kreydawn working mindlessly around it.

Macy shivered. The darkness here was almost as thick and heavy as she remembered it feeling in the Shadow Realm.

A low growl made the blood drain from her face. A DéHool led by a thick chain clenched in the fists of a giant Thrundoon stepped out from behind a low antiquated outbuilding at the edge of the clearing. Rune and Macy skidded to a halt.

"Brina now!" Rune yelled and Brina went invisible.

The DéHool snorted and watched her disappear, his nose following the direction she would have ran.

"Rune!" Macy tossed her last Glockshaw at him. He caught it mid-air, then took a step toward her and raised his fist. She bumped it once. "Go get 'em Blondie!"

Rune laughed as he ran the direction Brina had disappeared, while Macy ran toward the DéHool.

She drew her sword as she ran and bridged the gap between them quickly. She jumped into the air, landed on the wolf's back, and used the momentum to spring toward the Thrundoon holding the DéHool's chain. She forced her Kuna into the Kamud and it burst into blue flames as she swung. The Thrundoon barely had time to see what was coming before his head was severed from his body.

She landed on her feet behind the creature's twitching legs and flipped around to face the DéHool. It eyed her flaming blade and the body of its master on the ground. Hatred seethed from its red, pitiless eyes. It snapped and snarled, saliva drooling in thick ribbons from its teeth.

Macy moved the sword in front of her as the warmth of her Kuna flowed from her hands to the blade—her body trembled with power.

The DéHool lunged.

She ran forward and dropped to the ground, sliding on her back beneath the beast's belly, stabbing upward as she slid. The creature fell to its side with a howl, and Macy stood up, her arms covered in the wolf's blood.

New howls filled the air—the other DéHool had heard their fellow's cry. She shoved the sword, still glowing softly, into the sheath on her back.

The howls sounded closer. The clash of battle and chaos were everywhere. This is what Toke wanted. She was supposed to go—now. An explosion ripped through the air and huge silver boulders rained from the sky. Macy looked toward the clearing, and beyond where the Last Shard lay somewhere waiting for her. She licked her lips, swallowed her fear, and ran toward her destiny.

ooo

Tolen sat up and grabbed his chest. *Macy!* His mind rushed through the vision that had awakened him. A battle, *the* battle, the one he had seen. The one where she would face the ultimate danger. Flames, blood, and she retreated into the trees with a handful of Raksasha chasing her. A hazy image of Mahto and Sienn nearing the island danced across his mind and then the vision was gone.

He rubbed his eyes. How long before Mahto and Sienn could reach her? A heavy ache in his head made his stomach turn and he leaned over, thinking he was about to be sick. He took several deep breaths and swallowed. His head throbbed as he tried to get his thoughts in order.

Where was he?

It all came rushing back and he tried to jump to his feet, but his hands and legs were chained to the floor. Another chain, thick and heavy, was attached to a steel collar around his neck, forcing him to kneel in an uncomfortable, splayed position.

The room slowly came into focus. He was chained at the base of a large throne. Beside him were eight other sets of empty shackles like his own. The shackles were new, as was the throne. They all glistened with the strange metallic glint of the gate. He must be somewhere in the castle.

Where were the others? They'd want information, and if any of the others caved—if any of them told their captors who Tolen really was, they were doomed.

His heart sank. Blaze. Blaze, Quasar, and all those who had come to help him. Their blood would be on his hands.

He tried to turn his wrist to look at his watch. How much time had passed? He couldn't see it. Whether the Dak had taken it from him or it was crushed between his skin and the shackles he did not know.

Despair fought for a place in his heart and he fought against it. It wasn't over yet.

He closed his eyes and concentrated on enhancing his strength. He pulled against the chains and they creaked and groaned but didn't give.

He collapsed from the strain and the chains held him there suspended, pulling against his muscles, cutting into his skin.

He pulled the Kuna to his left palm and tried to conjure a fireball to send at the chain holding his right, but the fire would not leave his palm. He had to pull it back in before the pain of it made him pass out.

He lay there, trying to understand, when footsteps echoed across the dark floor. *Slap, slap*, it sounded like sets of bare feet.

Four creatures entered the room. Three he recognized, but the last was not anything he had seen before. He was huge, human in shape, but instead of skin, thick gray scales covered his body. His face continually shifted between something that resembled a lizard, a human, a Lafar, and some creature he couldn't name. It was disgusting to watch.

The other creature resembled something that would have fit in with Greek mythology, with thickly muscled human legs and tall furry boots that stopped at his dirty knees. He wore a loincloth made from the same type of fur as his filthy boots. But there the resemblance to human stopped. From the waist up he was a giant, black grizzly bear, but the eyes were the most terrifying; black, soulless, deadly. He'd faced these creatures before.

Kezgani.

The third creature was a Raksasha demon. A blood tracker. This creature knew what Tolen was.

Tolen shuddered against the chains. Two more followed behind the entourage and a cry escaped Tolen's lips. A Daklafar led Blaze into the room by a chain around his neck. His face was covered with blood. His lips were swollen and cracked, his right eye purple and puffed to a bloody slit. Blood from the cut on his mouth dripped from his chin, and his arms and legs bore the welted slashes of whip marks.

Angry tears burned the back of Tolen's throat and he fought again against the chains. "Let him go!"

The Dak strutted forward, kicking Blaze ahead of him. He muttered in his strange tongue and poked Blaze.

Blaze met Tolen's tortured gaze. "They want to know how the Ninth Chosen comes to be in the Shadow Realm with a treacherous Lafar."

Tolen swallowed. They knew. It was over. They would not let him survive.

Wait, *a* treacherous Lafar. Where was Quasar? "How long have we been here?"

Blaze shook his head and repeated the Dak's question, but barely lifted one finger.

"Days?"

Blaze shook his head and the Dak pulled back on his chain causing him to stumble.

Not days, an *hour!* There was still a chance… He just had to make sure they didn't kill him right away.

Blaze said something to the Dak in his own tongue and the Dak pointed a finger toward Tolen. Blaze shook his head and the Dak shouted. The Kezgani stalked over and lifted his fist.

"Wait!" Tolen shouted. "Wait, I'll talk!"

The creature stopped and Tolen looked at Blaze. "My name is Tolen Daedal Téloran. I am the Ninth Chosen. I'm here to save the Lafar from your reign. Now is your chance to surrender."

The Dak shouted again and the Kezgani backhanded Tolen. The blow rang through his ears.

The Kezgani paused in his next punch when a loud, angry hiss reverberated through the room. The Dak fell to his knees. The Kezgani knocked Blaze to the ground beside and quickly locked Blaze's unconscious form in another set of shackles.

The face that appeared, shimmering in the air above them, made Tolen's blood turn to ice. Daemon, the Demon Master.

"I knew you were simple minded, but when my Master saw you enter the grounds, I never imagined you would try something this stupid." Daemon sneered. "Your little stunt with the explosives did little damage. We'll be back on track in a few hours—once my Dak's finish off the rest of the Lafar hiding in the forest. All I need now is your face."

Tolen fought against the chains, his heart pounding. He knew. Daemon knew where the families were hiding. "How will you finish if you kill all your slaves?"

Daemon's eyes narrowed into slits. "Don't worry. Soon I'll have more than enough slaves, human and Hidden alike, to build a kingdom far greater than you can imagine, *Chosen One*." His lips pulled up in a disgusting sneer at the look of horror on Tolen's face. "So, how's your mother? It's so *helpful*, having her under my power."

Tolen wrenched himself against the chains; they cut into his flesh as he struggled to reach the image. "My mother will see you defeated. She's stronger than you, you evil piece of filth!"

Daemon bared his teeth and nodded toward the gray-scaled creature.

The creature walked over and touched Tolen's forehead. With a shudder of pain-filled horror, Tolen watched as the creature's features melted away and turned into a mirror image of himself.

Daemon licked his lips with his black forked tongue. "Hmm, yes, I think that will do perfectly. It should be easy to get the Seeker to hand over the Last Shard to me now, don't you agree?"

Pain lanced through Tolen as he realized Daemon's plan.

The Demon Master laughed and Tolen stared into his evil yellow eyes. "I will kill you for this!" he growled.

Daemon's eyes narrowed once before he barked out an order and disappeared.

Tolen fought against the shackles that tore into his flesh as the Raksasha, Kezgani, the Dak, and Tolen's evil twin walked out of the room.

53 THE AHWAY

MACY KEPT CLOSE to the trees, following the pull of Bastian's glowing shard toward an unseen source—hopefully the Last—as it pulsed and sent surges of joyous anticipation flowing through her body. It was impatient. It took extra concentration to keep it from rushing her.

The glow of the fires started by the explosion cast shadows as she ran, making it harder to hide, but the diversion had worked. So far, no one had noticed her. The battle sounds and screeches were behind her, in the clearing. Toke was right—their numbers might have been few, but, like a wasp in a beehive, they were stronger, fiercer, and had created plenty of havoc. Her stomach twisted. What if…?

She shook her head. No, this was what she was supposed to be doing. She grasped Bastian's shard in her hand as its urgency increased. Its power frightened her. She had held it back all this time, afraid to let it consume her, afraid to connect. It seemed too powerful, too overwhelming, too…*much.*

She licked her lips. She could feel what it now wanted. Her own shard had felt this way when she first connected to it fully, but could she do it? Would she be strong enough to control it, to *use* it? She clenched it tighter in her fingers. If she wasn't strong enough to control Bastian's shard, how could she be stronger than the temptation of the Last?

Her hands shook as she dodged behind trees, wrestling with the decision to become one with Bastian's shard. Her heart pounded and the shard pulsed with heat and light. It was waiting, hoping. Her thoughts paused on another fear, another reason to be afraid of connecting with

Bastian's shard. The Fallen. If she connected, would they be able to see her? Battle shrieks met her ears and she knew she didn't have the time to dwell on what ifs.

She took a deep breath, leaned against a tree, closed her eyes, and directed her thoughts to Bastian's shard.

I-I'm ready. I ask for your full allegiance. Let us be one. As soon as the thought came to its conclusion, she felt the change begin. A rush of adrenaline coursed through her veins, and Bastian's shard became so hot she could no longer hold it in her hand. It fell from her fingers and landed against her heart. She looked down and watched as it molded back to her own shard, a single bright blue line sealing the two together again. A burst of warmth rushed through her body—the incredible amount of love and acceptance became so overwhelming that she dropped to her knees. This was not at all what she had expected.

As the power of Bastian's shard—no, *her* shard—flowed into her body, her mind became incredibly clear. Their shards *loved* them. They were equal partners in every way. That was the true purpose of the shards. They were guides and companions—giving them direction and pure strength when they needed it most. A silent friend. A reminder of the love of the Light. They did not control or overpower, instead they enhanced the power that already existed within its bearer.

Her heart felt as if it would burst. So powerful, so incredible, so amazing!

As she finally let go of fear and allowed faith and trust to take its place, the enhanced strength from the shard flowed through her entire body. Her pace quickened, and as she ran through the forest her mind stayed alert and focused. It was strange to let the shard guide her like this. The power was exhilarating, fascinating. She felt stronger than she ever had. It was not the kind of strength that came from using her gifts to enhance her physical strength, but the kind of strength that comes from confidence, love, and assurance. She knew who she was, knew her purpose, and she knew she was strong enough to succeed. The Last could not tempt her now.

A quiet laugh of triumph burst from her lips, but her joy was short lived—there was still a battle going on, a battle that could hurt her friends. She needed to fulfill her mission and get back to them. She quickened her pace. She could feel the dark creatures around her better than before, and as she glanced around she could see their life forces cast eerie blue light—for the first time she could literally see, not just feel their evil as it affected the Balance.

Her footfalls felt so sure she was positive she could have closed her eyes and still been able to run without hitting a tree or tripping. She ran swiftly, faster than she ever had, her magnified gifts allowing her to avoid the strange flickers of blue.

Her pace slowed when she began to notice piles of dirt sporadically throughout the forest. She stopped altogether when the piles became more frequent. A feeling of intense sadness swept over her and tears pricked at her eyes. She had no idea why until she stepped through a grove of trees to a scene that made her gasp and cover her mouth. Bodies lay everywhere—partially decayed, grotesque, horrific. Murdered. Women, children, old ones…all gone. Daemon's symbol had been burned down to the bone into their rotting foreheads. Tears fell from her eyes at the same moment a thirst for vengeance began to burn in her heart.

Her stomach heaved. She covered her nose with her shirt and began to retrace her steps slowly back into the trees, her senses on high alert. Daemon was here, somewhere. He was after the Last Shard. He was a skilled and horrifying monster. Would she be able to sense him the way she could sense the other Dark creatures?

Keeping her back to the slaughtered colony, she crept into the trees, all former exhilaration gone, replaced by determined focus. She must get the Last.

She followed the pull of her shard, this time with her Kuna pulsing gently, reassuringly, in her palms, her ears tuned to the slightest sound, and her eyes darting back and forth.

A soft, warm yellow light appeared about a hundred yards ahead and her shard tugged her attention toward it. She followed the prompting and moved cautiously, her movements barely a whisper across the bracken. Once close enough, she could see a creature standing in the circle of light. As she got nearer, she realized the light was emanating *from* the creature. It was huge, ten, maybe fifteen feet tall.

She quickened her steps and barely hesitated before stepping out of the trees.

The creature turned and Macy paused. He radiated light and peace, but was the strangest looking creature she'd ever seen. His lower half was that of a lion—huge paws tipped with gleaming golden claws, glossy gold fur—but the top half was a man, with lion-like eyes and a thick, wavy golden mane of hair. He wore a bright silver breastplate and clutched a long silver staff topped with a white stone in his right hand.

"Welcome McLacy Allicandra. I am Ahway Paetah. I have been waiting for you."

ooo

Blood dripped off Tolen's fingers into a growing puddle on the floor. Blaze remained unconscious.

It'd been too long since the creature with Tolen's face had left, too long since Daemon had threatened Macy. He had to get free! But somehow the Dark had found a way to use the strange sliver rock as a way to chain gifts as well. He couldn't call to Skyborne, he couldn't see the future. For once he was as ordinary as anyone, and it terrified him.

He yelled in agony as the metal dug into his skin. "Macy!"

"T-Tolen?"

"Blaze! Are you okay? Where are the others? Where's Quasar?"

Blaze shook his head and moaned. "I don't know." He looked at Tolen with an agonized expression. "They tortured Erid…he told them…then they killed him."

Tolen clenched his teeth. "I'm so sorry, Blaze. I led you into this." He pushed the guilt aside as best he could. "You said it'd been an hour?"

"Yes."

Tolen twisted, ignoring the pain, to look around. "I'm guessing it's been at least another thirty minutes since they left."

"What happened after they knocked me out?"

"The Mimicker shifted into my lookalike. Daemon's going to use him to get a powerful item that will allow him to free Darsapean. An item that will soon be in the hands of someone who trusts my face." Tolen's hands flexed and blood dripped from his fingers.

"Tolen, I—"

"We're going to get out, and I'm going to stop them." He tugged against the metal. "I can't use my gifts. Something in these shackles is blocking me. I need to figure out how to get them off."

Blaze looked at the shackles on his own wrists. "I've never seen anything like it."

Tolen groaned. *Think! There has to be a way out of this!* His watch chimed four weak notes and a tiny bit of strength returned to his arm. He twisted his wrist, now slick with blood, until the watch appeared from under the shackle. The face glowed blue and the bright rune—three quarters-dark sun, one quarter-light—appeared at its center, giving him an idea.

"Blaze, turn your head and close your eyes."

"Why?"

"I'm going to try something and I'm not sure what's going to happen."

Blaze looked confused, but closed his eyes and turned his face away.

Tolen looked at the symbol on the watch. He couldn't project his gifts from his body; there was no way he could escape these shackles by force. He needed something from the outside. Something not under the power of the metal. He remembered how the watch had shot a blast of light into his face when he was being overcome by his anger and almost killed Quasar.

"Tolen?"

"Keep your eyes closed. I'm going to count to three, on three I want you to pull against your chains, okay?"

Blaze took a deep breath. "Okay."

Tolen called his gifts to his mind. He sought out the Lóklana, its warmth, its peace. It was difficult, but slowly appeared. His shard warmed against his chest as the Lóklana light fought for release. He pushed the power into the watch and the chime became louder and faster.

Tolen closed his eyes and shifted his thoughts to his dark Dreamer curse, allowing it to confuse the watch, hopefully engaging the strange self-defense mechanism. "One!" His voice took on the horrible quality of the Dark and the Dreamer within him burst into being as a blackness in his thoughts trying to drown out the light. Horrible images, fears, and doubts blossomed in his mind, frighteningly powerful here in its own realm.

The watch vibrated on his wrist. "Two!" It sent a burst of energy into the air and Tolen knew it was working.

"Three!" Blinding light blasted from the watch and both of them were shoved hard against the chains. For a split second Tolen felt the power of the Dark being overwhelmed within the metal and shifted his focus to his love for Macy and his people.

The metal exploded off his body. He shut his eyes as bits of shrapnel pelted his skin. When it ended he looked over to see Blaze staring around in amazement.

The light in the room surged back into his body and he felt his wounds heal. The Dreamer within him hissed in defeat and rolled back into a dark corner in his mind, shackled in its own chains. The walls started to crumble around them, and they covered their heads as they ran.

Light and purpose burning within him, Tolen jumped two guards rushing toward them and had both their necks broken before they could lift their weapons.

Blaze stopped next to him, out of breath, clutching his side. Tolen touched the boy's forehead. "*Lon'adras.*" He felt Blaze's strength return the same moment his ragged breathing leveled out. "Let's go!" He tossed Blaze one of the guard's swords and took the other for himself.

His watch seemed to know the way out and chimed at each turn he was to take. He trusted it without question, his thoughts on saving the others, on getting to Macy. He didn't know how many creatures he killed as they ran, but he was covered in black blood by the time they'd searched the remaining cells, but came up empty. They sprinted for the open area in the castle grounds, smoldering from recently put out fires, hoping for signs of their friends.

He skidded to a halt when he saw the army waiting for him. Hundreds of Raksasha and Daklafar. "Get behind me," he whispered to Blaze.

Tolen knelt down on one knee and the ground rumbled beneath his hands. The creatures began to stumble. He pulled his Lóklana and Kuna to the forefront of his mind. As the heat within him rose, the light mixed with it in a welcoming way. He lifted his hands from the ground and sent white-hot fire into the throng. Creatures burst into ash. Those that survived the initial blast fled from the light.

"Come on!" He stood up and ran, still holding the light. "Head for the hole in the castle gate. I can see the forest!"

They were about fifty yards from the hole when Tolen saw something that flooded him with hope. Quasar ran toward them with all the other captives and Skye's army. He dropped his hold on the Lóklana and ran forward to grab Quasar in a bear hug. "You're not dead!"

"Not yet!" Quasar returned the hug and then grabbed Blaze. "It's good to see you alive, my boy." He ruffled Blaze's hair. "The families are in the forest, hiding. I escaped my guards, and was coming for you, but Skye met me half way. She said she saw you disappear through a gateway with a Daklafar and a Kezgani."

"It wasn't me. Let's get to the forest. I'll explain on the way."

54 THE LAST

THE AHWAY'S IMAGE shimmered. "Time is running out. I have been guarding the Last Shard, but the power in my spear is fading, I cannot hide my presence from the Balance much longer. There is too much darkness here. Daemon is close. You must take the Last away from here."

Macy nodded slowly. "Where is it?"

The Ahway pointed at the huge pine tree behind him and Macy's shard began to glow and pulse with excited energy.

Gold light issued from the ground around the tree. The Ahway stepped back as Macy knelt down and pushed the dirt away from the base to reveal a golden symbol burned into the bark. Two golden hearts entwined. Tears pricked her eyes as she continued to dig deeper.

Her fingers brushed something hard. She wrapped her hand around it and pulled it out of the ground. The red shard began to glow bright gold between her fingers. A wide golden dome sealed out every noise and image of the surrounding forest. A man's voice seemed to come from the walls.

"McLacy Allicandra. I am Eamun Woodlore, Keeper of the Last Shard, speaker of the Prophecy of the Ninth Chosen. The Last has chosen. The Keeper awaits."

The Last burst free from her hand and floated in the air above her. Her own shard lifted from her neck and floated up beside the Last. This made her nervous at first—she needed its power and protection—but the dome seemed to be acting like a shard itself. She felt no loss of power or strength.

The two shards did a sort of dance in the air, following each other, spinning faster and faster until they blurred together and appeared to become one shard. As they spun, they created the glowing symbol of two hearts entwined. Her cheeks split into a wide grin.

The shards stopped spinning, the Last attached itself to her necklace by a thin piece of delicate metal, and floated back over her head. As the shards touched her heart, she felt the weight of the Last as a separate entity. It had incredible power and majesty and she knew if she hadn't decided to connect to Bastian's shard, the heady power would have tempted her greatly. But now, the strength and purity she felt from that connection removed any lust for power the Last could have tempted her with. She was whole exactly as she was—enveloped and guarded by the love and power of her Watcher and the Light. Her heart held no envy or yearning for the Last's power, only an extreme desire to protect it and a consuming need to get it into Toke's hands so he could deliver it to the new Keeper.

"To be the Seeker of the Last Shard is a great responsibility. You have been given its trust. Only by your will can it leave your care; no one can take it from you. Protect it and it will protect you."

The dome disappeared and she saw someone standing beside the Ahway.

But it couldn't be…could it?

"*McLacy.*" She spoke her name with joy.

"Mom?" Macy's legs felt like rubber beneath her; they carried her forward awkwardly.

The woman nodded and opened her arms.

Macy rushed forward. It wasn't like hugging a real person—she couldn't feel flesh and bone—yet she was enveloped in incredible warmth and peace within the shelter of her mother's arms. She couldn't stop the tears from spilling over, and she shook with sobs as her mother held her close.

"Shh. Everything's going to be okay," she soothed. "Oh McLacy, I'm so proud of you!"

Macy looked up into her mother's glowing face. So much the same, yet different—perfect, flawless. "I look like you."

Her mother smiled.

"Dad?" Macy glanced around, but her mother's face fell.

"There is not much time. You've grown so much these past weeks. I'm so proud of you."

"Why are you here?"

"There are laws that govern the next life, just as there are laws that govern this one." Alli glanced at the Ahway. "I have been allowed to become a Restorer, a guardian of the future. Only because of the circumstances surrounding you at this time did the law allow me to come."

"What circumstances?"

"Those that affect the ultimate fate of Light's creations."

Macy's palms tingled. "You're here to make sure the Last Shard accepted me."

She nodded. "Daemon is not far. He knows the general area where Eamun hid the Last and he knows only the Seeker can find it. He is waiting for you." Her image shimmered and Macy reached out.

"Mom?"

She grabbed Macy's hands, it was like they were wrapped in a cloud. "There isn't time to say everything that needs to be said, McLacy. Just know that I love you, and I am with you everywhere you go."

"I love you, Mom." She swallowed back the pain. "I won't let Daemon get the Last."

"You are so brave and strong." Alli tilted her head and smiled. "I see why the Light selected you."

Macy shook her head. "Brave and crazy aren't the same thing."

She smiled. "Your father's fears have laid heavy on your mind. Learn what you can about his concerns, but do not let them sway you."

Macy thought about all she'd learned over the past few days compared with everything Bastian had ever taught her. "I won't."

"Good. The human race needs you. They may not have knowledge of the Hidden, but they still have something that makes them a threat to the Dark, and far more powerful than they'll ever realize. They are *free*. Free to be whoever they want, learn whatever they want, go after whatever they want. They are free to *become*. In one way or another they will choose Light or Dark by their actions and choices, but the Light has given them freedom to discover who they are and who they can be."

Macy nodded and her brow crinkled. "I've been thinking that because we created the Pact out of fear, we hugely limited ourselves from reaching our full potential, and only made things easier for the Dark." She looked up at her mom and bit her lip. "That might have sounded a little prejudiced. I'm not against the Hidden now or anything, I'm just no longer ashamed of my heritage."

Alli's smile widened. "As you shouldn't be, McLacy. Every race has an equally important purpose."

The Ahway raised his staff. "Allison."

Alli took a deep breath. "We must go."

"No, please. Not yet. Can't you stay with me a little longer?"

"This life is precious and so short, my McLacy." Alli pulled her back into her arms. "Don't spend any of it grieving for what is past. Your future is bright and beautiful and I will be watching over you every minute. We *will* be together again. That is the greatest gift of the Light. I love you."

"I love you, Mom."

55 BETRAYED

McLacy."The Ahway stepped forward. "The Light has a final piece of advice to offer you. You are gaining a better understanding of the Light and its purposes. Don't stop seeking truth. It will come as a great help to you in times to come."

Macy thanked the Ahway and stepped back as their glow began to fade. A huge part of her wanted to go with them—away from the weight of her destiny. But the other part of her ached to hold Tolen again, to stand beside him and face their future together.

The light disappeared, but the warmth still surrounded her. She carried it with her like a talisman as she pushed her way back into the darkness. The sounds of the distant battle met her ears, and with a silent plea, she ran to help her friends.

Macy shoved her way through the branches back toward the battle, not caring as they ripped at her clothes and tore at her flesh. She came to the clearing to see that Rune's explosion had blown apart one side of the gate, but the majority remained intact. A thick wall of Raksasha stood guard around it. Every time one fell to an arrow, another quickly took its place. They weren't fighting. They were being sacrificed as a living wall until the threat could be eliminated.

There was no way her friends could get through the creatures to destroy the gate.

She ran along the edge of trees until she discovered her friends battling a mass of Gungruin and other strange creatures. A flock of dead Shrieg lay around the scene. Two other people—a guy and a girl Macy didn't recognize—fought with them, wielding gifts of their own. Tolen's promised help?

She didn't have long to watch before they all were swallowed up by the overwhelming numbers of Raksasha.

The strain on their faces made her push her feet faster. Destroying the gate was no longer an option, they had to fight for their lives. Her Kuna built in her chest and she pushed it just to the surface of her palms. Her shard coursed with calculated anticipation and zinged with anxious energy. It was as if Bastian were right beside her, keeping her calm while her nerves begged her to react.

Macy rushed into the mob, stabbed a Gungruin in the back, and sent a burst of fire with her other hand into the face of a Gungruin rushing toward her.

The Last Shard seemed only to be watching as she moved through the horde almost effortlessly. It felt like a strange dance, perfectly choreographed. She hardly had to think. Her gifts flowed smoothly through her body. Strength seemed to come out of nowhere to feed her life force. She ran, jumped, parried, stabbed, and set creatures on fire. *Indestructible.* A grim smile lifted the corners of her mouth as she stabbed a Gungruin in the back just as it was about to grasp Rune, who'd been knocked to the ground.

His eyes widened in shock at her appearance before a huge grin lit his bloody face. He picked up his sword in time to cut the head off a large green creature. Macy lifted a fist and he knocked his knuckles against hers, a smile starting, before a deafening scream split the night.

Everything seemed to move in slow motion as Macy watched Keelyn jump in front of a row of six young men, all mirror images of Connell, her arms splayed wide. Another wave of creatures rushed forward, seconds away.

It wasn't until Toke ran over and dropped to the ground behind Keelyn that the reason for her scream became known. Macy's eyes followed Toke as he leaned over the real Connell, lying on the ground in a pool of his own blood, his eyes staring blankly toward the gray sky.

Blinding light burst from Keelyn's body and the Gungruin shielded their eyes. Brina appeared out of nowhere beside Toke. Rune rushed forward, his face twisted in pain, and raised his sword. Macy moved to join him just as an arrow slammed into Keelyn's stomach. Her light instantly faded and she fell to the ground. Time seemed to stand still for a single moment before Rune stabbed the nearest Gungruin, grabbed Keelyn, and carried her over to Toke, away from the attacking creatures. Macy couldn't tell if she was still alive. Rune stood up, his face now a mask of pure anger, and rushed back into the fight.

A wall of creatures moved in, blocking the way to her friends. She screamed and shot bursts of fire in every direction. *Keelyn can't be dead, she can't!*

She continued to shoot fire and swing her sword, the pile of black bodies around her grew, but still she couldn't get through.

A burst of silver light lit the trees behind the throng and suddenly Brina appeared beside her. Macy looked over long enough to ask, "Keelyn?"

Brina sidestepped a blade and stabbed a Raksasha in the heart. "Toke's put her in suspended animation—" She rolled out of the way of a spear and cut off the legs of the Gungruin Macy was fighting. "But if we can't get her off this island, her chances aren't good."

Macy twisted and curled around the creatures, keeping Brina to her left, but the Raksasha kept coming.

"Did you get it?" Brina asked.

"Yes," Macy panted, the use of so much Kuna starting to take its toll.

"Give me five seconds—kill what you can—as soon as you see me disappear, run."

"But—"

"WE CAN'T LET THEM GET THE LAST!"

Macy clenched her teeth, thrust both hands forward and screamed. Two fireballs burst from her hands and she twisted her fingers until the fire formed a thick flaming rope that wrapped around the six Raksasha surrounding them, melting them in half. She glanced left. Brina had disappeared. She sent another ball of flame hurtling toward the group that started to circle in around her. The force of the explosion knocked her backward, but she jumped up and ran forward, stabbing and blasting everything in her way, Keelyn's scream still ringing in her ears. The look on Rune's face burned behind her eyes.

She shoved her feet into the hard packed earth, dodging trees and rocks. Tears fell from her eyes and dried instantly on her cheeks.

"No!" Heat pulsed from her body as she caught sight of the clearing on her left.

She reached the edge of the clearing, the sounds of the following army close behind. Her lips tightened as a plan formed in her mind. A crazy and stupid plan that could probably get her killed, but right now she felt made of heat and flame.

If she could get through the Raksasha, maybe, just maybe, she could take out what was left of the gate. It would require that she use some of the Last Shard's power to increase her abilities, something she knew she wasn't supposed to do, but she felt no temptation for personal gain, only a heart wrenching desire to get the Last off this island and save her friends.

She scrubbed the tears from her eyes and scanned the trees, looking for one close to the wall of Raksasha. A tall maple offered a few branches that might give the advantage she needed. She quickly scaled the prickly bark and shimmied out to the edge of a long branch that extended toward the wall of creatures.

She closed her eyes and focused on the power coursing through her body, allowing it to just barely reach out to the Last Shard. When her Kuna connected and the red shard glowed gold, she nearly fell out of the tree. She couldn't hold on for long. The power was too intoxicating. Distracting. So much strength. Never had she felt her Kuna like this before. It had become a flame that if tendered too long would consume her. She was not this shard's Keeper. She closed her eyes and pulled the faces of her friends to mind. Tolen, Bastian, her parents. She only had to hold on just a bit longer.

She opened her eyes to see the Raksasha once again glowing poisonous blue. She dumped the remaining herbs to make Glockshaw together into one pouch. She breathed on the pouch and it lit instantly in her palm, beautiful, fiery orange.

She raised her arm and with enhanced sight marked the gate through the thickest wall of Raksasha. "*MI'NOHA!*" The ball of flame was too huge and bright to look at as it shot like a comet through the sky. It melted the wall of Raksasha and hit the gate with a resounding BOOM! The metal exploded, rained down from the sky, and something screamed. A bloodcurdling, furious scream.

The tree shook violently, she lost her grip on the branch and slid off sideways, barely holding on with one hand. The flames spread fast from the clearing, setting the forest on fire. The tree shook again, this time so hard the roots broke free and started to fall. Her hand slipped and the ground rushed up to meet her.

When she came to, her hands and feet were bound in shiny metal chains with the same strange shimmer as the gate. Clenadium? She looked up to see Tolen standing above her, his arms held behind his back by a Thrundoon, his face bloody, his eyes nearly swollen shut. He could barely stand. "Tolen!" She screamed. He glanced her way, but his eyes were dazed.

She tried to stand but fell over before she could even get up to her knees. She tried to call the Kuna to her palms but it wouldn't come. The metal burned against her skin as if it were drawing the heat of the Kuna into itself. It was draining her gifts!

The trees rustled nearby and a cold, cruel laugh she would never forget made her stomach lurch.

Daemon stepped out from behind the wall of Raksasha and walked over slowly, calmly, completely unconcerned with the sounds of the battle behind them. His horns seemed to be slithering in the flicker of flames from the burning forest. His yellow eyes did not hold the fear of the defeated, but the pride of the triumphant. She must not have damaged the gate as much as she'd hoped. "I must thank you for the gifts." He growled softly. "First, your pathetic boyfriend tries to save you, and of course fails, and now you get to pay a ransom to save him." He flicked a speck of dust off his blood-red cloak. "The Last Shard please." He held out a scaly hand and wiggled his black clawed fingers.

Macy licked her lips. Daemon wanted the Last in exchange for Tolen's life. With Macy as the Seeker, he knew he could take it from her, but he wouldn't have access to its full powers unless she willfully gave it to him. Her blood seemed to freeze in her veins, the world went silent, and all she could see was Tolen standing there, bleeding, *dying*. But if Daemon got the Last Shard, it was the end for everyone. He'd bring Darsapean back; a world with Light would end.

She swallowed and placed her bound hands over the shards. "No. I won't give it to you."

"Hmm. Pity. You must not love him as much as he thought." He nodded toward the Thrundoon. "Kill him."

The Thrundoon threw Tolen to the ground and raised his sword above his head.

Tolen cringed away from the sword and moaned, his eyes rolling. He wasn't tied in the metal rope. Why wasn't he using his gifts? The Thrundoon began to lower the sword and Macy screamed.

"Stop! Don't kill him!"

Her gifts were not working, and Tolen was obviously too weak to use his, *but* he was the *Ninth!* With the power of the Last Shard, he could get them out of this!

Dread raced through her heart and pulsed from her shard as the only option shot through her mind. But she had to risk it. She had to! She fought against the doubt as she ripped the Last from her necklace and threw it as hard as she could. "Tolen, catch!"

Tolen rolled back and caught the shard with both hands. A twisted smile curled his lips.

Macy's heart sank at the same time Tolen's face started to shift and blur.

The face she loved melted into the gray-skinned doom of a Gungruin.

She lurched forward and tried to grab the shard before he could pass it to his master, but thick roots wrapped around her, dragging her back.

Daemon sneered as he curled the Last Shard in his fist.

What had she done?

56 DAEMON'S PLAN

Tolen explained to Quasar about his double as they ran for the forest. "Horrid skin changers," Quasar mumbled in disgust. He motioned the group ahead as they neared the trees. "Have they reached her?"

"I can't tell. My Second Sight is too hazy. I don't know if it's this realm or something else." Tolen shook his head.

"Even if Daemon gets the Last from Macy, he cannot access its full power," Quasar added.

"It'll still be more power than we want him to have." Tolen panted.

Quasar nodded gravely, and pointed ahead just as Skye whistled.

Tolen glimpsed movement through the trees as the people began converging. The sounds of shrieking Daklafar met his ears. They had little time before the army regrouped and came after them.

They stopped just inside the tree line and Quasar glanced over his shoulder. "Now would be a good time to open that gateway, Tolen."

"I'm going to open two. One to Hunsí's village for the refugees, but the other I want to open near Macy."

"Do you think you can?"

Tolen took a deep breath. "I have to try."

Quasar stepped back, and Tolen motioned for Skye. "Skye, follow the owl through the gateway. Hunsí's village will be a safe place for your people."

"What about you?" Skye asked.

Tolen glanced away. "There's somewhere I have to go. But I promise you'll be watched over." He looked at Quasar. "Protect them."

Quasar shook his head. "No, Tolen. I'm going with you."

"So am I." Blaze stepped over and grabbed Tolen's shoulder.

More stepped forward and pledged themselves to Tolen. In all, twenty of the youngest fighters chose to go with him, including Skye and two of the other captains.

Tolen's heart swelled with gratitude. It took hardly any effort to open the first gate. He felt a wave of homesickness as Hunsi's village came into view. A wall of at least fifty villagers, including Kichaya and Bren, stood ready with blankets and baskets of food. His heart swelled with gratitude for his people as they welcomed the refugee Lafar into their village with open arms.

They waited until the last person made it through and the gate closed before Tolen began the chant to open the second gate. He wasn't positive where Macy was, he was relying on what he'd seen and the pull of his gifts to know where to put the gate. He was deep in concentration when the first arrow slammed into a tree above their heads.

"Hurry!" Quasar shouted.

Tolen heard arrows fly, but he wasn't sure if they were from his side or the enemy's. Slowly, the air started to shimmer and a vague picture of a dark forest met his eyes. In the distance, he heard waves lapping against a rocky shore and could just make out a fire burning in the distance. This had to be it. "Let's go!"

He turned around and started shoving the fighters through the opening. The Daklafar and more Dark creatures rushed forward, intent on reaching them before they could escape. Quasar jumped through and grabbed Tolen by the shirt to tug him over. An arrow grazed Tolen's leg, he dropped his sword and fell through the gate into black icy water.

He came up gasping for air and waved his arm above him toward the gateway, willing it to close. He saw the angry faces of a dozen Daklafar almost to the hole before it collapsed with a hiss.

"Tolen, are you all right?" Tolen hadn't realized Quasar was holding him above the water, swimming with one arm.

Tolen nodded. "The arrow barely grazed my leg. I can heal it when we get to shore." He looked around but couldn't see much in the dim light. "The others?"

"Already there. Come on." Quasar helped Tolen to the rocky shore.

He healed his wound and enhanced his sight. The others sat perched on the rocks wringing out their clothes. The island was small. The rim curved away from them, and a tall, ghostly lighthouse stood sentinel against the strange dark sky. Hundreds of tracks were pressed into the sand, human and otherwise.

Tolen jumped up and raced into the forest. Quasar and Blaze met him stride for stride. The other Lafar, led by Skye, closed in behind. To go directly from one battle into another without a plan? So loyal. So *good!*

A huge fire cast an eerie glow ahead of them. Tolen skidded to a stop and motioned to the others around him. With quick instructions to Blaze and Skye, they each took a group of youth and split up. Tolen and Quasar ran forward; where there was fire, he was sure to find Macy.

They skirted the trees silently, sensing Dark creatures but meeting none.

Unease flowed into each step Tolen took. "Be careful. Daemon is close."

Quasar lifted his chin.

"There." Tolen pointed past the fire. "He's in the clearing up ahead."

They moved slowly toward the flames. They reached the edge of the trees, the heat of the fire uncomfortably close. Tolen shifted to the side and peered into the clearing.

A large silvery archway, an exact replica of the one in the Shadow Realm, stood towering in the middle. Nearly two-thirds of the arch had been blown apart, but Daemon stood beside it using his Nature Speak to call up roots to repair the damage. Up to this point he'd had to use unstable gateways to smuggle creatures here from the Shadow Realm. With a Gate that never closed he would be able to give millions of creatures of darkness unrestrained access to this world.

Tolen's heart thudded. They must destroy that gate!

Daemon lifted a particularly large boulder off the ground, giving Tolen a clear view of what was behind it.

His knees buckled and he grabbed Quasar's arm for support.

A hazy image of his mother hovered in the sky, enveloped in a cloud of blue mist. Her robes billowed behind her, her eyes were closed, and a trail of blue led down to where Macy hung limply from a thick pole.

Macy's arms and legs were bound, a gash on her forehead dripped blood down her face, off her chin and onto her shirt. A strange golden glow poured from her chest, mixed with the line of blue, and twisted toward a silver staff Daemon held in his fist. The Last Shard glowed from the tip of the staff, mimicking the Key that Tolen's mother had wielded in the Radia Revolution.

"What's he doing?" Quasar asked as he steadied Tolen.

Heat bubbled in Tolen's veins. "I think he's using his branded connection to my mother to control the Key, and Macy's life force to power it—keeping his own life force strong and unimpeded." His fingers tingled as memories from what he'd learned of the Key during his time with Hunsí came rushing to the surface. "He's not just building a gate, he's going to break down Misery. He's going to free Darsapean. If I can get to Macy, maybe I can interrupt the power." His eyes raked over the wall of hundreds of Raksasha guarding Macy, Daemon, and the gate, from any outside approach.

He started to run forward, but Quasar kept his grip on Tolen's arm.

"Wait! Use your head! If you run in there now the Raksasha will be on you before you even get close." He looked around. "Daemon doesn't know we're here. Let the Lafar draw away his forces. Weaken the enemy first."

Tolen's breath came in gasps. His heart battled with the logic in Quasar's words. "Where are they?"

Quasar pointed. "Surrounding now."

A crack sounded behind them and they spun around. A young man, near Tolen's own age with a blond disheveled ponytail, stepped forward. Blood ran thickly down his arm and dripped from his fingers. His face was so smeared with black and red blood it was hard to make out his features. He held a long sword with glowing blue runes in his uninjured hand. Tolen recognized him as one of the travelers with Macy.

Tolen stepped over and grasped the youth's arm before he could raise his Kamud. "I've seen your face with Macy, but I don't know your name. *Lon'adras.*" He trailed his fingers along the boy's injuries. The blood flow stopped, but he still looked grisly and the pain in his eyes remained.

"Rune. You must be the Ninth." He looked past Tolen toward the clearing toward Macy. "Is she—?"

"She's alive." Tolen fought to keep his voice steady. "But it looks like Daemon is draining her life force."

"What's the plan?" Rune's brow furrowed in concentration.

"We've got Lafar warriors surrounding the clearing to draw off the Raksasha. If we weaken Daemon's Guard, we should have a better chance to get to her. What kinds of creatures are here?"

"We killed the Shrieg, four DéHool and their Thrundoon, but there is still a mass of Gungruin, Raksasha, and a bunch of other creatures I've never seen."

Tolen nodded. His nerves stretched thin while he waited for the Lafar. The first arrows flew into the gathered Raksasha and Daemon shouted orders over his shoulder.

A pack of Gungruin ran into the forest while the wall of Raksasha around Daemon, Macy, and the arch tightened their ranks.

Tolen looked at Quasar and Rune. "You two run for Macy. Get through that wall and get her down! I'm going for Daemon."

"Tolen!" Quasar stepped in Tolen's path. "I will take the Demon Master. You two save Macy." He met Tolen's eyes once before rushing forward.

Daemon turned to see Quasar coming at him. He barely had time to lift his sword before Quasar struck. The two began a dance of blades as Tolen and Rune skirted the distracted Raksasha and headed for Macy, but at the base of her pole stood a wall of thorns.

Tolen pushed his will toward the wall, telling it to move and let him through. The six-foot-long spikes creaked and fought against Tolen's interference. They'd been formed by Daemon and the power was strong. Sweat beaded on Tolen's forehead as he focused against the power. The wall trembled as Quasar's incredible fighting skills demanded more of the Demon Master's attention. Tolen concentrated harder.

Daemon screamed and Tolen felt power leave the wall. He called the thorns away, and he rushed through the tiniest gap, ignoring the sharp tips grazing his flesh, unwilling to wait for the wall to finish its descent back into the earth. He sent strength to his legs to leap onto the pole above Macy.

His hands were a foot away and ready to grasp the pole when he smacked into an invisible force field and landed on his back, gasping for breath. Rune jumped forward and the same happened to him.

"What is that?" Rune yelled.

"Mom!" Tolen shouted. "Mom!"

Areen's face contorted with pain but the blue haze didn't thin. Her image was transparent, hazy, and Tolen knew she was probably still in the

Light Realm, having no idea Daemon was accessing her power.

They stood up and circled Macy. Her face was drained of color—ghostly under the churning sky. He could just make out the shimmer of his mother's shield blocking them from her.

"Macy!" Tolen shouted and her cheek twitched. "Macy! Wake up!"

A Raksasha rushed toward them, sword raised above its head, screeching at the top of its lungs. Rune swung and its head rolled across the ground. More Raksasha ran their way, drawn by the cry of their kin. Rune slashed and dodged, killing everything that came near, protecting Tolen's back.

"Macy!" Tolen screamed as panic surged through him. He tried to sense the force field, get a handle on how to destroy it, but he couldn't feel anything there to fight. Rune grunted and Tolen glanced back to see the Raksasha were getting closer, gaining.

His eyes snapped back to Macy. He had to get her down! He grasped his shard in his fist and pushed his deepest feelings toward her. Physically he couldn't pass that barrier, but their shards connected them. Love connected them. Destiny connected them. Nothing could block that. Nothing. *Macy, please wake up!*

Her eyes fluttered and opened slowly. They appeared blank and lifeless until they found Tolen's face. "Tolen?" her scratchy voice sounded far away.

"Yes, it's me, Mace! The real me. I'm here. I'm trying to get you down, but I can't get through the shield."

Macy looked down at the gold light flowing from her chest and started to struggle against the binds holding her. "Tolen! The Last. Daemon reforged the Key. He's going to release Darsapean. Stop him!" she squirmed. Tolen's heart sank. Not being the Keeper, Darsapean could not access the Last's full potential, but all he needed was enough power to break through Misery's defenses. "Tolen, behind you!"

Tolen twisted to kill a Raksasha who rushed past Rune. They were being overrun. "Macy, I can't get through. You have to do it from your side. You've got to break free!"

"I don't know if I can. It's too powerful!" She closed her eyes.

Tolen got as close to where his mother floated above them as he could. "MOM! Stop this!"

Areen's eyes flickered, but nothing changed.

"Macy!" Tolen spun around as the Raksasha plowed toward them. He lit them on fire, tied them with roots, blasted them with wind, but the creatures kept coming.

Tolen turned and jumped again at the invisible barrier but was thrown back. He scrambled to his feet. "Macy, please!" His voice broke. "Don't leave me!" An arrow slammed into Tolen's arm. He stumbled forward as another sliced into his leg. In a part of his mind he knew Rune must have fallen, but he couldn't take his eyes off Macy as he watched her life drain away.

Another arrow lodged in his side, just below his ribs, and he fell forward. Pain shot through his body, but the anguish of watching Macy dying right in front of him hurt so much worse. Despair encased him, dragging him down.

They were both going to die.

57 TOO LATE

Tolen watched Macy's eyes fly open. "Tolen!"

A wall of heat knocked him onto his back and the Raksasha cowered and scrambled backwards. A huge ball of golden light grew around Macy's body.

Areen's eyes fluttered open, and she surveyed the scene below in horror. She looked at Macy then back at her son. She threw her hands out and screamed. The blue mist disappeared and Tolen just caught sight of his mother's determined face. As Areen faded, the light around Macy increased. Her bonds melted and she drifted gently to the ground, landing on her feet. Her eyes burned fiery gold, her mouth hardened into a determined line.

The light surrounding her wasn't like his Lóklana gift—borrowed light. This was all Macy. This light existed in her. It was purity made into fire and strength. *Light's Aid.*

Tolen's heart soared as he watched her. She'd never been more beautiful…or terrifying.

The Raksasha ran away in earnest. Somewhere in the distance Daemon screamed, but Tolen couldn't tear his eyes from Macy as she shifted her stance toward the arch, raised her hands, and shouted, *"Y'na Ladonradi vasta! Y'nash mi'noha!" I am Light's aid! I give life to fire!*

Huge balls of flame shot from her hands and blasted into the arch with a resounding explosion that caused the entire island to tremble and quake. The gleaming rocks were ripped apart, shattered into a million pieces, and rained like glitter onto the ground.

"NO!" Daemon's shout echoed across the clearing.

The gold light faded from Macy's eyes and body as she ran to kneel by Tolen's side. He held one hand over the blood pouring from his side.

"Tolen! We've got to get these out so you can heal yourself."

But the joy he felt at seeing her whole, beautiful, and so powerful, overrode the pain in his body. He felt nothing but love and gratitude. He touched her cheek. "That was amazing."

She lifted her eyebrow. "Um, thanks. Now let's get these out, okay?"

He put his hand over hers on the arrow in his side, clenched his teeth, and pulled it out. He trailed his fingers along the wound and spoke the words of healing. As the blood flow stopped and his strength began to return, they were able to get the other two arrows out quickly. He healed the wounds and placed his fingers on the gash on Macy's forehead. "*Lon'adras*," he whispered. As the warmth trickled from his fingers to her injury and he felt it heal, he became fully aware that he was touching her again. They were together. It didn't matter in that moment that a battle raged around them, that they both had nearly died. She was there, in front of him. Alive. Perfect.

He stood up, pulling her with him. He pressed his hands to her back and lifted her off her feet, pulling her tighter to him. Their lips met and the fire that danced through his veins was intoxicating, the Kuna flowed from his body into hers, and her Kuna back into him, creating a molten bond. He'd kissed her many times, but never had it felt like this. Their lips moving as one, their hearts racing in time with each other. Time held no meaning. One year or five hundred would be enough if he could kiss her like this. Together they were fire and heat, love infused with light. He broke away to look in her eyes, but she grabbed his face with both hands and pulled him back to her lips.

Something stirred and Tolen spun around, pulling Macy behind him. But it was only Rune standing there covered in fresh blood. He jabbed a thumb over his shoulder and cleared his throat awkwardly. "We need to hurry."

Macy moved around Tolen to grab Rune's arm. They shared a pained look as Tolen stepped over and healed the worst of his wounds.

The three rushed back into the battle, killing Dark creatures and carving a path to the duel between Quasar and Daemon.

Lightning forked across the sky, highlighting the death match. Tolen knew from experience Daemon's strength was unsurpassed, but he'd never seen Quasar fight. Sweat dripped down Daemon's face, the muscles in his neck bulged, and his eyes were intensely focused. He continually called up roots to try and catch Quasar off guard, but the Lafar moved so fast his feet were a blur, his blade striking like a snake. Both opponents had bloody wounds on their arms, legs, and torso—Quasar's dripping red, Daemon's midnight black—but neither of them seemed hindered by them.

Tolen's heart had a single moment to soar, before Daemon called a root from the ground and this time Quasar was a split second too slow to side-step it. It wrapped around his legs, slamming him to the ground, and Daemon ran his sword through Quasar's stomach. Daemon stood over Quasar, chest heaving, the red shard gleaming from within the Key.

Tolen's gifts roared within him and he stepped into the clearing, alerting the Demon Master to his presence.

"Tolen!" Rune tossed him his sword and Tolen caught it midair.

"Tolen, wait!" Macy grabbed his arm. "Look, I know you have to fight him, but he has the Last. He's going to be even more powerful than before." She kissed his cheek and warmth filled his body. She was sharing her light with him. "Go, Tolen. Get the Last. Stop him."

With Light's Aid beside…

He nodded at Rune and called all his gifts to the ready. Relishing in the colors and warmth that flowed in and through him, Tolen ran toward the Demon Master.

Light burst from Tolen's body, brightening the clearing. The Dark creatures fell away from the light, but a shadow fell over Daemon, protecting him from the light. He beckoned Tolen forward with his bloody sword.

The dance started again. The last time Tolen had faced the Demon Master he'd been terrified, unsure, weak. This time he was still terrified, but he no longer questioned who he was or his purpose, and he no longer feared his gifts. This time he would face Daemon as the person he was created to be—the Ninth Chosen, wielder of all the Light's gifts, defender of all good people.

Where the light is, darkness cannot be.

Tolen raised his palm and sent a burst of white fire at Daemon, who sidestepped it easily and sneered. But the sneer quickly turned into a glare when he realized Tolen was manipulating the flame to surround the two of them, blocking Daemon from possible reinforcements and covering their small battlefield with uncomfortable light energy. This was no ordinary wall of flame. Pure Light infused its flickers, sustaining Tolen and pushing against Daemon's protection. The demon would have to kill Tolen quickly before the light drained his power.

Daemon rushed forward with his sword, but at the last minute swung the Key and knocked Tolen's feet out from under him. He jabbed his sword toward Tolen's heart, but Tolen rolled out of the way as roots snaked up and twisted around Daemon's ankles.

His yellow eyes churned with anger as he ripped free and charged Tolen again. Tolen twisted his hands and locked Daemon in a cloud of choking dust and debris.

Tolen could feel the drain. Despite the fact that he'd been battling Quasar, Daemon was no weak Raksasha, and far deadlier than the DéHool. He was a master killer whose evil heart drove him. He would never give up and Tolen knew he could not beat him. Not yet. Not when his gifts were still so new to him, and especially not while Daemon was in possession of the Last Shard.

Warmth surged into his limbs and he knew without turning Macy had joined the battle, she raised her own Kamud and they rushed the Demon Master together. Their swings in perfect sync, never getting in the other's way. A perfect dance of feet and blades. Tolen struck, Macy parried, then the roles would reverse. The Ninth Chosen was able to reach his peak with his trigger, Light's Aid, by his side.

…to death or victory.

Tolen felt their combined strength waning. It was time to end this. He met Macy's eyes for a split second, her face broke into a fierce grin, and she nodded.

"*Mi'noha!*" Macy shot a fireball into Daemon's face. He raised his arm to block the flame and Tolen shouted, "*Ma'sha! Tin'ruhl!*"

The owls circling the battle dove toward Daemon at the same moment a barrage of rocks and chunks of dirt began pelting him. He shouted, screamed, and swatted, but when the dust cleared, an owl held the Last in its talons, ripped free of the Key.

An image cut across Tolen's mind and he sent his will to the owl carrying the Last. Even Daemon paused to watch the events unfold, his face a mask of horror and anger.

The owl spiraled low and dropped the Last back into Macy's hands. Gold light burst from the shard as her fist closed around it. She closed her eyes and her thoughts flashed into Tolen's mind. Both their eyes turned to another battle between a small Lafar boy and a tall Gungruin taking place merely feet from where they stood. Macy cast Tolen a quick glance, he nodded, and she rushed for the other battle, stabbed the Gungruin, and then the golden light blurred them out of sight. When the light began to fade Tolen could see the Last shining from Blaze's fist. The Last Shard had claimed its Keeper. Blaze's bright violet eyes turned toward Tolen just as Daemon screamed.

Light poured into the clearing, pure white light, and its warmth and power surged past the wall of flame and slammed into Daemon's shadowy field.

The demon staggered.

The light slammed into him again and he fell to his back. Tolen risked a glance over his shoulder to see Macy holding her shard high, now standing with Rune and another girl with midnight hair separated into dozens of thick braids, holding their shards up.

The Chosen united.

Another vision filled Tolen's mind of all the Chosen throughout the world—their shards glowing, their unity banding them together in this single moment.

The time to issue the Call had come.

Tolen felt his connection deepen to all the Chosen. The light from his shard changed from blue to brilliant gold, as did the shards of all the Chosen he could see with his Second Sight. They had been Called. In his mind's eye, he saw them throughout the world, raising their shards, focusing their power toward the Ninth. He felt the power surge through his limbs just as Daemon regained his footing and barreled forward, murder in his eyes.

Tolen raised the Kamud to block the blow and their swords hit with a resounding clang. Daemon's speed increased and Tolen had to use every ounce of energy to keep up with the blows. His arms shook and he could feel the Kamud losing accuracy as his strength left him and therefore the sword. The wall of light dimmed and Daemon's sword grazed Tolen's side. He fell to one knee and twisted, feinting slightly left. Daemon rushed to strike a death blow, but his triumphant smile fell when Tolen rolled right and drove his sword deep into Daemon's side.

Holding the Last in front of him, Blaze ran forward to shatter Daemon's shadowy protection. The darkness faded and the Demon Master staggered. Tolen jumped up, his sword aimed for Dameon's heart.

"*T'kashti degani!*" Daemon screamed. A pillar of silver covered him, and Tolen's sword passed through nothing but air.

Tolen released his hold on the flames and turned to watch the horrified faces of the Dark servants as their master abandoned them. Most ran from the battle, crawling over each other in order to escape. Those who remained were quickly overtaken by the Lafar and a group of Radia Warriors Tolen hadn't even known were there.

Macy rushed forward, throwing her shoulder beneath Tolen's arm as his legs wobbled. Rune and the girl soon followed. Tolen noticed another girl with red hair suspended in a silver dome at the edge of the forest. Mahto and Sienn stood off to the side, bloody, but alive. He gave them a smile and a nod before his eyes moved back to Blaze where he now knelt by the body of Quasar.

He stepped toward them, keeping a grip around Macy's shoulders, and approached slowly, not wanting to see his friend this way. His heart was heavy as they dropped to their knees beside the two Lafar.

Tolen dropped his head to Quasar's chest. "I'm so sorry my friend. So sorry."

Silver light burst from Quasar's wound, the pool of blood beneath him glowed silver and began moving back into his body.

Tolen jumped back as Quasar's body was lifted up in a cloud of silver vapor, his arms spread like wings. His eyes opened and glowed silver as he was lowered slowly back to his knees.

"Quasar?" Tolen rushed forward to help him stand.

Quasar lifted his head and his eyes turned back to brilliant violet. "I cannot die until the Light deems my punishment fulfilled."

Tolen felt the pain in his friend's words and smiled sadly. He understood that in many ways, Quasar would welcome an honorable death. Tolen wasn't glad his friend was cursed, but he was grateful he hadn't lost him. Tolen gripped his shoulder. "Words will never be enough, but thank you. Thank you. Thank you for everything. We couldn't have succeeded without you."

Quasar dipped his chin and shook Tolen's arm.

"Tolen?" The purple-haired man stood above them. "I need your help." He gestured behind him toward the silver sphere.

Macy's voice quavered. "Toke?"

"Keelyn does not have long."

Tolen's legs shook as he hurried back toward the edge of the forest. Smoke clouded the area so he didn't see until he was standing beside the dome the body of a red-haired boy, similar in features to the girl, lying on the ground. In a flash of the past he saw what had taken place and his heart ached for the twin sister who would have to face a life without the brother who was her other half. Toke tapped a device on the ground and the dome faded. Wires and tubes stuck out all over the girl's body. Rune rushed forward to cradle her in his arms as Tolen stepped forward. He could feel the unspoken love Rune had for this girl. He placed one hand on her forehead and the other over the wound he could see in her stomach.

"*Lon'adras*," he whispered. The heat burst from his fingers, seeking out the damage and coaxing it to heal, but he knew the real pain she would awaken to would never fully heal.

Her eyes blinked slowly open and met Tolen's gaze. "I am so sorry for your loss." Her eyes brimmed over and Tolen stepped back, allowing Rune to give her the comfort only a loved one can give, and Toke to remove the tubes and wires. The other girl knelt beside them, her hand resting on the redhead's arm.

"Brina," Macy whispered to Tolen, pointing at the girl with the braids.

"And the twins?"

"Keelyn and Connell." Her voice cracked and Tolen turned to wipe the tears from her face.

As the conjured darkness began to leave the sky, they surveyed the devastation surrounding them by the light of the setting sun. Bodies and silver rocks littered the ground. The forest had fallen eerily silent.

All the Lafar were returning, shadowed closely by the Radia Warriors. He counted once, twice. Not one of his little army were lost. He sent a plea of thanks to the Light and smiled gently. This was a day of pain and sorrow, but also of hope.

A sigh of relief began to escape his lips when, without warning, another vision cut across his Second Sight and he staggered sideways.

The gate in the Shadow Realm glowed bright silver, the walls of Misery crumbled, and the air filled with maniacal laughter.

You're too late.

58 THE SERAPH

WE DIDN'T DO enough damage to the gate in the Shadow Realm. Darsapean is there now. I can feel him." Tolen clenched his fist, fighting against the truth that assaulted him. He stood panting, leaning against Macy, everyone but Rune and Keelyn gathering around him as the vision slowly faded.

He dropped to the ground. Macy sat beside him and put her arms around him.

Toke cleared his throat. "You did well, *Mindra*. You wounded Daemon and Macy's destruction of the gate here has protected this realm and destroyed Darsapean's chances of mounting a full-scale attack. He will have to use unstable gateways and build his army slowly. That is a great success."

"Yes, but we didn't destroy the gate in the Shadow Realm. Daemon had enough time with the Last to break down the remaining defense of Misery."

Toke sighed. "Yet, according to Quasar, you saved a large portion of the Lafar race." He pointed to the Lafar standing with Quasar. "I don't think there's a price to be put on that."

Tolen ran a hand through his sweaty hair.

"Take peace that you did the right thing at the *right* time." Toke's strange eyes were soft and honest.

Tolen felt Macy's thoughts murmur agreement and the anger slowly dissipated from his heart so peace could take its place. The right thing at the right time. *Whole in purpose and place.*

Macy touched his chin. "The Final Battle is going to happen. It's been foreseen. At some point Darsapean would have found a way to escape Misery. You did your duty Tolen. You are fulfilling your destiny."

"She's right, man." Mahto stood clutching Sienn's hand. "This was one heck of a battle. We needed you here, or we all would have died." He clapped Tolen on the shoulder.

"I'm glad you came, Mahto, Sienn. Thank you." He reached up and grabbed their arms.

"Couldn't let you have all the glory!" Mahto grinned and Tolen chuckled without humor.

Golden light began to fill the space. Everyone jumped to their feet as a figure appeared in their midst. It was a woman, inhumanly beautiful and wearing flowing golden robes. Her hair shone like a reflection on water and her eyes gleamed like brilliant silver.

She looked around at the crowd. "I am Seraph Landi. I come to speak for the Light. Daemon survived, but you have done well. You have saved more than one race this day. But you have also lost much." She looked at Keelyn, whose face was stained with tears, her hand on Connell's body beside her. "Take peace. His heart was pure. He is with the Light. Your sacrifice has not been in vain."

She paused and turned her eyes to Tolen and Macy. "You wish to find the Relics and sever the Pact."

They met the woman's eyes and Tolen felt as if she was looking right into his heart.

"Yes," Macy answered.

"This is a necessary desire, but there is much you both must know. As you go in search of the Relics, the Dark will stop at nothing to get them from you. As soon as you awaken a human, the Dark will seek to destroy them or turn them. The role of the Chosen will increase in necessity and difficulty."

"Once the Awakening begins," The Seraph turned her eyes to Macy, "this world will never be the same. It must be done with great care, and only you, Light's Aid, can begin it. You have felt only a measure of your strength this night. The full Awakening cannot take place until you complete your transcendence. Use the time until then to prepare, to learn, and to grow. You need to understand what you are going to face. I must warn you, tampering with the power of the Last will have a consequence. You had righteous intentions, but it was still not yours to use. The Balance will hold you accountable. You will now be tempted whenever it is near you. Beware that you do not tamper again with power that does not belong to you."

Macy bit her lip as the Seraph continued to speak. "You will have the ability to awaken one human at a time before you transcend. You must begin with the remaining eight descendants of the Nine. Find them."

She looked at Brina and Toke. "Find the father and you will find the path you seek."

She looked at Keelyn and Rune. "The past is your doom. Release it and you will find your future."

She turned her eyes to Blaze. "You *are* the Keeper of the Last Shard. You must learn why it chose you. Go to the boy Sashan and you will find your purpose."

She looked at Quasar. "The rescued Lafar are being moved to the Light Realm where they can heal in peace and safety. You have done well Seer. You have protected the Ninth and helped him on the path to his destiny. It is time now for you to protect the Keeper. You must go with him."

Quasar bowed.

She tilted her head at Mahto and Sienn, her eyes focused on Sienn's face. "Your father is among the recused Lafar. He did not abandon you when your mother died during your birth as you have believed. Find peace with your ancestry and you may be the bridge that finally unifies all Hidden kind." She looked at Tolen as she repeated his earlier words to Quasar. "It is time for this prejudice to end."

Macy squirmed beside him and he knew she was feeling guilty for her treatment of Nova and mistrust of the Lafar. He squeezed her fingers.

"You are extraordinary *Conchla Mindra*." The Seraph's silvery gaze warmed him. "Continue your path to its end and the Light will not fail you."

She glanced around the group. "Eight there are…" One by one, Rune, Brina, Keelyn, Toke, Quasar, Blaze, Mahto, and Sienn were covered in a pillar of light. "And the Ninth shall lead them with Light's Aid beside," the light touched Tolen and Macy, "to death or victory in the coming tide."

The golden light settled around each of the eight and a gleaming golden symbol, two hearts entwined, glowed in front of them. "You each have been gifted by a Seraph. The symbol will only appear when the Ninth is in need. Stay true to each other. Stay true to yourselves. Stay true to your purpose."

She turned to the rebel Chosen. "The Light knows your hearts and your desires. They will never forsake you." She looked skyward and disappeared in a pillar of gold.

The fear brought about by Darsapean's escape was pushed aside in the wake of the Seraph's visit. The last of the storm clouds and powers of darkness fled with her arrival. Tolen gathered with the little group of Lafar, Chosen, Radia Warriors, and Honitahai at the remains of the village slaughtered by Daemon as the first stars appeared in the sky.

Silent tears fell down everyone's cheeks as Tolen used his gifts to open a mass grave for Connell and the fallen villagers. Yellow-gold light filtered down the trees and bathed them in its warmth as he lowered the bodies into their places of rest. He whispered the words of the burial chant, allowing the dust to settle over the now sacred ground. A flock of owls circled over their heads, their hooting laced with sorrow for their Animashta friend, Connell. More birds and animals joined the song—the tribute—that could not be spoken more perfectly or beautifully.

Mahto and Sienn twisted their fingers and whispered to the plants. Wild flowers and grasses sprouted over the graveyard until Tolen knew it would be the most beautiful spot on the island. They continued to whisper and Tolen felt a gentle sigh from the island itself as it became cleansed from the effects of the Dark—the areas decimated by Daemon and his minions were being re-grown.

The song ended and they moved silently, respectfully, away from the empty village to a small clearing deeper in the forest. Macy lit a fire, and although they all should be exhausted, none of them felt ready to sleep. They sat around the fire talking quietly and eating bits of meat cake and herbs.

Skyborne appeared and landed on Tolen's shoulder. He smiled as the owl told him of the situation of the Lafar from the Shadow Realm. A refugee settlement had been set up within the Light Realm and they were being moved there from Hunsí's camp right this moment. There they could start over under the full protection of the Light, surrounded by the best healers.

"Quasar, Blaze, Skye?" Tolen spoke across the fire. "Your families are safe. The Lafar have reached the Light Realm." Blaze's grin could have lit up the night. The Last Shard reflected the light of the fire onto his gentle face. The Lafar leaned closer together and began talking in earnest. Quasar met Tolen's eyes and tipped his head. He knew what his friend was thinking—if Tolen had not followed his heart and saved Blaze, the Last would never have reached its Keeper. Tolen smiled, but it slowly melted into a hard line as Skyborne continued to deliver his news.

Tolen's father continued to heal, but his mother had been moved out of the citadel to a place where she could be more fully protected. Because of Macy, his mother had broken free of Daemon's power long enough to warn them Daemon's brand was allowing him brief moments of control. Her warning came at the same time another owl had arrived to tell them of the events unfolding on the island. They'd sent the Radia Warriors at once.

His heart clenched as the owl continued to explain his mother's plight. It was her thoughts that had betrayed them, her overheard knowledge that had sent the Dark to the gateway from the Light Realm to ambush Tolen, that told Daemon about Macy, that sent the army to destroy the village of old ones the Guardians had asked for help. She had had no idea and wouldn't be punished, but she could no longer be where she could hear too much and unwittingly put them all in danger.

The day would soon come when Tolen would be strong enough to destroy Daemon and free his mother once and for all—he would make sure of it.

Skyborne flew off and Tolen glanced at the faces around him. So much to do, but where to begin?

Macy sat close by his side, clutching his hand. Her eyes hadn't left his face the entire time he'd been listening to Skyborne. He touched her cheek with the back of his hand and motioned with his head toward the trees.

With a quick glance around they snuck away for a few moments alone. When the sounds of the bonfire were far in the distance, Tolen stopped and turned to face his purpose, his whole world. She reached up and wrapped her arms around his neck.

"We have a lot to do," he whispered.

She nodded and stared into his eyes. He could feel the love passing between them, through them, around them. "I think what we just faced was the easy part."

She nodded again.

"Darsapean is free. Every Dark creature imaginable is going to start showing up throughout the world, with who knows how many trying to get the Relics before we do."

Her lips formed a hard line.

He took a deep breath. "And I have no idea where to start looking."

She stood on her tiptoes and kissed him lightly on the lips. "That's okay. I do."

"Where?"

She pulled a small ring of keys from her pocket. "Whisper."

The End

The Chosen Chronicles: The Chosen Redemption

THE PRISONER

THE SMELL GAVE it away.

This was not an ordinary prison. Nor were his guards ordinary. From the outside they looked like normal prison guards—dirty brown uniform, black shoes, baton, gun on the hip. If he hadn't seen their eyes, maybe he never would have guessed this place was not as it seemed.

That is, if it weren't for the smell.

It wasn't the odor of human waste, sweat, and rotting food—the smell you would expect from a prison. It was the quieter sweet tang of death mixed with sulfur and earth. And something else, an unnamable smell that tickled his senses and triggered his fight-or-flight reflex.

The smell of evil.

Not all evil had a stench, just pure evil—the kind of stinking malignancy that meant the Dark lurked here in force.

The other humans in the cells on either side of his didn't know where they were. They still believed themselves to be in some god forsaken third-world prison—prisoners of war. He knew this because they still screamed when the invisible Tormentors came to them in the night to torture their minds, and pleaded their innocence to the careless guards who were nothing more than human pawns whose humanity had been blackened by the Dark.

What they didn't know? They *were* prisoners of war, but not a war of men, a war between good and evil, Light and Dark. A war that had been hidden from the sight of humans for centuries. He felt a pang of worry for his daughter, but shut the thought out as quickly as it came. The Tormentors would use it against him if they could, determined as they were to break him.

He'd managed to keep thoughts of her at bay until three days ago, when her face woke him from a dreamless sleep. Something had changed.

The creatures guarding this hell-on-earth became restless and more forceful in their torture of his mind, but though his body had weakened with time, his mind remained strong, and wholly his own. In ten years, they'd yet to find his weakness, and despite their increased visits, they were still failing. If they were to discover who he really was, who his daughter was, they would stop at nothing to learn his secrets.

One of the guards walked by his cell. He raised his chin and met the human creature's dead eyes with a look of loathing. The Darkened one bared its rotting teeth, but nothing more.

He was a prisoner that confused them, and in some ways, he frightened them. Their desperation told him his time was getting short. If they couldn't break him, they would kill him.

He was a human who knew too much.

APPENDIX

TERMS AND TITLES

Light: The source of all that is good.

The Guardians: Those who oversee and guard the realm of earth. They dwell within the Citadel of Light.

Light Realm: The dimension where the highest followers of Light reside. It is divided into two separate realms within the realm, Highest and Transitory. The Highest Realm is where the embodiment of Light itself resides, along with Seraphs, Ahway, and Mee'nah (see definition below), and those devoted followers of Light who have died on earth and passed through Light's Door to dwell with The Light forevermore. Transitory is the home of the Guardians, some deceased who are working toward progression to the Highest Realm, and a number of Spheres who protect the realm. The living can dwell here for brief periods to find healing and peace, but it is not a place of permanent residence.

Spheres: Have the ability to shield the power of another's life force from affecting the Balance, therefore hiding them from the Dark. They can sense the character of a person by the way they affect the Balance. They also have the ability to realign the cells within the body to heal almost any injury.

Balance: The force that binds humans and Hidden-kind. It shifts and sways with actions of good or evil. It is how the Light knows who to select as Chosen.

Life force: The matter, or intelligence, put into the body to give it life. Created with immense energy to power and control the physical body— the driving force. It will survive even after the physical body dies.

Dark: The source of all that is evil.

Shadow Realm: The dimension where Daemon, the Demon Master, resides. Home of the Shadow Prison where the Dark tortures its enemies. This is also where creatures of darkness—demons of the blackest nightmares—are released into the human world to torment mankind.

Misery: The phantom dimension used as a prison by the Light to hold the Dark's most powerful ally, Darsapean, leader of the armies of the Dark. A ruthless and horrible creature responsible for the deaths of hundreds of thousands of Hidden kind and Human kind during the dark days. He was imprisoned in Misery at the end of the Radia Revolution, a war that ravaged for nearly one hundred years. He is joined by thousands of other creatures so evil the release of which would mean an end to life as we know it on earth.

Hidden: The source of all the world's myths and legends. A people who came to the earth realm long ago. Humans can see Hidden kind if they are human in appearance and these Hidden can dwell with humans if they choose, but they must keep their gifts a secret. If they have Hidden defining features, (long ears, half-human/half animal, etc.), humans cannot see them because of the Pact.

Pact: An agreement made at the end of the Radia Revolution between Hidden and humans. A *shroud* was placed within the Balance that would shield humans from creatures of the Hidden world, including the creatures of the Dark. The following human generations would have no knowledge of the truth behind the myths.

Radia: The star that once gave life to the Hidden's original world.

Radia Shard: When Radia died, shattering into pieces, and the Hidden escaped to earth, she sent her shards to the Watchers to guard them and tame them. Once the Pact was formed, and Light did not want to leave the humans defenseless, the Watchers' shards divided in half, one half was sent to a human child the Light selected through the Balance. Through the shards each child could now see the Dark and was given one elemental gift to aid them in their duty. These became known as the Chosen.

Watchers: Watchers once had the ability to sense past, present, and future as it affects the Balance. Once the Pact was made, their Radia Shards split and their gifts became centralized to their Chosen wards whom they are to train and protect. Watchers also carry out orders given them by the Guardians, and oversee and educate the realm of Earth.

Chosen: Human children selected at six years old through the Balance to protect mankind from the monsters of the Dark.

The Ninth Chosen: A child of prophecy said to once again unite humans and Hidden in a Final Battle against the Dark for the fate of Earth. This child will have all the gifts of the Hidden within his life force.

Protectors: Those deemed to be completely loyal to the Light; warriors, overseers of all distribution of power among mankind.

Seraphs: Messengers and deliverers of the Light's justice and mercy.

Reckoners and Restorers: Those who are called by Seraphs or Protectors as either builders and guardians to countries, peoples, and individuals, or deliverers of justice.

The Lost Ones: Once Chosen, they remain good, but have become disenchanted toward the ways of the Light.

The Fallen: Watchers who have turned their talents to the Dark.

The Last Shard: In a final attempt to give hope to the human race after the Pact, the Last Radia Shard was sent to Eamun Woodlore, a Watcher, and with it he received the prophecy of the Ninth Chosen. This Last Shard holds more power and light within it than any other shard on the planet. Only the Keeper it chooses can wield its full power. If the Keeper dies, the Last chooses a Seeker as the only one who can find it and deliver it to the new Keeper.

Doogar: Dwarf-like creatures who live underground. Gifted in wood and metal work.

Lafar: Elves who are on the side of Light

Movan: Creatures with the ability to sense and manipulate bioelectricity. They are responsible for all of earth's technology.

Radia Warriors: Tall, powerful warriors whose sole duty is to protect Hidden kind from the monsters of the Dark.

The Order of the Nine Realms: The system of harmony that allocates the highest followers of Light. It is divided into three categories: *The First Realm of Three* contains those creatures so close to Light that they can only visit the earth for short periods of time: Seraphs, Ahway, and Mee'nah—creatures who fulfill duties only known to the Light. *The Second Realm of Three:* Guardians, Spheres, and Protectors. *The Third Realm of Three:* Watchers, Restorers and Reckoners, and Chosen.

GIFTS OF THE LIGHT/ CHOSEN ABILITIES:

All gifts are a connection allowed by the source, a union, it is not control.

Honitahai: Nature Speakers. They have the ability to grow plant life at will, as well as communicate with nature to seek aid.

Kunamin: Fire Wielders. They can create, manuever, throw, and snuff fire with their hands.

Télora: Earth Movers. They can ask the dirt to do their bidding, forming walls, weapons, and raise or level mountains.

Arwah: Wind Shifters. They can use the power of wind to aid them in any way.

Dicernan: Unseens. These can disguise themselves within the Balance and become invisible.

Leenwa: Water Callers. These can call to water and manuever it to meet their needs.

Animashta: Listeners. They understand animal's thoughts and communicate with them. They can project their own thoughts and desires into the animal's minds, as if they are sharing thought. It enables them to work together as a flawless team—so long as the animal is listening and willing. The animal always has a choice—it is not forced the way the DéHool are.

Lóklana: Radiance. These can call light in darkness from within the life that stores it.

CHARACTER INDEX:

Followers of Light:

Macy Allicandra Burdow: Chosen (human)
  o Parents: Max and Allison Burdow

Tolen (Parks) Téloran: The Ninth Chosen (Hidden-kind)
  o Parents: Daedal Téloran (Protector) Formerly held captive in the Shadow Prison.

Areen Téloran (Sphere)

Forrest Bastian: Watcher. His mortal life now complete, he has joined the Guardians. He still remains Tolen's and Macy's Watcher.

Jonas: Sphere and shield to the Unastra training camp

Quasar: Lafar

Hunsi: Chief of the Hinkta Honitahai tribe

Mahto: Honitahai

Sienn: Half Lafar, half Honitahai

Sashan: Watcher

Belahee'chay (Belch): Honitahai

Tashta: Village Mother—one who takes in the orphaned

Tahaka: Naiad, currently teaching in Hunsí's village

Kichaya: Commune and Hinkta Tribal Elder

Blaze: Lafar

Tokharian (Toke): Movan, leader of the Lost Ones

Rune: Chosen, Kunamin

Brina: Chosen, Dicernan

Keelyn: Chosen, Loklana

Connell: Chosen, Animashta

The Dominants: Those who are most powerful in the gifts and are responsible for training the Ninth.

O'shae—Arwah

Took'rah—Animashta

Kyndras—Leenwa

Dunrath—Télora

Nephen—Lóklana

Jun'tar—Kunamin

Ras'met—Honitahai

Vindi—Dicernan

Servants of the Dark:

Most servants of the Dark cannot come out in daylight.

Darsapean—Lord of the Dark, formerly imprisoned in Misery.

Daemon—Demon Master and High Captain of the Dark, resides in the Shadow Realm. His highest goal is to give control of this world over to the Dark by freeing his master, destroying all the Chosen, and annihilating or enslaving Hidden and human kind.

Shadow Wraiths—Thick, black, oily mist-like creatures who hide in storm clouds. Once they find you they use your fears to paralyze you, then you either become part of them, or they take you to the Shadow Prison.

Raksasha—Blood Trackers. Main purpose is to find and kill the Chosen. They resemble burned human skeletons, but with black fangs, overlong arms ending in long, razor-sharp, poisonous fingernails, and yellow eyes.

Night Demons—Blood drinking demons who pull themselves up from the ground to feed on the death of the battlefield. Their decaying flesh is covered with maggots and bloody scabs. They are bald, have no eyes, or legs. Night Demons are one of the most grotesque creatures born of darkness.

Divinators (crows)—Their eyes have been replaced by Oracle, or seeing stones. Whatever they see, their masters see.

Reconn—Chameleon type creatures. Not very powerful they are used mostly as scouts.

Phantoms—These mist-like creatures are placed within the dead or dying to reanimate and control them. Often placed in dead trees as spies.

Ookra—Small, with large heads, batlike ears sprouting tufts of dark hair, and overlarge hands ending in claws. Servants to the leaders of the Dark, they dwell in the Shadow Realm.

DéHool—Giant demonic wolves with red eyes. One of their greatest purposes is to hunt and destroy Watchers.

Daklafar—Once Lafar-Light Elves, but now serve the Dark. Once beautiful, they now are dark, filthy, and deadly.

Tormentors—Tall women with gray skin, lifeless black eyes, and floor length orange hair. Their screams cause unbearable pain. The dark uses them to extract information from their prisoners.

Kreydawn—Mindless creatures controlled by Suppressors.

Suppressors—Single-eyed creatures with no mouth. They control the Kreydawn.

Thrundoon—Huge men covered with black fur. Extremely strong. Masters of the DéHool.

Sundrák—Sentry's posted outside the cells of the Shadow Prison. Bald, translucent skin, no eyes, just an overlarge nose in the center of their face set above blood-red lips. They sense body heat.

Shrieg—Gigantic, venomous, bat-like creatures, often found with Raksasha or Daklafar.

Kinchomen—Lizard like creatures, more of a nuisance than dangerous.

Gungruin—Tall gray skinned creatures that can take on the appearance of anything they touch. Water is the only thing that can melt through their disguise.

Kezgani—Once Animashta until they followed the Dark. They now can shape-shift into an animal and withstand limited sunlight. Their animal side allows them to not affect the Balance in the same way most Dark creatures do, making them harder to detect.

Basic Hidden Language Dictionary:

Ladonradi—The Light

Degani—The Dark

Dembasi—Watcher

Iyahika—To Watch

Liosladon—May the Light lead and protect you wherever you may go.

Ladon—Light. Light come forth is Radi.

LaUnahi—Little Bird. Bastian's nickname for Macy.

To'—The

Y'na—I am

Hai—Here

Mindra—Chosen

To' Conchla Mindra—The Ninth Chosen

Vast—Fight

Pench Ni'yàlo—Be still

Lon'adras—Heal

Dón—For

Y' takra—Take me

Da'bay—Friend

Ke'ay—Help

Mea—Me

Chan'ta—Please

Mah'ne—Journey

I'kashti—Summon

Minradak-con-siadras—This ground is sacred and protected. The words spoken to bless the earth and make it burial ground, protecting those buried from the Night Demons.

To'conchla serith hune doocrah—The Ninth shall lead them.

Den aktra—Aid us

Den mea Tin'ruhl—Aid me Earth

Mi'no ha—Life to fire

Vin'akra—Life to wind

Ma'sha—Hear me animal

Win'tashta—Water hear my call

Tin'ruhl—Earth hear my call

Radi'non—Light come forth

Los'lon—Nature hear me

Vel'don—Veil me within

Words said to increase the body's natural abilities. Each word when said with intent has the power to speak to the life force and ask it to enhance that body part:

Konsh'la—The ears. Makes your hearing stronger.

Inreedo—The eyes. Makes your eyesight stronger.

Mig'nata—The body. Increases strength.

Lon'adras—heal, repair, return

Places of Interest:

Whisper, West Virginia: Macy's hometown

Waterton Lakes National Park, Canada: Home of the Hinkta Honitahai tribe

Poverty Island, Lake Michigan: Eamun's Island

ACKNOWLEDGEMENTS

THERE ARE SO many people to thank I could fill a whole book. Writing is a fun, scary, exciting, exhausting, wonderful thing. I could never do it if it weren't for the love and support of so many amazing people.

Thank you Brent, Rhett, Tyge, and all of my family for putting up with me and loving me while I follow this dream.

Thank you to my amazing parents for raising me to believe in the *Light*.

Thank you to all my sweet friends who constantly encourage and uplift me. Angie, I couldn't have survived another novel without our long conversations over hot chocolate and cinnamon bears!

Thank you KayLynn, Abbey, and Ellen, the best critique buddies a writer could ever ask for. This story is so much better because of you.

Thank you to my incredible beta readers and launch team buddies for your fabulous feedback, reviews, and shares. You guys are the bomb! These books could never have succeeded without you!

Thank you Katherine Armstrong Walters for the fantastic endorsement! You are a rockin' awesome author!

Thank you to my loyal readers who keep me motivated.

Thank you to Heather Godfrey—best editor ever—and all the crew at Snowy Peaks Media, KayLynn for a superb interior, *again*, Deborah Bradseth for yet another freaking awesome cover, and Julie Hess for lending your photography talent to my bio pictures.

I am truly blessed to be surrounded by, and inspired by, such incredible people.

ABOUT THE AUTHOR

K.A. PARKINSON WAS raised in a small suburb where she spent summers hiding under her bed with a book, a flashlight, and a bag of cookies. She began writing to give teens she mentored clean and inspiring stories that not only entertain, but teach powerful messages. *The Chosen Chronicles: A Chosen Path* is her third novel. K.A. resides in Utah with her husband and two children. If you would like to learn more about K.A., and the world of the Hidden, visit www.kaparkinson.com.

PRAISE FOR THE CHOSEN CHRONICLES

...K.A.'s writing is brooding and atmospheric from the gate. The battles are nothing short of explosive and the characters find their footing along the journey in a way that makes me believe in their difficult plight, and their reluctance to be what prophecy dictates... A Chosen Life is a highly entertaining read that deftly deals with finding one's place in a world that's out of their control, and the ever present battle of the light and darkness that surrounds us all. *–David Powers King, co-author of* Woven

If you enjoyed the first book in The Chosen Chronicles, you will not be disappointed with the second installment in the series, The Shadow Prison. Having learned he is the Ninth Chosen, Tolen begins rigorous training for his destiny and to find some way to rescue the father he knows is still alive. Teens will love the new aspects of both Tolen's and Macy's abilities as the action moves deftly forward. With action, danger, and romance, The Shadow Prison is sure to captivate new readers and current fans of the series alike. *–Teyla Branton | Bestselling Author*

There are a lot of supernatural fiction tropes that are getting really old really fast. Namely, the trope of special-girl-meets-mysterious-guy-and-learns-she's-more-than-she-thought-she-was. Adventure and training ensue, romance blossoms, and said girl ends up defeating the bad guy without any help. It's a story line that has worn a track in to the supernatural fiction section of Amazon, and I spend entirely too much time trying to find something that isn't…that.

Enter The Chosen Chronicles. Thank. Goodness…

I adore this story. Tolen is our oblivious male protagonist, who finds out he's more than he seems. He's scared and unsure and often needs to be protected by Macy, his de facto bodyguard when things get messy. Macy is hard-as-nails, and sometimes a little bit too abrasive for my taste, but she completely defies common expectations for female characters, which is really refreshing…

I highly recommend this book- the story is wildly entertaining, and it's hard not to love the characters. Be careful, though. It may cause a serious case of insomnia. :) –Megs (Amazon Reviewer)

Read more reviews or leave your own at www.amazon.com/author/kaparkinson